TIME CASTAWAYS
THE FORBIDDEN LOCK

The Time Castaways Trilogy
The Mona Lisa Key
The Obsidian Compass
The Forbidden Lock

Katherine Tegen Books is an imprint of HarperCollins Publishers.

Time Castaways #3: The Forbidden Lock
Copyright © 2020 by HarperCollins Publishers
All rights reserved. Manufactured in Germany.

Library of Congress Cataloging-in-Publication Data
Names: Shurtliff, Liesl, author.
Title: The forbidden lock / Liesl Shurtliff.
Description: First edition. | New York, NY : Katherine Tegen Books, [2020] |
    Series: Time castaways ; 3 | Summary: "The Hudson family prepares for a final
    showdown with Captain Vincent, who now has the power to change the past,
    present, and future"—Provided by publisher.
Identifiers: LCCN 2020028317 | ISBN 9780062568212 (hardcover)
Subjects: CYAC: Brothers and sisters—Fiction. | Time travel—Fiction. | Pirates—
    Fiction. | Adventure and adventurers—Fiction.
Classification: LCC PZ7.S559853 For 2020 | DDC [Fic]—dc23
LC record available at https://lccn.loc.gov/2020028317

Typography by Katie Fitch
20 21 22 23 24   CPIG   10 9 8 7 6 5 4 3 2 1
❖
First Edition

To my family—past, present, and future.
Don't let go.

You say I am a riddle—it may be
For all of us are riddles unexplained.

—Alfred Nobel, *A Riddle*

TIME CASTAWAYS
THE FORBIDDEN LOCK

1

The Time Tapestries

A sleek luxury cruise ship drifted peacefully on a calm Caribbean Sea, somewhere along the coast of Colombia. The air was balmy, just a slight breeze. The ink-black sky was sprinkled with stars. If you were to ask any of the many passengers on board the ship, they would likely say there was magic in the air that night, and they would be absolutely right. There was a certain magic in the air, inside the very ship on which they were currently sailing, and especially residing within the captain of the ship, Captain Vincent of the *Vermillion*.

Captain Vincent stood in his cabin preparing for the evening. He was dressed in his finest black waistcoat, black leather pants, and his favored pair of red Converse. He stood admiring himself in his mirror.

A white rat crawled out of the captain's waistcoat pocket and climbed upon his shoulder. He stared into the mirror with glowing red eyes. The rat's name was Santiago, and he knew the captain better than anyone. He knew his deepest, darkest secrets. He knew his greatest desires. He knew precisely how much sugar and cream he took in his tea. (Two lumps and just a drop.)

In short, Santiago was not your typical rat, except perhaps for the fact that he hated cats, detested birds, and was generally always in a foul mood, but otherwise he was quite unusual.

"How do I look, Santiago?" the captain asked, straightening his waistcoat and tightening his cuff links.

Clean, Santiago replied. To anyone else it would have just sounded like a few squeaks, but the captain understood the rat's meaning perfectly.

"Clean? Is that all?"

Santiago twitched his whiskers and tail. *Fine. Pretty,* he squeaked.

The captain laughed. "Yes, I *am* rather pretty, I suppose."

The captain's laughter stung Santiago's pride. Humans had so many words and expressions, and it was such a nuisance to keep them all in order. He wondered why anyone cared what they looked like at all. What did it matter? They all had eyes and noses and mouths, but no whiskers or tails and so were senseless and clumsy. Perhaps the captain should care more about *that.* He told the captain as much.

"You are perfectly right, Santiago," the captain said, his

eyes glimmering with mirth. "Perhaps I should grow myself some whiskers and a tail."

Santiago squeaked his indifference.

"Oh, lighten up, Santiago!" said the captain. "Remember this is a celebration of our triumph."

Triumph.

Yes. They had won, just like the time Santiago fought two other rats for a half-empty bag of pork rinds. That had been a *triumph.* The pork rinds were delicious.

But Santiago knew the captain's most recent triumph had nothing to do with pork rinds. He was talking about the things that had transpired on that beach, just days ago. Or was it weeks? Years? It all seemed to blur, a tangle of memories. They'd been with those Hudsons, whom Santiago detested, though he couldn't say exactly why. Maybe he didn't care for children in general, or *humans* in general (except the captain).

There had been words. Words, words, words. Humans were so full of words! But through the words Santiago understood one thing. The captain had found what he'd been looking for. Santiago remembered the thrill that raced through him as he took a small black stone and placed it in the center of his compass.

Triumph.

It felt like winning a full bag of pork rinds. Maybe two.

And then—*click*—as soon as the stone was inside the compass, the world stopped. Santiago stopped. Stopped breathing. Stopped moving. Stopped *being*. He felt nothing. Thought nothing. Became nothing.

And then—*click*—Santiago came out of the nothing, and everything was different. He wasn't certain how. Everything looked the same. The captain looked the same. He, Santiago, looked the same. He could see his reflection in the mirror—white fur, red eyes, magnificent tail and whiskers. But he felt different. He felt . . . *hungry.*

Hungry, except nothing seemed to satisfy him. What was he was hungry *for*? Pork rinds? Peanut butter? Caviar? He ate all those things. He ate until his stomach could hold no more. But the hunger only grew.

More, more, more.

Santiago sensed the same hunger in the captain, too, like a bottomless pit, only the captain didn't seem to mind it. He wasn't constantly trying to feed himself. Maybe it had something to do with that glowing stone, the one he'd put inside the compass. He wasn't wearing the compass anymore, at least not like he used to, but Santiago could see at the captain's chest the faint blue glow of that stone. Somehow it had become a part of him, seemed to be feeding him.

A knock came at the door.

"Come in," the captain said.

Two men entered—Brocco and Wiley. They were part of

the captain's crew, though they hadn't been with the captain as long as Santiago, and they weren't nearly as valued or as trusted. They didn't understand the captain like Santiago did. They certainly didn't know how he took his tea.

Brocco was dressed in a red-and-gold-floral tuxedo, his clumps of hair tied up with a gold ribbon. Wiley stood slightly behind Brocco wearing his usual brown suit, though he'd added a little flair by sticking a purple feather in his fedora. He was smoking his pipe, as he always did. They both bowed to the captain and viewed him with a mixture of fear and reverence bordering on worship. They had been like that since the captain's recent triumph.

Just the other day, Santiago had overheard Brocco and Wiley talking about what had happened that day on the beach. It was difficult for Santiago to completely understand what they were saying. Humans had words and ideas that were so foreign to rats. Through their many words he'd grasped only one thing. That day on the beach, the captain had become *immortal*.

But what was that, exactly? Was Santiago immortal too? He must be. Did immortal mean you were always hungry, always wanting *more*? Why would the captain want that?

"The party has started, sir, Your Excellence Majesty," Brocco said. "Your guests are waiting for you."

"Wonderful," the captain said. "Almost ready."

Wiley pulled his pipe out of his mouth. "You gonna

experiment on those people? Like you did the last time?" He said the word *experiment* with some amount of disgust. A dangerous tone to take with the captain, Santiago thought.

"Yes, Wiley," Captain Vincent said. "I told you I would need to conduct many experiments to test my powers, to understand how they work and their effects. I can't do what I want when I don't know what I can do."

"Yeah," Brocco agreed. "We can't just go changing things willy-nilly, Wiley. We don't want to make a bloody mess of the world."

"Of course not," the captain said. "We are not savages." He dusted the lapels of his waistcoat. Santiago helped dust off the shoulders with his tail.

"It just doesn't seem right," Wiley said. "Experimenting on those people's lives and all, without them knowing."

"If it bothers you that much, Wiley," the captain said, "perhaps you'd rather I experiment upon you? Would that make you feel better?"

Wiley took a few steps back. "No, sir. No, it would not."

"Then stop your moral philosophizing and go greet our guests. Make them welcome and comfortable. Hand out bags of gold and jewels, if it will clear your conscience."

"Yes, sir." Brocco and Wiley both bowed and left. Santiago whipped his tail at their retreating figures. He was thinking neither of them would last very long, for different reasons. Brocco was annoyingly eager. He tried too hard. Agreed too much. He could feel it grating on the captain's nerves. But Wiley was the opposite. He seemed to question more and more. He seemed hesitant. Must be all those books he read. Too many words in the head, too many voices. Wiley was confused, didn't know which voices to listen to or which words were the right ones. Of course, it was the captain he should be listening to, following. That should have been obvious, given his power. But for some reason it wasn't to Wiley. Santiago would have to keep an eye on him.

"Santiago, I'm afraid you will have to hide yourself tonight," the captain said, adjusting his crown. "You know my guests will not care for your presence."

All Santiago's enjoyment dissolved at these words. *Cruel captain!* Santiago hissed. *Santiago best! Humans slop!*

"Of course, Santiago, you are of more value to me than anyone," the captain said. "You are my most trusted adviser, my most faithful servant, but remember our mission. It's best if my subjects are in a relaxed state when I perform my experiments. Now go."

Santiago twitched with annoyance but obeyed. He crawled inside the captain's inner pocket. To appease himself, he chanted, *Most faithful, most faithful, most faithful,* over and over as the captain walked out of his cabin and headed to the upper deck. The captain would surely do away with Brocco and Wiley and all the rest sooner or later, but Santiago knew he would never discard *him.*

The *Vermillion*, able to transform into any kind of vessel, was currently a luxury ocean liner with rich interiors of crystal chandeliers, red tapestries trimmed in gold, and a grand staircase. It was supposedly a similar design to some famous ship, Santiago heard Wiley say. Apparently it had sunk in the Atlantic sometime in the early twentieth century.

But Santiago didn't care a whisker for any of that. He was here for the food. He was so *hungry*, and there were piles and piles of food of all kinds—colorful arrangements of fruit and vegetables, roasted game and fish and fowl, breads and cheese, soups and noodles, and delicacies of unknown origin. There were tall cakes decorated with flowers and pearls, small cakes topped with cherries, little lacy cookies, pastries with nuts and honey, small glasses of mousse with cream. Albert was currently piling a plate high with cakes and cookies.

Santiago's incessant hunger overwhelmed him. He scurried toward the food tables and started to nibble on a bit of lemon tart.

The party was a bizarre sight, even to Santiago who had seen some bizarre things in his unusually long rat life. It seemed like the guests had been gathered from all parts of the world and throughout every possible era. The captain had said he needed a good variety for his experiments, and so he had been collecting subjects. The one who stuck out most to Santiago was a woman wearing a dress as wide as she was tall, with her white-powdered hair stacked in a high pile of curls. Santiago thought she looked like a frilly, layered cake and had half a mind to go and nibble on the edges of her dress. At her side was a short man wearing an embroidered jacket and breeches and high-heeled shoes. Behind that strange couple was a group of people dressed in nothing but white sheets, and behind them a group wearing colorful silk robes with wide draping sleeves. There were girls in straight dresses with sequins and fringe, others in sweeping gowns, and some in large hoop skirts that knocked over glasses and furniture whenever they moved. There were several women wearing birds on their heads, which made Santiago hiss, even though he knew they were dead. There were men in full suits of armor, others in poofy shorts and tights, feathered hats, hunting leathers, suits, tuxedos, and robes. There was every pigment of skin and hair color, dark to fair, black hair, brown hair, yellow hair, red hair. The ball was a human smorgasbord.

A band started to play music. Santiago didn't care for music in general, but whatever this band was playing was absolute torture. So loud. There were people blowing through brass horns, beating drums, pounding a piano, and a man singing words into a microphone, as though putting words with music somehow improved them. It was bringing Santiago to the brink of insanity. It also seemed to be driving the guests insane, judging by the way they were moving. Some were hopping about, others twirling, others kicking out their legs front and back as though trying to fight off an attack.

Wiley was among those humans. He was flailing and twitching all on his own in ways that reminded Santiago of the time he'd witnessed a fellow rat's death after ingesting poison.

Brocco was bouncing around with a woman who appeared to be molting. The white feathers on her dress were floating everywhere. Several had landed on Brocco's clumpy hair and shoulders. He smiled, his diamond tooth sparkling.

When the captain arrived at the party, through their connection, Santiago felt the hunger in him, too, that bottomless pit.

More, more, more. It seemed to pulse along with the horrid music.

The band started another song, a slower, softer one meant for the humans to dance close to their chosen partners. Santiago calmed some, until the man started singing the words. Words about summer and sunsets and love.

Love. Humans everywhere at all times were always going on about love. He didn't understand it. He didn't understand a lot of human things. It was like putting a square inside of a circle. It might go in, but it didn't fit right. All the human thoughts and feelings inside of Santiago didn't fit. Love he understood least of all. It seemed to make humans do the most ridiculous things, like dance.

The captain must have felt the same way because he

stopped the party. He reached out his hands. He made a few motions, like he was turning invisible knobs and buttons, and then everything froze. The music stopped. The dancing stopped. All noise and motion stopped.

The entire ball was frozen. A woman's skirts were flared out from her spinning. A man was frozen mid-leap, both legs off the ground. Brocco and Wiley were frozen, too, their arms and legs bent at odd angles, their faces in unnatural expressions. Albert was frozen with a cake halfway to his open mouth, his eyes half-closed.

The only two animate creatures in the room were the captain and Santiago. The time freeze had no effect on them, except to give Santiago relief from all that chaos.

The captain went to Brocco and Wiley. He tapped on each of their chests and they both took deep gasping breaths as though they'd been underwater and had just come to the surface.

"Crikey," Brocco said, shaking himself a little. "I'll never get used to that. Feels like I've got spiders crawlin' all over me."

Wiley shivered, lit his pipe, and took a few puffs, looking around at all the frozen people. "What about Albert?" he asked. "You gonna unfreeze him?"

"No," the captain said. "He's not needed now."

Santiago knew the captain didn't really need Brocco and Wiley either. He didn't *need* anyone. But they could be useful.

The captain wove in and out of the frozen guests. He stopped in front of the woman who looked like a cake. The short man was behind her, half-covered by her wide dress.

"Oh! That's Marie Antoinette, isn't it?" Wiley asked.

"Yes," the captain said. "I thought her timeline might be an interesting one to work with, given her fate."

"Doesn't she get her head chopped off?" Wiley asked.

"She does indeed. Her husband too." The captain nodded to the man. "The fate of careless monarchs."

Wiley shuddered and puffed on his pipe.

"Lessons to be learned, eh, Your Majesty?" Brocco jested, elbowing the captain in the ribs.

The captain gave him a look that made him instantly stop.

"Lessons for *mortal* kings and queens," the captain said. "I am not susceptible to such a fate."

"Of course not."

"What would happen if someone chopped off your head?" Wiley asked.

Both Brocco and Wiley jumped back as the captain drew his sword and held it out to Wiley. "Why don't you try it and find out?"

Wiley shook his head and held up his hands. "No, sir, I'm good."

Santiago was a little disappointed. He wanted to know what would happen if someone tried to chop off the captain's head. Obviously he wasn't the least bit afraid of it.

The captain turned back to the woman called Marie Antoinette. He reached out and gently touched her throat. Wiley winced, turning his head, as though the captain was about to strangle her or break her neck. But he did no such thing. With a fluid motion, he drew out of the woman a swath of shimmery light blue material. It looked like water flowing in a stream through the air.

Pictures swam in the material, mostly of the woman, but other humans, too, and places and things. Santiago glimpsed a grand palace. Horses and fine carriages. Servants and children. A yappy little dog that made Santiago hiss. Mounds of food, especially cakes.

"That's the memory material, is it?" Brocco asked.

"Her time tapestry," the captain said. "It's her past, present, and future, all woven together."

The captain brushed his fingers along the watery material. The woman shuddered, as though the captain had stroked a cold finger along her spine. The captain lifted his sword and with a swift movement slashed the blade through the tapestry in several places. Both Wiley and Brocco winced at this, but the woman did not move. The captain rearranged all the pieces, pressing the fabric together, creating seams that were jagged and puckered, like scarred flesh.

The captain stepped back to observe his handiwork. The images seemed to be in a chaotic dance as they reorganized themselves, but they eventually settled.

"There now," he said. "Marie Antoinette's head has been saved."

Brocco clapped his hands. "Oh, that's nice, isn't it? Very kind of you to save her head like that."

"Yeah, but what about her husband's head?" Wiley asked. "You gonna save his head too?"

The captain turned to the short man hiding behind Marie Antoinette. The captain cocked his head, considering. "No, I think I'd like to try something different with him." He pulled out his time tapestry from his stomach (both Brocco and Wiley made disgusted faces) and then the captain took his sword and slashed through it in all directions, shredding it so the strings and fabric went all over the place.

He stood back to observe his handiwork. The pieces of the material hovered in the air for a moment, but soon they started to move and find their way back to one another, and the pieces wove themselves back together just as they had been before. The captain frowned. Santiago felt his disappointment.

"How about some guns, Your Majesty?" Brocco asked. "Sometimes a gun can do what a sword can't, eh?" He reached beneath his red tuxedo jacket and pulled out two pistols. The captain took one, cocked it, and shot at an image of the man's head in the fabric. Brocco and Wiley both ducked down as the bullet hit its mark. The tapestry absorbed the bullet like water. It rippled outward, distorting and scattering the images. The captain studied the effects, watching the people move and interact like characters in a play. He shot it again, experimenting with different angles or shooting it after slicing with a sword. "It's not quite the desired effect," the captain said, "but perhaps a move in the right direction."

"I don't get it," Wiley said. "Why don't you just travel back in time and shoot him in real life? That *is* what you are trying to accomplish, isn't it? To kill that Hudson man so you can steal his wife?"

Santiago twitched as a dozen different thoughts and emotions rushed through him at once. Triumph and loss. Desire and repulsion. Joy and rage. So many feelings clawed at each other. Too much, too much. Humans felt too many things at once. It made Santiago want to chew on his own tail.

"I could kill him," the captain said. "But that doesn't solve everything. I want him *gone*. Erased. I want him to never have existed. Only then can everything truly be set right."

"So why do you gotta deal with all this time tapestry stuff?" Wiley asked. "Why not just go back in time and kill his mother or his grandmother, make it so he's never born at all?"

"It's not that simple," the captain said, and he pulled more of the short man's time tapestry out of his stomach. "A person's life is hundreds of thousands of little threads, all woven together, and those threads are also woven into others' time tapestries, all of them connected, even if just by one little thread. I can go back in time and kill someone, but it doesn't erase their existence, and it doesn't necessarily erase the existence of their unborn children. They'll just be born to someone else, see, and their time tapestry might still play out in a very similar way as before, which is unhelpful to my mission. No, in order to truly erase Matthew Hudson, I need to destroy all the threads in all the time tapestries he's ever touched. It all needs to unravel completely, and the more connected they are to others, the harder it is to make it all come apart, see? So I can't just go back and kill Matthew Hudson. I need something more powerful than swords or guns."

"Well, the guns worked better than swords, didn't they?" Brocco said. "Maybe we should try some stronger stuff?" He opened his jacket to reveal an array of objects attached to the insides. It all looked like a jumble of balls and bundles of sticks to Santiago, but it seemed to unnerve Wiley. He backed up from Brocco a step or two.

"Ain't it a bit dangerous to be walkin' around with all that stuff on your person?"

Brocco shrugged. "You never know when it might come in handy. Better on me than *at* me, yeah?"

"Indeed," the captain said. "Go ahead, Brocco. Give it a go." He motioned to the fabric of the short man.

Brocco rubbed his hands together with childlike giddiness. "How about a grenade, eh? One of my favorites." He took out an egg-shaped object from his pocket. He pulled a pin and tossed it at the time tapestry. The tapestry absorbed the grenade, much like the bullet, and a moment later there was a muted explosion that reverberated throughout the ballroom. Santiago felt his bones rattle and his fur stand on end.

The tapestry swirled with a smoky substance. A sizable chunk of the fabric looked to be destroyed, but then the particles started to come together, weaving and knitting itself back together. They reorganized themselves in a haphazard fashion so that when it was complete the picture was blurry and jumbled, but nothing had been erased completely.

"Hmm," the captain said. "Not quite. What else do you have?"

Brocco reached inside his pockets and pulled out what looked like nothing more than a bundle of sticks. "Firecrackers! We can put on a show with these!"

And it was a show, but that was about it. The tapestry erupted in sparks and emitted some loud bangs, but it otherwise did very little to alter anything.

Santiago could feel the captain was getting bored, losing patience. Brocco seemed to sense this too and take it as a sign of danger. Perhaps the captain would see it as a failure if Brocco did not get something to work, and he was less forgiving of failure now. Immortality had the odd effect of making you *less* patient, rather than more, despite having all the time in the world.

"Wait!" Brocco said. "I got one more, saved the best for

last." He pulled out what looked to Santiago like a large candlestick. "Dynamite! We used this on a fair few bank robberies back in the day. Always worked wonders. Never fails! I once derailed a whole train with this stuff." Brocco wrapped the time tapestry around the stick of dynamite, then struck a match and lit the wick. It sparked and flared, traveling fast toward the tapestry. When it reached the end, the fabric absorbed the dynamite. And then nothing.

"Maybe it went out," Wiley said.

"Or it coulda been a dud," Brocco said. "No, wait!"

The tapestry suddenly flared with a bright light. It began to smoke, a thin vapor that swirled around the fabric like ghostly ribbons. It smelled to Santiago faintly sweet but rancid. The fabric began to burn and unravel. There was a flash and a small *boom*, a shower of sparks. The man came unfrozen for just a moment. He gasped for air. He started to flicker in and out like a sputtering candle. Finally he faded completely, leaving behind only a portion of his time tapestry.

"Where'd he go?" Wiley said, looking around as though he had simply hidden somewhere.

The captain bent down and picked up the fallen fabric, which instantly began to dim so there was no luminescence, only a dull glow, and the images within it faded to shadow. He turned the tapestry over in his hands, then inspected the cake-woman's tapestry. The images were again jumping around, reorganizing themselves.

"Did it work? Did it?" Brocco asked excitedly.

"Close," the captain said. "Very close indeed."

Brocco bounced on his feet and clapped his hands. "Shall we try it again? I can get more dynamite! Loads more. It's not hard to get. The boys and I used to use this stuff all the time back in the day."

"Maybe," the captain said, still inspecting the time tapestries. Santiago could feel the wheels turning and clicking in his brain, piecing things together. "We will need to run more experiments, certainly, but I think I should like to meet the person who invented this dynamite. Do you know who that is?"

Brocco opened his mouth and then shut it when he realized he didn't know the answer.

"Alfred Nobel," Wiley said, pulling out his pipe. "I've read some about him. Famous Swedish chemist, though I think his first passion was literature. Poetry. He wrote some fine poetry from what I recall."

"I do not care about his poetry," the captain said disdainfully. "Just tell me where and when I can find this Nobel."

"He's alive now, I believe," Wiley said, "though toward the end of his life. He lived in a fair few places around the world throughout his life and traveled a great deal besides. You could find him in any number of places."

The captain considered. Again, Santiago could feel the wheels turning in his mind, even if he didn't know precisely what he was thinking. He was cooking up a plan. "All right, then. I want to see this Nobel, but the timing is important. Wiley, I'll need you to do a bit of research on Mr. Nobel's life, see what moments would be best to insert ourselves in. A tragedy would be best. Something he would wish to be different. You know what I mean."

Wiley nodded. "I believe he has a brother who dies rather young. A tragic accident, very sorrowful."

Santiago felt the captain's neck twitch at the word *brother*.

"Better make sure Mr. Nobel actually mourned for his brother before we use that."

And Santiago felt that familiar sting of hate run through him from his whiskers to his tail. The captain certainly didn't mourn his own brother, and his death was no accident.

Wiley shivered a little, seeming to understand the captain's thinly veiled meaning. "I'll look it up in my library," he said.

"And I'll prepare our disguises!" Brocco said.

The captain nodded and dismissed them, and then the captain and Santiago were left alone in the midst of the frozen party.

"We're getting close, my friend," the captain said. "I can feel it. Soon the Hudsons will be gone and everything will be as it always should have been. Nothing will stand in the way of our happiness."

Santiago squeaked.

The captain shook his head. "How many times must I tell

you, Santiago, Mateo is on our side."

Santiago squeaked again. *How certain?*

"Positive," he said. "I know it doesn't seem like it to you, but I know better. Don't worry. You'll see. It will all come out right in the end. And the beginning. And the middle!" He tipped his head back and laughed. Santiago didn't laugh. It was not one of the things he'd learned to do since coming to meet the captain, and truly he didn't see what was so amusing. He couldn't help but think the captain had gone a little bit mad ever since his most recent triumph.

"Come, Santiago, let's enjoy the party a little before we go, shall we?" the captain said. With a few motions he unfroze time and the party was revived. The band started playing again, and the dancing continued.

Marie Antoinette seemed a little confused. She looked around for her husband, until the captain slipped into his place, and they danced together as if her husband had never been there at all.

Santiago went back to the feast and watched the spectacle as he ate and ate but was never filled.

More, more, more.

2

New Compass Tricks

June 5, 2019
Hudson River Valley, New York

Matt shot up from sleep, gasping for breath, sweaty and shaking. He looked around, saw the heaps of boxes and furniture, smelled the musty scent of old books and rusty tools, the silhouettes of sleeping bodies all around him. He was at Gaga's house, on her vineyard in upstate New York. Safe. He was safe. His family was safe. It was only a nightmare. But it had felt so real. So real he'd even felt the ground shaking beneath him. He could still feel it, he thought, or was that just his imagination?

The shaking stopped. Just his imagination, then.

Matt checked on his family, still asleep around him. They were all sleeping in Gaga's basement. The window wells provided very little light, and it was still dark outside anyway, but there was a night-light plugged into the wall. It cast a weak glow over the room so Matt could see everyone well enough. Corey was sprawled on top of his cot, arms and legs dangling off the sides, a bit of drool hanging from his open mouth. Ruby slept tucked neatly inside her sleeping bag with her hands placed under her cheek like a princess. A warrior princess, that is, as Matt noticed the sword handle sticking out from beneath her pillow. Jia slept on one end of the ratty plaid couch, her black hair cascading over the side. Pike was on the other end, curled up like a kitten, hands clutching her knotted rope. His parents were sleeping behind the couch. He could see the outline of his mom and hear his dad's heaving-breathing-almost-snoring.

They'd been sleeping like this for the last four nights in a row, cots and sleeping bags crammed together. Gaga thought it was adorable, a "giant family slumber party" she called it. She didn't know that it wasn't for fun so much as a survival instinct, though Matt wasn't sure that sleeping all in one room was any kind of protection against Captain Vincent now.

The nightmares only added to his anxiety. It was the same nightmare he used to have as a child. Almost every night it was the same. He and his family are having a picnic, or some-times they were playing a game of baseball, or just walking down the street together. In the nightmare he'd just had they were picking grapes together in the vineyard. Whatever the setting, they are always all together, his mom, his dad, Corey,

Ruby, and him, and they are happy. Then the sky darkens. Suddenly a strong wind rushes through. Something is coming. His mother tells them all to run. And they do. They all run. Except Matt. He can't seem to run. He's treading mud. And then his family starts to disappear. One by one they fade into nothing, or get sucked into the sky, or fall into some bottomless chasm. And then Matt wakes up, heart racing, drenched in sweat.

It's not that the dream felt particularly *real*. He knew it was a dream. It's just that it felt so possible now, like a warning, a premonition.

Matt reached for his compass tucked beneath his T-shirt. The Obsidian Compass, the time-traveling device that he himself had invented. Just a few turns of the dials and within seconds he could be not only on another continent but also in a different century. In the past few months alone, Matt had traveled all over the world, thousands of years into the past, and even once into his future. At first it had all seemed a grand adventure, but in reality the compass had caused a great deal of trouble, even destroyed lives, and who knew how many more lives it would destroy? Matt was starting to wonder if he'd made a mistake in building it at all. He'd had good intentions, but many a disaster can start with good intentions, he was learning.

But if he hadn't built the compass, he wouldn't even be here, nor would his mother, and therefore his father or Corey or Ruby or Jia and Pike. Or perhaps they would have all existed, but in very separate lives, not together. Either way, he didn't like to imagine his world without them, and they were all together because of the Obsidian Compass that *he* built. In that way, he reasoned, many good things can come from disaster. But would they be able to stay together? This was the unspoken question that hung over all their heads like a dark cloud, ready to burst at any moment.

Matt circled his fingers in rhythm over his compass, his mind going in loops and spirals. He'd gone over it again and again. Thirty-six hours ago, Matt and his family had stood on the shores of Asilah, Morocco, in the year 1772. He'd gone there with such hope, such confidence, to fix everything. But everything had gone wrong.

Matt lifted his hands to his face. He could barely see in the weak dawn light, but still the rootlike scars on his right hand were starkly visible. Thirty-six hours ago he'd seen identical scarring on the same hand of Marius Quine. That's when he knew without a doubt that he and Quine were the same person, just at different points in their timeline. When their hands had connected, they had erupted with such force and heat and power, Matt felt he would explode. He did, in fact. Both of them. But miraculously they didn't die, and when he was put back together, Matt was holding a black stone in the center of his palm. The Aeternum. The object that granted its possessor immortality and the power to manipulate time and events however they wished. As it happened, Matt had been in possession of the Aeternum all along and never knew it. It had been the stone in his bracelet that he'd worn since the age of six. Granted, it had been inactive until that moment he and Quine had grasped hands, but still, it had been in his possession.

No longer. Captain Vincent had the Aeternum now. Matt had watched as Captain Vincent had been altered, immortalized with unfathomable power to manipulate time, past, present, and future. Matt was honestly surprised they were still here at all, even now. There had been several discussions in the past two days (or arguments) about what they should do, whether they should stay or flee or try to do something to defeat Vincent before it was too late, but no one could agree on anything, mostly because they didn't know exactly what had happened three days ago in Asilah.

Everyone had been pestering Matt for answers and information about what had happened with Quine and Captain Vincent. He told them everything. Mostly. He told them how when he and Quine joined hands there had been some powerful reaction, and the Aeternum was fully activated, and then Captain Vincent took it and then they'd all been flung back in the universe. The activation of the Aeternum somehow reset things, and all their travels were set in reverse until the Hudsons landed back precisely where and when they'd all started in Gaga's vineyard.

There was only one detail Matt withheld from his family—the part where he had discovered that he and Quine were actually the same person.

He'd almost told Corey and Ruby and Jia. The first night they'd returned. The information was still so new to him, so mind-boggling, he felt he might explode with it. But before he could even begin to get it out, Corey had declared in a venomous tone that Quine was the real enemy in all this, that he clearly had teamed up with Captain Vincent and given him the Aeternum. Matt had tried to defend Quine, said he might have his reasons.

"Yeah," Corey had said. "To rip our family to shreds."

"He didn't seem all that bad when I met him. It didn't seem like he wanted to destroy us or anything."

Corey snorted. "We thought the same thing about Captain Vincent when we first met him. I don't think we can go by first impressions here. *Nice* doesn't always mean 'good.' It doesn't mean he's on our side."

"I think Corey's right," Ruby said. "We can't be naïve about these things anymore. We need to look at the facts."

Matt looked to Jia, hoping she would back him up, but she remained silent. She'd been unusually quiet since they'd returned from Asilah.

Matt could see he wasn't going to win this argument. He didn't know how to refute Corey and Ruby's logic. The facts as they stood were not in his favor. Matt knew he would do anything to protect his family, but he couldn't fathom the thinking or desires of his older self. Quine had even told him they were very different people. Where did Mateo end and Marius Quine begin? And when?

Without these answers Matt did not feel he could reveal his and Quine's shared identity. It was too much for them to deal with, and they were dealing with too much as it was. So he closed his mouth, tucked the information away. But it gnawed at him, like mice on a rope. The questions kept him awake and anxious at all hours. He felt increasingly alone.

The weather was unusually cold that morning. Definitely not summer weather.

When the rest of the household had woken, they'd all shivered and wrapped themselves in sweaters and blankets. Matt looked out the big kitchen window and saw that a heavy mist had descended over the Hudson River Valley. A light frost covered the ground. Uncle Chuck brought in a load of wood and lit a fire in the big fireplace in the living room. Gaga grumbled something about climate change and the world going to pieces.

Matt didn't think this was climate change, at least not in the way Gaga was thinking, but he feared she was right about the world going to pieces. Not that he could talk to her about it, because Gaga still knew nothing about anything that had gone on in the past few days. Or years, decades, centuries, however you wanted to look at it. She knew nothing about her family being a bunch of time travelers, nor the fact that Chuck was really her long-lost son, Charles, or that her husband hadn't really disappeared or died while hiking in Patagonia, but had, in fact, been kidnapped by a time pirate/maniac with infinite powers. Corey kept arguing that they should tell her, but both Mr. Hudson and Uncle Chuck kept putting it off. They said it wasn't quite the right time, though Matt wondered what would the right time be to share such information.

Shortly after breakfast, Matt sat with his family (plus Jia and Pike) at the kitchen table, huddled around a globe covered in little red dots and gold stars.

"Tell me again, Charles," Mr. Hudson said, staring at the globe. "Everything you can remember about where Vincent took you and Dad."

His dark hair was messy, and his glasses did nothing to cover the dark circles under his eyes. His mom had them too. Clearly Matt wasn't the only one having trouble sleeping.

Uncle Chuck, sitting next to Mr. Hudson, tugged his long silvery beard. "I don't know," he said. "It all happened so fast. I remember it was cold. There were icebergs, I think. And that's it. I didn't see anyone else. No people. No buildings. Nothing."

Mr. Hudson puffed his cheeks full of air and then let it out. "That's not much to go on."

A few days ago, before everything had happened on the beach in Asilah, Matt had discovered, quite by accident, that Chuck, his grandmother's quirky hippie farm manager, was actually Mr. Hudson's long-lost brother, Charles. The resemblance was quite clear now, but no one had ever suspected who Chuck really was because he was supposed to be Mr. Hudson's *younger* brother by six years. However, due to unforeseen circumstances involving time travel, Chuck was now a good two decades older, with long gray hair and a scraggly beard that reached his chest. He and his father, Henry Hudson, had both been abducted by Captain Vincent, who had mistaken them both for Matt's dad at different points in time. Captain Vincent had been trying to prevent Mr. Hudson from meeting or marrying Mrs. Hudson. Uncle Chuck had managed to get away, though he'd escaped into the wrong decade. He'd come back home to his mom and brother but never told either of them who he really was.

Now that they knew what had really happened to Henry Hudson, they were trying to figure where he might be, and if they could potentially rescue him. Only Uncle Chuck had seen the place where Captain Vincent had discarded him, but his information was proving to be not very useful.

"Since you say there were icebergs," Mr. Hudson said, "I'm thinking we should focus our efforts on the Arctic or Antarctic, but the time . . ."

"Maybe he took them to the Ice Age," Ruby suggested. "Like Tui."

Mrs. Hudson ground her teeth. Fatoumata, or "Tui," had been one of her crew when she had been captain of the *Vermillion*, someone they thought they could trust. But in the end she'd been working for Captain Vincent all along. She'd been the one to turn Matt over to Quine in order to give the Aeternum to Vincent. Turns out she never forgave Mrs. Hudson for leaving her crew to go off and get married and have kids. Matt wondered what had happened to her after that moment in Asilah, when they'd all been flung back in time and space. Had Captain Vincent gone back to get her? Or did he leave her there, her uses dried up?

"Did you see any woolly mammoths?" Corey asked. "Penguins? Polar bears?"

"No," said Uncle Chuck. "No animals. Just water and lots of ice. I'm sorry, that's all I got."

Jia suddenly gasped and covered her mouth.

Matt jumped and hit his funny bone on the table. "Ah! What? What is it?" he said while rubbing at his fizzing arm.

"I think I remember your grandfather," she said. "And you." She nodded toward Uncle Chuck.

"What?" Matt cried. "When? Where?"

Jia shook her head. "I don't know. It was so long ago for me, and you looked so different then, but I remember we brought a man on board at one point. Someone the captain didn't like, but the man seemed confused. He was scared. And then another man showed up, younger. It was you, I think." She nodded to Uncle Chuck. "And then he discarded you. It was the only time I'd seen him discard anyone. Before you, at least." She nodded to Matt, referring to the time he, Corey, and Ruby had been discarded on a barren island. Definitely one of the worst moments in Matt's life.

"You were the one who dropped the rope!" Uncle Chuck exclaimed. Matt remembered he had told them that someone had dropped a rope from the *Vermillion*. He had escaped by grabbing ahold of it before the *Vermillion* disappeared, but he never did find out who had helped him. Until now.

Jia nodded. "I wasn't sure it would do any good, but it didn't feel right, just leaving you there."

"Thank you. I owe you my life."

"I'm sorry I couldn't have done more."

"Perhaps you can," said Mr. Hudson. "Do you remember where or when Captain Vincent discarded them? Did you hear them speaking about it? Any details at all?"

Jia shook her head. "No. Nothing Chuck hasn't told you already. I'm sorry." She hung her head a little.

"Oh, Jia, *chérie*, don't be sorry." Mrs. Hudson put a hand on top of Jia's. "You've done so much for us, for my children, I only wish there was something we could do to repay you. And Pike too. You've both been such a help to our family!"

Pike barely looked up at the sound of her name. She was sitting at the table, fiddling with her knotted rope while staring at an open book. It was the book about famous scientists Matt's parents had given him for his birthday. Matt hadn't even cracked it open, but Pike seemed to like all the pictures. Occasionally, she glanced at Matt and his compass, like she was wondering when they were going to travel again.

Pike was still a mystery to Matt. She'd somehow stowed herself away inside of Blossom on their return from Asilah, bearing a note from Marius Quine saying she was "on our side." She was just as silent with them as she had been on the *Vermillion*. Matt was thinking there had to be more to Pike's story than what met the eye, but they had very little clues. They had no idea where she was from. Or when. Mrs. Hudson had guessed she was from a Nordic country, given her white-blond hair and fair skin, maybe Finland or Denmark. She had tried speaking a little to Pike in Finnish and Dutch. Pike had cocked her head like a curious kitten but remained mute.

"Is Pike her real name?" Mrs. Hudson had asked Jia.

"Oh, no," Jia said. "It's just a nickname. I have no idea what her real name is."

Matt had never considered this, but of course that made sense. According to Jia, shortly after Pike had boarded the *Vermillion*, she caught a huge pike fish with nothing but her rope and a string of paper clips. Brocco started calling her "Li'l Pike" and it stuck. Matt felt a range of conflicting emotions at this tale. Brocco had nicknamed all the kids on Captain Vincent's crew. Matt was "Li'l Professor." He had liked Brocco a lot, right up until that moment he found out he was helping Captain Vincent try to destroy his family. Maybe even then he was willing to give him the benefit of the doubt, until he shot Corey and almost killed him. The lines had been clearly drawn.

Mr. Hudson kept studying the globe, and everyone continued to offer different theories about where or when Captain Vincent could have taken their grandfather. The table started shaking. It jerked so hard, a table leg hit Matt in the knee.

"Corey, quit it," Matt said.

"Quit what?"

"Quit shaking the table."

Corey lifted his hands. "Dude, I'm not even touching the table. Back off." He glared at Matt, but the shaking stopped. Matt shook his head. Of course it had been Corey. He was always fidgeting, rattling things and knocking things over, but Matt didn't see any point in arguing with him. Corey had been a bit touchy since their return from Morocco. He hadn't joked nearly as much. He'd been through a lot, too, including getting shot in the arm. He said it was fine, good as new, but Matt caught him rubbing it every now and then or rotating it like there was a kink that he couldn't quite work out.

Gaga came into the kitchen just then with a basketful of laundry. She plopped herself down at the end of the table and started folding. Everyone stared at her like she was an alien that had just joined them for a meal.

"Why are you all staring at me like that?" Gaga asked. "Am I interrupting a secret meeting?"

"No, of course not!" Mr. Hudson said a bit too loudly. Mrs. Hudson gave him an exasperated look. He was perhaps a worse liar than Matt.

Gaga adjusted her square-framed glasses and squinted at the globe full of stickers. "Are you having a geography lesson or something?"

"Yep," said Corey, spinning the globe. "We just love our geography. Can't get enough."

Gaga frowned. "Matthew, don't you go trying to turn my grandchildren into a bunch of nerds like you. Let them have a little fun, will you?"

Mr. Hudson looked highly affronted. "They think geography is fun, don't you, kids?"

"Yep!" "Yes!" "Can't get enough." They all chirped perhaps a little too enthusiastically. Gaga looked dubious.

"We were just learning about Antarctica," Ruby said.

"Antarctica!" Gaga blurted. "Oh my Lord, that reminds me. You would not believe the things I was hearing on the news this morning. They found a family of penguins wandering around in the middle of the Gobi Desert! Can you believe it? Unbelievable. And if that wasn't enough, a blizzard hit Jamaica! Tourists are actually asking for refunds."

Matt glanced at his mom. Her eyes flickered toward him for just a moment. He wondered if these were signs of Vincent's new powers, of him meddling with time. How else could a flightless Antarctic bird suddenly end up almost ten thousand miles away, on a completely different continent? What else could explain a snowstorm in a tropical climate? They seemed like sure signs of glitches in the timeline. But the bigger question was, why hadn't Vincent tried to do anything to *them* yet? When would they have to face him again? Because it was surely a question of when and not if. The one "if" in question was if they would stand any chance against him now that he had the Aeternum.

"I'm telling you, the world is going to pieces," Gaga continued. "Scientists are beside themselves, trying to explain everything with climate change or whatever. Then of course there's always the preacher who says the world is coming to an end and we're all doomed, and I say what's the difference? Recycle and repent. Doesn't hurt to try both."

"Amen," said Uncle Chuck.

"Oh, Chuck, I meant to tell you," Gaga said. "I just saw some strange fissures in the vineyard. Maybe it was caused by that ridiculous storm, or maybe we have a mole again. Will you take a look?"

"Sure thing, Mrs. Hudson." Uncle Chuck put on his fishing hat and sunglasses and hurried outside as though he couldn't wait to get away.

"Everything's going to pieces around here," Gaga said, shaking her head.

Matt looked out the cracked window and watched his uncle walk into the ruined vineyard. Half the grapevines had been uprooted and scattered all over. Where there had been a quaint little cottage on the eastern end of the vineyard, there was now nothing more than a pile of wood surrounding a toilet. Gaga thought all the damage had been caused by a freak storm. Everyone else knew it had something to do with their recent time travels. Only Matt knew the whole truth. Just after they'd returned from Asilah three days ago, Matt had found a note pinned with a dagger to the willow by the pond.

This is only the beginning, it read.

Matt had thrown the dagger in the pond but kept the note. He had not shown it to the rest of his family. For one, he didn't know what the note meant, exactly. It was ominous and threatening, but too vague to get any real sense for what to expect or prepare for. It was just enough to send Matt's mind in endless spirals, thinking of all the things Captain Vincent could do now that he had the Aeternum. Discard all of them in different centuries. Kill his parents. Make it so none of them were ever born. Throw them all into a pit to rot. And that was the other reason Matt didn't share the note with his family. It would only add to everyone's anxiety, and they had enough already. Too much. Matt felt for his compass, still resting on his chest beneath his shirt. All that power and still he was helpless. He wished he knew what to do!

"Well, you all have fun with your geography lesson," Gaga said, standing up with her basket of laundry. "Let me know when you're ready to actually *go* somewhere and then I'll gain some interest."

After Gaga was gone, Mr. Hudson spun the globe around, tracing a finger over the little gold stars. "If only I had the map," said Mr. Hudson for the thousandth time. He used to have a map that showed the *Vermillion*'s location at any given time, but Captain Vincent had it now. He seemed to hold all the aces.

But Matt still had his compass. Vincent wouldn't be where he was now if it weren't for that. Matt had invented it, after all, so didn't that put him at the advantage? It seemed a logical conclusion, and yet Matt felt like the underdog here. But there had to be *something* they could do . . .

"Wait a second . . . ," Matt said, as a realization suddenly donned on him. "What if . . . ?" He didn't finish his thought. He pulled his compass out from beneath his shirt, lifted it over his head and set it on the table.

"Mateo?" his mom said. "What is it?"

"Jia, do you have a small Phillips screwdriver, some tweezers, and maybe a pin or needle?"

Jia rifled through her pocketed vest until she produced the requested items. Matt took the screwdriver first and pried open the top piece from his compass, revealing a tiny but intricate labyrinth of wires and cogs and gears, all smeared in a peanut butter–bubble gum concoction. (He'd made sure to give it a tune-up after their return from Morocco.) The smell of it made him feel like he was time-traveling. Even now, the ground almost felt like it was shifting beneath his feet.

Matt could barely believe he'd built this thing. Staring at it now he could see things he'd hardly noticed before, things he'd designed and built without fully understanding why he was building them, but now was starting to see a bigger picture.

He took the tweezers and started gently pulling things apart, removing small cogs, pushing aside thin wires, until he found the piece he was looking for, a thin metal disk. "I built a hard drive into the compass," Matt said. "I meant for it to store various calendar systems and earth's geographic coordinate system, so you know it would take us where and when we want to go, but there's a possibility that it could have recorded and stored dates and coordinates to which it has traveled."

"Genius! And you think you can access them?" Mr. Hudson asked.

"I think so, though I'm not sure exactly how. We might need to hook it up to a computer or a phone and see if we can decode it."

Matt had that nervous-excited feeling he always got when he knew he was onto something, and the clarity of when he could see how all the pieces fit together. "Let's see . . . if I hook this to this wire here and that there . . . ah!"

Matt fell back in his chair as the compass sparked and sputtered. And then something started flowing out of the compass. At first Matt thought it was just smoke. He must have triggered something, crossed some wires that weren't supposed to be crossed. But then he saw that this was not any regular kind of smoke. It was certainly a vapor of some kind, but it had a bluish glow. And it was forming images. People and places that were all too familiar to Matt.

3

The Return of the Vermillion

Matt gaped at the blue vapor pouring from his compass.

"That's Asilah!" Ruby said, pointing to the white building along the shore. "And look, there's Quine and Captain Vincent. It's showing when he got the Aeternum!"

It was like a shadow of the past. There was Quine and Vincent, both of them looking down at a small object in the palm of a scarred hand. Matt's hand. He was holding the Aeternum, the Chinese symbol glowing white-hot, and then Vincent plucked it from his hand and snapped it inside his own compass (which was technically the same as Matt's compass).

"Gee, you sure did put up a fight," Corey said.

"Corey, hush, he couldn't help it," Mrs. Hudson said, but Matt's face flushed anyway. He knew he really couldn't have helped it at the time. He couldn't move, but watching this moment made him feel guilty. Like he was somehow complicit. Which he was, futuristically speaking, so maybe his guilt was warranted.

The image faded. The dials turned of their own accord. Another image poured forth, a horizon of endless water in all directions.

"That's Nowhere in No Time," Ruby said. There were his parents, Corey, Ruby, Jia, Pike, and Uncle Chuck. And Tui, when they still thought she was on their side.

"I never knew the compass could do this," Mrs. Hudson said in wonderment. The dials kept turning, the vapor kept coming, showing them echoes of the events that had happened not long ago but felt like ages—the Chicago World's Fair, Yellowstone National Park, Wrangel Island.

It was coming close to the time he'd built the compass. There was Matt on board the *Vermillion*, the very first time he'd traveled, facing his mother before she was his mother, when she was still Captain Bonnaire. Her image flowed out of the compass and disappeared.

The compass paused. It didn't seem like any more would come out.

"That's the point you built the compass, isn't it?" Ruby asked. "I told you it wouldn't show before that."

"Well, it was a nice try anyway," Corey said.

Matt poked a little at the compass and it started to spark again. The dials clicked and the bluish smoke poured out the ghostly images, more of Chicago and other places, but clearly from a different point of view—Captain Vincent's. Jia gasped as she saw herself being discarded from the *Vermillion* several times. There was the battle at the Met, and then before that all the Hudson children's travels with Captain Vincent, when they thought he'd been their friend. India and the 1986 World Series and stealing the *Mona Lisa*, and the first time the three Hudson children boarded the *Vermillion*, which was supposedly only a few months ago but felt like lifetimes. He even looked younger to himself, Matt thought.

Then there were all the times Captain Vincent had tried to kidnap the Hudson kids. It seemed like he'd tried nearly every day for all their lives. The *Vermillion* posed as buses, taxis. The ice cream truck where Brocco, dressed in a red cape, tried to lure all the kids aboard with Popsicles.

"It seems kind of miraculous that he didn't get us sooner," Ruby said.

"Maybe now you can appreciate how hard your father and I worked to keep you safe," said Mrs. Hudson. "He tried more than even I realized."

"It was inevitable," Matt said. "We were going to board sooner or later."

"I know," Mrs. Hudson said. "I just hoped it would be later."

It was the first time Matt had heard his mother acknowledge that all of this was supposed to happen. He'd always felt she wanted to keep them out of the time-travel business entirely.

The dials kept turning, the pictures flashing of the crew of the *Vermillion* on various missions, stealing art and money and treasure, and every now and then returning to New York, but not necessarily in any kind of chronological order. Matt found it incredibly strange to see these images of himself and his family, in random order, like watching old family videos, but ones you didn't know had been taken, like a spy camera.

"We must be getting close," said Jia. "That one was not long after I came aboard."

An image poured forth of the vineyard all lit up. "That's our wedding day," Mrs. Hudson said. She reached out almost as if she wanted to touch it.

"It'll be the next one," said Mr. Hudson. "He would have come straight to the wedding after figuring out his mistake with Dad."

The dials turned. Another image flashed.

"That's it!" Mr. Hudson shouted. "That's Dad!"

An image poured out of the compass of a man who looked very much like Mr. Hudson, but with a short beard and no glasses. He wore a flannel shirt, much like the ones Gaga always wore. He looked terrified. Next to him was a young man, no more than twenty.

"And that's Uncle Chuck!" Corey said.

"Matt, stop the dials if you can," said Mrs. Hudson. "Check the date and location."

Matt held the dials in place. "Sixty degrees north and eighty-five degrees west."

Mr. Hudson quickly went to look at the globe, tracing his finger along the lines. "That's in the Hudson Bay! The *Hudson* Bay! Vincent *would* dump him there, that unimaginative ba—"

"The date, the date!" shouted Mrs. Hudson, cutting off her husband. "We've got nothing if we don't know the date."

Matt studied the dials. "The year is 1611, and the month is May, no, June—" The table started shaking, and the dials of the compass slipped.

"Corey, stop shaking the table!" Mr. Hudson shouted.

Corey threw up his hand. "Why does everyone always think it's me? I'm not doing anything!"

The tremor grew stronger. It vibrated the floors, shook the walls and ceiling.

"Earthquake! Earthquake!" Gaga shouted, running into the kitchen. The smoky image of Grandpa Hudson was still hovering in the air. Mr. Hudson quickly swiped his hand through it. "There's an earthquake! Everyone get under the table. Oh! My vineyard!" She pointed out the window.

Matt looked. His jaw dropped. The vineyard had split clean down the middle, forming a ravine that was widening and deepening every second.

"Uncle Chuck!" Corey shouted. "Uncle Chuck is out there!"

He pointed to where Uncle Chuck was, right in the midst of the splitting vineyard, clinging to a few grapevines while the earth literally fell out from under his feet.

The ground shook more violently. And then the window shattered.

Matt shielded himself as glass flew over the table and floor. A cold wind gusted through, knocking over chairs, a mug of coffee, and the compass. Its loose pieces scattered. Matt fell to the trembling floor and crawled after the pieces. He gathered them all up, tried to put them back together, but the ground was shaking so hard it was impossible.

Another window shattered. Pictures fell off the walls.

"Get everyone to Blossom, Belamie," Mr. Hudson said. "I have to go help Chuck."

"Be careful!" Mrs. Hudson called after him as he raced out of the house.

The house tilted violently. Everyone went sprawling. Matt clutched the pieces of his compass to his chest as he fell. Flaming logs spilled out of the fireplace. Cinders and ash billowed out. The living room rug caught fire. The fire spread quickly. It caught on to the drapes and the room began to fill with smoke and flame. The smoke detectors started beeping.

"Fire! Fire!" Gaga ran to the kitchen and came back with the fire extinguisher, but by that time the fire had spread well beyond containment by a single fire extinguisher, and she couldn't figure out how to use it anyway.

"Why are these things so impossible!" she shouted as she shook the red canister. "I'm going to sue whoever made this thing! Where's my cell phone? Somebody call the fire department!"

"Gloria, we have to get out of the house now!" Mrs. Hudson shouted and then coughed. "Everyone outside now!"

Corey and Ruby were already running for the door. Pike ran to Jia, still clutching the book. Jia took her hand and they ran. The wall cracked. The ceiling groaned. The light fixture crashed to the floor. Matt was still frantically trying to get the pieces back into the compass as the smoke thickened and the flames crept closer to him.

"Matt!" his mom shouted. "What are you doing? Get out of the house now!"

Matt clutched the pieces of his compass and hurried out of the burning, smoking house.

Outside, the ground still shook violently. The vineyard was completely gone. Now there was a small canyon in its place. It continued to widen and deepen. Mr. Hudson was on the edge of a cliff, pulling Uncle Chuck to safety.

The house was now engulfed in fire. Flames crawled out the windows and licked the sides of the house. Gaga pulled her phone out of her purse and dialed 911. "Hello! My house is on fire! My address is— What is *that!*"

The sky above them was churning. Dark clouds rolled toward them. Matt thought it almost looked like a whale swimming through the sky, and then the whale burst through the clouds.

"Is that an airship?" Gaga said. "What is an airship doing *here*? What is happening!"

The side of the airship was emblazoned with a black compass and red *V*. It was the *Vermillion*. It came barreling toward them on a wave of black clouds.

Corey cursed under his breath.

"We gotta get out of here," Ruby said.

"Like *out* out," Corey said.

And Matt realized they meant they had to time-travel. Of course they did, but the compass was still in pieces! Quickly, Matt tried to get the pieces in order. He'd gotten it mostly put back together, but there was a piece missing. He must have dropped it somewhere, either inside the burning house or outside. Either way, he didn't have it and there was no way the compass would work without that piece.

"Everyone to Blossom!" Mrs. Hudson said. They all ran toward the bus.

Chuck's orange Volkswagen bus was still stuck in the porch where they'd crashed it just three days ago. Jia had done some maintenance to it to make sure it was in working order, but Gaga hadn't wanted the car removed until she could make sure her house wouldn't collapse when it was moved. It was collapsing anyway now.

Everyone hurried to pile into the bus. Mr. Hudson and

Uncle Chuck appeared at the same time, both of them out of breath and covered with dirt.

Uncle Chuck started Blossom's engine. He slowly pulled out of the house. The roof groaned and scraped against the top of Blossom as they backed up. Matt could see the *Vermillion* in the side mirror.

"Yo, bro," Corey said. "You going to get us out of here or what?"

Matt searched hopelessly around for the little piece. What could he do?

"Hello?" Gaga said. "Hello, yes, we were cut off before. I said my house is on fire!" She was talking on her phone again. It was an old flip phone. Totally outdated. Matt zeroed in on it, an idea forming. It was probably a stupid idea, probably wouldn't work at all, but he had to try *something*. He felt a wild desperation overtake him, survival instincts kicking in. "Yes, my address is— Ah!"

Matt snatched the phone out of Gaga's hands and cracked it in two pieces.

"Mateo, what are you doing?!"

He ripped open the case, searched the innards until he found what he was looking for. The transmitter. It was basically the right shape and design. He knew it was a Hail Mary, but it was his only shot. Matt popped it out and handed the broken phone back to Gaga, who stared at it in disbelief.

The airship was descending.

"Bro, get us out of here!" Corey shouted.

Matt shoved the transmitter inside the compass. He replaced the central dial and clicked it into place, then turned the dials as fast as he could.

Please work, please work . . .

Blossom revved her engine and spun her wheels. Dirt shot up in angry sprays all around them. There was a low growl, like some giant beast was opening its maw to swallow them. Matt grasped on to his mom as they shot away.

4
Bad Day

Henry Hudson was having a bad day. One for the books, as his own father would have put it. It had all started when Gloria kicked him out of the house. Or maybe he'd kicked himself out. He wasn't sure anymore. They'd been fighting. It was the usual stuff—work, money, leaving the cap off the toothpaste. Just regular fights that regular couples have. Gloria had told him he was a hard man to live with, and he told her that if he was such a hard man to live with maybe she'd be better off without him. He knew this was the wrong thing to say. He had a bad habit of saying the wrong things at precisely the right moment.

"Maybe I would be better off," Gloria said coldly. "Maybe you'd be better off on your own as well."

"I'll go take a hike, then," he said.

"Make it a good long one! You can hike your way to Patagonia for all I care."

So he did. Well, he didn't hike to Patagonia. He didn't even know where that was, though he'd never admit that to Gloria. He went to the Catskills, trying to find some peace in the trees and fresh air. Nature was his church, he always said. On Sundays when Gloria took the boys to church to pray and sing, he'd head for the hills. Gloria said that was just fine by her so long as he came home in time for dinner.

Henry had a feeling he was not going to make it home for dinner.

He'd noticed the strange man about halfway through his hike. He didn't think anything of it at first. Plenty of people hiked around these trails. It was when he went off the trail that he started to worry. The man followed him. Henry even made random and unreasonable turns, but still the man followed. Finally, Henry turned back and confronted the man.

"Excuse me, are you lost?" Henry asked.

"I don't believe I am, not if you are Mr. Hudson."

Henry was startled. The man spoke in a British accent. He was younger than Henry, late twenties or early thirties, dark-haired and ruggedly handsome. He looked and sounded like one of those actors on the British dramas that Gloria was always watching that Henry couldn't stand. (Though he wouldn't dare say that to Gloria.) The man wore all black, except for his shoes, which were red. Henry thought that was an odd fashion choice, but not as odd as the sword hanging on his waist. That wasn't something you saw around these parts. A rifle, maybe. But a sword?

"You are Mr. Hudson, aren't you?" the man asked.

Henry got a bad feeling in his stomach. "No, I'm not. Wrong guy. I don't know any Hudson." He turned away from the strange man, ready to hightail it out of there. But he didn't get a chance. The instant he turned around, something hard came down on his head and he was out.

When he woke, he found himself on a ship. An old ship, something he'd seen in pirate movies. Three tall masts of white sails. Henry tried to sit up. He groaned. His head felt like it had been split in two by a jackhammer. He couldn't remember what had happened. How did he get here?

"I apologize for the inconvenience," said a voice. "I'm afraid I have to relocate you now. It won't take long." Henry turned and saw the strange man who had followed him on his hike, the one with the sword and the red shoes.

"Relocate me . . ." Henry looked around. They were in some kind of lake or inlet of the ocean. He saw bits of land and rock, but no signs of civilization. Not so much as a telephone wire. And it was cold, very cold. He started to shiver.

"What do you want?" said Henry. "You want money? You'll have to take me home for that. I didn't bring my wallet, you know. Take me home, and I'll give you all the money in my wallet, plus a vintage bottle of wine. Best in the Hudson Valley."

The man pulled out a bottle of wine and took a swig. A sickening horror overcame Henry as he looked at the label. The wine was from his own vineyard.

"Why are you doing this?" Henry said. "What do you want?"

"Let's just say your interests are not mine, Matthew Hudson."

"Matthew? I'm not Matthew. Matthew is my son. I'm Henry."

The man's eyes narrowed. He got right down in Henry's face, observed him more closely, and then he swore and threw down the bottle of wine. The thick bottle didn't break, but wine spilled all over the deck and splashed onto Henry's clothes.

"Look, I think there's been a misunderstanding," Henry said, holding up a hand. "Whatever it is, I'm sure we can work it out. Just . . . just take me home and we'll work it out."

The man ignored him. He gave some sort of signal to someone who must have been standing behind Henry. Before he could even blink, he was knocked out again.

When Henry woke, hours or days later, he had no idea, he found himself in a much smaller boat that was being slowly lowered down the side of the ship. But he wasn't alone. There was another person in the boat with him, a young man, late teens or early twenties. He looked familiar to Henry, though he couldn't place why until he turned and met eyes with him. Henry felt a jolt in his heart. Those eyes. They were Gloria's eyes. He'd recognize them anywhere. Gray and full of life and laughter, though there was more fear than laughter in them now.

"Dad?" the young man said. "Dad, is that really you?" His breath smelled of wine. He was probably a little drunk and confused. Maybe he was some unknown relative, a niece or nephew of Gloria's he didn't know about. She had siblings who lived far away.

"Who are you?"

"Dad, it's me. Charles. Your son."

Henry laughed a little. "Charles? Charles is only six."

"Dad, you've been missing for over twelve years."

"Twelve years?" How hard did they hit his head? Maybe that maniac had given him brain damage. Maybe this was all just one big hallucination.

They were about halfway down the ship now. The young man who claimed to be Charles (he *did* look like Charles) started to shiver. He was wearing a tuxedo, a rose pinned to his lapel.

"Did you just go to the prom or something?"

Charles shook his head. "Wedding."

"Aren't you a little young to get hitched?"

"Not mine. Matty's."

Henry's eyes widened. Matty was getting married. And he was missing it. How much had he missed?

"It's Matty he's really after," Charles said, nodding up to the man above. "I think . . . I'm not positive, but I think he stole his woman or something. Belamie. That's the girl Matty's marrying. Pretty. Smart. Mom loves her, and she doesn't like any of the girls we've ever dated, you know."

"No, I don't know," Henry said, and his heart suddenly ached terribly, thinking of all the things he would miss, had missed, in his sons' lives. And Gloria. He thought of how he'd spoken to her that morning, or however long it had been, and he was filled with sorrow and regret. This could not be the way they parted. This could not be the way his life ended.

They hit the water. The ropes were pulled up, and the ship started to move away from them. Henry looked around and noticed the oars in the bottom of the boat.

"Grab an oar," said Henry, hard determination in his voice.

"Huh?" Charles said.

"We're not getting left behind here. Start rowing."

They started to row, keeping up with the ship at first, but then something strange started to happen. The water began to bubble around the ship, and the ship itself began to change.

A rope dropped down, and though he couldn't explain it, Henry knew if they didn't grab on to that rope right that second, they would be stuck here forever.

"Grab ahold, Charles!" said Henry. He hefted his son to the rope. Charles clung to it and then the ship moved and he was pulled out over the water.

"Dad!" Charles cried. "Hang on!"

He reached out to him as he swung over the bubbling, churning water, clinging to the rope, but Henry knew it was too late.

"Tell Gloria I love her!" he shouted. "And Matty too! I love you!"

And then the ship was gone. And Charles too. It had just . . . disappeared.

The little boat tipped and swirled in the eddies until it calmed to a gentle rocking motion. Silence. Henry stared at the place where the ship had been. It had just disappeared, and now he was utterly alone. Lost.

Henry had never minded being alone, in fact he enjoyed it. Of course, he always knew he would eventually get back to Gloria and the boys, but now he didn't think that would be the case. He never cared for being lost. He was not accustomed to it. He was used to being oriented, knowing where he was.

Henry floated aimlessly in the boat for hours, huddled and shivering in the corner of the boat. He thought maybe he should row to land, try to find help, but he saw no signs of civilization anywhere, and what if the ship returned and he missed it? Or what if someone else came along? But he was hungry, and his head was pounding. He couldn't think.

The sun set. It grew colder. Henry began to shiver violently. He started to lose his sense of reason or any feeling of hope. He reached in his back pocket and took out his wallet. He always carried pictures of the boys and Gloria. Charlie was only five in this picture and Matty eight. He had a gaptoothed smile and front teeth too big for him. How could it be that Matty was getting married? That Charlie could be so grown up? And Gloria . . . what had happened to her? What had she made of all this? Did she think he'd run away? Left her? Did she find someone else? Everything had happened so quickly, he hadn't thought to ask Charles these questions.

If only he could go back. He'd do things differently. He didn't care how many years had gone by. He didn't care if Gloria was old and gray, or if his own children were now older than he was. He just wished he could see them, even if only for a few moments, so he could say how sorry he was. That he loved them so much. Always.

These were Henry Hudson's thoughts as he drifted aimlessly in the Hudson Bay. Finally, exhaustion overcame him. He curled up on the bottom of the boat and pressed the pictures of his family against his chest. He wrapped his flannel shirt as tightly around himself as he could and fell in a fitful, shivering sleep.

As dawn approached on the other side of the bay, small ripples formed in the glassy surface of the water, and underneath it began to bubble and churn again.

Henry sat up, leaned over the side of the boat. Would the ship appear again? Was there hope for escape after all?

The water bubbled and swirled. A dark shadow formed deep in the water. It got bigger and bigger. Something was coming. It was coming right underneath him.

The little boat began to spin. Henry grabbed on to an oar and tried to row himself out of the way of whatever was coming. But it was too late. A ship burst through the surface, spraying water, making waves and whirlpools. Henry spun out of control. The boat nearly capsized, but he used the oar to gain some control.

The ship was not the same as the last one, he didn't think. It was smaller, but it was moving fast and coming straight for him. It was going to crush him.

Henry held on to the oar. "Well, this is it, I guess," he said aloud, because he felt he should have some final words, even if they were only spoken to himself. He thought of Gloria, their two boys, the future he would never share with them, and then the ship collided with Henry Hudson.

5

Time Chase

Alpine Rail, Switzerland

Blossom bumped and rattled through space and time. Matt tried to keep hold of his mom, but Blossom became a human popcorn machine, and they were forced apart. Elbows and knees knocked into heads and stomachs as they traveled until Blossom stretched and widened and they landed with a jolt. Matt was thrown against a window. He heard the *oof*s and groans of people tumbling about, getting squished and crushed, but eventually everyone settled. Matt sat up. He looked around to make sure everyone was there and alive.

Blossom had transformed into a train with simple cushioned benches and tables next to large picture windows looking out on green mountainsides. Mrs. Hudson was sitting on top of one of the tables, grabbing the sides for support. Gaga was in the aisle, groaning and clutching at her stomach.

Mr. Hudson was next to her, bleeding at the forehead. His glasses were cracked and twisted on his face. Uncle Chuck looked dazed, his hair and beard a tangled mess, but he didn't look hurt. Corey was helping to release Ruby, whose foot had been caught beneath a bench. Jia and Pike were seated neatly on one of the benches like regular passengers.

"Where are we?" Mrs. Hudson asked, looking out the window.

They were winding slowly up a mountainside. Green, sunny valleys were spread out below them. Quaint little villages dotted the land with whitewashed cottages and churches and farmland. The hillsides were scattered with flocks of goats and sheep.

"Switzerland," Matt said. "The Alps." It was one of the locations Matt had memorized. He'd seen a picture of it in a book in Gaga's house and thought it looked so peaceful and beautiful. He had imagined them living in secret in a tiny cottage in the mountains. It was even prettier in real life. He'd never seen such green.

The train tracks dipped and stretched across a valley, straight through a village. "I don't understand," Gaga said as they passed little white houses, a herd of sheep, a woman hanging out laundry on a line. "We're in *Switzerland*?"

"It's okay, Mom," Mr. Hudson said. "We can explain."

"What about that? Can you explain that?" Gaga pointed.

Another train appeared ahead, coming straight toward them, a red *V* blaring on the front. It was the *Vermillion* again.

"Matt," his mom said.

"I got it." He started turning the dials to the next location on his list. "Everybody hold on." Everyone ran to grab on to something. Just before the trains collided, Blossom jerked away and they were plunged in darkness again.

South Pacific Ocean

Blossom transformed into an old fishing boat, a single sail billowing in the wind. They were all piled together in the middle. Matt was sandwiched between Corey and Ruby, with Ruby on the bottom.

"Get off!" Ruby shouted.

When he freed himself, Matt squinted at the bright light of the sun reflecting on the water. They were on the open sea, no land anywhere in sight.

"Where are we now?" Mrs. Hudson asked.

"South Pacific Ocean," Matt said.

"What?!" Gaga shrieked.

Even though Vincent had Mr. Hudson's map, Matt thought it might be harder for him to track them in the middle of the ocean. He seemed correct in that assumption. They bobbed on the surface of the sea quite calmly, except for Gaga's hysterics.

"Matthew! I demand to know what's going on! What just happened to my house? What is that thing Matco has? And who is Vincent? Is that the maniac who tried to kidnap the children?"

But before anyone could answer Gaga, something large shot through the water about fifty feet away.

"Guess you thought wrong," Corey said grimly. It was a speedboat. It moved around in a circle until it spotted the Hudsons and then it sped toward them. The *Vermillion*'s flag waved in the wind.

Brocco was driving the boat. Wiley and Albert stood next to Brocco, bracing themselves as they sped over the choppy water. There was another man with them, too, a new crew-member, a pale man with light brown hair and a beard, wearing a suit that could come from any number of eras and countries. He was holding some kind of case in his arms. Matt couldn't focus on the man too long, though, because of Captain Vincent. He was standing on the bow, somehow maintaining perfect balance as the boat bounced over waves. He looked to Matt like a flying demon, a very handsome and well-dressed flying demon in red Converse. Santiago, the captain's white rat, sat on his shoulder, glaring straight at Matt with his evil red eyes.

Mr. Hudson cursed under his breath.

"Time to move again," Mrs. Hudson said.

Matt turned the dials again.

Dhaka, Bangladesh

They landed on a road and nearly crashed into a motorbike. The bike beeped and swerved around them, but then they were faced with a cow in the middle of the road. Uncle Chuck, now in the driver's seat, swerved around the cow and steadied Blossom, back in her bus form.

The road was jammed with cars, buses, motorbikes, carts and carriages, animals and people. There didn't seem to be any traffic rules. Everyone just sort of did what they wanted and worked around everyone else.

"Did we travel to the circus this time?" Gaga asked. She was looking pale.

"Bangladesh," Matt said.

"Of course," Gaga said dryly. "I should have known."

Matt had chosen this location specifically because he'd read that it was a crowded and confusing city, which he hoped would make it difficult for Captain Vincent to find them.

"Where's our next stop? Mars?" Gaga asked.

If Matt knew how to travel to outer space and thought they'd survive it, he would travel to Mars. Maybe Vincent wouldn't be able to follow them there.

They came up to a huge roundabout. In the center was a circular pond with a sculpture of a giant water lily. Suddenly the sculpture exploded and a car flew out of the center.

Matt didn't wait to confirm that it was the *Vermillion*. He turned the dials of the compass again.

And again.

And again.

They bounced through time and space like an out-of-control, transforming bouncy ball. He took them to the Amazon, to the North Pole, the South Pole, the Grand Canyon, and the Serengeti, from their present day to the fifth century BC. But no matter where they went, no matter what time, Captain Vincent and the *Vermillion* were there. It was all so chaotic, Matt wasn't even sure what Blossom had turned into half the time. He heard the groans and cries of his family as they traveled erratically from ocean to land, night to day, and year to year. Matt was accidentally slapped and kicked and knocked at every turn, and after the fifth or sixth turn of the dials, his stomach grew queasy. His head felt like it might implode. But he kept going. It was either keep moving or face Vincent. And they couldn't face him. Matt didn't know what would happen if they did, but he knew he didn't want to find out.

He lost track of where or when they went. He had exhausted his memorized list. Dates and coordinates seemed to pop into his head at random and he just turned the dials. Sometimes they were boats in the middle of the ocean, or a lake, sometimes they were a car or a bus in a city. It all started to meld together. There were explosions, shouts, and screams, and Matt didn't know where or who they were coming from, if his family was getting hurt, or if he was, or someone else. At one point, Blossom nearly landed on top of a lone man in a boat. He was waving at them, probably afraid they were going to crash. And they did. Matt turned the dials right away, but he felt the jolt of Blossom colliding with the man's boat before they disappeared. Matt had a horrible feeling that they'd done damage to the man's boat, maybe even hurt the man. But what could he do? They couldn't stop. They had to keep going.

Through all the transformations, Blossom and the *Vermillion* seemed to be carrying out their own battle, circling and racing each other, weaving in and out of the other's paths, coming dangerously close to crashing. It was unclear if anyone was in control of the vehicles. No one seemed to be driving the *Vermillion* or Blossom, from what Matt could see. In every formation, Wiley, Brocco, and Albert seemed to be standing by, waiting for the captain to do something. Wiley was always holding a large piece of paper in his hands. Mr. Hudson's map.

And there was the stranger on the *Vermillion*, the one holding the case. Matt could see him a little better now. He was a pale man with light blue eyes. He had a very solemn, severe expression. He was carrying his case like he was guarding a precious treasure. There were moments he saw the man looking toward him with a confused sort of expression, like he was seeing something that didn't make sense to him. Matt didn't have the energy to try to puzzle that out. He was too busy turning the dials of the compass, too busy trying to keep them alive.

Blossom turned into a train again, a rickety steam engine, very basic and bare. Blossom seemed to be losing her steam. Or the compass, or maybe both. The train huffed and groaned as she chugged along, slowly.

Matt was losing his own steam. He didn't think he could go on. The rest of his family was in bad shape too. His dad was leaning over Gaga, who was keeled over clutching her stomach. His mom had her head to the floor, pressing her fingers to her temples. Jia and Pike were both curled up behind the seats. He could see only their feet. Uncle Chuck was limp in the engineer's seat. Matt did not know if he'd passed out or if it was worse than that.

Matt was not certain where or when they were. They'd landed in another storm. The car was open on both sides so they were exposed to the elements. Rain lashed down and the sky cracked with lightning followed by booms of thunder. They were chugging slowly between narrow, rocky cliffs and brown, snowcapped mountains, the opposite of the lush green Alps. It was cold, wet, dreary, and lifeless.

A horn blared in the distance. There was the *Vermillion* again, also a train, coming up alongside them on a parallel track. Matt knew he needed to move, to turn the dials of the compass, but he found he couldn't move. His fingers were leaden, his strength sapped. He just needed a minute to rest.

The *Vermillion* was now even with them. The car doors were open between the two trains. They were running so closely together, Captain Vincent could take one step and board Blossom. And he likely would have had Mrs. Hudson not drawn her sword and attacked him with everything she had, which was clearly very little. Captain Vincent easily blocked her blows and retaliated. He smiled like they were playing a delightful little game. Matt could tell he wasn't really putting up a fight, but more egging her on, allowing her to drain the last of her strength.

Ruby and Corey crawled to Matt. Both of them seemed fine. How were they fine? "We'll never be able to lose them while they have the map!" Ruby said. "We have to get it back."

"How?" Matt said. "I don't think they're going to just hand it over."

"We have to steal it, duh," Corey said.

"Okay," Matt said, too tired to even put up a reasonable argument. "Go steal it then."

Corey stood up and saluted Matt. "Aye, aye, captain!"

And before Matt could register what was happening, Corey took a running leap from the side of Blossom and landed on the *Vermillion*.

"Corey, no!" Ruby shouted.

He barreled into Captain Vincent, who stumbled back into the rest of his stunned crew.

"Corey!" Mrs. Hudson shouted.

It all happened in a few seconds. Corey snatched the map right out of Wiley's hands. Brocco made a grab to take it back, and in doing so the map ripped in two pieces. Corey shoved Brocco, then made a run for it back to Blossom. Their parents were right there, reaching out to him. Corey took a giant leap, but Albert was behind him. He grabbed Corey by the shirt. Ruby screamed. Matt screamed. He was sure that Corey was going to fall right between the trains.

But then Captain Vincent reached out his left hand. He made a few strange motions, like he was writing something in the air, and Corey stopped. He froze midleap, the torn map in his clenched hand. Matt looked around, stunned, as he realized that *everything* had stopped. The world seemed to have frozen right in the middle of the action, like a film on pause. The wind ceased. The rain hung in the air like a million tiny crystal droplets and spears. The air was perfectly still, unnaturally quiet. And it wasn't just the storm that had been stilled, Matt realized. His entire family, and Jia and Pike, had been paused in time, just like three days ago in Asilah, when Captain Vincent had gotten the Aeternum.

Matt tried to stand up, but he was very weak. He could hardly move, and then he thought it would probably be better if he stayed where he was anyway because Captain Vincent hadn't seen him. He didn't seem to know that Matt hadn't been frozen like the rest of them.

Captain Vincent put his sword back in his scabbard. He went to the pale stranger, touched him on the chest. The man took a deep, gasping breath and was revived.

"Let's get to work," Captain Vincent said.

"As you wish it," the man said. His voice was deep and gruff. He had a European accent, German, Matt thought, or maybe Dutch. He took his case and followed Captain Vincent to the edge of the train car, right in front of Matt's parents, who were both reaching for Corey. Captain Vincent waved a hand at all the stilled raindrops so they moved aside like a curtain. It made a strange sound, something like tinkling glass and sloshing liquid. Matt shifted a little to keep out of view, which was a mistake. The stranger turned his head and locked eyes with him. Matt froze, held his breath, but he was certain the man knew he was awake, that he had seen him move, and now he would tell Captain Vincent.

But he didn't say anything. He simply lifted an eyebrow at Matt, then turned his attention back to Captain Vincent. Interesting.

"Where do you wish to begin, Your Majesty?" the man asked.

Your Majesty? Was Vincent a king now? Of what? The world?

"Him, of course," Captain Vincent said, nodding toward

Mr. Hudson. "That should solve a great deal, I think, though perhaps not all. We might need to do some work on her as well." He nodded toward Mrs. Hudson. "And the children, depending on the results."

What was he talking about? What did he mean by "work"?

Captain Vincent reached out and grabbed Mr. Hudson by the throat. Matt gasped, thinking he was going to strangle his father, but then the captain released his grip and pulled something away. Matt had no idea what it was. It was shimmering blue, almost fluorescent, and it flowed from his dad's throat like a watery, sparkling fabric. Images floated within the material. Matt saw his mom, Corey and Ruby, himself and others, scenes from his father's life. It looked similar to the smoky vapor that had come out of Matt's compass, though this material looked more solid and vibrant, like it was a living thing.

The stranger opened the case he'd been guarding and pulled out a long cylinder. It looked to Matt like a stick of dynamite, but this couldn't be any normal explosive. It had a strange iridescent glow, similar to the material flowing out his dad's throat. It looked and *felt* alive. Matt could feel it, even from his hiding spot. It made his blood rush.

The stranger handed the dynamite over to the captain. Matt felt panic rise in him. Whatever the captain was going to do to his dad, he was sure it wasn't benign. He could not stand by and watch. He had to do something. Anything.

"Stop!" Matt shouted as he jumped forward and then quickly retreated. The stilled droplets of rain poked and sliced him when he came against them, like hundreds of glass shards dangling in the air.

"Mateo!" Captain Vincent said, in his congenial but oily voice. "How glad I am to see you." Santiago, sitting on Captain Vincent's shoulder, hissed at Matt, his traditional greeting for him. "Come now, Santiago. Aren't you glad to see our friend Mateo? Or is it Marius Quine now?" He turned back to Matt. "Are you going by your true identity yet? I am not entirely sure when that change happens."

Matt felt the blood drain from his face. He knew. Captain Vincent knew he was Marius Quine. How did he know? What did that mean? He didn't have time to work that through his brain. There were more important things at stake in this moment. "Don't touch my dad," Matt said. He tried to step forward but got jabbed again with the shards of rain.

Matt touched his cheek and winced at the sting. Bright blood smeared on his fingers.

"Be careful, Mateo," Captain Vincent said. "The world is a precarious place even outside of time. For mortals, at least." He took a white handkerchief out of his jacket and held it out to Matt. Matt hesitated, wondering if there was some trick in this.

"I'm not trying to trick you," Captain Vincent said. "Here." He tossed the handkerchief. Matt caught it and pressed it to his bleeding face without taking his eyes off Captain Vincent. He was closer to him now, and they weren't traveling, so he had a better view. At first glance he looked the same as he always had ever since Matt had first met him. A handsome man with dark hair and eyes, a neatly trimmed beard around his chiseled jaw, wearing his usual black clothing and red Converse. But Matt could see the differences too. They were subtle but unmistakable. He had a strange aura about him, a sort of bluish glow that seemed otherworldly. Anyone else might mistake it for an effect of the light, or your own failing eyesight, but in the dim light of the storm it was noticeable. The other thing Matt noticed was the scar, or rather the lack of it. The captain was supposed to have a scar on his right cheek, where Matt had sliced him with a sword. Granted, it could have been any number of years for the captain since that time, but Matt was certain he had cut him deep enough to make a permanent scar that no amount of time would heal. But the scar wasn't there. There wasn't even a trace of it.

Captain Vincent, seeming to know what Matt was staring at, reached up and brushed the spot where the scar should have been. "Another benefit of the Aeternum," he said. "I don't bleed anymore. Nothing can hurt me. The Aeternum truly does mend all that is broken."

Where was the Aeternum? The compass? Matt searched for the gold chain and the small bulge at the captain's left sleeve where he usually kept it, but he didn't see it. His compass did not heat up against his skin like it always did when it was in its own presence. It remained cool and lifeless around his neck.

"It's gone," Captain Vincent said, once again seeming to read Matt's thoughts. "Or I should say it's a part of me now. No one can take it from me. I *am* the Aeternum. And now I'll be able to fix everything to how it always should have been." He took his eyes off Matt and glanced toward Mrs. Hudson.

Matt instinctively took a step toward her. Both she and Mr. Hudson were reaching out toward Corey. They looked like wax statues, something from Madame Tussauds. "What did you do to them?"

"Nothing," Captain Vincent said. "I simply stopped time. Humans are highly attached to time. But not you and me. We are different."

Matt was reminded of Quine's words. "We have always been different. We have different rules." How was he different? He didn't have the Aeternum. Even when he had it, he hadn't known what it was, hadn't known how to use it. He was pretty sure he wasn't immortal. He could bleed. He was fairly certain he could die.

"What about him?" Matt nodded toward the stranger. He'd been completely silent and almost as still as everyone else. He barely glanced at Matt when he spoke.

"He is a regular human being," the captain said, "though

an intelligent one, I'll grant him. He knows how to choose sides wisely. We look forward to the time you join us."

"I'm not joining you," Matt said, disgusted.

The captain smiled at him like he was an obstinate toddler. "I know you think I am your enemy, Mateo. But I am not. I never have been."

"Fine," Matt spat. "Then go away and leave us alone. We won't bother you if you won't bother us."

Captain Vincent chuckled. "I'm afraid that's not the way this is going to work. There won't be any kind of truce or compromise. I'm simply going to make things right. You'll understand eventually. One day you'll come to me and tell me just about everything I need to know in order to succeed. You know how I know? Because you already did."

"What are you talking about? No, I didn't!"

Captain Vincent just shook his head, still smiling at Matt in that patronizing way that made him want to gouge out his eyeballs. "Remember how I said when we first met it wasn't the first time for me? Remember the *Mona Lisa*? The message? The key?"

The hair on the back of Matt's neck prickled. He'd almost forgotten about that time he'd stood right in Captain Vincent's cabin, and the captain produced his own Mets hat that had contained a secret message inside of it that had essentially set him on the path to getting the Aeternum. Which essentially Matt had given him. "I've known we were on the same side from the very beginning. You might not know it yet, but you will. I promise."

Matt shook his head. No, he wouldn't. It didn't matter what his future self had done. There had to be an explanation. Vincent was trying to harm his family, and Matt would never, *never* allow it. No matter what.

Captain Vincent brushed the watery material flowing out of Mr. Hudson's throat.

"What is that?" Matt asked.

"This is a time tapestry," the captain said. "Our time in the world, everything we see and do, everyone we come in contact with, is woven into our very beings, creating a tapestry of our lives." Captain Vincent pulled more of the material from Mr. Hudson. Flashes of images shone in its rippling, iridescent folds. Matt, Corey, and Ruby, and their mom. Everywhere was his mom.

"The Aeternum made it possible for me to access it so I could change it as I wished, change things in the past, rearrange. Or erase completely. I've found that's a better way to take care of some problems. Just make them go away. Here. I shall demonstrate now."

Captain Vincent lifted that strange, glowing stick of dynamite and wrapped it inside of Mr. Hudson's time tapestry.

"What are you doing? Stop!"

"Don't worry," Captain Vincent said. "It will only be a moment, and then all will be just as it always should have been." He struck a match and lit the wick. It hissed and started to burn. The fabric began to tremble as though it could sense a threat.

Matt was panicking. What could he do? He wasn't good in these kinds of situations. He needed Corey and Ruby. What would they do? He glanced at Corey, frozen in midair, his father's map crumpled in his hand. Corey wouldn't think so hard. He'd just act. And Ruby . . . Matt's eyes landed on Ruby's sword in the scabbard at her side. He pulled it out and before he could second-guess himself, he leaped. The tiny spears of rain sliced his face as he soared through the air, sword raised. He landed on the *Vermillion* and slashed the sword down with both hands over Captain Vincent's wrist, slicing through skin, snapping bones. Captain Vincent made a beastly kind of growl as his hand was severed clean off. It fell between the two trains and disappeared, along with the strange dynamite.

Mr. Hudson's life tapestry spun back into his throat, but Matt couldn't take his eyes off Captain Vincent's handless wrist. There was no blood, only skin, sinew, and bone. And then, to Matt's shock and horror, the skin began to knit itself together, healing with incredible speed. The flesh swelled and split into small fingers that thickened as they lengthened. The captain's hand was regrowing itself.

Matt backed away. He let go of Ruby's sword. It fell between the train cars, and then . . .

Boom!

The dynamite must have exploded beneath the trains. A flash of blue light erupted, and with a sudden jolt, the timeline started again. Everything went back into motion. Matt toppled over as the trains suddenly started moving. The rain went back to regular liquid rain. Corey continued in his leap. Albert still had ahold of his shirt, but Mr. and Mrs. Hudson both grabbed on to Corey's hand and pulled him over, and they all rolled in a big heap.

Matt didn't think twice. He scrambled to his feet and took a running jump back to Blossom. As soon as he landed, he grabbed his compass and turned the dials. He set the compass to the only time and place he could think of in that moment. Blossom immediately began to transform. The rocky cliffs and mountains seemed to shrink.

Then Matt heard a scream. It was Jia. "Pike! What are you doing?!"

A pale little blur leaped across to the *Vermillion*.

"Stop! Don't go yet! We need to get Pike!"

But it was too late. They were traveling now.

The last thing Matt saw before they disappeared was Captain Vincent reaching out his freshly grown hand toward them. He came so close, Matt could have sworn he felt it graze his scraped and bleeding cheek.

6

Stowaways

New York City

Matt was not certain what Blossom was transforming into, but it was definitely not a train or a boat or a car. The surface beneath him became cool and smooth, some kind of metal. He slid along its surface until he caught onto a thin pole. He felt a powerful rush of wind, heard the sputtering roar of an engine.

They burst through the darkness, into bright light and a shock of cold air. Matt's stomach jumped to his throat as they plummeted about twenty feet in a second. They were in the sky. Blossom had transformed into an airplane. It was a very old-fashioned airplane, with wide double wings connected by thin metal poles. Matt was sitting on top of one of the wings, clinging to one of the poles. Jia was on the same wing as him, clinging to another pole. She was shouting. Matt couldn't hear her, but he knew she was shouting for Pike.

Uncle Chuck was at the controls of the plane, with Gaga crouched behind him. This plane didn't have a cockpit, just a few gears and levers, and a watch-like instrument mounted on a pole.

His parents and Corey were still in a heap, a big tangle of arms and legs. He could hardly tell where one started and the other began. One of the arms, his dad's it looked like, was hanging on to a pole.

But where was Ruby? Matt looked around. He couldn't see her. Had they somehow left her behind? They couldn't have. She had stayed on Blossom. Only Corey had jumped to the *Vermillion*.

Then he spotted her. Or her hands at least. She was hanging off the edge of the wing! Her two hands were clinging for dear life to one of the poles.

The plane rattled and dipped. They rose up and then plummeted again. Matt felt like his stomach was being twisted and flipped inside out. But he had to get Ruby. Slowly and carefully, he made his way to her. Ruby looked up at him with pure terror in her eyes. Holding tight to a pole with one hand, Matt leaned down and shouted in Ruby's ear, "Swing up a leg!" She swung a leg up enough for Matt to catch it and pull her over the wing. Ruby wrapped her arms tightly around Matt's neck, but then the plane tilted, and Ruby grabbed on to one of the poles.

They were flying a little lower now. Matt could see sky-scrapers and bridges and the ocean. They were soaring over New York. Home. That was all Matt could think of in those last moments. He just wanted to go home with his family.

They were headed toward the Brooklyn Bridge. There was clearly something going on there. Matt thought he could see quite a bit of commotion, like traffic had come to a full stop on the bridge, but he couldn't see what had caused it. Maybe there had been an accident.

They flew on, wrapping around the Statue of Liberty. A giant bird was circling the crown. Its wingspan was enormous. What kind of bird was that? An eagle? A condor, maybe? It looked bigger than any bird he'd ever seen. The bird landed on the crown of the Statue of Liberty, stretched and folded its wings. Matt squinted, studying the bird's profile. It sort of looked like a pterodactyl. But that was impossible.

The plane circled around the Statue of Liberty again. Matt could tell Uncle Chuck was trying to decide where they should land. Water or land? If they landed in water they could crash and drown, and if they landed on land they might crash and burn, not to mention possibly injure or kill innocent people.

The plane dipped, then raised a bit, then dipped again. They got lower and lower. It looked like Uncle Chuck had decided on a water landing. As they first touched the water, Matt thought perhaps he should turn the dials again, see if he could nudge Blossom to transform into a boat or ship, but it seemed Blossom was one step ahead of him. After the first few splashes, Blossom began to shift. The plane's wings folded in like a bird landing on water. The body of the plane stretched and widened into a long boat. A mast shot through the center, right in the place where Corey was tangled up with his parents. A single square sail unfurled and puffed out in the wind. The boat rocked violently. Water splashed over the sides, soaking Matt's already wet shorts and sneakers. Gaga was curled up in the fetal position on the bottom of the boat. Uncle Chuck tried to stand and take a few steps, but instantly fell down and stayed there.

Matt braced himself on a bench and turned all around, searching for any signs of Captain Vincent or the *Vermillion*. A water taxi approached, and he almost thought he saw the compass and V symbol on the side, but it was only a white life preserver with a few red stripes. He kept his fingers poised on the dials of the compass. He jumped at every movement, any boat, ship, or ferry, near or far. He searched for the symbol of the *Vermillion*.

Someone touched his shoulder. Matt flinched and whipped around, breathing hard. But it was only Ruby. "It's okay," she said. "It's just me."

Matt nodded. "You okay?" he asked. Ruby's face was flushed, and chunks of hair had been pulled free of her braid, but she didn't look hurt.

"I'm fine, thanks to you."

Matt looked around one more time. No *Vermillion.* No Captain Vincent. No time pirates. He took a breath as though it was his first in ages and slumped down to the floor, overcome with exhaustion and dizziness. He felt as though he'd been put through a shredder and then hastily glued back together. It was all very tenuous. He could fall apart at any moment.

Ruby knelt down beside him. "Matt, your face . . . What happened?"

Matt touched his cheek and felt the sting. He looked at his fingers, saw the blood. Somehow the sight of it made the pain bloom everywhere. His arms were cut up, too, and his shirt and shorts were in shreds. It was a miracle they were still on his body.

His mom was suddenly there, and Corey and his dad. His mom's hair had been ripped free of its ponytail and was a wild mess. His dad's hair was also crazy, his glasses askew, and his face extremely pale. Matt automatically looked at his throat, searching for any sign of injury from where Captain Vincent had pulled that watery material. His time tapestry. He couldn't see anything, but he couldn't believe it hadn't had some effect.

"Dad," Matt said. "You okay?"

"Yeah, buddy, I'm okay."

"You sure? Count your ABCs and sing your numbers."

His dad gave him a funny look. "I think the one we need

to worry about is you, bud. You look like you've been in a war zone."

Matt winced as his mom brushed his cut-up face, frowning. "Oh, Mateo, what happened?"

"The rain," Matt said.

"The rain?"

"It was sharp."

They all looked at each other. "Maybe he's talking about the window at Gaga's house," Ruby said. "It shattered, remember? Matt was right in front of it."

"Plus he always gets really bad time sickness," Corey said. "Maybe he's lost his mind this time."

"Well, that was some pretty intense time traveling," Mr. Hudson said. "I'm a little woozy myself. You two okay?"

Ruby shrugged. "I feel fine."

"Me too," Corey said.

Matt marveled at his brother and sister. He couldn't understand how they were both still standing. They never seemed to be affected by time travel. They never got time sick. Matt wondered if that had anything to do with the fact that their parents were born in different centuries, and that somehow made them biologically fit for time traveling. It was an interesting theory. Maybe one day, there would be many more children born of parents in different centuries. They could run all kinds of studies on the effects. But Matt was getting ahead of himself.

Jia came tumbling into his view. She was crying. "We have to go back for Pike!" she said. "She jumped onto the *Vermillion* just before we left!"

"I'm sorry, *chérie*, but I'm afraid we can't go back."

"We have to! We have to!" Jia cried hysterically. Matt had never seen her so beside herself. "You would go back if it was Matt or Corey or Ruby!"

"This is different," Mrs. Hudson said. "Pike very clearly chose to cross over to the *Vermillion*."

"She didn't mean it! She didn't know what she was doing!"

"We can't be sure of that," Mrs. Hudson said calmly. "It could be part of Vincent's plans. It could be another trap."

"You mean the way *I* was a trap?" Jia said in a hard voice. "Do you wish you hadn't saved me?"

"Of course not," Mrs. Hudson said, taken aback. "Oh, Jia, I'm so sorry. That's not what I meant. I only—"

"Hello?" said a very irritable voice. "Anybody want to help me out here?"

They all froze and looked around the boat.

"Who's that?" Ruby asked.

Matt looked up, squinting in the sunlight. Two stout legs were dangling from the mast.

Corey groaned. "Oh no! You have got to be kidding me."

Jia wiped her tears. "That sounds like Albert."

"How did he get here?" Ruby asked.

Matt remembered how Albert had been reaching for

Corey as he was jumping across. He must have lost control of himself and jumped across, too, just before they traveled.

"Hello!" Albert spoke in his usual haughty tone. "It's rather rude to leave a person just hanging like this! If I fall, I could break my neck!"

"Oh no! We wouldn't want that to happen!" Corey shouted.

"Corey, that's enough," Mrs. Hudson reprimanded.

"I'll go help him down," Mr. Hudson said, which was easier said than done. Albert was not very cooperative when it came to following Mr. Hudson's directions, so eventually Mr. Hudson just yanked on both his legs so Albert was forced to let go. Mr. Hudson caught Albert as he fell but clearly wasn't prepared for Albert's bulk. Albert landed right on top of Mr. Hudson, who let out an *oof!* Albert rolled off him, grumbling about incompetence. He brushed himself off, straightened his glasses, and smoothed his hair. Finally, he noticed the group of people staring at him. His face drained of color in an instant.

"Oh no," he said. "I've been taken hostage by the enemy!"

Corey snorted. "Are you kidding me? Us take *you* hostage? I'd rather cut off my right arm than be forced to spend time with you. You're a stowaway, that's what you are, and we're going to discard you the first chance we get. In fact, let's throw him overboard now."

Albert backed away, looked around for some place to run, but seeing that he was trapped on a boat floating down a river, he decided on another tactic. He stood up straight, lifted his chin. "It doesn't matter. Captain Vincent will save me."

"Sure," Corey said sarcastically. "I'm sure you're top of mind for him right now."

"You won't be laughing after the captain is finished with you," Albert said. "You're all doomed."

Corey rolled his eyes. "Don't listen to him. He's full of it."

Albert's eyes darkened. His nostrils flared, making him look even more piggish. "You think I'm lying? I've seen what Captain Vincent can do now. He's more powerful than you could ever imagine."

Matt thought of the time tapestry, and that strange dynamite the captain had almost used on his dad, the way it erupted beneath the train. He knew Albert was telling the truth. But there were still things he didn't know or understand, and as long as Albert was gloating Matt decided he should try to get some information out of him.

"Who was that other man who was on the *Vermillion*?" Matt asked. "What was he doing for Captain Vincent?"

"That's Al—" Albert began, but then stopped and reconsidered. He seemed to pick up on what Matt was trying to do. "That's none of your business." He clamped his mouth shut.

"You'd better tell us," Corey said, "or we'll throw you overboard, and I have a hunch you can't swim."

By the expression on Albert's face Matt guessed Corey's hunch was correct.

"Corey, settle down. We'll do no such thing," Mrs. Hudson said.

"But, Mom! He's withholding information. He's the enemy! This is war! Shouldn't we at least torture him a little? Break a few fingers? Hold him underwater until *just* before he drowns?"

Albert tucked his hands behind his back and backed away a few steps.

Mrs. Hudson got down in Corey's face and stuck her finger in his chest. "You won't harm a hair on his head. He's only a child."

"I'm not a child!" Albert protested.

Mrs. Hudson turned on Albert and regarded him with a cool gaze. "Very well, then. You are free to go. You are not our hostage. We don't take prisoners. We can drop you anywhere you wish here in the city, and you can wait for Vincent to rescue you. Is that what you wish?"

Albert's eyes darted around. He moved his feet in a way that reminded Matt of a toddler doing a potty dance.

"I'll take your silence as your desire to stick with us," Mrs. Hudson said. "We will feed and protect you, but you will not be our prisoner, even though you deem us the enemy. You are free to go whenever you like. If Captain Vincent should return, you may return with him, if that's your wish."

Albert didn't seem to know what to do with this

information. He studied Mrs. Hudson with suspicion, trying to find the trick in her words.

A loud groan turned all their attention to the other side of the ship, where Gaga and Uncle Chuck were. Gaga slid down against the side of the ship, her face a pale shade of green.

"Yikes, I almost forgot she'd come along," Mr. Hudson said. He went to Gaga and knelt down beside her. "Mom, you okay?"

Gaga shook her head back and forth with her eyes closed. "Never again. Never, never, never."

Matt could only imagine how she was feeling. It was a terrible way to experience time travel in any case, but especially for the first time.

Matt closed his eyes and tried to steady his breathing. Captain Vincent popped into his mind, unbidden, pulling swaths of that time tapestry from his dad's neck. Matt wasn't sure exactly what the captain had been about to do, but whatever it was, Matt was sure they'd dodged a big bullet. But he wasn't sure they'd be able to dodge another one. That had been too close. The captain was sure to take better aim the next time. But what could they do? He didn't understand what they were up against.

"How cool is this?" Corey said. "I think Blossom turned into a Viking ship!" He was standing at the front of the ship, holding on to the carved head of a dragon. The ship was long and narrow, the single sail striped orange and white.

"That doesn't make sense," Ruby said. "We're not in the Viking Age."

No, they certainly weren't. They were sailing down the East River, toward the Brooklyn Bridge and the bay. The temperature was cool with a slight breeze, but not too cold that they were uncomfortable. The sun shone so brightly on the water, Matt had to squint in order to see. He wished he had his Mets hat. Where was it now in the timeline? He wondered. The last time he'd had it was when he'd accidentally traveled to the *Vermillion* back in Chicago, 1893, when his mom was still captain. Captain Vincent had grabbed it off his head. What had he done with it? He showed it to Matt when he'd boarded the *Vermillion* for the first time, but it had the message about the *Mona Lisa* in it then, and Captain Vincent said Matt had given it to him, so that didn't totally line up. He hadn't put the message inside his hat yet . . .

They were closer to the Brooklyn Bridge now than when they'd been in the plane, and Matt could tell something was definitely happening. Maybe it was one of those protests about climate change, or it could be a parade. As they drew closer, though, it looked more like a battle. On one end of the bridge was an army of men in full armor, not unlike the ancient armor he'd seen displayed his entire life at the Met. They had swords and shields, spiked balls and chains and double-sided axes. On the other end looked to be a Roman army, with red tunics, gold breastplates, and feathered helmets. They had swords and shields, too, and spears and bows and arrows and chariots pulled by armored horses.

"Maybe they're filming something?" Uncle Chuck suggested. Matt remembered they'd tried to give him this excuse when they'd traveled to the Ice Age and saw woolly mammoths, but Matt was pretty sure that wasn't what was happening here.

"You sure we didn't travel to the Viking times?" Corey asked. "Or Ancient Rome?"

"We couldn't have," Ruby said. The bridge wouldn't be there, nor the Statue of Liberty or any of this." She gestured to all the buildings of the city. They were definitely in New York City, close to their own present if they were judging by the buildings and bridges. But even there, when Matt looked more closely, things were different. He couldn't say exactly what, but it seemed like certain buildings were out of place, others missing, like the One World Trade Center. He knew exactly where that building stood, but he couldn't see it now. Maybe this was before it had been built? But after 9/11? He didn't see the Twin Towers either.

"What's the date, Mateo?" Mrs. Hudson asked. "Where did you set the dials?" She walked slowly toward him.

Matt checked his compass. Truthfully, he hadn't been paying all that much attention to the date when he'd turned the dials, only the place. "It's . . . uh . . . 2019 . . . no 1902 . . .

no . . . ah!" The dials were going haywire, particularly the time dials, which were shaking back and forth.

"Let me see," his mom said, stepping gingerly to take a look. Corey, Ruby, and their dad gathered around, too, leaning in to observe the compass spinning its dials in Matt's hand.

"I've never seen it do this before," Mrs. Hudson said, her brow knit.

"Maybe it's because time has been disrupted," Ruby said. "The compass doesn't know where or when it is, because the *world* doesn't even know."

It wasn't a bad theory, Matt thought, but he wasn't sure how helpful it was to know. Mrs. Hudson continued to frown at the compass.

"It might be that the compass just needs some repairs," Matt said. "I lost a piece just before we traveled. I had to add a spare part at the last minute from Gaga's phone, but it was only a temporary fix."

"Lucky that it got us this far, I suppose," his mom said. "Can you fix it?"

"I'll need some tools and materials, but yeah, I think so."

"Corey, do you have my map?" Mr. Hudson said. Corey looked down at his hand as if he'd forgotten what was clenched in his fist. He slowly held out the crumpled map to his dad.

Mr. Hudson took it and carefully unfolded it. He set it down on the bench and tried to smooth out the wrinkles. The map was torn completely in half. They had the piece with the Northern Hemisphere, so most of the earth's landmasses, except the southern tip of Africa, the majority of South America, and all of Australia. That was helpful, Matt thought. At least Vincent wouldn't be able to track them if they stayed out of those areas, and they'd be able to track him if he traveled in any of the places they could see on the map. But then Matt saw that no one would be tracking anyone. There were no symbols on the map, none that glowed to tell them where or when the *Vermillion* was currently located, nor any dark markings to show where it had been before. The map was broken.

Mr. Hudson's hands trembled a little. They all knew how much he loved this map, what it meant to him. To all of them. It was the thing that had brought their family together.

"I'm sorry," Corey said softly.

"No, it's okay," Mr. Hudson said, his voice a little hoarse. He carefully folded up the torn map and slipped it in his back pocket. "Better destroyed than in the hands of Vincent. He can't track us now, at least."

Albert, standing a ways off from the group, snorted.

"Is there a hog on board?" Corey said, looking around. "Oh, no, it's just Albert."

"Corey," Mrs. Hudson warned.

"Call me whatever names you like," Albert said. "Captain Vincent doesn't need your silly map. He'll track you down in other ways."

"Well, he's not here now, is he?" Corey said.

Matt silently had to believe Albert was right, though, and by the looks on the rest of his family's faces he could see they felt the same. But no one said it aloud. That was too much.

They were sailing around Battery Park and out toward the Statue of Liberty. Matt saw those large birds again on top of the crown. Still there was no sign of Captain Vincent or the *Vermillion*, though Matt's heart raced whenever he saw another boat or ship.

"Hey, where's my sword?" Ruby was frowning at her empty scabbard.

Matt suddenly remembered that he'd dropped it on the *Vermillion*, after he'd chopped off Captain Vincent's hand. "I'm sorry," Matt said. "I took it. I was trying to stop Vincent, and I lost it."

Ruby frowned. "What are you talking about? I would have remembered if you had taken it."

"Stop Vincent from what?" Mrs. Hudson asked at the same time.

Matt wasn't sure how to explain. He was still processing everything that had just happened, and he was still woozy and weak from all the travel. But he could see he would have to try his best because everyone was staring at him like he was deranged, including his parents. Never a good sign.

"When Blossom was a train," Matt explained, "just before we came here, Vincent stopped time. Everything stopped.

The train, all of you, even the rain was frozen in midair. That's what I was trying to explain earlier. The rain became still and turned hard, like shards of glass. It hurt when you touched it. Anyway. you were all just frozen like statues."

"But you weren't?" his mom asked, looking at him with a creased brow.

Matt shook his head.

"How come?" Corey asked.

Matt shrugged. "I don't know. I just wasn't." Matt did his best to explain what had happened, but it was very jumbled, and he could see by the looks on everyone's faces he wasn't making much sense, but the worst part was when he tried to explain what the captain had done to Mr. Hudson.

Everyone gasped. Mrs. Hudson paled. "What do you mean he pulled something out of his throat?" Mrs. Hudson inspected her husband right away, searching his throat for a wound. There was none.

"It wasn't like he was pulling out organs or anything," Matt said. "It was something I've never seen before. He called it a—"

"A time tapestry," Albert supplied, clearly unable to hold back his knowledge. "Captain Vincent can pull it out of anyone, and change things as he wishes."

"And he did that to me?" Mr. Hudson said, putting a hand to his throat.

"I stopped him before he could do anything," Matt said.

"I used Ruby's sword and I . . . chopped off Vincent's hand."

"You chopped off Vincent's *hand*?" Corey said. "And I didn't get to see it? That is so unfair!"

Matt did not think it was nearly as cool as Corey thought it was. If there was anything cool about it, it was the part where Captain Vincent regrew his hand right before his eyes, but he never got to explain that part.

"Well, there doesn't seem to be any harm done," Mr. Hudson said. "I'm fine. I still remember my ABCs and one, two, threes."

"Let's check, just to make sure," Corey said. "Recite 'em."

Mr. Hudson obliged, and then they all took him through a series of questions.

"What's the capital of Alaska?" Ruby asked.

"Juneau."

"How did I get this scar?" Corey asked, pointing to a thin scar beneath his chin.

Mr. Hudson laughed. "You jumped off the top of a playground because you thought you were Superman."

"Most disappointing moment in my whole life."

"Where did you go to college?" Ruby asked.

"Undergrad at Columbia. PhD at Oxford."

"What day did we get married?" Mrs. Hudson asked.

Mr. Hudson looked at her, confused. "I never got married. Who are you, anyway?"

Mrs. Hudson paled. Mr. Hudson started laughing.

"Oh, that is so not funny!" Mrs. Hudson slapped him on the chest, but he just wrapped his arms around her.

"August 7, 1999. Best day of my life." He kissed Mrs. Hudson.

"Gross. No PDA, please!" Corey said, but Matt didn't mind it so much, he realized. Watching his parents, the way they looked at each other, made him feel safe. All was right with the world as long as they were together. They were the most unlikely pair, centuries and continents apart, but they belonged together. They were lucky. Matt hoped one day he'd have what his parents had. He automatically glanced over at Jia, but she wasn't paying attention to the scene. She was sitting on a bench, hunched over something.

Matt went over to her and saw that she was looking at a book. It was Matt's book that Pike had been reading, the one about famous inventors his parents had given him on his birthday.

Jia looked up at him. Her eyes were so incredibly sad, Matt felt his heart squeeze inside his chest.

"I'm sorry," he said. "About Pike. I wish there was something I could do."

Jia looked back down at the book. "I was supposed to take care of her," she said, her voice a bit raspy. "I was the one to find her first on the *Vermillion*. Did you know that?"

Matt shook his head. He remembered Jia telling him once that Pike had been found in the *Vermillion*'s food pantries, eating a pile of sugar.

"Captain Vincent didn't want her to stay at first," Jia said, "but I convinced him because I thought she was so sweet-looking and we couldn't figure out where or when she had come from. I couldn't bear the thought of her being discarded and all alone in the world."

"I'm sorry I couldn't stop her," Matt said. "By the time I saw her leap across I'd already turned the dials, and we just had to get away from Vincent. If you had seen what he was doing to my dad . . ."

Jia shook her head. "It's not your fault," Jia said. "I should have done something sooner, said something . . ."

"What do you mean?"

Jia looked at Matt. He'd never seen her look so serious. She opened her mouth. Matt knew she was about to tell him something important, but they were interrupted by a loud thumping.

"Hey, what's that sound?" Ruby asked.

Thump. Thump. Thump.

It sounded like someone was pounding on a door.

"It's coming from over there," Corey said, pointing to the other end of the ship. They all moved in that direction. Mrs. Hudson drew her sword and took the lead, shepherding her children behind her.

The thumping grew louder. Then a muffled voice could be heard.

"Hello? Help!"

"There!" Ruby said, pointing to a small boat turned upside down on the deck of the ship. Someone had to be underneath it.

"Another stowaway?" Uncle Chuck said.

"Maybe Brocco or Wiley got caught on Blossom like Albert," Jia said.

"Careful," Mrs. Hudson said. "It could be a trap. Matthew, Charles, lift it up, please."

Mr. Hudson and Uncle Chuck both stepped forward and lifted the boat. A man crawled out.

"Phew," he said, sitting up. "Thanks, I thought I was maybe going to die in there, and before that I thought I was going to die out there." He pointed to the water, then looked around and seemed to realize he was not wherever he had been before. Then he looked at Mrs. Hudson's sword pointed at him. "And I guess maybe I'm still going to die?"

It was not Brocco or Wiley. Matt didn't know this man, and yet he looked familiar. He just couldn't think why.

Someone gasped. Gaga stumbled forward. "Henry?"

And then it clicked in Matt's brain. This was Henry Hudson, his long-lost grandfather.

7
New-Old Family and New New York

Matt was trying to understand what was going on. Henry Hudson was on Blossom. Henry Hudson, his dad's dad, who had been discarded by Captain Vincent in the Hudson Bay in 1611. Somehow, in all the chaos, Matt must have traveled there and picked him up. He remembered the lone man in a boat, how they'd crashed into him during their time chase with Vincent. That must have been his grandfather, Henry Hudson. Somehow, they'd pulled him along with them.

Henry Hudson looked a lot like Matthew Hudson, except with a beard and no glasses. They were about the same age, which meant he'd just been catapulted roughly forty years into his future.

"Henry, is that really you?" Gaga said.

Henry squinted at Gaga and then his eyes went wide. "Gloria?"

Gaga's face went from pale green to just plain green. She

swayed on the spot. Matt thought she might faint, but then she stumbled to the side of the boat, leaned over, and vomited in the water. Mr. Hudson went to her and patted her on the back. Mrs. Hudson handed her a handkerchief. Gaga took it and wiped her face, then turned back around to face her husband, who she believed had died decades earlier.

Henry stumbled to his feet. His clothes were definitely from the 1980s. "Gloria, is that really you? I don't understand. You're so . . . you're so . . ."

"Old?" Gaga supplied.

"Yeah . . . I mean old*er*. And still beautiful. I mean . . . How long have I been gone?"

"That depends on who you ask," Uncle Chuck said.

Henry cocked his head at Uncle Chuck, studying him. "You look like my great-uncle Bill."

"I'm sure that's a great compliment," Uncle Chuck said.

"Will someone *please* tell me what's going on?" Gaga said. "Have I gone completely crazy? Or are we all dead? We're dead, aren't we? And this is"—she looked all around—"some strange in-between place."

"No, Mom," Mr. Hudson said. "You're not crazy, and you're not dead. I can explain."

"Wait, *Mom*?" Henry said. "Hang on. You're not Matty, are you?"

"Yeah . . . hi, Dad."

"Boy, time really does fly."

"Somebody tell me what is going on right now!" Gaga shrieked.

"I will!" Mr. Hudson said. "I just . . . I'm not sure where to begin."

"How about at the beginning," Henry said.

Mr. Hudson laughed. "Which one?"

"Oh, come on," Corey blurted. "It's not that hard." He turned to Gaga and Henry. "Listen up. We're time travelers, okay? Our whole family. Matt invented a time-traveling compass, our mom is three hundred years old, and we're being chased by a bunch of time pirates, one in particular named Captain Vincent. He's the maniac who abducted us before. And he's Charles, your son and our uncle." He pointed at Uncle Chuck.

Gaga's mouth opened, but no words came out. She looked at Mr. Hudson, and then Mrs. Hudson, and finally Uncle Chuck. She stared at him long and hard. "Charles. You're . . . *Charles*?"

"*Charlie?*" Henry said.

"We call him Uncle Chuck," Corey said. "It just sounds better."

"Chuck . . . Charles," Gaga said, still staring at her long-lost son who was now nearly the same age as her. "But . . . but that's impossible. You can't be . . . You can't be . . ."

"Hi, Mom. Hi, Dad," Uncle Chuck said with a little wave.

"I don't understand," Gaga said. You've worked for me for nearly forty years! I would know my own son if I saw him!"

"Not unless you were expecting him to be thirty years older than he should be," Corey said. "Time travel. It's a beast."

"And who are you supposed to be?" Henry asked, looking down at Corey. "My great-grandfather or something?"

Corey laughed. "Close. I'm your grandson."

At this Henry's eyes nearly burst out of their sockets. "My *grandson*!"

"Yeah, you got three of them. Grandchildren, I mean. I'm Corey, and that's your granddaughter, Ruby." Corey motioned to Ruby, who waved and smiled. "She's my twin, but we are nothing alike. And that's your other grandson, Matt, or Mateo, so you don't get him mixed up with our dad. We are also nothing alike, but not in the same way that Ruby and I are unalike. He was adopted from Colombia and is a total genius. He invented the Obsidian Compass, which is how we time-traveled to rescue you, and I guess it's also how you got discarded in the first place. Ironic, huh? Or is that not the right word for this situation?"

"Is there a word for this situation?" Henry Hudson said. He was looking at Matt now, who wished he could disappear. Why did Corey have to point out all that? Was he trying to embarrass him or just being a total blabbermouth? He felt so exposed, and he would have liked to have made his own introduction to his long-lost grandfather.

"Okay . . . okay, so you're all Matty's kids. And is this your mom?" He nodded to Belamie.

"Oh, sorry, Dad," Mr. Hudson said. "So . . . this is my wife, Belamie."

Mrs. Hudson held out her hand. "It's a pleasure to meet you, Henry."

"Charles told me you were getting married. That was yesterday for me, but he was much younger then . . . though still older than I had left him. So, I'm guessing the wedding happened a while ago?"

Mr. Hudson nodded. "Twenty years. Sorry you couldn't be there."

"Guess I got a lot of catching up to do. A daughter-in-law . . . grandchildren . . . Wasn't expecting that for a couple more decades, but okay. Life comes at you fast sometimes, I guess. And who are these two?" Henry asked, nodding to Jia and Albert. "You're not my great-grandchildren, are you?"

Jia shook her head, then looked to Matt as though she didn't know how to explain herself.

"This is Jia," Matt said. "She's my . . ."

"She's our friend," Ruby said.

"But sort of, like, Matt's *girlfriend*," Corey added.

"Shut up, she is not," Matt said, feeling his face heat up. Now he couldn't even look at Jia. He glared at Corey instead.

Why did he always have to ruin everything by opening his big mouth?

"And you are a friend of the family, too, I assume?" Henry asked Albert.

"Ick, no way," Corey said. "More like a family enemy."

"Corey," Mrs. Hudson chided.

"What? It's true." He turned back to Henry. "Albert's in league with Vincent. That's the guy who discarded you. He's here by mistake, and now he's our hostage."

"He's *not* our hostage," Mrs. Hudson said.

Albert kept his head down and didn't say anything, which Matt thought was probably wise, given the circumstances. Maybe he wasn't their hostage, but he certainly wasn't one of them.

"Man, this has been the weirdest day," Henry said, and then looked back at Gaga, who was still staring at him like he was a ghost. "Gloria, I'm so sorry. The way I left . . . and you never knew what really happened . . ."

Gaga shook her head. "No, it's not your fault. And I'm sorry too. If I had only known . . ." She then turned sharply to Mr. Hudson, her expression turning severe. "Why didn't you tell me? Why didn't you tell me *any of this*?!"

Matt backed up a bit. Corey and Ruby did too.

"I told you we should've told her," Corey said under his breath.

"Mom, we're really sorry," Mr. Hudson said. "We honestly didn't know about Charles or Dad until a few days ago."

"You should have told me the instant you knew!" Gaga said. "And not just about your father, but all of it. I assume you thought I wouldn't notice anything strange was going on?"

"I . . . well . . . ," Mr. Hudson stuttered. Gaga bulldozed right over him.

"All this time I thought I was going crazy. I thought I was seeing things a few days ago when I looked out the window to see you and Belamie chasing after the kids in Chuck's hunk of junk bus, when suddenly it disappeared into thin air, right before my eyes. And then a fluke storm rolled through, nearly destroyed my entire vineyard, and then you all reappear moments later, and everything seemed fine. I'm fine. We're all fine. But then I've heard you all these past few days, whispering and conspiring who knows what. And then I start hearing about penguins in the desert and snowstorms in Jamaica, and an earthquake hits New York, and a monsoon floods everything and destroys my house *and* vineyard, and then a pirate ship appears and then . . . and then . . . my son who I thought had run away and my husband who I'd thought had died both suddenly appear, but my son is the same age as me and my husband's four decades younger! And you thought that would all somehow escape my notice?!"

"I'm sorry," Mr. Hudson said. "I just . . . we didn't know how to tell you, or if it would even be helpful."

"News flash," Gaga said. "It's always helpful for a grieving widow to know that her dead husband is actually still alive. How did this happen? And *why*?"

"I wouldn't mind a few details myself," Henry said.

"We know this is all a lot to take in at once, for both of you," Mrs. Hudson said. "We'll tell you everything, we promise."

"Yes, you will," Gaga said. "Every last detail. But not here. If I have to spend another minute on this boat, or whatever it is, I *will* go crazy."

Matt didn't doubt it. He could see his usually very with-it grandmother unraveling before his eyes. She was breathing hard, clutching at her chest, her face in a grimace. Her usually sleek silver hair now resembled dandelion fluff with half the fluff blown away.

"Can we go home?" Ruby asked. "I think we'd all be most comfortable there."

"We can't go back to the vineyard," Mrs. Hudson said.

"No, I mean home home. Like our apartment?" Ruby nodded toward the city, the familiar skyscrapers sparkling in the afternoon sunlight.

Yes, home, Matt thought. It felt like they'd been away for ages, and Matt suddenly ached for their apartment, his own bed, the familiar things and smell.

"I don't know," Mrs. Hudson said. "It seems like just the place Vincent would go to find us."

"Maybe not," Jia said. "In all the time we came to New York, Vincent never did want to set foot in your apartment. He never even tried. I think that's why he sent Pike to steal the letter instead of going himself."

Jia frowned and looked away. Mentioning Pike must be painful for her, Matt thought.

"He *did* always try to kidnap us when we were outside, never when we were home," Ruby reasoned. "So maybe it really is the safest place for us to be."

"And maybe he won't think to search for us in New York in any case," Matt added. "He found us at Gaga's house. I'll bet he'd think we would think it wouldn't be safe to go home, so maybe it's actually the safest place we could go right now."

"That all seems oddly reasonable," Mr. Hudson said.

"And besides," Ruby said. "Even if he did think we'd go home, he wouldn't know when to go. He can't know what date we traveled without the map."

"Maybe, but Vincent isn't the only risk in going home," Mrs. Hudson said. "What if we're there right now? We don't know what the date is, exactly, with everything being so mixed up. We could run into ourselves, which could do just as much damage as Vincent could inflict on us, maybe even more."

Matt thought not, but he didn't say so. Given what he'd just witnessed, he was guessing Vincent could do quite a bit of damage. "Where else would we go?" Matt asked. "I don't think we'll be able to travel right now, anyway. Not far, at least. I can probably get us home, but it wouldn't be safe to do much more than that. The compass needs some mainte-nance. I lost a piece. It could take a few days to fix it."

"Can't we at least try?" Ruby pleaded. "We'll be careful, and if we hear anything then we'll leave right away."

"Belamie, everyone's exhausted," Mr. Hudson said. "My parents have been through the wringer. We need a place we can rest. And I, for one, would prefer to go home."

"I second the motion," Gaga said.

Uncle Chuck raised his hand. "Third."

Mrs. Hudson finally relented. "All right. We can try going home, but any sign of trouble and we leave right away, agreed?"

They all nodded.

"Matt, if you hold the time dials and just set the location dials it should work."

Gaga groaned. "Oh no. Please, no, don't do that . . . that thing . . . whatever it is. I can't take it."

"It's okay, Mom," Mr. Hudson said. "It's almost over." He turned back to Matt and whispered, "Make it as smooth as you can."

Matt did his best to make the travel smooth, and Blossom turned back into her original bus form. It was a bit cozy at first, but then Blossom, seeming to sense their discomfort, widened and stretched to create a bit more breathing room. Blossom was now more the size of a motor home.

"She seems to be getting better at transforming," Mrs. Hudson noted.

Matt nodded in agreement. He had noticed certain similarities between Blossom and the *Vermillion*, the way they transformed, the feisty, almost sarcastic personalities of the vehicles. He wondered if it was just the effects of the Obsidian Compass and if it would have that effect on any vehicle. Or could it be that Blossom and the *Vermillion* were actually the same vehicle? It was a crazy notion, and yet it weirdly made sense. He guessed only time would tell. Only time would tell a lot of things. Or maybe it wouldn't. Maybe it would just keep bringing more and more questions, making more and more chaos. There didn't seem to be much order to the universe anymore.

They landed on Fifth Avenue, right near the museum and only a couple of blocks from their apartment, but there was no chance of them getting through all the traffic. Fifth Avenue was completely jammed because not only were there cars and buses and taxis, but also horse-drawn carriages where neither the horses nor drivers seemed to understand what was going on. There were policemen on the streets, trying to direct traffic with their whistles and batons, but it made little difference, and they seemed just as confused as anyone.

"This is supposed to be Manhattan?" Henry said, looking

out the window as a covered wagon pulled by oxen passed by. "Did we go back in time?"

"We couldn't have," Ruby said. "There are too many modern buildings."

"The timelines have been disrupted," Matt said. "Different times and places seem to be breaking up and getting meshed together."

They parked Blossom right in front of the Metropolitan Museum of Art, between a warhorse in full armor and an old Model T. Everyone tried to get out the side door at once until Mrs. Hudson yelled at the kids to calm down and let their grandmother out first. Uncle Chuck and Henry both assisted Gaga out of Blossom. Corey and Ruby were next to jump out, followed by Albert. Matt climbed out and then realized Jia wasn't with them. He turned back to find her tucking the book Pike had been reading inside her vest.

The city was a circus. Not an actual circus, but some kind of time circus. People wandered the streets, all in clothing from different eras. Some looked completely lost and terrified, while others looked around in wonder, pointing and jabbering in all different languages at the buildings, the cars, the people. Across from the museum, Central Park looked like it had been turned into a zoo. The trees were full of gorillas and monkeys and brightly colored birds that were clearly not native to New York. A herd of zebras trotted along the paths.

"I always knew Manhattan was a melting pot," Uncle Chuck said, "but this is something else altogether, isn't it?"

"This is Vincent's doing," Mrs. Hudson said, frowning at all the people.

"Looks like he doesn't really know what he's doing, does it?" Mr. Hudson said.

Mrs. Hudson didn't say anything, just kept frowning at the chaos. A group of men wearing togas passed them, speaking in what sounded like Greek.

"What's going on at the museum?" Ruby asked. A legion of soldiers in blue coats with tails, white breeches, and tall hats with feathers stood on the steps of the Met. In front of the soldiers was a short man wearing a similar but more decorated uniform. Instead of the tall hat the other soldiers wore, his was like an upside-down boat sitting sideways on his head. He spoke loudly in French. He seemed to be issuing some kind of proclamation to the crowd before him, though most were not listening.

"Who is that dude?" Corey asked, pointing.

"And what's he saying?" Ruby asked. "Something about a castle?"

Matt listened and interpreted it in English as best he could. "He says the castle is his and that he is the emperor of this land. Those who resist his rule will be thrown in the dungeons or put to death."

Mr. Hudson squinted at the man. "He sort of looks like

Napoleon Bonaparte. Hang on, I think that *is* Napoleon Bonaparte!"

"Looks like you're not getting your job back any time soon, huh, Dad?" Corey said. Mr. Hudson's face dropped.

"Let's get home," Mrs. Hudson said, ushering all the children. "Come on." They started walking, but then Mrs. Hudson looked back. Albert was still by Blossom. He looked like he wasn't sure if he was invited or should follow.

"You're free to do as you like, Albert," Mrs. Hudson said. "Wait here for Vincent if you want, but if you want to stay with us, you're going to have to keep up." She turned around and started walking without looking to see if Albert followed. But he did, because where else was he going to go?

Matt kept close to Jia as they walked. She hugged Pike's book to her chest. She didn't seem like she wanted to talk, so Matt didn't say anything, even though he wished there was something he could do to comfort her.

"So," Corey said, addressing Henry as they walked. "What should we call you?"

"Call me? What do you mean?"

"Well, you're technically our grandpa, right? But you don't look like a grandpa. You look younger than our dad! So it would be kind of weird to call you Grandpa, don't you think?"

"I do," Henry said. "I guess you can just call me Henry."

Corey screwed up his face. "No. I don't think that's right. We can't call you *Henry*. It's like calling our dad Matthew or a

113

teacher by their first name. Totally disrespectful. We have to give you some kind of title. Like how we call Grandma Gaga, you know?"

Henry glanced at his wife who was clearly avoiding eye contact with her husband. "How did you come to call her Gaga?"

"Mateo couldn't say Grandma Gloria when he was little," Ruby said. "He called her Gaga, and the name stuck."

"Much to my chagrin," Gaga mumbled.

"Well, I like it," Henry said. "Seems to suit you. More than Grandma, anyway."

"Ha. Ha," Gaga said dryly.

"Hey, I got it!" Corey said. "We could call you Haha! Get it? I mean your name is Henry Hudson, and I'll bet if Matt had tried to say that when he was little, it probably would have sounded like Haha, wouldn't it?"

Henry Hudson wrinkled his brow. "Ha-ha?"

There was a moment of silence, and then a strange sound emitted from Gaga, sort of like water sputtering from a hose, and then she let out a loud snort. "Haha! Haha!" she doubled over laughing. At this point everyone else cracked up, too, though whether it was more at Gaga's glee or the name itself, no one was sure.

"Haha it is, then," Henry said, smiling at Gaga, who now had tears streaming down her cheeks, and then her face suddenly crumbled, and her laughter really turned to sobs. All the merriment of the moment shriveled up in a hot second.

Mr. Hudson went to his mom and wrapped an arm around her. "It's okay, Mom. Everything will get worked out."

Henry (or Haha now) stepped toward Gaga, but then paused. He looked completely helpless.

"Come on, Henry," Mrs. Hudson said, putting her arm through his. "We're almost home and then you can rest. I know it's been a long day for you."

"Yeah," he said. "Sure has."

Matt thought he could use a rest as well. His brains felt like scrambled eggs. Vikings and Roman armies taking over the Brooklyn Bridge, Napoleon Bonaparte taking over the Met, his long-lost grandfather coming back, not to mention everything that had happened before all that. Matt wondered if there would be any home to come home to, and even if there was, would it remain? Would his family? Would they ever be free of the threat of Captain Vincent?

8
Home Again

When they reached their apartment door, Mrs. Hudson motioned for everyone to be quiet, in case their past or future selves were home for some reason, and slowly put the key in the lock. It turned and clicked. She opened the door just a crack and called inside, "Hello? Anybody home?"

No one answered. Mrs. Hudson pushed open the door. Matt saw just a glimpse of the dining room and kitchen. All was still and quiet.

"We'd better do a search," Mr. Hudson said.

Mrs. Hudson nodded. "Wait here," she said to Matt and the rest. She pulled out her dagger and went inside.

Mr. Hudson took one of Mrs. Hudson's swords off the living room wall and held it like a baseball bat as they proceeded to search every room, under every table, chair, and bed, and behind every curtain and cupboard. When they at last deemed it safe, the rest all shuffled inside like weary soldiers coming home from battle. All except for Albert. He stood on the edge of the entryway, as though he were on the edge of a cliff.

"Albert, either come in or stay out, but shut the door, please," Mrs. Hudson said. Albert quickly stepped inside and shut the door. He then stood in the hallway like a help-less lump. It looked like he was waiting for someone to greet him and take his coat. Matt wasn't about to try to make him feel comfortable. It wasn't as though Albert had gone to any lengths to make him and Corey and Ruby feel welcome on the *Vermillion*.

Matt looked around. Everything in their apartment was as he remembered it—the furniture, the photos and paintings, mementos, and knickknacks. His mom's swords and knives on the wall (minus the one his dad had taken down). The only major difference was the blank wall above the dining table, where the map used to hang. The empty frame was on the floor, leaning against the wall. Mr. Hudson was looking at it like a loved one who had just died.

The apartment felt strange to Matt for some reason. Off. Even though it looked the same, it almost felt like a replica of their home, and not their real home at all. A set in a play. Maybe it was because they had been away for so long, and so much had happened since the last time they'd come here. So much had changed. Matt had changed. When had that hap-pened, exactly? Was it in a moment? Or had it been a gradual thing? How much more would he change before this was all over?

Corey went to the living room and turned on the television.

"Corey, no television right now, okay?" Mr. Hudson said.

"Wait just a second," Corey said as he flipped through the channels. "I want to see what they're reporting on the news."

"I'd like to see that myself," Haha said.

"You probably won't be able to get the news in this mess," Gaga said.

But they could. Corey landed on a news channel with a blue banner that read *NYC's Dinosaur Crisis*. It showed footage of the Statue of Liberty, closing in on the crown where a grouping of pterodactyls had nested. So Matt *had* seen pterodactyls on top of the Statue of Liberty!

"Cool!" Corey said. "The dinosaurs are back! Do you think we got a T. rex?"

As if the news had heard Corey's questions, next they reported dinosaur sightings in other parts of the city, including a herd of velociraptors wandering the subway tunnels, and a female *Tyrannosaurus rex* that had taken over Yankee Stadium and was now laying eggs. "All games have been canceled for the foreseeable future," the anchor stated, "and citizens are advised to keep away as the female T. rex is particularly volatile while nesting." The footage showed a *Tyrannosaurus rex* roaring and tearing its teeth into the seats of Yankee Stadium, flinging them over the field. Helicopters were circling.

"Wahoo! Go, T. rex!" Corey shouted until Ruby gave him a look. "Sorry, but it *is* kind of exciting."

"It's all fun and games until someone gets their head bitten off," Ruby said.

"Hey, how are the Mets doing anyway?" Haha asked. "What did I miss? We were shaping up to be a pretty good team when I left."

"We won the World Series in 1986," Mr. Hudson said.

"No way!" Matt couldn't get over how alike his dad and Haha were, both in looks and sound. It was seriously weird.

"We were there!" Corey said. "We went to Game Six."

"Isn't that a little before your time?"

"We time-traveled there," Matt said, remembering with a mixture of emotions the night that he'd almost caused the Mets to lose the World Series, but in the end was basically the reason they'd won, because he'd caused a glitch in the timeline with the stone in his bracelet, which, unbeknownst to him, was actually the Aeternum, the very powerful object Captain Vincent had been looking for all along. It had gotten him out of a couple of tight spots, actually, before he and Quine activated its full power and gave it to Vincent.

"One of the greatest games in history," Mr. Hudson said. "You really should have been there."

"Could we, though?" Haha asked. "I mean, with your

time-traveling thing?" He nodded to Matt's compass.

Matt shook his head. "Not a good idea. Overlapping with ourselves could cause some serious damage. We already caused a glitch overlapping with Dad."

"We can find all the games on YouTube," Corey said.

"YouTube? That a video store?"

"Sort of." Matt suddenly realized there was a lot more to catch Haha up on than just their lives and baseball.

Next up, the president has declared a state of emergency . . .

"Corey, turn that off," Mr. Hudson said. "We don't need any more news today."

Corey switched off the TV, and quiet settled over the apartment.

"Gloria," Mrs. Hudson said. "Why don't you go lie down in our room? I'll bring you some tea."

"Tea?" Gaga said. "Oh, no, I think I'll need something stronger than tea."

"I don't think we have any wine in the house, Mom," Mr. Hudson said.

Gaga waved him off and went to the kitchen, teetering a little. She was clearly still off-balance from their travels, and maybe a little off mentally as well, because she opened the freezer and stuck her head inside.

"Mom?" Mr. Hudson asked. "What are you doing?"

Gaga didn't answer. She rifled around in the freezer. A few packages of frozen vegetables fell to the ground, and then Gaga emerged with two pints of Ben & Jerry's Chunky Monkey.

"Hey! Where did that come from?" Corey asked. "Mom doesn't ever buy ice cream!"

"I know," Gaga said as she opened a drawer and grabbed a spoon. "I keep a secret stash for when I come to visit. Been doing it for years. Sorry, Belamie, but your love of vegetables is a little intense."

"How did I not *know* this?" Corey said.

"Are you sure it's not expired?" Mr. Hudson asked.

Gaga pulled off the lid and stabbed the spoon into the ice cream. She scooped out a big hunk, stuck it in her mouth, and let it sit there for a moment. "Tastes fresh to me." She grabbed a handful of spoons and plopped everything down at the dining table. "Dig in, everyone. And start talking. Your days of mystery are over."

It took hours to explain everything. And another pint of Chunky Monkey. (Corey could not get over this revelation.) By the time they reached the bottom of the third carton they'd told Gaga and Haha everything, albeit in a very haphazard fashion, all of them telling their own piece of the story and talking over each other. Mrs. Hudson told her true history and how she and Matthew met by means of his magical map.

"I'm surprised I didn't guess it before," Gaga said. "I mean, don't get me wrong, Belamie, you're very intelligent, and I always liked you, but it's not really a shock to me that you're not from this century."

Mrs. Hudson seemed a little offended by this. "What do you mean? I've always been able to blend into society."

"Ha!" Gaga laughed. "Blend, my foot. You slice apples with hunting blades, and you used to think Ben and Jerry were my very helpful neighbors instead of an ice cream brand!"

They all laughed as Mrs. Hudson's face flushed. "Well, what was I supposed to think? You told me every time there's a crisis in your life you go straight to Ben and Jerry and they always help you out no matter what. How was I supposed to know you were talking about ice cream?"

"Because everyone knows that?" Corey said.

"Exactly!" Gaga said, pointing at Corey. "I mean, there are odd people who live under rocks, but this was something else entirely."

Matt, too, had memories of his mother's odd ineptitudes, blank spaces of knowledge of common, everyday things. He hadn't thought much of it at the time, just chalked it up to the fact that she was an immigrant and English was not her first language, but after he learned the truth it made much more sense why she'd never learned how to ride a bike, or when she thought a jump rope was some kind of weapon, or why she could never quite understand how the internet worked.

Uncle Chuck and Haha both told their strange tales of how they'd been abducted by Captain Vincent. Apparently, when

Haha had gone for a hike, Captain Vincent had mistaken him for Matthew Hudson, then realizing he'd gotten the wrong person, went back and took Charles Hudson, thinking *he* was Matthew, then discarded them both in the Hudson Bay in the year 1611.

"I managed to escape," Uncle Chuck said, "thanks to Dad and Jia"—he nodded at Jia, who flushed and looked down—"but I got dropped off in the wrong decade, and well, that was that."

"Oh, Charles," said Gaga, placing her hand on top of his. "My baby boy. You've been here all these years, and I didn't even know it. But how could I? I admit, I always thought there was something familiar about you, but how could I possibly have known? Oh, Charles!" She broke down and wrapped her arms around her long-lost son.

Chuck stiffened. He looked helplessly at his brother. Mr. Hudson nodded his head, smiling, and Chuck tentatively put his arms around his mother and patted her awkwardly on the back. "It's okay, Mom. I'm here now."

Matt caught Corey grimacing. Ruby gave him a sharp look, but Matt couldn't blame him. The whole scene *was* a bit weird. A mother comforting her son who was now about the same age as her.

After a long embrace in which Uncle Chuck looked more trapped than anything, Gaga finally released him and pulled away. She dabbed at her eyes with the edge of her sleeve.

"And, Henry . . . ," Gaga said, but then she seemed to lose her words.

"Gloria, I'm so sorry," Haha said. "I can't imagine all you've been through, what you must have thought happened."

"Well, at least I know you didn't run off with some floozy, like Patty Chesterton always said."

Haha sputtered a laugh. "Is that what that busybody told you? And you believed her?"

"Not really," Gaga said. "I told the boys you disappeared while hiking in Patagonia."

"Ha!" Haha said, slapping his knee.

"What's so funny about that?" Corey asked.

"Because she actually told me to hike to Patagonia!"

Gaga looked away, but Matt could see her neck was reddening.

"Why did you tell him to hike to Patagonia?" Corey asked.

"I don't know," Gaga said. "I think I saw Patagonia on your father's atlas and it just came out."

"But why did you tell him to hike there?"

"We were having a fight," Haha said.

"It was not a fight!" Gaga said. "It was a disagreement."

"Sure, a very loud disagreement."

"What did you fight about?" Corey asked.

"Corey, mind your own business," Ruby chided.

"I don't remember," Gaga said, still turning away. "It was too long ago."

"I remember it like it was yesterday," Haha said. "Oh wait, it *was* yesterday. We were fighting about toothpaste."

Corey made a face. "Toothpaste? Who fights about toothpaste?"

"We fight about it all the time!" Ruby said. "You're always leaving the cap off and the toothpaste gets squirted all over the drawer."

"And you always squeeze from the top instead of the bottom," Matt said. It drove him nuts.

"And you put the toilet paper on the wrong way!" Ruby shot back.

"I do not. You do!"

"Seriously, it doesn't matter which way it goes," Corey said. "You're such weirdos."

At this Haha started laughing and then Gaga joined in. It seemed this was very similar to the argument they'd had before Haha had disappeared. But Gaga's laughter quickly dissolved into tears once more. "Oh, what are we going to do now?" she cried. "The vineyard is gone, our lives are all mixed up, and it doesn't sound like that maniac Vincent has any intentions of allowing us to all live happily ever after together."

No, Matt had to agree.

"I'm so sorry, Gloria," Mrs. Hudson said. "And, Henry. If I'd had any idea Vincent would do this . . ."

"You'd what?" Gaga said, her voice bitter through her

tears. "Not have married Matthew? Stayed where you were?"

Mrs. Hudson closed her mouth and shrunk back a little. Mr. Hudson put his arm around his wife. "Belamie is saying she's sorry, that's all. We were all doing what we thought was best at the time. None of us could have predicted all that it would affect. Surely you can appreciate that."

Gaga took a deep breath. "I can. I'm sorry, Belamie. I know it's not your fault, and maybe there's nothing you can do, but it's all just . . . so overwhelming."

"We have to do something," Ruby said. "We can't give up. We have to fight."

"Yeah," Corey said. "Nobody messes with the Hudsons and gets away with it! This means war!"

"Whoa, there. Hold your horses," Mr. Hudson said. "We're not quite ready to run off to battle just yet."

"We couldn't even if we wanted to," Matt said. "The compass needs repairs."

"And we all need some rest," Mrs. Hudson said.

The last drama of the day was the sleeping arrangements. Gaga usually slept in Ruby's room when she visited, but with Jia and Albert, as well as the sudden and very unexpected return of Henry Hudson, it made things awkward, to say the least. After about ten minutes of volleying ideas back and forth it was settled that Gaga would sleep in the master bedroom, Mr. and Mrs. Hudson in the living room to "keep an eye on things" (in other words, make sure their children didn't sneak away in the middle of the night, as they had been known to do). Henry and Uncle Chuck would sleep out in Blossom, under the guise that they would "keep eyes on the street" in case Vincent should approach.

Matt wanted to tell Jia that she could sleep in his room but then wondered if that would be weird, then wondered why he would wonder if it was weird. They'd slept in the same room plenty of times before, just as if they were brother and sister. But they *weren't* brother and sister, and he had no wish to be. But what did that mean? And what if *he* just felt that way and she didn't? While Matt was working through these thoughts, Ruby offered for Jia to sleep in her room, and before Matt could say so much as a good night she was gone. Matt watched her go with a weird mixture of longing and relief. He was starting to feel that relationships of any kind were far more complicated than even the most complex math. There was no formula. No proof. And sometimes they could throw you some serious curve balls, as both his parents and grandparents could attest.

"Albert, you can sleep in the boys' room," Mrs. Hudson said.

"What? No!" Corey protested. Albert didn't look any more pleased by the idea.

"Where would you suggest he sleep?" Mrs. Hudson asked. "The bathtub?"

"That's a good idea," Corey said. "Maybe he'll wake up smelling better."

"I'm not sleeping with *them*," Albert said. "They'll probably murder me in my sleep!"

"Probably," Corey said. "Why can't he just sleep out in Blossom?"

Mrs. Hudson gave a long sigh and pressed her fingers to her temples. "If you two don't stop it this instant I'm going to make you wear the 'get-along shirt.'"

Corey made a horrified expression. "You wouldn't!"

"Watch me."

Matt sniggered until his mom said, "Don't think I won't shove you in there, too, Mateo," and he stopped. The "get-along shirt" was legendary in their family. It was a huge T-shirt that Mrs. Hudson would make the kids wear together whenever they fought. It was usually Corey and Matt, or Corey and Ruby, but occasionally all three of them had to wear it, and then things got really squishy and horrible. Corey clearly had strong enough memories to shut his mouth.

"Albert will sleep in your room," Mrs. Hudson said with a note of finality. "And, Corey, you can make his bed for him."

Corey pressed his lips into a thin line and stomped away.

Their bedroom looked just the same as Matt remembered. Their bunk beds took up most of the room. Matt's top bunk was made up neatly from the day they'd left for the vineyard. Corey's bottom bunk was still a tangle of blankets and sheets. He never made his bed, no matter how much Mrs. Hudson nagged him. "What's the point?" he always said. "I'm just going to sleep in it again." The old Shea Stadium seats sat beneath the window, a few T-shirts and hoodies draped over the arms.

On his desk were some of Matt's old school assignments, a Rubik's cube, completed (he could do it in under a minute), and a few books and magazines. *National Geographic* and *Science Today*. Relics of his life before he'd boarded the *Vermillion* and made the Obsidian Compass. Everything was familiar and just as he'd left it, but just like the rest of the apartment, it all felt alien, something from another world.

Matt changed into his pajamas and brushed his teeth. When he came back, Corey was violently placing sheets and blankets on a blow-up mattress while Albert stood in the corner.

Matt climbed up into his bunk bed and crawled beneath the cool blankets. He couldn't remember ever being so exhausted and wired at the same time. His brain was still going in circles, remembering all that had happened since that morning at Gaga's house. He ticked it all off in his mind. The compass reversal. The storm. The time chase. Facing Captain Vincent. Seeing the time tapestry pulled from his father. Chopping off Captain Vincent's hand. Escaping by a nose, but not before Pike leaped to the *Vermillion*.

Mr. and Mrs. Hudson came into the room. Mrs. Hudson brushed her hands through Matt's hair and kissed him on the forehead. "Good night, *chéri*. I love you."

"Love you too."

"Good night, bud," Mr. Hudson said, tousling his hair. "You did good today."

They repeated this to Corey on the lower bunk. Matt caught Albert staring at them with a kind of longing, like he wished Mrs. Hudson would tuck him in and tell him she loved him, too, and Mr. Hudson would call him "bud." It gave Matt a squeamish feeling. It was like coming out of a restaurant with a full stomach only to see a hungry child with hands outstretched. There were different kinds of hunger. Matt hadn't realized until now that Albert had been starved for a long time. It didn't make him like him, but maybe he despised him a little less.

"Good night, Albert," Mrs. Hudson said. "Let us know if you need anything."

Albert started a little. His cheeks flushed like he'd been caught stealing. He nodded stiffly, then quickly lay down on the blow-up mattress. He pulled the covers up to his chin and closed his eyes.

Mr. Hudson switched off the light as they went out.

The room was quiet. Matt didn't think either Corey or Albert fell asleep in five seconds, but it's not as if they were going to chitchat.

9

The Initials

Matt awoke to someone tapping him on the shoulder. He shot out of bed. "Whaaaa?! What's happening?"

"Shhhh! Calm down, it's only us."

It was Corey and Ruby. They both were standing on the edge of his bed with flashlights. Their faces looked ghoulish.

"What are you doing?" Matt asked.

"Secret sibling meeting," Corey whispered. "Come down."

Barely conscious, Matt slid down from his bunk. He looked at the clock. It was 2:03 a.m. Had they set an alarm so they could meet in the middle of the night, or had they still not gone to sleep?

"Bathroom," Corey whispered. "We don't want to wake Albert."

They all crowded into the small bathroom, still using only the flashlights. It was pretty squishy and uncomfortable.

"What's going on?" Matt whispered.

"I'd like to know the same thing," Ruby said. "Corey woke me first, said he needed to talk to us."

"I have to show you something," Corey said, and he waited, like he was trying to build anticipation, but Matt only felt annoyed.

Clearly Ruby felt the same because she said in a whispered huff, "Then show us something already so I can go back to bed!"

Corey reached inside the pocket of his pajamas. "The map is not the only thing I came away with from Captain Vincent," he said. "When we landed in New York, I found this." He pulled out a square of cloth and laid it flat on the floor. Both Corey and Ruby focused their flashlights on it.

Matt recognized it right away. It was the handkerchief that Vincent had given to him when he'd frozen time during their chase. There were the smears of his own blood, now dried to a rusty brown. He wasn't sure what the significance of it was. Clearly Ruby didn't either.

"You dragged us out of bed to show us a bloody handkerchief?" Ruby hissed.

"No, look here," Corey said, pointing to the corner of the handkerchief. Some letters had been embroidered into the cloth in pale blue thread. Matt hadn't noticed those before. Of course he wouldn't have in the moment. He was far too focused on Vincent and keeping him from destroying his family. Matt leaned in and squinted to see the letters more clearly. They were very loopy letters, but Matt could read them clearly.

V. Q.

Ruby gasped. "Oh no . . . you don't think . . . ?"

"I do think," Corey said. "Vincent is a Quine! It makes perfect sense. This confirms that Marius Quine is really on his side because they're somehow related!"

"Related how, do you think?" Ruby asked.

"I don't know. Maybe Quine is Vincent's father or brother. Or he could be his son!"

Matt almost threw up right there and then. He was glad Corey and Ruby couldn't see him. He was sure his face was green. This couldn't be. There had to be another explanation. Some mistake . . .

"Do you think Mom knows?" Ruby said. "That Vincent is a Quine?"

"I don't think so," Corey said. "My guess is he kept it from her on purpose. He was playing her all along. They both were."

"I'm not sure we should be so hasty in drawing conclusions," Matt said. "It's possible this is just coincidence. There are plenty of last names that begin with Q."

Corey scoffed. "Really, bro? Still going to try to convince us that Quine's on our side?"

"He *is* on our side," Matt said, sounding more convinced than he actually felt.

"He also said Pike was on our side," Corey said, "and where is she now? When are you going to wake up? Quine is messing with you."

"You have to admit, Matt," Ruby said, "the fact that Vincent got the Aeternum from Quine makes it look pretty clear, no matter what he said to you in Asilah."

Matt didn't say anything. He was glad now, very glad that he hadn't told Corey and Ruby or anyone the truth about his true identity. It would have been a mistake considering this new revelation. They wouldn't understand. Matt didn't understand. He was trying to reorder everything in his brain. Vincent had just told him he was not the enemy, that they were on the same side. Vincent said Matt, at some point in his future, had already come to Vincent in his past and helped him figure out what he needed to do in order to get the Aeternum, thereby assuring him that they were on the same side. And Vincent knew Matt was really Marius Quine, or would become him at some point in his future. And if they really did share a name . . . if they were family . . . No. He refused to believe this. It couldn't be. Matt stared down at the handkerchief as if he could force the letters to change somehow. "Are you sure that's really a *Q*?" he asked. "Could be a fancy *O*, couldn't it?"

Corey rolled his eyes. "You know, I think you don't want to admit that you were wrong about Quine, that he's been against us all along, because then you have to own everything that happened in Asilah and everything that's happening now and will happen, whatever that is."

Matt flinched. "I'll admit I've made mistakes, but I'm not wrong about Quine."

"How can you think that?" Corey spat. "Everything points to him being in league with Vincent. He handed Vincent the Aeternum! They have the same name, for crying out loud!"

"You don't know *why* he did that," Matt said. "And even if they do have the same name, so what? We have the same name. Doesn't mean we're always on the same side, does it?"

Matt regretted the words as soon as they left his mouth. Even in the shadows, he could see Corey's and Ruby's expressions. They looked as though he'd just slapped them across their faces.

"No," Corey said coldly, "I guess it doesn't."

Matt held Corey's gaze until the shame boiled over and he looked away. He wished he could take those words back. He should say he was sorry, but somehow the words wouldn't come out.

"Let's not fight," Ruby said. "It doesn't help anything. Let's just focus on what we can do. We can't go back in time and change anything. We know that doesn't work, so we have to look ahead."

"You mean travel to the future?" Matt asked, his voice squeaking a little. He'd only traveled to the future once, and it was on accident. And up to this point, nobody had been able to travel past June 1, 2019, because that was when

Matt had invented the compass.

Ruby shook her head. "I don't think traveling to the future will help us any either. I've been thinking . . . you guys, we've been so focused on time travel, on the past or the future, we've forgotten the most important thing. Our present."

"How do you mean?" Matt said.

"The present is the only time we have real control over. Right now, this very moment, everything we do or say we're choosing. Don't you see?"

Matt didn't, but he didn't want to admit it. Corey wasn't afraid though.

"No, I don't see," Corey said. "I mean, I agree that right now we're choosing to be here having this conversation, but there are, like, a thousand things that brought us to this moment that we *didn't* have any control over, you know? I mean, if Vincent were to show up right here and now and blast us all, there wouldn't be much that we could do. And what if he goes to our past and changes things? Then what?"

"Our past selves would fight," Ruby said. "We'd fight to stay together, and our present selves should too. And our future selves. Whenever or wherever Vincent goes to pull us apart or make us disappear or whatever, we can't let him."

"But that's just it," Matt said. "It's not about us *letting* him or not. With the Aeternum, Vincent *can* tear us apart. He can change things and we won't have any control over it. He controls everything."

Ruby shook her head. "No, I don't think so. Oh, how do I explain this? I don't even fully understand, but I can *feel* it! I think we're missing something really important, guys. Something about us, our family. Vincent wants to tear us apart, but so far he hasn't been able to, and we can't let him. We have to keep fighting, refuse to let go. We have to stick together."

Corey and Matt just stared at her. Matt thought Ruby was vastly oversimplifying things. Sweet as her sentiment was, he did not think they could fight Vincent simply by "sticking together." Corey seemed to feel the same.

"Okay, so what should we do?" Corey said. "Superglue ourselves together or something?"

Ruby rolled her eyes. "You're not getting what I'm saying."

"No, I'm not," Corey said. "I don't get any of this. Do you, Matt?"

Matt just shrugged. "I guess I sort of do? But not really."

Corey snorted, shaking his head. "I'm going back to bed. I'm sorry I woke you two up. This is going nowhere." He grabbed the handkerchief and stuffed it back in his pocket, then started to stand.

"Wait!" Ruby said. She held out her fist into the beam of her flashlight. "For luck."

Matt glanced at Corey, who raised an eyebrow at him. Matt put his fist next to Ruby's, and Corey finally stuck his in, completing their three-way family fist bump. But it felt weird. Like some tether between them had come unraveled.

Matt went back to bed, but any thoughts of sleep were long gone. The initials from the handkerchief swirled in his brain. *VQ* . . . It couldn't be. There had to be some mistake. Or it was a coincidence. Or something. Matt could not, would not accept that he was on Vincent's side, that they couldn't be related in any way. They didn't even look alike. (As an adopted child he knew that disproved nothing, but still.)

But then he remembered how Vincent had told him he'd visited him before he came on board the *Vermillion*. Matt had given him his Mets hat, which had contained a message leading him to the *Mona Lisa* and the key that ultimately led him to the Aeternum. All signs that he was trying to help Vincent. But why? They couldn't be on the same side. Marius Quine had said they weren't. Hadn't he? Matt tried to recall their conversation from Asilah. Quine said he didn't care for Vincent. But he gave no other details or clues as to their relationship or what would happen in his future. He only said it would be difficult. That more sacrifices would have to be made. And he wouldn't tell him when or why he changed his name to Marius Quine. Or was that supposed to be his name all along?

Everything was a blur, Matt thought, including himself.

10

Vincent's Plans

It was clear that no one slept well, if at all, because they were all up at the crack of dawn, except Gaga, who was still recovering from time sickness. They all had dark circles under their eyes. Albert eyed everyone like they might attack him at any moment. Matt noticed Jia's face was slightly puffy, like she'd been crying all night. He'd almost forgotten Pike was no longer with them, and he felt a twinge of guilt that he hadn't been able to stop her or go back and rescue her.

"Hey," he said to Jia when she came into the kitchen. "You doing okay?"

She nodded. "I'm okay."

And then he remembered that she had wanted to tell him something before, when they'd first landed on the river in New York. He was about to ask her about it, but she abruptly left him and went and sat next to Ruby at the dining table. Matt tried not to feel hurt, but it was hard not to. Jia had always preferred him. He wondered if she blamed him for what happened to Pike. Probably. Everything was his fault, wasn't it? Or maybe she was regretting her decision to side with his family. She was starting to see how hopeless it all was and wished she'd stayed loyal to Captain Vincent. It's hard to feel good about choosing the losing side. Maybe that's what she had almost told him yesterday.

Mrs. Hudson dug through their pantry and freezer and found enough ingredients to make a big pot of cinnamon oatmeal with brown sugar and frozen blueberries. But their pantry wouldn't feed them all for any length of time. However much time that may be. Mr. Hudson said he would try to go out later and see if the corner grocer was still in business, but Mrs. Hudson killed that idea as fast as it was brought up. She said there was no way she was allowing him to go out on the street in broad daylight. Vincent or one of his crew could be out there. Then Mr. and Mrs. Hudson got in an argument about who was in more danger from Vincent, him or her, and the kids simply watched them fight like they were watching a tennis match. Finally, Uncle Chuck and Haha ended the fight by coming in the door with their arms full of groceries. Both of them looked a little worse for the wear. Their clothes were stained and rumpled and their hair was tangled.

"Whew! It's a jungle out there," Uncle Chuck said, setting the groceries down on the counter. "The whole economy is going up in smoke. Nobody's taking cash anymore, but we managed to trade a few things to get some groceries. Figured we'd need some with our large crew." They all watched him as he unloaded a bag of potatoes, apples, bananas, and some cans of food that didn't look like they were from this century.

Haha set his groceries down too. "Anybody watch the news this morning? I want to see what they're reporting now."

Matt went and turned on the TV in the living room and everyone gathered around. Their cable was out now, but he managed to get a few local news stations. It certainly wasn't good news. An anchorwoman who looked like she was from 1985 was reporting more bizarre sightings and incidents throughout the city—a herd of buffalo stampeding down Broadway and the disappearance of several buildings including St. Patrick's Cathedral. Napoleon had now proclaimed himself emperor of the entire city. The mayor and most elected officials were currently in exile on Ellis Island with no apparent plans. Also, the Brooklyn Bridge had apparently been taken over by the Romans. The Vikings had retreated and taken refuge in Grimaldi's Pizzeria, which Corey said wasn't such a bad loss when you really thought about it.

"All right, that's enough news for now," Mrs. Hudson said, shutting off the television. "Everyone sit down for five minutes and eat your breakfast."

They all sat, except Albert, who remained apart from the group like they might be carrying the plague.

"Come on, Albert," Mrs. Hudson said. "I'm sure you're

hungry." Albert seemed to be having another internal battle of whether he should accept food from the enemy, but eventually his appetite won out. He timidly walked toward the table. Mrs. Hudson pulled out a chair for him at the end of the table and set down a bowl of oatmeal, to which Albert mumbled a thanks.

Haha tried to make small talk with Gaga, asking her questions about the vineyard or the house, but seeing as both had been utterly destroyed by Vincent it didn't go well.

Matt kept looking at Corey, wondering if he was going to show the handkerchief to their parents and bring up Vincent and Quine and the possibility of them being related. He didn't, though, and Matt was relieved. He still had a hunch that his mom suspected the connection between Matt and Quine but didn't want to bring it up for whatever reason, probably for the same reason he did not confess it. Neither of them wanted to face the truth and what it might mean for the future.

Albert emptied his bowl of oatmeal in less than a minute. Mrs. Hudson offered him seconds. Matt could tell he was trying to resist but failed in the end. He could also tell he was trying to resist liking Mrs. Hudson, but this was also difficult. Matt had never known anyone to not like his mother the instant they met her.

"You're Captain Bonnaire, aren't you?" Albert asked after he'd been staring at Mrs. Hudson for a full minute.

Matt noticed his dad stiffen at this question, but his mom didn't skip a beat. "I was," she said. "But not anymore. You can just call me Belamie."

Albert made a face like he thought calling a grown married woman by her first name would be highly inappropriate. "Why did you leave Captain Vincent?" he asked baldly.

"Shut up, Albert, that's none of your business," Corey said with a growl in his voice.

"No, that's all right," Mrs. Hudson said. "It is his business on some level." She then looked at Albert with an unflinching gaze. "Vincent and I had some good times together, but people change. I wanted a different life than he did. Different things. I wanted my family. There's nothing quite like family, wouldn't you agree?"

Albert looked away and shrugged. "I wouldn't know. I'm an orphan."

"Me too," Mrs. Hudson said.

Albert looked surprised by this. "You are?"

Mrs. Hudson simply nodded but didn't explain further. It was her trying to bring her parents back that had caused their deaths in the first place. Just one paradox of time travel.

"Captain Vincent said he would bring my parents back," Albert said, lifting his chin a little. "Maybe if you hadn't betrayed him he would have done the same for you."

Mrs. Hudson smiled gently at Albert. "Maybe. But I wouldn't ask for that."

Albert looked confused. "Why not?"

"Because I've come to find it's dangerous to always focus on the past. Even if you can change it, even if you do get what you want, there will always be regrets. There will always be something you wish you could change. I'd rather focus on the present and the future. That's where all the possibility is. Right here and now. It's where I found my true family."

Matt couldn't help but think of what Ruby had said to him the night before. *The present is the only time we have real control over.*

Albert considered this for a moment. He took another bite of his oatmeal and chewed as though he were chewing on his thoughts. "Captain Vincent plans to take you back, you know. He's going to change the past so you and him don't end up together." He nodded toward Mr. Hudson.

Mrs. Hudson stared at Albert, unblinking, but Matt saw a vein in her forehead pulse.

"What does he intend to do?" Mr. Hudson said softly, calmly. "Kill me before we meet?"

Albert shook his head. "That's what Brocco suggested. He wanted to just go back in time and shoot you before you two met, or your mother before you were born."

Gaga let out a little whimper and clutched at her chest. Haha put a hand on her shoulder.

"But Captain Vincent doesn't think that's good enough," Albert said. "He said there's still ways it could go wrong. He intends to make it so you don't exist at all, so no one can even remember you."

"He can do that?" Ruby asked in a small voice. "He can just . . . erase people, and everyone's memory of them?"

Albert nodded. "Yes. It took him some time to figure out. He had to get some help, but he can do it." His eyes flickered to Matt. Matt wondered if he was referring to that man with the case, the one whose identity he refused to reveal.

"But . . . ," Ruby said, "if our dad doesn't exist, then *we* won't exist."

"You and I won't," Corey said. "Matt's safe." He didn't even look at Matt when he said it, but he could hear the bitterness in his voice.

"Matt may still exist," Albert said, "but he won't be Matt anymore."

Matt stiffened. "What's that supposed to mean?"

"Just what I said. You can't be Mateo Hudson if the Hudsons don't exist, can you? So, you'll become someone else. Your whole life will be different."

Matt felt an icy chill come over him from the top of his head, traveling down to his toes. He started to tremble. He thought maybe he would have a seizure when suddenly Ruby grabbed his hand and squeezed it until it hurt. She must have done the same thing to Corey because he gasped. Matt could almost hear Ruby's thoughts shouting straight into his brain. *We have to stick together! Don't let go.* Matt glanced at Corey, but he kept his gaze down.

"So now you know," Albert said. "I'd prepare if I were you. You don't have long."

Mrs. Hudson let out a breath. She went to the kitchen and started to wash dishes. Mr. Hudson followed her, leaving the rest of them at the dining table with cold oatmeal and somber thoughts. Albert went on eating like nothing had happened. Matt wanted to dump his own bowl of oatmeal on Albert's head, but then he really didn't want to have to wear the "get-along shirt" with him. Corey seemed to be having similar thoughts. At least they still had that in common. They could be unified in their mutual hatred of Albert. But he was guessing that wasn't going to be enough.

11

An Eye for an Eye

Nowhere in No Time

Santiago was *starving*. The well of hunger seemed to be growing bigger inside of him. When their chase on the Hudsons was finally over, he scurried to the pantry and ate and ate and ate. He ate a bag of cheese puffs, three Twinkies, and six packages of peanut butter crackers. The salt made him thirsty. He found a can of that syrupy brown drink on the shelves. He climbed up and swiped the can with his tail so it fell to the floor. It sprayed and bubbled everywhere, all over the walls, the floor, and his fur. He licked up the bubbly, sticky stuff, allowing it to fill in the cracks of all the food he'd eaten. And still he felt empty.

More, more, more.

He hadn't felt hunger like this since *before*. Before he'd met the captain and he'd been just a regular rat living on the shipping docks in San Pedro Bay. His memories of that time were hazy. There wasn't much to the life of a rat, but he remembered one thing quite clearly—he was always hungry, always scrounging for scraps of food, fighting over them with the other rats or cats or seagulls. And that was his life day in and day out, until those three children, the Hudsons, appeared out of nowhere one rainy night. They smelled like peanut butter. Santiago *loved* peanut butter. So he followed the scent, but instead of a meal, when he'd found the source of the peanut butter smell, he'd gotten a searing shock. The next thing he knew he was flying through the air. He was on fire, burning from the inside out. His mind was shredded. New pathways formed, new connections, new sounds, new thoughts and feelings. So much, so much. But there was all the food he could eat and no other rats or cats or seagulls. Just him and the captain and whatever stray humans he gathered to do his bidding.

That reminded Santiago. He hadn't heard the captain's voice in a while, hadn't felt his feelings. Perhaps he'd gotten a little too far away. He didn't like that feeling, either, of being separated from the captain. It felt like losing something very necessary, like his tail or his sense of smell. He squeezed beneath the pantry door and went in search of the captain, sniffing around, trying to catch that thread between them.

He heard voices above him. He climbed up to the rafters and peered through one of the holes into Wiley's library. He sniffed at the musty smell of all the books. Words, words, words. Some humans hoarded words like rats did food. Santiago did not understand it. Words couldn't feed you. They couldn't keep you alive. Worse, they sometimes confused and complicated things, which could lead to death. Words were weak. They were for fools and cowards, like Wiley and Brocco. They were both in the library now, spitting worthless words back and forth at each other, as humans like to do.

"I don't know what to tell you, mate," Brocco said. "You know the captain is not so forgiving of mistakes."

"But you could help me!" Wiley said desperately. He was frantic, flailing his arms about. He was holding the map, the one he'd stolen from the Hudsons. It was crumpled and torn. "You could back me up, tell him it was an accident and there was nothing either of us could do about it."

They were discussing their last mission, Santiago guessed. The chase on the Hudsons had not gone as well as the captain had hoped, and to top it all off, Wiley had lost the map they had relied on to track the Hudsons. He knew it didn't matter so much. The map wasn't essential to their plans, but Brocco was right. The captain was not forgiving of mistakes.

"I don't want to be discarded!" Wiley cried.

"That makes two of us," Brocco said. "Don't ask me to get mixed up in this. You're the one who was holding the map."

"But for the sake of a friend? Please, Brocco! You have to

help me!" He got down on his knees and grabbed Brocco's hand.

The captain appeared in the library just then, followed closely by Mr. Nobel. Santiago hadn't sensed the captain's approach. He must have been distracted. But now that he was here, he sensed that tether between them, and the complex web of feelings that inhabited the captain, as well as that bottomless pit of hunger.

Brocco yanked his hand away from Wiley when he saw the captain. Wiley jumped up and backed away, trembling. The captain gave a wry smile, as though he knew exactly what they had been doing before he entered. Of course, he would have heard anything Santiago heard.

"Your M-majesty," Wiley said. "I want to apologize. For the loss of the map. It took me by surprise, you see. I couldn't do nothing about it. The Hudson boy just ripped it out of my hands."

The captain said nothing. Santiago felt a twitch of annoyance, a flare of anger at the mention of *Hudson*. It would have been better if Wiley had simply kept quiet, as he usually did, but he blabbered on even more.

"Maybe we could go back and get the map again!" Wiley suggested. "At another time. We could, couldn't we? I'll do it. I'll make the plans and everything. The risk will be all mine. You can take me back to before and I'll steal the map. Easy peasy. I'll be slippery as oil. Like a shadow! I'll—"

Wiley's speech cut out as the captain shot forth his arm and grabbed Wiley by the jaw. Wiley froze, his face caught in a silent scream.

"You know what, Wiley? I think you were a much better time pirate *before* you learned how to read."

Wiley's eyes widened so the white parts shone all around. He clawed at the captain, but he was powerless. The captain drew out Wiley's life tapestry from his jaw. He pulled and pulled, looking at the various moments of Wiley's life. There were so many books. Books in stacks and piles. Wiley turning page after page, eating all those words like they were a fine meal. The captain drew his sword and sliced the piece where Wiley was learning how to read, sounding out each of those nonsensical symbols, turning them into words and stories.

"Mr. Nobel, if you please," Captain Vincent said, holding out his hand.

Without a word, Mr. Nobel opened his case and pulled out another of his special explosives. Captain Vincent wrapped that scrap of Wiley's life tapestry around it and lit the wick. The fabric burned, disintegrated, and disappeared. The remaining pieces of Wiley's life tapestry knit back together and retracted back inside of Wiley. When he came to, he took a huge gasp of air and fell to the ground, clutching at his head.

"What did you do? What did you do?"

"An eye for an eye, Wiley. Isn't that in one of your precious books?" The captain nodded to the book that was still clutched in Wiley's arms.

Wiley looked down at the book. He squinted at the cover, blinked a few times. He opened the book and turned the pages, shaking his head as though trying to clear his vision.

"The words," he said. "What happened to the words?" He turned the pages. Page after page. "My words! My words! I can't read them!" Wiley dropped his book. He clutched at his head and let out a guttural scream that sounded more animal than human. He fell to his knees before the captain and clasped his hands together. "Oh, please, Captain, please! Please don't take away my words! Anything but that! Anything!"

Santiago felt the captain's total lack of feeling. There was not an ounce of sympathy in him. He had no use for it. "I was the one who gave you words in the first place, Wiley," the captain said. "I have every right to take them away."

Wiley wept like a child. "My words, my books!"

Brocco put a hand on his shoulder, frowning, then took it away. He glanced nervously at the captain. "I don't mean to question your judgment, Captain," he said cautiously.

"Then don't, Brocco," the captain said.

"'Course not. Wouldn't think of it. But I was just curious, how will we plan missions without Wiley's reading? Wiley planned half our missions from his library."

"Honestly, Brocco, do you really think I need any of this in order to carry out my missions?" Captain Vincent said, gesturing to the library. "Do you think I need any of you?"

Brocco made an audible gulping sound. "N-no, Your Majesty," Brocco stammered, "but we still want to help you. We'll do anything for you, anything at all, won't we, Wiley?"

Wiley made no response. He was still crying, collapsed over a stack of books.

Brocco took off his hat and placed it over his chest. He got down on one knee and bowed his head. "We will be your most faithful, most loyal subjects."

Santiago hissed. *Santiago most faithful!* But no one paid him any mind. Not even the captain.

"I'm sure you'll do all you can to assist me," the captain said. "It was my own mistake to go after the Hudsons when I did. I'll admit to that. I was greedy. I wanted to witness them falling apart. I wanted to see it with my own eyes, the looks on their faces, the knowledge of their lives and their love draining from them, but we can't get too emotional about these things. The goal comes before showmanship. We only need to find one Hudson to stop them all. I'll stop them before they even start."

A vision of a plan raced through Santiago's mind, where they would go, who they would unravel, who would stay.

"Clean yourselves up," the captain said, "and prepare for travel."

Brocco helped Wiley up off the floor, still crying and clinging to a pile of books.

Santiago could not feel sorry for him. Captain Vincent could have done much worse to him than take away his books. Wiley should consider himself lucky. They were all lucky to be part of the captain's crew. Wiley was especially lucky he had not been discarded. So what if he couldn't read? Clearly the words had done nothing but muddle his senses.

Santiago scurried after the captain. He climbed up his leg and perched on his shoulder. He squeaked in his ear.

"I quite agree," the captain said. "He got exactly what he deserved. Everyone does, you know, one way or another. The Hudsons will get what's coming to them."

Santiago squeaked again. It wasn't that he disagreed with the captain's plans, but he had his concerns. One in particular.

"I've told you before, Santiago. Mateo is not the enemy. You will see soon enough. So will the rest of his family, I believe. They'll come to see he's not really part of their family at all. And then they won't even be a family anymore." He laughed and then he looked over at Santiago sitting on his shoulder.

"Ugh, Santiago," the captain sneered. "What have you done to yourself?" Without any warning, the captain shoved Santiago from his shoulder, and he fell to the wooden floor with a thud. He squealed as he wriggled on his back. The captain looked down at him with pure disgust.

"You're filthy," he said. "Don't show yourself again until you're clean." He turned on his heels and walked away without a backward glance.

Santiago finally righted himself. He hissed at the captain's retreating back. *Mean captain.* He turned his head and saw how his coat was matted and sticky, no longer white but a dull gray. Bits of peanut butter and cheese puff were stuck in his fur. The captain was not wrong. He was a mess, but still . . . he did not think his filth warranted such brutality.

Santiago nibbled on some of the cheese puff bits stuck in his dirty fur. He was still hungry.

12

A Few Answers

It was 3:00 a.m. and Matt was wide awake. He'd had the nightmare again, the one where all his family disappears, and now he couldn't go back to sleep. So he just lay there in his bed, holding on to his compass. It still wasn't fixed. After the conversation at breakfast yesterday, he'd retreated to his bedroom and worked on it almost all day. It felt pointless, if he was being perfectly honest, after the things Albert had told them about Captain Vincent's plans, and what would happen to them all. To Matt. Still, he couldn't just sit around. He had to do something, fix something.

Everyone else had been in a sort of haze, ambling around like zombies with a dark rain cloud hanging over their head. Jia had mainly kept to herself, reading the book Pike had left on Blossom. She seemed to be avoiding everyone, especially Matt. Things were weird between them for some reason. He wished they could just go back to their easy friendship. He couldn't tell if he was the one being distant or if she was, but there was something blocking the way of their friendship. Was it him? Or was it what had happened to Pike? Or was it just everything? Maybe there were some circumstances where you just couldn't be easy with each other. They had to be soldiers right now, not friends.

Gaga and Haha seemed to have recovered a bit from the shock of all that had happened, but now there was the question of where they could go from here. Last night Matt overheard Gaga ask his dad if there wasn't any way of going back and fixing this so she and Henry weren't decades apart. Mr. Hudson said it wasn't impossible, but there wasn't anything they could do about it right now, not with everything that was going on.

And what was going on, exactly? What did their future hold? The things Albert had told them haunted Matt every moment. Could Captain Vincent really make his dad not exist? Make him, Matt, a totally different person with a different life? He thought of the initials on the handkerchief. The Aeternum must create an alternate universe, he was thinking. Because his dad existed now. So even if Captain Vincent erased his existence, there would always be some space in the universe where he did exist in some form or another. He couldn't just make something not exist, right? That was just basic physics. It all had to go somewhere.

But Matt knew his thoughts were all theoretical, and who

knew if anything he understood about the universe even applied in this situation? Who knew how it all really worked in reality? Matt considered himself a smart person, but he knew in the grand scheme of things, he was about as knowledgeable as a flea.

A light flicked on outside Matt's door. He heard a bit of shuffling, the opening of drawers and cupboards. It had to be one of his parents. Matt climbed out of bed, careful not to step on Albert, and slipped out of his bedroom.

He found his mom standing at the dining table with a steaming mug of tea and one hand pressed to her temple, like she was trying to stanch a headache. She seemed to get a lot of headaches lately. Maybe it was all the time travel, a touch of time sickness. Matt stepped into his mom's line of sight. She whipped out a dagger and jumped from her seat, spilling hot tea all over herself. "Ah!" She winced and cursed under her breath.

"Sorry!" Matt rushed to the kitchen and got a towel.

"You'd think an expert with blades would know not to handle knives while drinking hot beverages," his mom said while blotting up the mess. When it was all cleaned up she finally looked at Matt and then at the clock. "Why are you awake, *chéri*?"

Matt shrugged. He didn't want to tell his mom about the nightmares, partly because he didn't want her to worry any more than she already was, and partly because he felt saying it out loud would make it even more real and solid in his own mind. He just wanted it to fade away, to forget.

His mom ran her fingers through his hair. "You're turning into an insomniac like your mother." She patted the chair for him to sit next to her. He did and she wrapped a strong, comforting arm around him. He leaned against her and breathed in her scent—a mix of soap, old leather, metal, and varnish. The smells of home.

"Mom?" Matt asked.

"Yes?"

"Can I ask you some questions?"

"About?"

"About my adoption. Where I came from. And maybe some other things."

"Of course, *chéri*. You know you can ask me anything."

Matt nodded. His parents had never tried to hide anything from him. As soon as he could understand, they had told him that he'd been adopted and what that meant. He knew he came from Colombia, that his biological parents were unknown, and that was pretty much it. He'd never cared to know more. His parents were his parents as much as if he'd been born to them. Corey and Ruby were his brother and sister. End of story. And that was all still largely true, but with the recent revelations about his identity, as well as Captain Vincent's, he felt he needed to know more, even if his mom didn't like the questions, even if he didn't like the answers.

"When you adopted me," he asked, "where did I come

from, exactly? I mean, where was I found?" He knew he had been adopted in Santa Marta, a small seaside city in the Caribbean, but he didn't know where he'd come from before that, and he could tell by the look on his mother's face that this was not an insignificant question, but she still answered, as she said she always would.

"The agency told us you were found somewhere in the jungle," she said. "They believed you had come from one of the tribal villages, but even when government officials investigated, no one claimed you. There were no missing babies, they said. They speculated you'd maybe been born to some young woman who was frightened and not ready to have a child, and she abandoned you in a place where you'd be easily found by someone who would take you."

"Who found me?"

"A tourist, they said. Someone who'd been hiking to Ciudad Perdida."

The Lost City . . . Matt had read a little about Ciudad Perdida in *National Geographic*. It was an ancient ruin, predating Machu Picchu, that had once been a great civilization until Spanish conquistadors invaded. He wondered if his origins could have anything to do with that place.

"Do you know the name of the person who brought me in?"

"No. They did not wish to have their name on the record," his mom said.

"But they knew my name," he said. Matt had memorized every word of the adoption papers he'd gotten from Vincent. *Liaison claims infant's name is Mateo. Requested name to remain in adoption terms.*

"Yes," Mrs. Hudson said.

"Didn't that make you wonder . . . ?"

"Yes," Mrs. Hudson said plainly.

Matt's mind was buzzing in erratic circles. He had half a mind to travel to Colombia at the time of his adoption and see who brought him in, maybe question them. But the compass was still in pieces, and anyway, he didn't think he could handle any more revelations right now.

His next question he did not want to ask. He'd rather spare his mother the pain as well as the awkwardness of asking it, but he knew he had to. "I have some questions about Vincent."

His mother stiffened but nodded. "What do you want to know?" she said in a calm voice that did not match the rest of her body.

"Well . . . I guess I wanted to know if you knew what Vincent's last name was?"

Mrs. Hudson's brow furrowed. "His last name?"

"Yeah, like how our last name is Hudson. And your name before you married Dad was Bonnaire. And Captain Vincent's last name is . . . ? Pretty sure it's not just Vincent, is it?"

Mrs. Hudson shook her head. "I never knew his surname."

Matt found that hard to believe. Was she lying to him? To protect him or spare his feelings?

"I know that seems crazy considering how . . . well we knew each other," his mom said, her cheeks coloring a little. "But if you understood Vincent's history, it's not so surprising. He hated his family. He was all too glad to shed his family name and never speak of them again. So he was always just Vincent to me. Or Vince. I never suspected anything deceitful in it. I, too, had things I never wished to speak of in my past."

"What do you know about Vincent's past? His family?"

Matt vaguely remembered Wiley telling him something about Vincent not getting along with his brother, that he had run away from home and that was when he'd met Belamie Bonnaire, Matt's mom long before she was his mom.

"I know some," Mrs. Hudson said. "Vincent didn't like to speak of his family or his past, but he shared bits and pieces every now and then when his guard was down. Vincent was born in Cornwall, England, the second son of a wealthy lord. His father always compared him to his older brother, and Vincent always fell short. He came in second at everything. Vincent's relationship with his father had always been strained, but it was worse with his brother. When his parents died and his older brother inherited his father's title and estate, he took pains to make Vincent miserable. He withheld the living promised to him by his father, and just to add salt to the wound, he stole the girl Vincent had loved all through childhood. His brother didn't care for the girl one whit, but he knew it would drive Vincent mad if he married her. So he courted her, and he being the elder brother with the lands and title and money . . . well that's just the way things were. She was young, and her parents of course saw it as the superior match, so they became engaged. Vincent left before his brother's wedding. He joined the Royal Navy, and we met a year or so after that. The rest you know well enough."

Matt wondered how different things would have been for him and his family if Vincent's brother had treated him differently, or better yet, if he'd had no brother at all. If he'd been his father's heir, he likely never would have left home, never would have met Belamie Bonnaire and gotten so entangled in all their lives.

"Did he ever see his brother again?" Matt asked.

Mrs. Hudson hesitated a moment. She seemed uncertain as to whether she should share what she was thinking or remembering. "Only once that I know of," she said. "After we'd been together for a few years, Vincent learned that his brother and his bride had both died. He didn't tell me how or when it happened, or even how he had learned of it. He grew quiet and reclusive. I left him alone. I thought he was mourning the loss of his first love, and maybe even his brother a little, even if they didn't get along. I thought maybe he'd forgiven him, because if they hadn't quarreled Vincent never would have left home and so he never would have met me.

"One day, shortly after he'd gotten the news of his brother's death, he asked me to take him to his brother. He told me he wanted to make amends with him, before his death. We knew he could do nothing to prevent it, but perhaps he could mend the breach between them. I thought it showed strength of character. I never would have believed he was capable of what he actually did." She shivered and closed her eyes as though trying to block out the memory.

"I didn't go with him," she continued. "Vincent said he needed to go alone, and though I worried about him, I wanted to be respectful of his wishes. So I stayed with the rest of the crew on the *Vermillion*, as a ship at the seaside, just below Vincent's family's estate. I waited for him late into the night and grew increasingly uneasy. I worried something might have happened to him. I still didn't know the details of his brother's death, and what if Vincent was in danger? Just before dawn, I decided I had better go after him. That's when I saw an orange glow up on the cliffs. Vincent's family estate was engulfed in flames.

"I shouted for the crew to prepare for travel. And then I saw him. Vincent was standing at the bow of the ship, sipping a goblet of wine, watching his own family estate burn to the ground as though it were a beautiful sunrise. He smelled of smoke and kerosene."

Matt was starting to get the picture pretty well, but his mom continued.

"I asked him what had happened," Mrs. Hudson said.

"And he told me he'd gotten wind that his brother and new bride died tragically in a fire on their wedding night, and he realized that it was *he* who set the fire. Just as I had been responsible for my parents' deaths, he would be responsible for his brother's death, only in his case he would enjoy it. Why not be the one to light the match and have his revenge?

"We never spoke of it again. I tried to tell myself that it wasn't so bad, that his brother had been really horrible to Vince and maybe he deserved it. Vince could be so kind and gentle, it was easy to forget his streaks of anger and how vindictive he could be. Forgiveness had never been a virtue to him, only a weakness. It made no sense to forgive those who'd wronged you. But revenge? That made sense. People should get what they deserved.

"Later, when our search for the Aeternum intensified, Vince said if he had the power to change the past, he wouldn't kill his brother, and for a moment I thought he truly regretted his actions. I felt such relief. He wasn't a cold-blooded murderer. Just a man in pain. But then he explained further. I'll never forget what he said. 'Death doesn't remove the stain of their existence. It still doesn't give me what I want. When I have the Aeternum, I'll make it so he was never born at all. I'll make my own family, my own kingdom. The one *I* choose.'"

Mrs. Hudson shivered a little.

"What about Marius Quine?" Matt asked. "Do you think he's on our side? Or Vincent's?"

Mrs. Hudson shook her head. "I can't say. His actions, his communications seem to contradict themselves. I don't know if he's changing his mind over time, or if he has some other kind of grand scheme I can't comprehend, or if he's just different people at different times."

"What do you mean different people?"

"People change. I was a different person when I was Captain Bonnaire. That was me, but I'm not her anymore, you know? I went from Captain Belamie Bonnaire the time pirate to Belamie Hudson, the wife and mother who likes her swords and knives. The same and yet not. So I suppose Quine could be on our side at times and then not at other times. I don't know."

Matt shivered. He wanted to believe that he was on his family's side always, but future evidence would suggest otherwise. What would happen between now and then? What kind of person would he become? Would there ever be a circumstance where he, Mateo, could decide that *they* were not his family?

He wanted to say no. Never! But the truth was, the discovery of who he really was, and this possible connection with Vincent, had turned him upside down, so he didn't feel like he could definitively say anything. Nothing was certain. Nothing was so fixed that it could not be broken. His mom knew that better than anyone.

Matt felt dizzy. He started to tremble, almost like he was

going to have a seizure, but then his mom placed her warm hand on his cheek, and it steadied him.

"Hey." She looked him straight in the eyes. "I need you to know, to never forget, that you are my son. You will always be my son, no matter what happens to any of us. I've known it from the moment I set eyes on you. Past, present, or future, we are family. Do you understand?"

Matt nodded.

"I love you, Mateo." She kissed his forehead.

"I love you, too, Mom."

Matt rested his head against his mom's shoulder. She started to hum a tune and then she opened her mouth and sung the words. It was a French lullaby, one she used to sing to him when he was little, when he had the same nightmare that woke him up tonight. She must have known then.

When you feel lost and all alone
Look to the sky and you'll find home
The stars will guide you back to me
They shine for all eternity

His mother finished singing. She kissed the top of his head, and they sat in silence for a minute. Usually he would have felt comforted. The fears and dark thoughts would dissipate, but tonight's nightmare made them extra potent. The fear clung to him, like wet clothing, cold and chafing to his soul.

13

Changing Tides

1995
London, England

Matthew Hudson knew that the map he'd found in London was unique, but he had no idea it would change his life. Or more specifically, end it.

He found the map at a little flea market. He wasn't much for flea markets, but when he saw a stand displaying old maps he stopped. Most of them were tourist trash, crude and inaccurate replicas of old maps of various parts of the world. And then he saw a map that was something else altogether. A world map on thick vellum. He couldn't place what time period it came from. It seemed both at once old and new, and something about it called to him. When he touched it, the land lines shimmered and shifted. He wanted to study it, but not here.

"How much for this one?" he asked the seller, whom he

couldn't even see behind all the displays.

"Oh ... uh ... I don't know. What do you think it's worth?"

Matthew raised an eyebrow. It sounded like a kid. Maybe they were manning the stand for their mom or dad. He reached in his pocket. He was low on cash. He was low on everything. Money, energy, inspiration. His studies were sucking him dry. He only had a few coins in his pocket. "How about fifty pence?" he suggested.

"Sure, okay." A small hand reached out.

He felt a little guilty. He was probably ripping this kid off, but he was broke, and it wasn't his problem if the owners hadn't properly instructed the child on how to sell to customers. He handed over the money and rolled up the map. "Thanks," he said.

"Enjoy!" said the kid.

Matthew showed the map to his professor, who was almost as fascinated by the map as Matthew. The land lines seemed to shift to accommodate different eras. It also had a strange watermark stamped all over it in varying shades, a circle with a *V* at the center. Maybe it had something to do with Vikings? Or perhaps it was *V* for *Victory*. It could be a war map. Or a treasure map. There didn't seem to be any particular pattern. The markings were scattered all over the world, land and ocean, though mostly land, and they didn't seem to coincide with any one people or particular event. His professor wasn't sure it could be used academically, but he told Matthew he should hang on to it. You never know. The map could lead to any number of interesting things. Historical artifacts or a burial site. Treasure. As a child Matthew had fantasies of finding a map that would lead him to hidden treasure, like a pirate. He thought he'd let those childhood fantasies die, traded them in for serious scholarly pursuits, but somehow this map had unearthed that old longing for magic and adventure.

When he returned to New York, Matthew hung the map up in his apartment, just like a souvenir. He studied it closely for a while, taking down dates and locations, trying to find some kind of pattern. Sometimes new markings seemed to appear that he hadn't noticed before. Or maybe they hadn't been there before. He wondered who had made the map, how, and why. What purpose did it serve? Was it a toy? Or was it somehow useful?

One day, as he was getting ready to go to a Mets game with a friend, he noticed a new marking appear on the map, very different from the others. It glowed like the blue base of a flame. It was in New York, right in Manhattan, not far from where he was. He promptly forgot about the Mets game and his friend. He grabbed a compass from his desk, took the map down from the wall, and ran out the door.

The coordinates took him to Saks Fifth Avenue, but he saw nothing out of the ordinary, just pedestrians minding their business, cars and taxis, a woman walking her dog, a man in a suit leaning against the building, smoking a cigarette.

Matthew unfolded the map. The symbol on the map was still there, still glowing. When he looked up again, a woman emerged from the store. Matthew Hudson's heart stopped dead in his chest. He couldn't quite say what it was about this woman that slapped him so silly, but he knew she was anything but ordinary. It wasn't only that she was beautiful. Matthew had seen plenty of beautiful women in his life, and they never had this effect on him. It was something else, an otherworldliness, a certain energy. She was *different*. He wanted to meet this woman. He thought maybe he could offer to help her, since she had several bags and packages. That wasn't creepy, was it? He wasn't experienced in approaching strange women. He wasn't much experienced with women at all. He'd always been very shy with girls. They always made him feel awkward and tongue-tied. He simply had no confidence when it came to those things. But this woman, for whatever reason, made him feel bold. He had to talk to her. He just had to.

But before he took a step, a taxi pulled up. In all respects, it looked like an ordinary taxi, except for two things. It was full of people, surely more passengers than there were seat belts, and in the place where there would usually be an advertisement on top of the car, there was instead a symbol. It was exactly the same symbol that showed up all over the map in varying shades, a compass with a *V* at the center. In this case, the *V* was bright red.

The woman shoved her packages in the trunk. She looked over her shoulders both ways, clearly checking to see if anyone was watching. Her eyes locked on Matthew. They stared at each other for a moment, and then her face spread into a smile, almost like she recognized him somehow. Matthew Hudson's heart nearly leaped out of his chest. She gave him a wink and got inside the very crowded taxi.

Then something happened that Matthew Hudson wasn't sure he really saw or not. The taxi drove off and disappeared. *Truly* disappeared. One moment there, the next gone. He looked at his map. The symbol was still bright, but it was no longer glowing.

From that moment on Matthew was obsessed. He could barely take his eyes off the map. When he was at home, it was on the wall in front of his desk. He looked at it about every five minutes. If he was forced to go out, to class or to work, or home to visit his mother, he always brought the map with him. His mom teased him about it once, asked if he'd found any nice girls to date on that map of his.

Matthew would never mention the mysterious woman to his mother. She'd think he was crazy, and on some level Matthew thought she would be right, but he couldn't get the woman out of his head. Who was she? Where did she come from? Where had she gone? And *how*? How had the taxi just disappeared like that? He had to know. He had this feeling that he was meant to find this map, that he was meant to cross paths with that woman, for whatever reason. Sometimes he saw glowing new markings appear, as he had in New York, but they were always too far away, and would often disappear before he could even make travel arrangements. Even if he could, he didn't think he'd have much luck, not if the dates that hovered over the glowing symbol were correct. They were all over the place in time, as far back as 44 BC and even into the twenty-first century AD. Eventually Matthew figured out what was going on. As improbably as it seemed, the woman was a time traveler, and this map was somehow tracking her movements.

It was almost a year before he was able to see the woman again. He almost missed it. August 24, 1996. He was trying to write a paper for one of his classes, glancing at the map every now and then, as was his habit. Then he saw it. The symbol was glowing blue, just like before. In New York City. Right now.

Matthew grabbed the map and raced out the door. He hailed a taxi. Checking the coordinates he saw that it was in the theater district. He found her at *Les Misérables*. She was with a group of people, all of them dressed up, but she perhaps more than any of them. She was wearing a red dress. She looked stunning, like a movie star. Lots of people looked at her, but she didn't look back at any of them. She was clearly with someone. A handsome man who had a hand around her waist in an extremely possessive manner. Matt's heart sank.

Had he been a fool obsessing over this woman for the past year? She could be married for all he knew. She could have children, for crying out loud.

He almost left, but then she looked up and their eyes met. Matthew started to move toward her. She said something to her friends, and then she turned abruptly and walked out of the theater. Her group followed, and they all got into a limousine. But before she got inside she stopped at the vendor selling hats and T-shirts. She grabbed a Mets jersey, then looked up. Their eyes met again. He could tell she was confused, scared. She knew, just like he did, that something strange was happening, but neither of them knew what, exactly.

"Ma'am, you going to pay for that?" the vendor said.

The woman didn't say anything. She jumped into the limousine.

"Wait!" Matthew called, running after her.

"Hey!" The seller pounded on the window. "I'll call the police! I got your license plate number!"

But he didn't. The limousine didn't even have a license plate, and seconds later, it disappeared.

The vendor cursed.

"Here," Matthew said, pulling a twenty out of his wallet. "I got it."

"Nah, man," said the vendor. "You don't have to pay for the thieves."

"Neither should you," said Matthew. "Please. Allow me."

The vendor thanked him. Matthew walked home, his mind buzzing.

It was another year before he saw the mark again. August 3, 1997. As luck would have it, this time it was at the convenience store just down the street from him, which was fortunate as he probably would have missed her had she been anywhere else. When he walked in, he found her stuffing things in her bags. Was she *stealing*? Matthew found he didn't care. He thought it somewhat amusing, actually. She tossed items in her shopping bags, cosmetics, creams, snacks. Then she stopped in front of the book section. Ah, a reading thief. Matthew was terribly amused, especially when he saw that what she picked up was a sultry romance novel, the kind his mom would buy and try to hide.

The woman looked up, met eyes with him. Matthew smiled, waiting for recognition to come to her. It didn't. This struck him as very odd. She had seemed to recognize him before. But then Matthew realized, if she really was a time traveler, as he suspected, it was possible that their timelines were mixed up. While he had seen her twice before now, this could be the first time she was seeing him. And the first time he had seen her may not have been the first time she had seen him.

The woman looked around as though maybe he was smiling at someone else, but there wasn't anyone else in the store, so she finally looked back at him, staring him down with a bold confidence that Matthew found completely irresistible. She held up the book, smiled, and tossed the book in one of her bags.

Matthew almost started laughing. The woman grabbed something around her neck, a watch of some kind, it looked like. She twisted some knobs or dials on the watch. She looked up at Matthew, winked, and blew a kiss, right before she disappeared.

She *disappeared*! Into thin air. Matthew ran out of the store, looked up and down both ends of the street, but the woman was nowhere to be found.

Game on, he thought. He was going to get to the bottom of this.

He didn't have to wait long. The symbol appeared on the map the very next day, this time at the bay. He raced down as fast as he could. He had a feeling this time she was testing him, waiting to see if he would show up. When he arrived, he didn't see her. But there was a man dressed all in black wearing red Converse. Matthew recognized him. He was the man who had been with the woman that night in the theater. He was looking at Matthew with cold hatred, and Matthew knew he had done something to anger him, though he wasn't sure what. Sure, he was kind of obsessed with the guy's girl-friend (assuming she was his girlfriend) but he hadn't done anything. He hadn't even talked to her.

"Good evening," said the man in black in an oily British

drawl. "Looking for someone?"

"I was, actually," Matthew said. "But it looks like I'm in the wrong place."

"Indeed," the man said. "The wrong place and the wrong time."

The man smiled as though he thought something was amusing. He took a step toward Matthew, who had a hard time not flinching or recoiling with fear. He wasn't sure what it was about this man. Like the woman, he seemed to have an otherworldly quality about him, but not in a good way. Something was off about this man.

"My mistake," he said. He turned around to leave, only to come face-to-face with two other men. He didn't recognize either of them, though he was sure he would have remembered if he'd seen them before. The one on his right was a young black man wearing an old-fashioned suit and smoking a pipe, something out of a 1930s gangster film. The other was a white man with thick clumps of hair sprouting out of his head like a plant. His clothes seemed to have been pulled out of a costume bin, including a red cape and purple cowboy boots. He also had a gun. He smiled, revealing a clear tooth that sparkled like it was made of diamond.

Matthew felt alarm bells going off in his head. He needed to get away, but where could he go?

"Don't worry," said the man in black. "This will be the last mistake you ever make."

And before Matthew could move or say another word, the man in black grabbed him by the throat. He was paralyzed.

The man pulled Matthew close to his face so he was forced to look in his eyes, dark, depthless, almost inhuman. His heart raced. He tried to move, told his arms to swing, his legs to run, but they wouldn't obey.

"Whatever did she see in you, I wonder?" the man said.

Who was he talking about? The woman? That couldn't be. They hadn't even met. It looked like they never would.

"Ah, well, I suppose we'll never know," the man said. "Because she never will see you, and you will never see her. In fact, you won't exist at all."

The man then pulled something from Matthew's throat. It almost felt like he was unraveling him, pulling out his blood and sinew by some invisible force. But there was no blood or sinew. Streams of watery material poured out of him, shimmering, iridescent. What was happening? What was that? He saw people in the material. Himself at various moments of his life. His mother. His father! His brother, Charles. And there was the woman. She was holding a baby, smiling up at him. She seemed to glow with the purest love and complete joy. Matthew's heart almost burst inside his chest. He tried to speak, to shout, but no sound would come.

"You are probably wondering what is happening," Captain Vincent said. "I know how frustrating it is to be left in the dark with no explanation, so I will tell you. Your existence is in the way of my happiness, and so I'm sorry to tell you that I must eliminate it altogether. Actually, no. That is incorrect. I'm not sorry at all."

He brought out what looked like a stick of dynamite. It glowed blue, just like the symbols on the map. The man wrapped the shimmering fabric around the strange dynamite. The woman holding the child disappeared in its folds.

The fabric began to disintegrate. Matthew felt no pain, but still he was terrified. The world seemed to be fading. He felt he was being sucked into a black hole. His own reality of existence began to slip. Who was he? Where was he? What was happening to him?

The last conscious thought of Matthew Hudson was fixated on that mysterious woman.

14

Unraveling

Matt was getting restless. The others were too. They'd been cooped up for three days. Only Uncle Chuck and Haha had gone out once more to get food and supplies, and they came back with news that a battle was happening in Central Park that looked to be from the Civil War. Matt could hear the cannons and gunshots from their apartment. The news reported more strange happenings, not just in New York City, but in other parts of the world too. Buildings were relocating themselves. Landmasses were spreading, sinking, or crashing together. The Eiffel Tower had disappeared completely. Wars were breaking out all over the place. And people were disappearing and reappearing in different times and places. The whole world was in chaos.

Matt still had not fixed the compass. He was having a hard time replacing the piece he had lost back at Gaga's, during the storm, and he didn't have all the tools he needed, so everything took longer. A couple of times he thought he had it, but then he'd run a test and it wouldn't work and he'd have to take it all apart again.

Tensions escalated as the family began to argue over what they should do once the compass was fixed, whether they should stay put or move somewhere else. Mr. Hudson felt they should stay put, while Mrs. Hudson thought they should keep on the move.

"The longer we stay in one place the more likely it is that Vincent will find us," Mrs. Hudson argued. "We have to keep on the move."

"What are you suggesting?" Gaga said. "That we time-travel from place to place and century to century for the rest of our lives like a bunch of . . . of . . ."

"Pirates?" Corey said.

"Not pirates," Mrs. Hudson said. "That's Vincent. Not us."

"Castaways," Ruby said. "We're time castaways."

"I don't want to be a pirate *or* a castaway," Gaga said, pulling at her silver hair. "I want to go home! I just want to live what's left of my life!"

Haha tried to comfort her, patting her awkwardly on the back. "It's okay, Gloria. At least we're together." But this only seemed to make Gaga cry harder.

"I'm sorry, Gloria," Mrs. Hudson said. "We're doing the best we can."

"It doesn't really matter what you do or where you go,"

Albert said. "Captain Vincent will find you anyway."

"Well, he hasn't found us yet," Ruby said. "Maybe he's not as powerful as you think."

Albert simply shrugged. "Believe what you like."

Jia was unusually quiet throughout all these arguments, Matt noticed. She mostly stared blankly out the window. Occasionally, she reached inside one of her vest pockets, but she never brought anything out that he could see. Matt tried to talk to her, ask her how she was doing, but she avoided him, preferring to spend her time with Ruby. The most she ever spoke was when Mr. Hudson brought out a stack of board games to fight their restlessness. Chinese checkers was at the top, and upon seeing it Jia became indignant.

"Ridiculous name. There's nothing Chinese about that game at all."

"How do you know?" Matt said. "You didn't live in China that long. It could have been invented after your time."

"It's on the box." Jia lifted the lid of the box where the information and instructions were printed on the inside. "And maybe I didn't live in China that long, but I remember my cultural heritage."

Matt felt he had struck a nerve with Jia. He knew she did not like to discuss her past, and he told himself it was none of his business and she would tell him when and if she felt like it. But he couldn't help but feel a tiny bit hurt that she hadn't confided in him a little more. He didn't even know what era she was from, only that she was an orphan from China. Sometimes Matt got the feeling Jia was hiding something from him, but then he told himself that was probably just his own paranoia because *he* was actually the one hiding something from everyone.

They didn't play Chinese checkers. Haha wanted to have a chess tournament, and Matt soon learned where his dad got his competitive board-gaming nature. Haha beat out everyone and gloated after each win, until it came time to play Matt. Matt had always been a natural at chess. He declared checkmate on Haha in six swift moves. Haha was flummoxed. He thought maybe it was a fluke, or that Matt had surely cheated. Matt played him again and beat him in four moves.

Haha scratched his head, laughing a little. "Okay, how did you do that?"

"Matt's a genius, duh," Corey said.

"None of us have ever been able to beat him at chess," Ruby said. "He doesn't operate on the same level as the rest of us."

"Well, I suppose that makes sense," Haha said, "considering how you built a time-travel machine and all." He kept frowning at the chess board, rubbing his chin.

Matt frowned at the board too. He wished all this time-travel stuff could be as clear to him as a game of chess, all black and white, that the moves would reveal themselves in combinations of letters and numbers. But when it came to time travel there was so much gray and fog. Even if Matt fixed the compass, he wasn't sure what their next move should be, how to predict Captain Vincent's moves, or Quine's. He could feel himself going crazy.

Corey didn't help any. He kept going on about the Quine thing, and how they needed to find him and take him down somehow, though no one could even begin to guess how. Well, Matt had a guess, but what was he supposed to do, sell himself out? Maybe that was the answer.

Late that night, when everyone else was asleep, Matt sat working on the compass at his desk. He could still hear the clanks and rumblings of whatever battle was happening outside. A huge shadow passed over his window and when he opened the blinds there was a pterodactyl sitting on the fire escape, folding in its huge wings. Matt studied it. For a moment he forgot about all the chaos and simply marveled at this prehistoric creature before him. Unlike the more reptilian creature he'd always imagined, this pterodactyl actually had small, tufty feathers. Its crest was bright red and its eyes were surprisingly catlike, wary and intelligent. If they could wade through the chaos, Matt thought, scientists and historians could probably learn more in a few short weeks of real-life interaction with the past than they could in a lifetime of digging and research. Time travel wasn't all bad. Like anything it just needed some regulation. But how could anyone regulate such a thing?

The pterodactyl made a sound between a growl and a shriek and flew off.

Matt placed the center dial back on the compass and gave it a short twist. Before he knew what was happening he was gone.

When he appeared again, he didn't know where he was. The space was dim and foggy. He took a breath and coughed as dust entered his lungs. He was in a small room with bunk beds. After a moment he realized it was his own bedroom, his and Corey's. Those were their bunk beds, covered in dust. There were the baseball stadium seats, his desk, his books and magazines and clothes.

He went out to the main area of the apartment. Everything was gray, covered in a thick layer of dust. One section of the wall was blown out, and Matt could see the city beyond, only there was no city. It was in ruins and completely unrecognizable to Matt. Some buildings had been reduced to rubble, others were partially standing. There were hills and mountains. People and animals roamed the land aimlessly. He could see a herd of giraffes. This couldn't be New York. But this was his apartment. He must have traveled to the future, far into the future for this much change to have happened. He looked down at the dials and his heart did a little leap. He'd gone to June 10, 2019, only days from the time they'd left the vineyard, which meant this could only be a day or two in the future. How could everything have changed so drastically in such a short space of time? What happened? Where was his family? Had they left? Were they here? Maybe they were hiding?

"Hello?" Matt called. "Mom? Dad?" He went to his parents' bedroom. The bed was unmade, but there was no one there. He went to Ruby's room. No one. His heart began to pound. Whatever had happened, it clearly wasn't good. He needed to get back. When had he left? He'd disappeared so quickly and he hadn't been paying much attention to the time. It was around 11:00 p.m., he thought. He didn't want to overlap with himself, so he'd go back at midnight the next day. That should be safe. As long as he returned while everyone was still asleep, he should be okay.

He was just about to turn the dials when something caught his eye, something on the dining table, a thick piece of paper. He picked it up and shook off the dust. It wasn't paper but a piece of cloth. It was Captain Vincent's handkerchief, the one with the initials *VQ* on them. Why was it on the table, out in the open? What did that mean? Had Corey shown it to his parents and everyone? Did this have anything to do with what happened here?

Matt dropped the dusty handkerchief and quickly turned the time dials to take him back to when he'd left. The room spun and the next thing he knew he was in his bedroom again. The dust and destruction was gone. It was clean and bright. Too bright. The sun was shining through the windows. The sun . . . That wasn't right. It had been night when he left. Corey's bed was empty and so was Albert's. He looked down at his compass and his stomach dropped. He'd accidently returned at 12:00 p.m. instead of a.m.! He hit himself in the forehead. How could he have been so careless? He really should have designed the compass in military time to avoid this very mistake. His mind raced. He could fix this. He could travel back, wake up in his own bed. . . .

His bedroom door flew open. There was Corey. He looked from Matt to his compass and back to Matt. His eyes narrowed and darkened. "You're in *so* much trouble." Corey grabbed Matt's arm and yanked him out of the bedroom like he was some kind of criminal.

"Ouch! Let go of me!"

"He's back! I found him!" Corey announced as he pulled Matt into the dining room where everyone was gathered around the table—his parents, Gaga, Ruby, Jia, and Albert. Mrs. Hudson had her hands at her temples, but as soon as Matt entered she stood quickly and rushed toward him. He thought she was going to embrace him with relief that he'd returned, but instead she grabbed him by the shoulders so her nails dug into his arms. She shook him a little. "What happened? Where did you go?"

"Nowhere. I—"

Corey scoffed. "Oh, brother, quit with the lies already."

"I'm not lying!"

"Matt," Ruby said. "You've been gone for *hours.*"

"We've been looking everywhere for you," his dad said. "Your grandfather and uncle are both out looking for you now." Matt was surprised by the harshness in his dad's voice, the wariness in his eyes.

"I'm really sorry," Matt said. "I can explain. The compass is fixed, see?" He held it up, but no one seemed to be all that impressed.

"Yeah, we guessed that much," Corey said, then turned to their parents. "I told you he's been traveling behind our backs."

"What? No, I haven't!" Matt said. "I was fixing the compass, and then when I put it back together I traveled. It was an accident, just like on my birthday!"

"Where did you go?" his mom asked.

"I went to the future, I guess, just a day or two. I stayed right here in the apartment, and—"

"Did you see us?" his mom interrupted. "Did you see yourself in the future?"

Matt shook his head. "We weren't there. Something happened. An explosion or something. No one was there. We have to get out of here. This place is going to be torn apart any time now."

"Don't listen to him," Corey said. "It's a trick."

"What are you talking about?" Matt said angrily. "Why would I want to trick you?"

"I don't know," Corey said. "Maybe because you've been tricking us all along. Maybe because you're not who we thought you were. Maybe because you're not really on our side at all."

Corey nodded toward the dining table where everyone was sitting. Matt glanced at the table and saw the handkerchief laid out exactly where he'd just seen it in the future. So Corey had shown it to everyone else while he'd been gone. They knew now that Vincent was a Quine. But there was more on the table that he hadn't seen in the future. The note from Vincent that he'd found on the willow tree in Gaga's yard, and the scrap of paper he'd torn off from Quine's letter, the part that completed the poem and confirmed Matt's true identity. His mother, at least, would have been able to put it together. *Bring Mateo to me. We are one and the same.* They must have searched his things for any clues as to what had happened to him or where he'd gone.

"It all makes sense now," Corey said. "*You're* Marius Quine!"

"I still don't see how this can be true," Ruby said. "That's Matt. Our brother. He can't be Marius Quine. He's just . . . Matt . . . right?"

"No, he's not just Matt," Corey said. "Don't you see? It all makes sense now. We always thought Marius Quine was the inventor of the compass. But then we found out Matt had invented the compass, and so we thought Quine was somehow the bad guy. But then Matt was there with Quine when Captain Vincent got the Aeternum. Vincent always favored you when we were on the *Vermillion*, because he knew who you really were, that you two were related somehow."

Everyone looked at Matt, waiting for him to confirm. He felt like he was being backed into a corner. He had no defense, nowhere to run or hide. He couldn't keep his secret any longer.

"It's true," Matt finally said, casting his eyes downward. "Quine and I. We're the same person."

"I knew it," Corey said with part triumph and part derision. "I *knew* you were hiding something from us."

"How long have you known?" his mom asked, her voice a bit hard, and he realized right then he'd made a mistake. He thought she knew already, and maybe she suspected, but he should have told her right away.

"Since that day in Asilah."

"When Quine gave Vincent the Aeternum," Corey said, every word dripping with disgust. "When *you* gave him the Aeternum! So that's it then. You're on *his* side."

"No!" Matt said. "I'm not, I swear."

"Then why didn't you tell us?" Ruby asked.

"I don't know," Matt said. "I guess I didn't understand it myself. I still don't. I didn't want you guys to think I was against you."

"Congratulations," Corey snarled. "That's exactly what we think."

"Enough, Corey," said Mrs. Hudson. "Mateo is your brother, no matter what."

"No, he's not," Corey said. "He's an impostor. Don't you get it? He's *manipulating* us! He's like a master puppeteer. Quine made sure you adopted him, somehow, so he could infiltrate our family, right from the beginning, and tear us all apart."

"That's a horrible thing to say," Mrs. Hudson breathed.

"It *is* horrible," Corey said. "But it's true. We have to face the facts."

"No," Ruby cried in a small, quivering voice, so unlike her usual confidence. "Matt would never do that to us."

"Maybe not Matt," Corey said. "But Quine would. Because he already did. And one day Matt will become Quine. Maybe he has already. You've been working with him, haven't you? Sneaking behind our backs, having secret meetings."

Matt shook his head. "I haven't. I only saw him that day in Asilah . . . and just once before that, but he was invisible, so I didn't really see him!"

Corey huffed a laugh. "You're such a liar. You've been traveling behind our backs. I'll bet the compass was never broken at all. You just wanted to be able to travel on your own, plotting who knows what with Captain Vincent while we all sit here and freak out."

Everyone looked to Matt, waiting for an answer, for him to refute what Corey were saying. But he had no answers. He felt like a mouse being backed into a corner by a bunch of feral cats. He had no defense, no way out. He looked for anyone who might be on his side, but everyone was looking at Matt like he'd just had a mask removed, revealing something grotesque and alien. Even Jia was looking at him with her lips pursed, her brow knit. She hadn't said anything through all of this. He couldn't tell what she was thinking or feeling, if she was angry or confused. Maybe both. Albert was the only one who did seem surprised or angry. He just stared at Matt with curiosity rather than accusation.

Matt wished he could disappear. He could, he realized. He had his compass. He could disappear right now, leave all this mess until he could figure things out. He started to reach for it, then stopped. He couldn't do that. He couldn't just leave his family like that. They had to work this out together. That's what families did. Corey, however, noticed only the movement Matt made for his compass, unaware of his inner thoughts.

"Oh, no, you don't!" Corey rushed at him. There were screams and shouts as Corey attacked. Matt fell back and had the wind knocked out of him. They rolled on the floor, knocking into chairs and walls.

"Corey, stop!" Ruby shouted.

Matt tried to shove Corey off, but Corey had always been bigger than him, and stronger. All Matt could do was try to protect himself. And the compass. Corey grabbed the chain and tried to tear it off Matt's head, maybe tear his head off too. Matt grabbed on to the chain. He wouldn't let go of the compass, no matter what Corey or anyone believed. He'd built it. It belonged to him.

Corey gave up on the compass and went directly for Matt, punching him in the ribs and stomach, shouting rage-filled insults and curses that under any normal circumstances would have gotten him grounded for life.

"Matthew, get Corey off him," Mrs. Hudson shouted.

Mr. Hudson tried to pull Corey off, but he was in such a rage he flung his elbow back, hitting Mr. Hudson right in the nose.

"Traitor!" Corey shouted as he punched Matt in the chest and stomach. "You're nothing but a lying, traitorous . . ."

There was a strange sound, a kind of humming or a buzz, like a beehive. At first Matt thought it was inside his head, an effect from Corey's punching, but then Corey suddenly stopped hitting him. He looked around as though he heard the noise too. It seemed to be coming from everywhere and nowhere in particular. It grew louder.

The door flew open and Haha and Uncle Chuck came running in the door. "We didn't find him, but—" Uncle Chuck's eyes landed on Matt. "Oh good, he's back. Listen, there's something strange going on. Things appearing and disappearing all over the place. I think it might be wise for us to—"

Haha cut him off. "What in the name of Peter, Paul, and Mary happened to you?!" He was looking at Mr. Hudson. His nose was bleeding from Corey elbowing him in the face, but that's not what Haha was referring to, Matt was pretty sure. He was referring to his hands. Mr. Hudson held up his hands, and Mrs. Hudson gasped. They were blurry, like someone had taken an eraser and smudged them.

"What's happening to Dad?" Ruby said in a trembling voice.

The apartment started to vibrate, the walls and ceiling, rattling the table and dishes.

"It's Captain Vincent," Albert said. "He's taking him now. He's changing things. In the past."

"No," Mrs. Hudson breathed. She reached out and grasped for her husband's fading hands. Her fingers moved right through him, like he was a ghost. "No, no, no. Matthew."

"Belamie . . . ," Mr. Hudson said, reaching out a fading hand.

"I told you," Matt said, pushing Corey off him. "I told you something was going to happen! We have to get out of here!" Matt pushed himself up from the floor and teetered as the ground continued to shake.

"If you knew something was going to happen it's because *you* caused it!" Corey shouted. "This is your fault!"

"Stop fighting!" Mrs. Hudson shrieked. "Stop it right now! We have to go!" Mrs. Hudson grabbed Mr. Hudson by the arm, which was still solid, and pulled him to the door.

"You can't run from this," Albert said. "It's going to happen no matter what."

But Mrs. Hudson didn't listen to Albert. "Everybody, let's go!"

They didn't pause to take anything. They all ran out the door, but as Matt was on the threshold he realized Jia was still standing in the apartment.

"Jia, come on!" he shouted.

"China," Jia said.

"What?"

"We have to go to China."

What was she talking about? "Jia, we have to get out of here now!" Matt ran back inside, grabbed Jia by the arm, and pulled her out the door.

By the time they were outside, Mr. Hudson stumbled and fell to the ground. His legs were fading.

A strong wind swept through the street. A flock of birds scattered from a tree. Then the birds disappeared midflight, as if invisible hands were snatching them out of the air, sucked into some invisible fold of space.

"Oh, the poor birds!" Gaga exclaimed.

"What's happening to them?" Haha asked. "Where are they going?"

"We have to go to China," Jia said again, as if she were in some kind of trance.

"We have to get out of here," Mrs. Hudson said as she watched the birds disappear. "Let's go. Everyone to Blossom. Chuck, help me with Matthew, please." They both hoisted him up, fumbling a little with his fading arms and legs.

Everyone started running. Except Matt. Just like in his nightmare, he couldn't seem to move. Everything around him seemed to be moving, but he couldn't. He felt like he was standing in the midst, observing everything like theater in the round.

"Mateo! Run!" his mom called. She was reaching for him while holding on to his dad, who was still fading. Matt could hardly see his features at all.

Something snapped.

Matt felt it more than heard it. It was like a rubber band had been pulled too tight and finally it broke. There was a brief moment of stillness and silence. That was all the warning he had.

"Belamie," Mr. Hudson said, reaching for her, but his faded hand went right through her face. Mr. Hudson began to disappear or, more accurately, unravel. That shimmering fabric, the time tapestry Matt had seen Captain Vincent pull out of his dad's throat, was spilling out of Mr. Hudson now. The tapestry unraveled, and the threads flew away on the wind. Mrs. Hudson screamed as she tried to hold on to him, hold on to those unraveling threads, but they slipped through her fingers as easily as water.

"Dad!" Matt shouted.

The last of the time tapestry unraveled, and Mr. Hudson was gone.

Mrs. Hudson fell to the ground, clutching her head.

Ruby started screaming.

Matt whipped around. Ruby was looking down at her hands, her mouth open in horror. They were blurry. Corey's too. Matt took a step toward them when the pavement beneath his feet cracked. The earth began to split open. He almost fell between the cracks but was saved by someone who grabbed him from behind and pulled him back, Haha, he thought, and then they ran to go help someone else.

A building in front of Matt completely collapsed, swallowed up by the earth, and then the earth pushed up, forming a sheer cliff. People were screaming and running in all directions. Some of them disappeared just like the birds, as though invisible hands were snatching them between folds in the sky, and others appeared out of nowhere. Matt saw a few cowboys on horseback pop into being, then a group of people who looked like they were from the Stone Age, and a herd of giraffes.

The earth continued to widen. A deep, bottomless chasm opened. Ruby screamed as her legs began to blur and she fell. Corey followed after her. Matt suddenly seemed to unlock. He dove after Corey and Ruby. He grabbed Corey by the arm. "I got you!" he said. He tried to reach for Ruby, but someone else had her. Matt glanced over and was shocked to be looking at himself. He was dirty and bruised and covered in scrapes and cuts.

"You!" Corey shouted, looking back and forth between the

two Matts. "What are you doing?!"

"I'm trying to save you!" they both said at the same time.

"No you're not!" Corey shouted. "You're killing us!"

Both Corey and Ruby were fading, their limbs dissolving in their grasp. Matt couldn't hold on. The other Matt couldn't either.

"This is your fault!" Corey shouted at both Matts. "You did this to us!" His face started to blur.

"I'll fix it!" Matt pleaded.

"I promise I'll fix it!" pleaded the other Matt, and then another Matt appeared and reached for Corey and Ruby.

"Matt, don't let go!" Ruby cried. Her voice sounded distant, almost like a whisper even though she was shouting.

"I won't! I promise!" all three Matts said at nearly the same time so it sounded like an echo. He wouldn't let go. He would go with Corey and Ruby, wherever they were being taken. The three of them were supposed to stay together. They had always stayed together.

But his promise was in vain. He was no match for whatever forces were at work. Corey's arm dissolved in Matt's grasp. It slipped through his fingers. He tried to hold on, tried with all his might to pull them toward him, but it was like trying to hold on to air.

Both Corey and Ruby screamed as they unraveled and faded away.

15

Nightmare Come True

"No!" Matt shouted. He tried to jump in after them, but the earth crashed back together, closing the chasm and rising up in a rocky wave. Matt went up and then slid down like a giant playground slide, only it ripped at his legs and bottom and was far from fun. He couldn't tell what happened to the other Matts. They'd disappeared or something, but they weren't his concern.

Lightning cracked. The sky seemed to shatter like a fallen snow globe, only the snow was pouring *in*, and not just snow, but rain and hail the size of quarters. Matt covered his head with his arms. The ground tilted. The whole world was fragmenting, crumbling, folding in on itself. The earth fell and rose like waves in the ocean, creating new levels and dimensions.

Matt tumbled and rolled as rocks and hail and lightning shot down all around him. He curled up in a ball, shivering, as the hail beat down, but it was Corey's words that hit and stung him the hardest.

This is your fault!

You did this to us!

This is your fault!

Your fault!

Your fault!

Matt took his compass and with trembling icy fingers turned the time dial back. He knew it wasn't logical, and at the same time it was the only thing he could think of to do. He had to do something. He needed to save his family. Somehow he knew he could. There had to be a way. He turned the dial back two minutes. That was all he needed. Two minutes to rescue them.

It felt like someone picked him up and threw him twenty feet. He landed on the edge of that chasm where Corey and Ruby were now sliding down. His past self dived for Corey. "I got you!" Matt reached for Ruby and grabbed her by the upper arm.

"You!" Corey shouted. "What are you doing?!"

"I'm rescuing you!" Matt said at the same time as his past self. His past voice echoed in his head.

"No you're not! You're killing us!"

They were fading again. Matt couldn't hold on.

"This is your fault! You did this to us!"

"I'll fix it!" the other Matt pleaded.

"I promise I'll fix it!" Matt pleaded again, and then another Matt appeared.

"Matt, don't let go!" Ruby cried. "Please!"

"I won't! I promise!" all three Matts said, even as Ruby's arm dissolved in his grasp and Corey slipped through past-Matt's fingers.

Both Corey and Ruby screamed as they unraveled and faded away.

No.

No, no, no, no, no!

Matt turned the dial back again, three minutes this time. He knew it was madness. He knew the rules and the consequences of time travel, that his actions were only causing chaos and solving nothing, but he also couldn't accept what was happening. He would break the rules, bend them to his will. He had to.

He was thrown back again, like time was spitting him across the universe. He landed just behind the past-Matt, right as the earth split apart and he was about to fall into the chasm. Without a thought, Matt reached forward, grabbed himself by the collar, and yanked himself back.

The sky boomed and crackled with lightning.

Matt sprinted toward Corey and Ruby, but the cowboys appeared right in his path, and then the cavemen, and the giraffes. By the time he got around them he could see he was already too late. Corey and Ruby were unraveling, fading.

Why did he stop to rescue himself? It was a stupid thing to do and at the same time the only thing to do. Just like what he was doing right now. All three of his selves.

"I promise I'll fix it!" pleaded the first Matt.

Matt knelt down next to the second Matt and reached for Corey and Ruby, trying to grasp on to those unraveling threads.

"Matt, don't let go!" Ruby cried. "Please!"

"I won't! I promise!" he said with his two past selves.

He reached and grasped for those unraveling threads with more desperation than he'd ever felt in his life. He started to shake. Stars were popping in the corners of his eyes and a great rushing sounded in his ears, like the crashing of waves. He knew he was having a seizure and that he was about to black out, but he held on to those threads.

Some invisible force pulled at him, sucked him in. Into where, he didn't know. It was like the threads he'd been so desperately trying to hold on to were a current and he got caught in it.

He was weightless now, adrift. He tumbled along the current, twisting and spinning. He saw flashes of people and places, Corey, and Ruby, and himself. He saw the remnants of their lives together. The current split off into other currents that connected to other currents. He was swimming in a web of some kind. A web of memories spun over lifetimes and generations. He saw people and places both familiar and foreign. He saw his mom, his dad, Corey, and Ruby. He saw himself. One thread led to another—flashes of baseball games, school, when they'd first boarded the *Vermillion*. He even saw the moment their parents met, just before it unraveled and disintegrated. He tried to reach for these things, hold on to them, but he was powerless to move or act. He could only be carried away on this current.

Matt started to lose the sense of things, the sense of space or time, and of himself. Where was he, exactly? How long had he been here? Seconds? Years? Somehow he had the feeling that he had been here both seconds and years, if that were possible. Forever and no time at all. Was there a difference?

He saw a light ahead. He thought maybe that was death and he was heading right toward it. A hand reached down to him. He saw a blurred image of someone, like the person was underwater, only Matt was fairly certain it was he who was underwater. Or whatever he was under or inside. He was inside a time tapestry, he thought. But not just any time tapestry. It was Corey's and Ruby's. He didn't want to leave it. He didn't want to let go, but he had the feeling that if he stayed here much longer, he would unravel too, and that would be the end. His consciousness was already fading.

He grasped on to that hand.

It was like a plug had been pulled from a bathtub. Matt spun as he was sucked in a downward spiral. The images he'd seen before reversed themselves, flickering so fast he could barely discern them. Corey and Ruby flashed before him. He made one final reach, wrapped his fingers around those shimmering threads and willed them to stay with him.

With a gurgling, slurping sound he came spewing out of the current and back into the world. He landed on the hard, broken earth. He rolled a few times, then crashed into a wagon wheel. He remained curled up on the ground as the rain and hail continued to descend, but a few seconds later it stopped as quickly as it had started. The wind died down. The clouds in the sky dispersed.

Someone shook him a little, patted his cheek.

"Matt! Matt!" someone cried. "Wake up!"

Matt gasped and sat up. He looked around, hoping that what he had just seen was only one of his nightmares and his family would be standing all around him, making sure he was okay. But they weren't there. Only Jia stood before him. He saw no sign of his family. He had to go back again. He had to save them. He moved for his compass again, but Jia grabbed his arm.

"Matt, stop," she said. "It's no use."

Matt jerked his hand away. "I have to save them!"

"Matt . . ." Jia's eyes filled with tears. She trembled as the tears spilled over her cheeks. "Oh, Matt, I'm so sorry."

And it was her tears that broke Matt, that finally made him realize that he couldn't save them. There was nothing he could do except make it all worse. He'd failed.

Jia wiped her tears and sniffled. She had welts on her face and arms from the hail, a few scrapes on her face. Her vest was torn and dirty. One of the pockets had been ripped off completely. It was a weird reaction, but he looked on the ground for whatever tools of hers she might have lost. He should like to recover something. But as he searched he finally became aware of the destruction and chaos all around him. It looked like another world, a different planet. This surely couldn't be Earth, let alone Manhattan. He didn't see any sign of his home, not any of the buildings with which he was so familiar, not the dry cleaner's, or the drugstore, or the bakery. He couldn't see the Met, not even Central Park. There were sudden cliffs and mountains jutting up between unfamiliar and very random buildings. In one place there were little grass huts jumbled together, and next to those what looked like half of an Egyptian pyramid. A more modern building stood behind Matt, and it took him a moment to realize that it was his own apartment building, miraculously still standing, though half the front had been ripped away so it looked like a doll's house. He counted up the levels and could see where his apartment was. This was the scene he'd been viewing when he'd traveled to the future. And now he knew it was his fault.

Your fault.

Your fault.

Your fault.

He closed his eyes and saw Corey and Ruby, the looks on

their faces just before they'd unraveled and disappeared.

"Oh, Matt, look!" Jia said. Matt opened his eyes. His chest flared with the smallest hope that Jia had seen someone in his family, but she was pointing down at his hand. He was holding something and hadn't even noticed, probably because it was weightless and felt like little more than air. It was a couple scraps of those shimmery, translucent threads he'd been so desperately grasping for.

"What is it?" Jia asked.

"I think it's a bit of Corey and Ruby, or their time tapestries, anyway," Matt said. Somehow he'd been able to hold on to them.

"That's good, then, isn't it?" Jia said. "It might be able to help somehow."

"How?"

"I don't know."

Matt held up the bits of tapestry to catch the light. He saw no images within them, only faint shadows. One of the threads fell away and disintegrated before it hit the ground. Matt almost felt like something had shriveled and died inside of himself. He wasn't sure what, a feeling, an essence of something, and then that faded too, and he was left with a blank space. He carefully folded the pieces of fabric and tucked them inside his pocket.

A movement caught the corner of Matt's eye. He looked up to see Albert approaching them, walking from their dilapidated apartment building. He was completely un-harmed. He must have stayed inside the building the whole time. He must have known there was nothing they could do to get away or stop what had happened. The sight of Albert filled Matt with a sudden rage. All reason and sense left him. He growled and charged at Albert. Albert squealed and tried to run away, but Matt tackled him and took him down.

"Where did they go?" Matt shouted as he pinned Albert to the ground. "Where did Vincent take them? What did he do?"

"I don't know!" Albert said. "I don't know anything!"

"Liar!" Matt shouted. "You are nothing but a dirty, rotten, pigheaded liar!" He punched and slapped Albert.

"Matt, stop!" Jia cried. "It isn't his fault!"

Matt could barely hear Jia. He kept punching and clawing at Albert until someone pulled him off, someone a lot bigger and stronger than Jia.

"Whoa there, Matty." It was Haha. He spoke to Matt like he was some wild animal that needed to be contained. Maybe he was. He was growling and spitting like one. Haha held on to him until he finally stopped thrashing and he slumped in his grandfather's arms. Haha wrapped him tightly in a hug.

"It's okay. It's okay. It'll be okay."

But it wasn't okay. Matt buried himself in Haha's chest. When Matt finally pulled himself away, Haha still held on to him, just in case he flew off the handle again. Albert scooted away from him on the ground. His lip was bleeding, and his glasses were twisted and cracked. Matt felt a small amount of satisfaction, but it faded quickly, swallowed up by despair.

There was a coughing sound. Uncle Chuck emerged from behind a fallen pillar. He was dusty and had a few scratches on his face but otherwise looked okay. "Geez Louise, I thought this place had gone to pieces before, but it's really in shambles now, isn't it?"

Shambles wasn't a strong enough word, Matt didn't think. The city was unrecognizable. It was a smorgasbord of time and space. Where there had been buildings and streets there were now hills and small mountains with water trickling down in little streams and waterfalls. There were cars and bikes and wagons pulled by oxen and horse-drawn carriages trying to make their way through the rubble and chaos. The cars honked their horns and the horses neighed and reared back, and people shouted at one another in different languages. In less than a minute Matt recognized Mandarin, English, French, German, Italian, Spanish, Russian, and more that he couldn't place. There were fashions from every era imaginable. Modern jeans and T-shirts, women in 1950s-style poodle skirts, long dresses and hooped skirts, men in knee-length knickers with stockings and shoes with big buckles and powdered wigs. There were the Stone Age people Matt had seen appear, dressed in leathers and furs, speaking in a language Matt had never heard before. One of them was approaching a giraffe with a spear until another woman stood in front of it with her arms outstretched. She shouted until the man backed away. Everyone looked frightened and confused. One man in a toga carrying a scroll knocked into a man in an African tunic. They both yelled at each other in their own languages and then moved on.

"Where's Gloria?" Haha said. "Have you seen her?"

Matt shook his head. Maybe she had disappeared too. He didn't want to say it though.

"She was in Blossom, wasn't she?" Jia said.

"Yes," Uncle Chuck said. "Where's Blossom?"

They looked all around. Matt wasn't sure he could even say which direction the car had been parked. Maybe it had been carried away in the storm, disappeared like so many people and things. Then Matt noticed the Alice in Wonderland statue from Central Park. It was lopsided and half-buried in the side of a hill, but Matt remembered they had parked Blossom somewhere near that statue. He looked all around until he spotted it. At the top of one of the newly formed hills, about fifty feet high, was Blossom, her front wheels dangling precariously over the edge.

"There," Matt said, pointing.

"What the beetle juice?" said Uncle Chuck. "How did Blossom get up there?"

The side door of Blossom slid open. Gaga poked her head out. "Henry?" she called. "Anyone? Help, please!" Her voice echoed over the ravaged city. Some people stopped and looked up at the old woman in the bus on top of the hill, but no one seemed obliged to help her.

"Don't move, Gloria! I'm coming!" Haha said.

"Me too, Mom! Be right there!"

They both stumbled over fallen trees and rubble and started to climb the hill. The dirt was loose, and Uncle Chuck slid down a bit, but Haha caught onto him and helped him up. When they finally reached Blossom, they carefully helped Gaga out. The release of her weight caused Blossom to tip. The bus teetered for a few seconds then rolled down the hill.

"Oh no!" Gaga cried.

"Look out below!" Uncle Chuck called out in warning. People screamed and ran out of the way as Blossom barreled down the hill. When she reached the bottom, she rolled to a stop in front of a giant stone sculpture of a lion. Matt recognized it as one of the stone lions that stood at the entrance of the New York Public Library, either Patience or Fortitude. It had to have been flung halfway across the city to get to this spot. It certainly showed evidence of a journey, with a cracked mane and a missing bottom half.

Matt heard a groan. He searched for the source of the sound and found a woman curled up on the ground half-buried in branches, bits of glass and broken marble, and hailstones the size of golf balls. His heart nearly leaped out of his chest.

"Mom!" Matt shouted, rushing to her. "Mom, are you okay?"

Jia helped him move the debris away from Mrs. Hudson and gingerly lifted her to a sitting position. She had a gash on her head. Blood trickled from her hairline down the side of her face.

"What happened?" she said, looking around. "Where am I?"

"There was a storm," Jia said. "It's over now. Don't worry, it's going to be okay."

"Where's Vince?" Mrs. Hudson looked around. "Where's the *Vermillion* and my crew?"

"Vincent isn't here," Matt said. "We haven't seen him."

"Of course he's here," Mrs. Hudson said irritably. "I'm here, so why wouldn't he be? And who are you two? Have we met before?" Mrs. Hudson gazed from Jia to Matt, and then her eyes lit up with recognition. At the same time Matt's breath caught.

"You," she said. "I've seen you before."

"Of course you have," Jia said. "That's Matt. Your son."

Mrs. Hudson placed a hand on her bleeding head and winced. "Son?" she said. "What are you talking about? I don't have a son."

16
Mom-Not-Mom

Matt took a few steps back. The woman before him was not his mom. This wasn't Mrs. Hudson. This was Belamie Bonnaire, younger than Matt's mom by at least twenty years. She looked almost exactly as Matt had seen her that day he'd traveled to the *Vermillion* and found her fencing with a younger Captain Vincent. She was even in her Mets jersey. How did this happen? No one else seemed to have gone back in time. Gaga and Uncle Chuck looked their same old selves, and Haha his same young self. This must be some kind of glitch from whatever just happened, a repercussion from Captain Vincent changing the past.

"You." She spoke sharply, glaring at Matt like he was a rat. "I just saw you. You are that boy who snuck onto my ship."

Matt's mind whirled. She was talking about the time he'd first time-traveled. He'd gone to Chicago and found himself inadvertently on the *Vermillion* when his mother had been captain and possessor of the Obsidian Compass. His mother had no idea who he was, had no memory of him except a vague instance of him sneaking onto her ship. Whatever Captain Vincent had been trying to do, he'd done it. He'd broken time. He'd broken his family. He'd taken everything away. His father, his brother, his sister, and in a twisted way, his mother too. He was not sure which was worse—to erase your family, or to erase you from their memory.

"You were on my ship," Mrs. Hudson said again. "I just saw you there. You were spying on me. What did you do, then? Clearly you disrupted something. Where is Vince?" She looked around. "And where in the world am I?"

Albert approached them. He glanced warily at Matt and kept his distance. "Don't worry," Albert said in his usual pompous tone. "The captain will come. For both of us."

Belamie looked Albert up and down. "Captain? Captain Who? And who are you?"

"I'm Albert. I'm one of Captain Vincent's *loyal* crew."

Now Belamie looked at Albert like he was nuts. "What on earth are you talking about? This is all madness. I need to get back to the *Vermillion*." She reached for something at her chest, the compass, Matt realized. "What . . . where?" she said, looking down at her chest.

Matt instinctively reached for his own compass, and the

movement alerted her attention. Belamie's eyes narrowed. Before Matt could make another move, she pounced and grabbed him by the hair.

"You little thief!" She clawed at the compass, trying to pull it off him, much like Corey had done before. But his mom was much stronger than Corey, and certainly a more skilled fighter. She yanked back his head by the hair and lifted the compass to take it off. Matt was able to twist himself so she couldn't, but in doing so, the chain tightened around his neck. Belamie twisted the chain further so it bit into his skin and cut off his airways.

"So you weren't spying on me, were you? You were stealing!"

Matt saw stars spark in the corners of his eyes. Oddly, all he could think was that it was absolutely not normal that for the second time in less than a month his own mother, or more like his *pre*mother, was threatening to kill him, and if he survived this moment and ever returned to a normal life, he might need some serious therapy.

"Stop! Belamie! What are you doing?" Matt heard Gaga shriek.

"No one steals from Captain Bonnaire!"

Both Haha and Uncle Chuck pulled Belamie off Matt, forcing her to release the compass, though not before it ripped into Matt's skin. He fell back, gasping for air. Jia knelt down to help him up while Uncle Chuck and Haha struggled with Belamie. It quickly became clear that this wasn't a fair fight, not by a long shot. Uncle Chuck, though a head taller and probably a solid hundred pounds heavier, was too old and slow, and Haha, much like Mr. Hudson, did not have a mean bone in his body. Belamie, meanwhile, was strong, quick, and agile, and though Matt had never thought of his mom as mean, she certainly didn't hold back in a fight. She easily maneuvered out of both of their grasps, twisted Uncle Chuck's arm, took his legs out from under him, and slammed him to the ground. She drew her sword and pointed it right at his heart, then drew a dagger and pointed it at Haha.

Gaga screamed and jumped in front of her husband.

"Gloria, no!" Haha said as he pushed her out of the way.

"Please don't kill them!" Gaga cried. "I just got them back!"

Belamie looked at Matt. "Give me back my compass. Now."

Matt shook his head, holding tight to his compass.

"Give it to me, or I'll kill them all."

"Matt, just give it to her," Gaga said.

"I can't. She doesn't understand."

Belamie pressed the tip of her sword into Uncle Chuck's chest. "You have ten seconds. Ten, nine, eight . . ."

"Give her the compass!" Gaga yelled.

"If I give her the compass she'll leave us!" And he couldn't let her leave. Even if she didn't know him, even if she thought he was nothing but a thief, he could not lose his mother after everyone else.

". . . seven, six, five . . ."

Matt's mind raced. What could possibly convince his mom that they were on the same side? She didn't remember him, at least not as her son. She only recognized him as a spy she'd caught on her ship. She saw him as a threat, especially as he had the Obsidian Compass, the one thing she prized above all others.

". . . four, three . . ."

"Mateo!" Gaga screamed.

Matt reached for the compass. He had to give it up. He couldn't be responsible for the death of the rest of his family, and he certainly didn't want his mother to murder them. But just as he was about to pull it off, Jia stopped him and shouted, "We know where the Aeternum is!"

Belamie stopped counting, though she kept her blades pointed at Uncle Chuck and Gaga and Haha, who all seemed to have stopped breathing.

"What did you say?" Belamie asked.

Jia kept her hand on the compass. "The Aeternum," she said. "We know where it is." Matt frowned at Jia, but she kept her gaze on his mom. What was she doing? They didn't want her to know that Vincent had the Aeternum, did they?

Belamie stared at Jia. Jia stared right back. She didn't so much as flinch. Belamie turned to Matt. "You. Your name is Mateo?" She appraised him with a furrowed brow. Matt was thinking, hoping, that maybe she was remembering him.

Maybe she had some inkling of who he was and their connection.

"Yes," he said, hope rising. "My name is Mateo."

"And are you associated with a man called Marius Quine?"

His hope fell. Now he understood. She did not recognize him as her son at all, or anyone personally connected to her. At this particular point in her timeline she only knew the name Mateo as it related to her search for the Aeternum, because of that line from the poem in Quine's letter.

Bring Mateo to me . . .

Matt wasn't sure what to say now. She wasn't interested in him as her son, only in how he could bring her the Aeternum. Perhaps he could use that to their benefit somehow.

"Yes, I know Marius Quine," he said.

"Is he here now?" Belamie asked, looking around as though he might appear out of thin air, which certainly Matt knew Marius Quine could do, but did not think he would at this particular moment.

"No," Matt said. It wasn't really a lie, Matt didn't think. He wasn't Marius Quine, truly. Not yet. Marius Quine was his future self, not himself at present.

Belamie turned back to Jia. "You. You said you knew where the Aeternum was?"

Jia nodded. "I do, and we can help you to get it."

"But you must promise not to harm any of us," Matt said.

Belamie looked between Jia and Matt. "If you know where

the Aeternum is, then I assume you are also seeking it, in which case why should I trust you? I'm not interested in sharing it. Not with you anyway."

Matt knew his mom was speaking about Vincent and their plans to get the Aeternum together. The very thought made him want to vomit.

"What we seek is none of your business," Jia said boldly. "The point is we do know what you seek and we're the only ones who can lead you to it. It's up to you. You can choose to follow us and agree to our terms or kill us all and continue your quest on your own. But I can promise you, you won't find what you're looking for. Not without us."

Matt held his breath. He was not sure he agreed with the bargain Jia was offering. Watching his mother-not-mother, he wasn't entirely certain she *wouldn't* kill them all, just to get the compass. She was staring at it now. He could practically hear the thoughts going round inside her head.

Aeternum or compass?

Finally Belamie seemed to come to a decision. She removed the sword from Uncle Chuck and the dagger from Haha. Matt and the others let out a collective breath. Haha put down his hands and backed away until he was next to Gaga, who grasped his hand with both of hers. Uncle Chuck rolled over and got to his feet. "Whew," he said, brushing a hand over his forehead. "Geez Louise! For a moment there I thought you were really going to skewer me!"

"I still could," Belamie said with cool indifference. "Now what are your terms?"

"First, you must promise not to harm any of us," Jia said.

Belamie nodded. "And second?"

"You must promise not to steal the compass," Matt added.

Belamie's mouth tightened. "Fine," she said between gritted teeth. "I won't harm any of you, and I won't steal the compass, even though it is *mine*."

"Promise," Jia said.

"On my honor as a time pirate."

Matt knew that his mother, Belamie Hudson, would never break her word, but he had a feeling that Captain Bonnaire's honor as a time pirate was somewhat watery, especially knowing that she was in league with Vincent at this time, and even more especially when he saw her glance at his compass with a fierce possessiveness. He needed a stronger assurance than just her word as a time pirate, a promise she would never dare break.

"Promise on the graves of your parents," Matt said.

Belamie flinched as though he'd just pricked her with a needle. Her eyes widened. "How do you . . . how dare you . . ."

"Your parents drowned in a shipwreck," Matt said solemnly. "You went back in time and tried to save them, only to be the cause of the very storm that ended their lives. This is the main reason you want the Aeternum, isn't it?"

The color drained from Belamie's face, as well as all her

bravado. She looked more like a little girl just then, one who'd been slapped hard in the face and was about to cry. Matt almost regretted bringing it up, but he knew it was necessary.

"I promise on the graves of my parents," she said. "I will not harm any of you, and I won't steal the compass."

Matt nodded, satisfied. Belamie recovered herself, drew the mask over her emotions. "Well, then, let's get on with it. Where's the Aeternum?"

"China," Jia said automatically.

"China," Belamie repeated. "Why?"

"I should think that would be obvious to you," Jia said. "The insignia for the Aeternum is a Chinese character."

Matt nodded. Yes, that was smart thinking. He wasn't sure what game Jia was playing, but he could play along. Clearly she'd thought this through in ways he had not. "It's in Quine's letter," he added.

"We must go to China," Jia continued. "We must visit the Kangxi emperor. He knows things about the Aeternum. About its *effects*." She made a brief glance at Matt then, and he knew she was speaking more to him. In the storm, before his family had disappeared, she kept saying they needed to go to China. Where was this coming from? What did she know? Why hadn't she said anything before now?

"I've already *been* to China," Belamie said impatiently. "More than once. And I've tried to speak to the Kangxi emperor. I've tried to speak to *several* emperors. It's impossible. The emperor lives in the Forbidden City. *No one is ever allowed inside the Forbidden City,* and even if we could get inside, we wouldn't get anywhere near the emperor. He's too heavily protected. No one sees him without an express invitation."

"That is where I can help," Jia said, a slight smile on her face.

Belamie scoffed. "You think *you* will be able to get us an invitation? Why? Because you are Chinese? Don't be naïve, girl. Very few of his subjects are allowed to see him. He's practically a god to his people."

"It's not because I'm Chinese," Jia said calmly. "Emperor Kangxi is my father."

17

Qvejing

Matt stared at Jia. He was trying to process the words that had just come out of his friend's mouth, but they weren't computing. He didn't understand. Jia had told him she was an orphan, that she had grown up in an orphanage in China. Was she lying then or now? Maybe she was lying now to convince his mom. That had to be it. If she really was the daughter of the emperor of one of the greatest empires in all history, she surely would have told him. She wouldn't have pretended to be an orphan all this time, would she? Jia glanced at Matt with an apology in her eyes that only confused him more. He had a thousand questions, but he couldn't question her now.

Albert was looking at Jia like she'd just sprouted a third eye. If Jia was telling the truth now it was news to him too. Small comfort, Matt thought, but at least he wasn't alone in his confusion. Gaga, Haha, and Uncle Chuck also looked surprised at this news but of course they barely knew Jia, and there had been so many surprises for them in the past few days, they didn't seem to need to question.

"Emperor Kangxi is your father," Belamie repeated.

Jia nodded. "Yes."

"Well," Belamie said. "That's better than nothing, though can you guarantee an audience with him? I'm not sure Chinese emperors are accustomed to spending a great deal of time with their children, especially not their daughters."

Jia winced a little at this, but she kept her composure. "He'll see me. I promise. When I show the guards this, they'll bring me right through." Jia reached inside one of her vest pockets and pulled out a large coin, about two inches in diameter, made of bronze. Matt squinted, trying to make out the details. At first glance it almost looked like a smaller version of the Obsidian Compass, three circles within each other, and several numerals and symbols all around. There was a triangle at its center and inside the triangle there was a symbol, some Chinese character that Matt could not decipher, but he had a hunch it was the Chinese character for eternity, the very same as the insignia for the Aeternum.

"It's the Qing dynasty amulet," Jia said. "The emperor only gives them to those he most trusts. I promise once the emperor sees this, he will grant me an audience."

"Well then," Belamie said, looking almost pleased. "It seems we have a mission. We must go to the Forbidden City and speak to Emperor Kangxi. But first, does anyone have any of that magic headache medicine that comes from the future? You know what I mean?" She touched her bleeding head gingerly. "I feel like I've just been trampled by a herd of buffalo."

Matt felt the same.

"There's a medical box inside the bus," Jia said, nodding toward Blossom, which was now surrounded by a group of curious cavemen. "I'm sure there's some in there, and I can help you clean the wound on your head."

"Very well," Belamie said. "Lead the way."

Matt sat on a toppled pillar, staring blankly at the wreck-age of the city. The pillar looked like it had come from the Met. He didn't see any other signs of the museum. He didn't want to think what had happened to it. He did not want to think about how many people had lost their lives from this, whether they had died, were displaced in time, or ceased to exist altogether. He did not want to think or feel. He just wanted to sink into a hole and disappear.

The others were at Blossom. Jia was helping them get patched up with her box of medical supplies. Matt had some cuts that probably needed cleaning and bandaging, but he didn't want to go over there. He couldn't be around people right now, especially not his mom-who-wasn't-his-mom. She had just snapped at Jia and ripped the bandages away from her. Matt had to look away.

He glanced at the cavemen about twenty feet away who

were rummaging in the wreckage, picking things up, putting them in sacks if they looked like they were useful. One woman got extremely excited over a twisted piece of metal. She demonstrated to her companion how she could throw it on the ground with all her strength without breaking or bending it. Another man was collecting shards of glass, admiring them as though they were incredible treasures. Matt observed a young boy dressed in all leather and fur, a head full of bushy dark curls, pick up a baseball glove, the laces ripped. He turned it over in his hands, poking at it. He placed it on his head and smiled a big gap-toothed smile. Somehow that did it for Matt. He broke. He started to cry and once he started, he couldn't seem to stop. He trembled so violently he thought he might be having a seizure.

Someone touched his hand. Jia. He hadn't noticed her come over, but she was sitting beside him now. She didn't say anything, just held his hand while he bawled. He caught his mom watching. She looked like she felt sorry for him, but what could she do? She couldn't comfort him. She didn't even know who he was. That thought only made Matt cry harder. Gaga touched Belamie on the shoulder, said something to her that made her turn around and go with her mother-in-law, who was not really her mother-in-law. Not now. Maybe not ever.

Eventually Matt's tears ran out. He wiped his face on his T-shirt and took a few shuddering breaths. Jia handed him a bottle of water. He took it and chugged the whole thing in about five seconds. He hadn't realized how thirsty he was.

"Is Emperor Kangxi really your father," Matt asked, "or were you just making that up?"

Jia took a deep breath. "He really is my father."

"Why didn't you tell me before?" It came out angrier than he meant.

"Why didn't you tell me that you're really Marius Quine?"

Matt winced. In all the chaos, he'd almost forgotten that his identity as Marius Quine had been exposed, that he too had been keeping secrets. He could tell by the look on her face, though, that she wasn't angry about it. She didn't seem to be holding it against him the way Corey had. Corey. The look on his face. His words.

This is your fault!

Matt closed his eyes, trying to dispel the image of his brother and sister unraveling right in his hands, the feel of it. "I didn't know until a few days ago," he said. "It was confirmed when we went to Asilah. I guess I was shocked at first, and then I didn't know how to explain myself. Even though I knew it was true, that I was Marius Quine, I didn't understand what it meant, and the more I found out the worse it looked. I really don't understand who I am. I just feel like I'm . . ."

"A riddle," Jia offered.

"Yes. A riddle."

"I feel that way sometimes," Jia said, "like one moment I'm one person, and the next moment I'm someone else entirely, and I'm not sure which one is the truth. There's Jia, Repair Master of the *Vermillion*. Jia, friend and ally to the Hudsons. And then there's Quejing, daughter of Emperor Kangxi."

"Quejing? Is that your real name?"

"Yes, but I prefer Jia."

"Where did the name Jia come from?"

"My mother," Jia said. "That was her pet name for me."

Matt was sorting through his Chinese vocabulary. He knew *Jia* could mean "good," or "family," or "beautiful." He thought all those fit Jia, but he was thinking of the latter meaning in particular. Even with the dirt and grime all over her, she was beautiful.

"No one else ever called me Jia besides my mother," she continued. "I was always Quejing. So when you came to China and called me Jia, that's how I knew I could trust you."

Matt was startled by this. "When I came to China?"

"Sorry, I'm getting ahead of myself. You came to China. To speak with my father. Of course, it was years ago for me. *You* haven't gone yet. But I know you will, because I know you did. Because if you hadn't, we never would have met. I never would have boarded the *Vermillion*."

"Wait, what? Hold on. Captain Vincent's the one who brought you on board the *Vermillion*. He told me he picked you up when he'd come to China in search of the Aeternum."

"Yes," Jia said. "But it was *you* who brought me to him. It was you who got him to take me on board."

"Okay," Matt said, trying to still the whirling mass of thoughts in his mind. "Does Captain Vincent know who you really are, then?"

"No, no," Jia said. "He's always believed I was an orphan, just as you did, and it's not really a lie. I *am* an orphan, practically speaking. My mother died from fever when I was young, maybe four or five, and it's not as though my father would raise me like your father would. He's the emperor. He is father to all of China, no time to visit or play with his children, especially not a daughter." She spoke these words with a bitterness that belied pain. "After my mother died, my life in the Forbidden City was . . . not pleasant. I was clothed and fed and cared for as one of the royal household, but there were some members of my family who were . . . unkind. I spent a lot of time hiding. It was the only time I felt safe, and there were many places to hide in the Forbidden City, lots of secret tunnels and hidden passages to explore. One day, I found myself at a secret passage to the Hall of Supreme Harmony. That's my father's throne room. No one was allowed there except the most important of guests. I started to turn back, knowing I'd be punished if I were caught, but then I saw something that almost made me faint."

"You saw yourself," Matt said. He knew the feeling, the utter weirdness of being in your own presence.

Jia nodded. "I didn't know it was me though. I thought I was my mother. I looked very much like her, from what I could remember."

"She must have been very beautiful, then," Matt said without thinking, and then felt his face burn with embarrassment.

Jia smiled and blushed a little. "I thought perhaps it was my mother's ghost, that she was visiting my father as an angel from heaven. Maybe she had come to rescue me, tell him all the injustices I had been suffering and make things right, take me away from the Forbidden City. And then you found me. You seemed to come out of nowhere, so I can only assume you time-traveled to me, though at the time I thought you, too, were an angel from heaven. It was strange. I wasn't at all afraid. Well, maybe at first, but then you called me Jia, and you were so kind and gentle, and there was something about you that felt familiar. I can't explain it. I even felt it when we truly met for the first time on the *Vermillion*. It was sort of like déjà vu, I guess."

Matt nodded. He had felt the same, a link between them that went beyond the here and now. "You were foreremembering," he said.

"What?"

"It's a time-travel effect. You were foreremembering me. Because we had met at different points in time, your past and my future."

Jia nodded. "Yes. I guess that makes sense. I foreremembered you, and I felt like whatever was going to happen was supposed to happen, like it was my destiny. You took me away. It was like we were flying in a whirlwind, and then you brought me to the *Vermillion* and put me under the charge of Captain Vincent."

"And Captain Vincent didn't seem suspicious at all that I brought you to him?"

"No, on the contrary. He seemed very pleased. You were speaking in English to each other, so I couldn't understand you then, but Captain Vincent took me on board without hesitation. I wasn't afraid because I honestly thought I was in a dream, or that I'd died and the ship was going to take me to heaven, to my mother."

"And then when it didn't?"

Jia shrugged. "By the time I figured it out, I was used to my life. I was happy. I almost forgot about my old life. I never spoke of the Forbidden City. I never spoke Chinese. We never went back. Captain Vincent and all the crew believed I was an orphan, so I made up stories about living in an orphanage in China, and eventually I believed them too. The lines between make-believe and reality started to blur. But then you came, and Corey and Ruby, and slowly I began to wake up. I knew things were going to change. I wasn't sure how, but little by little I pieced things together. I began to suspect maybe Captain Vincent was not as good and kind as he seemed, and I knew we would eventually go back to China, that it hadn't been my mother I'd seen at all, but myself. And you . . . you were at the center of everything."

Matt took a moment to absorb all of this. Everything had been turned upside down. He couldn't believe he'd never known, that Jia had never told him any of this, not even given him a hint. But she was innocent, really. He was clearly the one behind all of this, so it was his own motives he had to guess at.

"Did I give you any instructions for when you were on the *Vermillion* with Captain Vincent?" Matt asked.

"A few," Jia said. "You told me to wait for you, and when you came, I should convince you to stay, though I wasn't supposed to tell you anything about meeting you in China, or anything about my past. I was just an orphan. That's why I never told you. Because you told me not to."

Matt remembered, when he'd boarded the *Vermillion*, how there seemed to be something deeper going on than just a fanciful adventure, especially when he'd seen his and Corey's and Ruby's names carved in the mast of the ship. That was the first time he'd experienced foremembering himself. He just could never have fathomed how deep it all ran—past, present, and future.

"You also gave me this." Jia held out the amulet she had shown his mom as proof of her heritage. "You told me to keep it safe, that I would need it when I returned to the Forbidden City."

"How did I get it?"

"I don't know, but it's lucky that you did. It's the key to gaining an audience with the emperor—my father."

"Why do we go to the Forbidden City in the first place?" Matt asked. "I mean, I'm all for going and rescuing you, but I'm assuming there's more to it than that."

Jia shook her head. "I've had the same question. You took me away almost as soon as you came, so I didn't get to stick around to see everything that happened after that. I do know that my father was a brilliant astronomer. He was famous for it and had one of the best observatories in the world, and so I've always assumed it had something to do with that."

"Astronomy?" Matt said.

"Yes, you know. The study of the stars and planets?"

"I know what it is, I just don't understand what it has to do with anything."

"Maybe something. Maybe nothing. But it's likely he'll have some idea about the Aeternum, otherwise, why would the Qing dynasty amulet have its insignia?" Jia held up the amulet so it caught the light. Matt could see the symbol at the center was indeed the insignia for the Aeternum. That couldn't be coincidence.

"I guess we're going to China, then," Matt said.

Jia nodded, took a breath. "I guess so."

"Are you scared?"

"A little."

"Me too." Which was probably the biggest understatement of the universe. His father, brother, and sister had just disappeared before his eyes. His mother didn't remember him anymore. Everything in the world was either mixed up, falling apart, or disappearing. And he was at the center of it all, somehow. There was so much he didn't know, and what little he did know he didn't understand.

Jia took his hand again. "It will be okay. In the end."

"How do you know?" he said, his voice quivering a little. He wasn't so naïve as to believe this could end like the fairy tales. Sometimes you don't get your own happily ever after.

"Because," Jia said. "I believe in you, Matt, and I will do whatever it takes to help you get your family back."

Matt squeezed Jia's hand. He was so grateful she was with him now. If she weren't, he was sure he would fall apart.

Matt looked back toward the grown-ups. Gaga, Haha, Uncle Chuck, and Belamie sat on a lopsided park bench. Gaga was talking to Belamie, and Belamie kept glancing over at Matt.

"Why don't you go talk to her," Jia said, patting his hand. "I'm going to go check on Albert." Albert was sitting alone on the side of Blossom, looking dejected. Matt did not feel sorry for him.

Matt walked over to where the grown-ups were sitting. Belamie watched him as he came toward her, scrutinizing every inch of him. A Band-Aid was placed over the cut on her forehead. She looked tired, and yet Matt could see that she was tense, ready for a fight.

"So," Belamie said when he'd stopped a few feet from the bench where she and the others sat. "You're supposed to be my son, are you?"

"In the future, yes." Matt forced himself to meet her cold, steely gaze, painful as it was.

"You don't look like me," Belamie said baldly. "Nor Vince, though *she* seems to think Vince isn't your father either."

"He's not. And anyway, I'm not your biological son. You adopted me."

Belamie looked dubious. "But what happens to Vince? Does he . . ."

Matt shook his head. "He doesn't die. You chose someone else. My dad. Matthew Hudson."

"Matthew," Belamie said a bit wistfully. Maybe the name pricked something in her memory—her forememory. It gave Matt some hope, but then she straightened, lifted her chin. "The *Vermillion* is my home, my whole life, and I would never leave Vince. He and I are inseparable."

"You're not together now, are you?" Gaga said.

Belamie winced. "That was not of our choosing. Something happened. One minute I was on my ship and the next . . ."

"And the next you were thrown into some unknown place, surrounded by people who think they know you but you don't know them?" Haha said. "I know the feeling. It was your boy-friend who did that to me, you know."

"I'm sorry, explain to me again who you're supposed to be?" Belamie asked. "My future brother-in-law?"

"No, I'm Henry. I'm supposed to be your future father-in-law."

"He's my husband," Gaga said, "and this is our son Charles. He's your husband's younger brother."

Belamie looked between Haha and Uncle Chuck. She shook her head. "I'm sorry, I think you've got them a little mixed up. Surely he's your husband," she pointed to Uncle Chuck, "and he's your son?" She pointed to Haha.

"Nope," Uncle Chuck said. "I'm the son, he's my dad. Time-travel mishaps."

"All at the hands of your *wonderful* Vincent," Gaga said bitterly.

Belamie shook her head. "It can all be fixed," she said, "once I find the Aeternum. Everything can be made right. So let's go. Off to China."

"Now?" Matt said.

"Yes now. You said you could take me to the Aeternum. So take me."

"But—"

"You gave me your word," Belamie said sharply. "And I gave you mine, and I always keep my word." She placed her hands on her sword. Matt swallowed. He was about to say they could go now when Gaga spoke up.

"We're not going anywhere tonight," Gaga mumbled from the bench, her eyes closed.

"Agreed," Haha said. "I've had about all I can take."

"Me too," Uncle Chuck added.

"You stay here, then," Belamie said. "None of you are needed on this mission, anyway."

Gaga nearly flew off the bench. She advanced on Belamie with fire blazing in her eyes. Belamie jumped back, startled. "Over my dead body!" Gaga boomed. She held up a shaking finger. "I have lost my husband, my son, and then my other son, and two grandchildren to your time-travel nonsense. I may look like an old lady, but I will not let Mateo out of my sight for one second, and if you try to pull a fast one on me, I will rip you apart with my bare hands! I won't need a silly sword."

Belamie stared at Gaga, mouth slightly agape. Matt had to bite his cheeks to keep from laughing. Haha and Uncle Chuck had both risen halfway from the bench, preparing to interfere in another fight and looking rather fearful about it.

"We can leave in the morning," Gaga said with a bit of a growl in her voice. "You're chasing after eternity, aren't you? What's one more day in the grand scheme of things?"

"I . . . ," Belamie began, but seemed to have lost the argument. She sighed. "Very well. We can stay the night."

Gaga smiled. "Thank you kindly," she said in a sweet voice

that made Belamie flinch. Maybe there was still some tether there as her mother-in-law, Matt thought. It gave him a small bit of comfort, until his mom turned to him and snapped, "We leave at first light, understood?"

Matt nodded. Clearly there was still a tether between them as mother and son, even if she didn't recognize it.

They got some of Uncle Chuck's blankets out of Blossom and set up a crude camp right there in the midst of the wrecked city. Belamie kept her distance from Gaga, and Gaga kept close to Matt while she barked orders at everyone, which seemed to annoy Belamie, as she was used to calling the shots, but she clearly didn't want to cross Gaga again. Matt was intensely grateful he still had his grandparents and Uncle Chuck. He'd lost those dearest to him, but he still had some family in this world. That was something. But even this thought seemed to be tempting fate. What if they were taken away from him too?

Uncle Chuck brought out some of the food they'd stored in Blossom for emergencies (like the one they were in)—some canned stew, granola bars, and fruit cocktail. A few people, seeing that they had food, made attempts to steal some, but between Gaga's snarls and Belamie's sword, it was made crystal clear that no one would be stealing from them.

"Poor souls," Jia said. "I wonder what will happen to all these people? Where will they go?"

Matt didn't want to think about it too much, because it

was simply too much. He couldn't worry about everything.

They ate their food in awkward silence. Albert continued to look at Belamie with a mixture of fear and awe. He had only just met Mrs. Hudson, and it seemed to jar him to see her as the legendary Captain Bonnaire. She paid him no mind, almost pretended that he wasn't there until Albert spilled some of his stew, and some of it splattered onto her boot. She snapped at him and Albert recoiled. Ordinarily Matt would have been delighted to see Albert get a bit of chastising. It served him right. But in this case it was only heartbreaking. Belamie Hudson was always kind to everyone.

They all settled down to sleep, finding spots inside or around Blossom. Belamie remained close to Matt. He tried to imagine that she wanted to protect him as his mother, but he knew it was more about the fact that he had the compass. She wasn't going to let it out of her sight, and Matt had a feeling she wouldn't close her eyes until she knew he was asleep.

But sleep was miles away for Matt. The events of the day swirled in his brain. His dad. Corey and Ruby. The way they had unraveled and disappeared.

This is all your fault!

Don't let go, Matt!

The image of them, their voices in his head, it made his heart race and pound in his chest. He tried to redirect his thoughts, think of something besides the horrors of the day. He counted to a thousand. He did multiplication in his head.

He listed off the elements in the periodic table. None of it helped. Finally, he started humming a song, almost without thinking.

Belamie sat up very suddenly.

Matt stopped his humming. "What's wrong?"

"What is that?"

"What's what?" He sat up and looked around, thinking she must have seen or heard something in the dark that looked suspicious or threatening.

"That melody you were just humming."

"Oh." Matt suddenly realized what he'd been humming to himself. "You—my mom, I mean—used to sing that to me. When I was little, whenever I had a nightmare, she'd sing it."

"My mother sang that to me," Belamie breathed. She looked at him, held his gaze. Matt could almost hear her singing those words to him now in her low, warm voice.

When you feel lost and all alone
Look to the sky and you'll find home

He saw just a flicker of the mother he knew, and maybe a bit of recognition for her as well, but it was gone as soon as it came.

She clammed up. Her face became a mask. "It's a fairly common song, I think," she said, and she lay down again.

Matt lay back down, pulled his blanket up to his chin. That burning ache returned to his chest. He reached inside his pocket and pulled out those scraps of time tapestry. Another thread pulled away and disappeared, and again Matt felt something unravel inside of him, like a corresponding thread in his own soul had just disintegrated. The feeling was gone in an instant, though, and he clutched the fabric tightly in his fist until he finally fell asleep.

Matt woke to gray light and a roaring engine. He jumped up from his sleeping place on the ground, thinking it must be the *Vermillion* and Captain Vincent. His mom must have thought the same because she was on her feet in an instant, searching for the source of the engine. Albert, too, scrambled to his feet, tripping over his blankets.

"I'm sure that's the *Vermillion*," he said. "Captain Vincent's come to rescue us!"

But it wasn't the *Vermillion*. It was a military tank, rolling through the wrecked city. A soldier was sticking out of the hatch with a loudspeaker. "All persons in the city are to report to the pyramid! Food, supplies, and fresh water will be distributed. Medical treatment is available." Another soldier popped up and repeated the words in Spanish, then French, Russian, Chinese, and a host of other languages, including Greek and Latin. Clearly, they knew they were dealing with unusual circumstances.

"At least there's some kind of order in this chaos," Gaga said, wrapping her knitted blanket tightly around her shoulders. Matt was glad to know that something was being done to help all these displaced people. They were all time castaways now. He wondered how many more there were throughout the world and all of time. Maybe his dad and Corey and Ruby hadn't really disappeared, but had been discarded into another time and place, and they only needed to find them. But when he thought about the way they had disappeared, how they had seemingly come unraveled, he felt whatever had happened to them was altogether different than what had happened to these people. He closed his eyes, and the images of Corey and Ruby surfaced in his mind, each of them clinging for life, Ruby begging him not to let go. But he couldn't see their faces. Not clearly, anyway. They were distorted somehow, like they were underwater, and when he reached for them, they disappeared. He only heard the echo of Corey's words.

Your fault.

Your fault.

Your fault.

He opened his eyes, looked down at his clenched fist. The scraps of their time tapestries were still there, but it looked as though they had faded. Or maybe they were just dirty. He didn't want to let go of them, but maybe he shouldn't be touching the tapestries so much. He folded them back up and slipped them in his pocket.

"I think we'd better leave now," Belamie said. "We don't want to get swept up in all of this." She gestured to all the people around them who were now starting to make their way toward the pyramid, holding on to what few belongings they had. It was like a dozen rivers of humans all flowing toward the pyramid.

They packed up their things and cleaned up their general camp area. Matt thought it hardly mattered, given the state of things, but Gaga was insistent that they not be "litterbugs."

Uncle Chuck distributed more granola bars for breakfast, and Haha brewed some coffee for the grown-ups on the little gas stove in Blossom. With a cup of hot coffee in her hands, Belamie warmed toward Haha a little.

"You remind me of someone," she said, studying Haha's face. "We haven't met before this, have we?"

Haha looked a bit awkward. "Don't think so. You're probably thinking of my son. We look a lot alike."

"No, we don't," Uncle Chuck said. "I take after Mom."

"I meant my other son. Your brother."

"Oh. Right. My brother." Uncle Chuck shook his head a little. "Brother . . ."

After everything was picked up and stowed away, they all piled inside of Blossom. Albert hesitated at the door. He kept looking around, clearly hoping the *Vermillion* would appear and rescue him, but there was no sign of the ship or the captain.

"Get in, Albert," Jia said. "Time to go."

Albert frowned but got inside and shut the door.

Somehow it felt more crowded inside Blossom, even

though they were fewer in number. Maybe it was because they weren't as comfortable with each other. They had to shift a few things around a bit, and Matt felt a small pang when his mother tossed one of Ruby's sneakers aside and muttered something about how hideous the future fashions were.

Uncle Chuck sat in the driver's seat with Gaga in the front passenger seat. Haha was crouched in the spot between them. Albert and Jia sat in the back seat, on opposite sides, leaving Matt and Belamie to sit together at the small table. Matt pulled the compass out from under his shirt. His mom's hand twitched when she saw it, and he almost thought she was going to try to steal it again, but she took a breath and folded her hands in her lap. Still, she looked at it with a longing that made Matt uneasy. Even with the promise she had made, she believed the compass rightfully belonged to her. Oddly, in a roundabout way, it did. He did give it to her, after all. Or Quine did, anyway, and he always felt she understood how to wield it better than he did, even though he had invented it.

"Uh . . . ," Matt said. "I'm not sure where or when we're going, exactly?"

They all turned to Jia. "Oh!" she exclaimed, as though she had forgotten her role in all of this. "I'm sorry. Let me think . . . We need to go to the late 1600s, I think around 1680?"

Belamie scoffed. "You think? You don't know?"

Jia shook her head. "I'm sorry, I don't. I was very young when I left, only six or so."

Belamie rolled her eyes. "Well, this is turning out just as I thought. A bunch of children trying to take charge. Try sometime in 1688. That's what Quine's letter specifies. Set the dials sometime in that year, that should set us right. And the coordinates are thirty-nine degrees north and one hundred and sixteen degrees east. That will take us outside the walls, at least. I've never been able to travel directly into the city. You *don't* want to take us directly into the city. We'll be killed on the spot."

"Not while I'm with you," Jia said.

"We'll see," Belamie said, clearly not sure she believed Jia really could gain them an audience with the emperor, even if she was his daughter, but Jia seemed confident. That was enough for Matt.

"Set the dials, Mateo," Belamie said.

Matt obeyed. Blossom's engine roared to life. The bus began to shift, and they were off.

18
The Kangxi Emperor

1688
Beijing, China
The Forbidden City

Jia had never before been so nervous for any mission in all her days as a time pirate, and she had to work extra hard to hide it. She didn't want anyone to see how scared she was, how uncertain, especially Matt. She couldn't let him down, not after all that he'd been through, so she squared her shoulders and held her head high, even though she was a wreck inside. She was going back to China. Back home. *Home.* What a strange, powerful word, that it could stir so much inside of her, things that lay dormant for years. She'd almost forgotten who she really was, where she came from. She had told the story of her being just an orphan from China so many times for so long, she had almost come to believe it herself.

They landed in the moat surrounding the Forbidden City.

Blossom had transformed into a junk, a small Chinese ship, flat-bottomed with two orange-red sails.

The Forbidden City was surrounded by a wide moat and closed in by high stone walls. Only a few sloped, red-tile roofs could be seen above them. Jia had never been outside the walls of the Forbidden City, save for the few moments before Captain Vincent took her on board the *Vermillion*. In her younger days, this had been the whole world.

"It doesn't look like time has been disrupted here," Matt said.

No. It looked just as she remembered.

They sailed toward the edge of the Forbidden City, where guards were posted with swords.

"They look kind of serious," Matt said. "What if they don't believe who you are?"

"Then we're in trouble," Belamie said. She kept her hands on the hilt of her sword, though Jia knew it wouldn't do them any good, no matter how skilled and fierce a swordswoman she was. If Jia did not convince the guards, they'd be lucky to be taken prisoner. But she wasn't going to let Matt believe for one second that they might be in any kind of danger.

"They'll believe me," Jia said. "When I show them the amulet." She brought it out of her pocket. It too had almost been forgotten, pushed to the bottom of her memories.

"Let me do the talking," Jia said. "The rest of you should remain quiet unless directly spoken to, understood?"

They all agreed, even Belamie. They were all looking to her now.

When they reached the edge of the moat, Jia greeted the guards. She had, of course, practiced her Chinese plenty with Matt, and done some studying on her own from time to time, but she had always been a little reluctant, and the words had never felt quite right coming out of her mouth. Now, as if returning to this place and time had unlocked something in her brain, the language seemed to slip off her tongue without a thought, as though she had never left. It felt oddly comfortable, and to her surprise, empowering. This was her native tongue, and she was speaking it in her native country, in her original era.

The guards were stiff and eyed the odd grouping with deep suspicion, especially Albert, Jia noticed. He was so pale and completely not Chinese in every way, but then Jia showed them her amulet, and their expressions and stances changed drastically. They each bowed low to Jia and helped everyone out of Blossom. Matt stepped beside Jia.

"I know I can't take these dudes," he whispered in her ear, eyeing the guards and their armor and weapons. "But I'll be your moral support."

She smiled. "Thanks. You're my hero." And she knew that he really would be very soon. She wondered how it would all play out. In her memory, she saw herself speaking to her father on his throne, and then Matt appeared and took her away, but she was never quite sure why, and she still didn't fully understand. There must be a reason.

The guards led them through the gates of the Forbidden City, past smaller buildings where servants lived. She saw a few of them repairing the roof of one of the buildings, others repairing faulty steps or pillars. The Forbidden City had thousands of servants and craftsmen and guards, all of them living within the walls, never allowed to leave or have their own families. This was their entire life. She squinted, trying to see if she might recognize any of them, but they were too far away. When she was little, before she left on the *Vermillion*, one of her sanctuaries had been the craftsmen's quarters. She knew no one would look for her there, and it was where she first fell in love with building and fixing things. For hours she watched her father's servants carve and craft and forge. One of the servants had taken a liking to her, had even forged her a little hammer and taught her the basics of craftsmanship and engineering. She touched the little hammer she always carried with her. Li Lianying. That was his name. She'd forgotten so much, but it was all coming back now, like a veil was being lifted.

They walked through gardens of orchid and magnolia trees in full bloom, ponds with lotus blossoms floating on top. The smells brought back memories. The wives having tea in the gardens, always strategizing for power and influence, the children playing games around them, having lessons with tutors. Jia always running, always hiding.

Her heart skipped a beat as they walked along the stream that ran through the city, and she saw a group of children, about seven or eight of them. Some of her siblings, she realized. She recognized some of them, even remembered their names. There was Prince Yinxiang, and Wenxian, her sister closest to her in age, though her mother never allowed them to play together. Wenxian was a princess of the first rank, a daughter of an empress, while Jia—or Quejing—had merely been the daughter of one of the emperor's consorts.

"Who are they?" Matt asked quietly, nodding to the children.

"The emperor's children, a few of them anyway."

"A few? You mean he has more than that?"

"Yes. I can't remember how many exactly. It was hard to keep track."

"The Kangxi emperor had three dozen children," Belamie interjected from behind them in a dry, matter-of-fact tone. "Twenty-four sons and twelve daughters."

"Thirty-six kids?!" Matt exclaimed in a whisper though his voice squeaked a little. "How is that even possible?"

"Well, he had several wives," Jia said. "My mother wasn't his only wife, you know."

"Oh," Matt said, and seeing the discomfort on his face suddenly made her uncomfortable.

"It was a common practice among emperors in China,"

Belamie added. "One of the emperor's most important duties was to produce an heir in order to ensure that their lines continued to rule and the empire would thrive. Having many wives to bear him many children ensured this."

Matt nodded. "Right. Makes sense."

Jia had never given much thought to her family dynamic, how it would seem to someone outside her time and country. To her it was just the way things were. But now, after viewing it through Matt's eyes, she was suddenly self-conscious of how strange her family must seem. Matt must have sensed her discomfort because he leaned in and said in a low voice so only she could hear, "It's all good. I mean, it's not like I have the most conventional family on the planet." He glanced briefly at his mom, who didn't know him, and his grandmother and uncle, who were roughly the same age.

Jia smiled a little. She had traveled enough to know that families came in all varieties and sizes. Family meant different things at different times and places. Sometimes it was about survival. Sometimes it was about power and names and bloodlines. And sometimes it's just about love and wanting to be together. This was why she often thought the Hudsons were the most wonderful family in the whole world, because they *chose* each other. She had wished more than once that she could be a part of the Hudson family, a true member of their crew. But now the Hudsons were no more, and though it might mean nothing to the rest of the world, it seemed as great a tragedy as any she'd witnessed, and her heart ached for Matt. Oh, how she hoped her father could help them!

The guards led them to another set of gates, these ones extremely tall, painted red and gold. The door opened to a spacious courtyard. At the end stood a large square building with many red pillars and a sloped, double-tiered red-tile roof. Jia paused for a moment to take it all in.

"Is that your father's palace?" Matt asked.

She nodded.

"The Hall of Supreme Harmony," Belamie said, her own voice full of awe. "The most sacred building within the Forbidden City. This is the place where the emperor was crowned, where he held his wedding ceremonies, and where he meets with his most important guests." Clearly, she'd researched this place a good deal. Jia had done a little bit of her own research in Wiley's library, but to her this place was more than just a sacred building. The very pillars had memories inside of them, the walls full of stories of those who built them and those who had lived inside of them, including herself.

The Hall of Supreme Harmony was raised on three layers of marble platform. Stone dragons surrounded the curved red-tile roof. When it rained, the water would pour from their open mouths, spilling on the stone tiles below. Jia suddenly had an image of her standing beneath them in the rain, letting the water pour over her head. She made believe it was a magical potion that would transform her into a swan so she could fly away, beyond the walls of the Forbidden City.

The steps leading up to the palace took them alongside a great marble relief carved with nine dragons frolicking amidst waves and clouds, playing with pearls.

Albert reached down as though he would touch the marble relief. Jia gasped a little, but before Albert could touch it, Belamie grabbed his arm and yanked him away.

"What are you—" Albert protested.

"Don't touch anything, you fool," Belamie snapped. "The emperor has executed men for lesser offenses."

"What offense?" Albert said. "It's just a bunch of stone. I can't hurt it by touching it, can I?"

Jia did know something about this relief. One of the royal tutors had taught her and her siblings that the relief was carved on a single slab of marble that weighed more than three hundred tons. It had been transported from miles away, in the dead of winter, with hundreds of men and horses pulling it on roads of ice.

"This marble relief is sacred," Belamie said. "To touch it would be to disrespect the many lives given and sacrificed for its creation. Now keep your hands to yourself and do as you're told. I won't have you ruining my mission with your clumsiness."

Albert slumped. Poor Albert. He never could win with anyone, it seemed.

"This place is out of this world," Uncle Chuck said, looking all around as they climbed the stairs. "Amazing what we humans can build and create."

"It is stunning," Gloria said. "I've always wanted to visit this place. Remember how we wanted to travel here for our honeymoon, Henry?"

"The Catskills were just as good, weren't they?"

Gloria laughed. "Good enough," then she looked back up at the Hall of Supreme Harmony. "It's even more magnificent than any pictures I've seen."

Jia felt a great sense of pride in her home, which was something, she realized, she'd never truly felt before.

"When am I supposed to, you know, rescue you?" Matt whispered. "You said I took you away the same day you arrived, right?"

Jia shook her head. "I don't know. We'll just have to wait and see. It will become obvious when, I'm sure."

"Okay," he said. "You're the boss, boss. Just tell me what to do."

She nodded, gave him a weak smile. She wasn't so sure she wanted to be the boss. It felt heavy, yet tenuous.

When they reached the top of the marble stairs, the guards told them to wait while they announced them to the emperor. Jia stared straight ahead. Her heart was hammering in her chest. She wasn't ready for this. Not in any way. She certainly wasn't dressed appropriately, with her modern jeans and tool vest, her hair hanging limp and unkempt. She was still dirty and dusty from the storm. They were all a mess. Her father could send her to the dungeons just for the way she looked. And then there was the matter of how she was to address her father. There were so many rules of decorum here in the Forbidden City and she had forgotten all of them. Should she bow? Kneel? Should she speak first, or did he? Should she speak at all?

Matt whispered in her ear. "Breathe. It's going to be okay."

Jia did not realize she'd been holding her breath. She let it out. Matt took her hand, held it tight. She was so intensely grateful Matt was here with her now. She was certain if he wasn't, she'd fall apart. That, she realized, was part of what made a family too. People who held you together made you stronger, better.

Guards opened the doors of the palace and told Jia she could see the emperor now. Jia stepped inside. The rest of the group started to follow, but the guards blocked their path.

"Only the princess," one guard said.

Jia's heart started to hammer even harder. Alone. Of course, she knew that's how it would be. She had seen only her future-self meeting with her father, but somehow she hadn't really translated that to the other end. She hadn't prepared herself for this, mentally.

Belamie tried to argue with the guards in broken Chinese. She told them that she was the girl's personal guard and must accompany her. Jia could see the guards stiffening, reaching for their swords. She knew they would have no patience with disobedience and wouldn't hesitate to respond with swift violence. If anything more happened to Matt's family, Jia didn't think he would survive it, and she would never forgive herself. She held up her hand to silence Belamie.

"It is the custom," she said. "You cannot see the emperor without express invitation."

"But—"

"You must wait here," she said with a command in her voice she didn't know she possessed. It surprised her as much as it seemed to Belamie. "For your own sake as well as mine, you will stay. I will plead your cause to the emperor and ask if he will see you."

Belamie pressed her mouth in a tight line. She nodded and stepped back.

Jia looked back at her friends, who all looked worried, even Albert, and especially Matt. "Don't worry," she said. "It will be fine." She said these words as much for her own sake as theirs, maybe more.

As Jia entered the Hall of Supreme Harmony, she was hit with the heavy smell of incense and perfume. The interior of the palace was ornately decorated, mostly in red and gold. The imperial dragon was on nearly every surface and object in the room—spiraling around the pillars, stitched into tapestries, painted on the walls. She had read stories from other countries of fierce dragons that breathed fire and wreaked havoc over kingdoms, but in China dragons were playful, frolicking creatures, a symbol of power and strength and good luck. She hoped now that was true and that they would bring all those things to her.

In the center of the room, surrounded by four golden pillars, was the imperial throne, set on a high dais, and sitting on the throne was the emperor, her father. He looked exactly as she remembered the last time she had seen him, both years ago and no time at all. Somewhere in this palace was her younger self, spying from behind one of the tapestries, believing that she was her mother, somehow back from the dead.

Jia approached the throne. The emperor was dressed in imperial yellow, embroidered in red and gold, symbolizing that he was the center of the universe, like the sun, and everything revolved around him. He wore his hair in a long braid, his beard combed into a short point at his chin. On his head he wore the red crown, a narrow stem of pearls sticking up from the center.

Now in his presence, Jia suddenly remembered what she was supposed to do. She got down on her knees and prostrated herself before her father, touching her forehead to the ground.

"Rise," her father said. Jia obeyed. She felt his gaze upon

her, and at last she built up the courage to look at him. Jia felt something flare in her chest. This was her *father*, and though she barely knew him, she felt a strange sense of connection. They were linked by blood, by time and place.

There was movement on the emperor's right, and Jia was startled to see that there was someone else by his side. It was a boy about her own age, dressed in robes of embroidered blue silk. His head was shaved to the scalp in the front and the rest tied in a ponytail at the back. Her breath caught in her throat as she met eyes with him. It was Yinreng, the crown prince and her half brother. As heir to the throne he was naturally often with the emperor, but if he had been here in this moment before, Jia had forgotten. She must have blocked it from her mind, along with so many other memories. But they came rushing back now, like water from a broken dam. She remembered all the times Yinreng bullied her, teased her about her low rank. She remembered the time he pulled her hair so hard it ripped from her scalp. And there was the time he stole her doll, the one possession she had from her mother, and threw it in the fire, then forced her to watch it burn.

"Who are you?" the emperor demanded. "Why have you come? And how did you get this?" He held up her amulet.

Jia's tongue had gone dry. She did not know how to speak. She wanted to back away, run away. She could not do this.

But she thought of her friends waiting outside, of the Hudsons, of Matt. This wasn't just about her. She was here for

Matt, for his family, and, she had to assume, the fate of the world. She could not fail.

Jia raised her chin and squared her shoulders. "I am Quejing, Princess of the Second Rank, born of Jing of the Wanggia Clan." She didn't stutter or tremble, even though she was trembling on the inside. Maybe the dragon luck was helping her.

There was a moment of silence. The emperor studied her. "Jing is dead, and her daughter cannot be as old as you."

Jia's heart clenched. *Her* daughter. Not our daughter. He did not claim her as his own.

"I know Quejing," Yinreng said. "She is much smaller than this girl. This girl is an impostor. She must have forged the family amulet. She and those who came with her are clearly trying to infiltrate the Forbidden City. This is a coup, Father."

The emperor stiffened. His eyes narrowed on Jia. She could tell he was being persuaded by Yinreng. "Who are you truly? Who sent you?"

"I am Quejing!" Jia said desperately. "I have traveled through time, from the future. I have come to warn you of terrible things that are happening in the world and ask for your help!"

Yinreng laughed. "The future? Father, I warned you. You have been too soft with your security. We must lock up this girl and her friends and interrogate them, torture them, if we must."

The guards took a step toward Jia, waiting for the emperor's command to seize her.

Jia started to panic. How could she prove to her father who she was when he hardly knew of her existence at all. But Yinreng knew her. Maybe it was him that she needed to convince. And perhaps in convincing him, she could convince her father of more than one truth.

"If I am an impostor," Jia said, looking straight at Yinreng, "how could I remember that day you locked me in a chest for hours and when I was found you pretended I had locked myself inside? How could I remember the time you forced me to eat cockroaches, or the time you broke the porcelain vase and then blamed me, even cut my hand with one of the shards to make everyone else believe it?" She held up her hand to show the faint scar. "How could I remember all the times you chased me, hit me, blamed me? And not just me, but all our brothers and sisters—Yinzhen, Yinzuo, Wenke, Chunque. Remember how you cut Wexian's hair? How you burned Yunsi's arm with incense and threatened to burn his face if he tattled?"

Yinreng looked alarmed, fearful even. His eyes flickered toward the emperor, but he quickly composed himself.

"Lies," he hissed. "None of that is true. You are making up stories to manipulate our father and turn him against me!"

"So you admit that he is my father as well as yours?" Jia said, trying to suppress a smile.

"I . . . no . . . ," Yinreng stammered. Jia knew she had to seize this moment, trample on Yinreng while he was off-balance.

"I am Quejing, daughter of the Kangxi emperor. I have traveled into the past and the future, and I have come to warn you of disruptions in time that have caused great devastation and will cause more if we don't stop it. I have come to you for your knowledge and wisdom in these matters, not just for our own sake, or the sake of China, but all the world."

Yinreng opened his mouth to speak, but the emperor put up a hand to silence him, all the while keeping a steady gaze on Jia. She looked right back at him. She didn't move. She didn't even blink.

"My guards told me your boat appeared in the moat quite out of nowhere, as if by magic. By what power have you traveled to me today? What is the method, I mean, for traveling through time? Were you transported here by your own power or the power of something else?"

Jia took a breath. She needed to be clear and concise.

"A compass," Jia said. "A very special compass, one of a kind. The inventor is here with me now. He is just outside the palace door."

"With his magic compass, I assume," her father said.

"Let the guards bring him in," Yinreng said. "Let's have a look at this compass and see if it really does what she says.

If she's lying we'll know she's an impostor. If she's telling the truth then we will have gained a great treasure that will make us all the more powerful."

Jia panicked. Why had she been so thoughtless? She couldn't think of anyone worse to have the Obsidian Compass than Yinreng. He'd destroy the entire world with his greed and malice. "It would be foolish to attempt such a thing," Jia said, trying to keep her voice even. "The inventor is very powerful, and time travel is not a game. You know nothing of the rules and consequences. If you make a mistake, you could cause incredible chaos and destruction, even your own death."

"I gather not all your travels have been pleasurable?" her father asked.

"There have been . . . unintended consequences," Jia said. "Many people have suffered. Again, that is why I am here. We've come to ask for your knowledge and wisdom. For your help."

"And how do you suppose I can help? I am not a time traveler. I know nothing of what you have endured or caused."

"But you understand the world!" Jia said. "It is well-known throughout the world, even in the future, that you are a wise and learned man, very knowledgeable with astronomy and the workings of the universe. We think if you hear our story you might be able to help us understand the things we are missing and set the world right again."

Jia stepped back and bowed her head. She had said her piece, and now she could only wait for her father to decide. Whatever his decision, it would be final, and there would be nothing she could do to alter it.

19
Jìnzhǐ Suǒ

Matt thought he would go insane waiting for Jia to come out of those tall red doors. She had been gone for only minutes, but each second felt like an hour, and he couldn't help but imagine all the terrible things that might be happening. What if her father didn't believe her? What if he thought they were all impostors? Would he kill her on the spot? Then come for the rest of them? Would they torture her to try to get the truth? What was Matt supposed to do?

He was supposed to save the young Jia. But when? How? Why? Should he go and find her? And then what? Jia told him it would become obvious when he was supposed to save her, that he would know what to do. Nothing was obvious to him now except that he was worried out of his mind.

Belamie paced back and forth in front of the doors. She was clearly worried, too, but for different reasons. She wasn't worried about Jia's safety or well-being, only the Aeternum. She didn't care about what had happened to him or their family. This, too, was making Matt feel crazy. He tried to remember his real mother, the one who knew and loved him, but he was having a hard time thinking of what she was like. Was she always so impatient, so brusque with people? He tried to picture her with his dad, the way they looked at each other and made it seem like the entire world revolved around them, but he couldn't see it. He couldn't even picture his dad's face. And Corey and Ruby. He couldn't picture their faces either. He had this weird feeling that something was slipping from him, but he didn't know what it was or how to hold on to it.

"Belamie, sit down," Gaga said. "You're making me dizzy." She, Haha, Uncle Chuck, and Albert were all sitting on the steps below the doors.

"I don't want to sit," Belamie snapped. "And don't call me Belamie. My name is *Captain* Bonnaire."

"Oh, good grief, you're not *my* captain. But go ahead and keep pacing. It's clearly entertaining the guards."

Belamie glanced at the guards, and when she saw the expressions on their faces, she did stop. This relieved Matt's nerves some, until she turned her attention on him. She leaned against the marble stair railing, folded her arms, and stared at him, frowning.

"There's something I'd like you to explain to me," she said.

"Okay."

"You said I chose a different life. That I left the *Vermillion* and Vince for . . . another man."

Matt nodded. "You did. You do."

"But Vince doesn't die."

"No."

"And . . . he was okay with me leaving?"

Matt hesitated. "Not exactly."

Gaga sputtered something between a laugh and a cough. "He was furious! That's how Henry got taken away, you know."

"Why would he take you away?" Belamie asked Haha. "I wasn't going to marry you, was I?"

"I think your boyfriend got us a little mixed up," Haha said. "He thought I was Matty. He abandoned me in the Hudson Bay. I thought I was going to die until these guys showed up."

"Vincent tried to change things after you left him," Matt explained. "He tried to keep you and my dad from being together. First, he kidnapped my grandpa, thinking he was my dad. Then he did the same to my uncle, right at your wedding." He nodded to Uncle Chuck. "He never could get rid of Dad."

"Until now," Uncle Chuck said, heaving a sad sigh.

Belamie looked between them all. Matt thought surely she was horrified by what Vincent had done, but then a smile suddenly crept on her face and she chuckled softly.

"What's so funny?" Matt asked.

"Vince," Belamie said, shaking her head. "No one can

double-cross him and get away with it. It's one of the things I like best about him. He'll go to the ends of the earth to make things right."

Matt was too shocked to speak. His own mother was telling him that what had just happened to their family was just, deserved, even.

"Make things *right*?" Gaga said, disgusted. "Your *Vince* destroyed innocent people's lives. He ruined an entire city and who knows how much of the rest of the world. He tore apart your own family, basically murdered your husband and children and altered your past so you don't even know what's happened to you!"

"First of all, no one is innocent," Belamie said. "And anyway, that's impossible. He can't change the past. The Aeternum is the only thing that can really change timelines, and what do you mean he murdered my *children*?" Belamie asked. "I have other children in the future? More, supposedly, besides you?"

"You have twins," Matt said.

"Twins!" Belamie exclaimed, clutching both her head and stomach.

"I know," Haha said. "I was shocked when I met them too. But they're really delightful. You'll like . . . what are their names again?"

"Gordon and Riley," Uncle Chuck said.

Matt frowned. "Corey and Ruby."

"Oh, right. Sorry. My brain is a bit fuzzy." Uncle Chuck shook his head.

"Ruby," Belamie said a bit wistfully. Her eyes lit up at this name, a spark of recognition. Matt knew it was her middle name, and her own mother's name.

"Ruby looks just like you," Gaga said. "Acts like you too. She's a fiery little thing."

"Good with a sword too," Matt said. "And Corey is funny. He always made you laugh." Matt winced even as he said the words. *Made you laugh.* Past tense. He had no present now. And possibly no future.

"I was there the day they were born," Gaga said, "and I've never seen so much love in anyone's face as I saw in yours, Belamie."

Belamie seemed to look inward, almost as if she were trying to picture her children in her mind. "But they're gone now? What happened to them?"

"Vincent . . . took them away," Matt said.

"How? He kidnapped them? Discarded them?"

"Something like that," Matt said. He was tiptoeing around this now. They had convinced his mom that they knew where the Aeternum was. That was the leverage they had in getting her to cooperate with them. If they lost that, if she knew Vincent already had it, he didn't know what would happen.

Matt glanced briefly at Albert who gazed back at him

with a bored, indifferent look. Albert knew very well what had happened, perhaps even more than Matt did, but he didn't say anything. He wondered how long that would last.

"Your father," Belamie said. "The one I supposedly choose over Vince. What was his name again?"

"Mateo," Gaga said.

"No, I'm Mateo," Matt said.

"Oh. Yes," Gaga said. "Sorry. I'm getting old."

Matt frowned. He'd never thought of Gaga as old, and she'd never been forgetful. "His name is Matthew. Matthew . . ." Matt tried to say his last name but couldn't for some reason. It was like it had suddenly slipped into a fog. He shook his head. "His name is Matthew . . ."

"Huh . . . Huh . . . ," Uncle Chuck began but couldn't seem to finish.

"Hurston," Haha said. "Matthew Hurston. He's my son."

Hurston . . . Was that it? How on earth could he have forgotten his own last name?

The doors suddenly burst open, and Jia came out, her eyes sparkling, her cheeks flushed. Matt ran to her.

"It's okay," she said. "I spoke to my father. He has invited us to dine with him tonight! He has agreed to help us."

"That's great!" Matt said. "I knew you could do it."

Jia beamed.

"Did you ask the emperor about the Aeternum?" Belamie asked.

Jia's smile slid off her face. "Not quite," she said, wincing a little. "It was a little difficult to explain things. Yinreng was there, the crown prince."

"Would he be your brother, then?" Matt asked.

Jia nodded and shivered a little. "Half brother. I didn't think it would be wise to give too many details. Yinreng is not trustworthy."

Belamie looked a little skeptical. "But the emperor has invited all of us to dine with him tonight?"

"Yes," Jia said. "His servants are preparing our quarters now. We'll be very well taken care of."

Just as she said these words, a servant approached and bowed to Jia. He addressed her as *Gōngzhǔ* and told them that their quarters were ready now and to follow him.

"*Gōngzhǔ*?" Matt questioned.

Jia blushed a little. "It means 'princess.'"

Princess . . . yes, of course she was a princess. She was the daughter of an emperor.

"Well then," he said, stepping back and holding out his arm, "after you, *Gōngzhǔ*."

Matt thought Jia must have impressed her father quite a bit, because they were basically given a palace to stay in. It was an enormous house, richly furnished, with a spacious, open main room twice the size of Matt's apartment, and many more rooms surrounding it, each with their own bathroom.

Unsurprisingly, Jia noted right away how she would like to update the plumbing so they could have flushing toilets, but before she could get too far in her plans, a servant came and told her she needed to prepare for supper with the emperor. Another servant lifted her hair between two fingers and looked over her filthy state, frowning in particular at her bulky tool vest. "We have much work to do," he said without any tact. Jia gave Matt an exasperated look as she was pulled away by both servants and disappeared into a room.

Jia wasn't the only one who would have to endure a fair bit of grooming. They were each given their own servant to attend to them. One of the servants approached Chuck and stroked his long beard, chattering on about the different ways he could groom and fashion it.

"What's he saying?" Uncle Chuck said.

"He likes your beard," Matt said.

"Oh, why thank you," he said, patting his beard. "Took me a quarter of a century to get it this way, and a lot of conditioner."

Two more servants approached Gaga and Haha and guided them each to separate apartments.

Matt's servant's name was Tong. He was a small, cheerful old man who was delighted to find that Matt could speak some Chinese and instantly started chattering away. Matt only understood about half of what he said, but he gathered their presence in the Forbidden City was a very exciting thing.

Tong prepared Matt a bath, for which Matt was grateful, as he was starting to feel quite itchy from all the dirt and grime on him. As he removed his clothes, he was careful to take out the scraps of time tapestry from Corey and Ruby and set them under a washbasin where he could retrieve them later.

While Matt soaked in the soapy bath, Tong started to brush and style his hair. He first tried to style it in a bun on top of his head, but it wasn't long enough for that. Next he brought out a razor and told Matt he would shave the front of his head.

"It is a good style," he said. "Very Chinese. Just like Crown Prince Yinreng." Aside from the fact that Matt really did not want his head shaved, he also did not think it would go over well with Jia if he came out looking like her brother whom she clearly despised and feared. He declined as politely as he could and told Tong he would rather keep his hair the way it was. The servant sighed, disappointed. Matt got a sudden flash of the first time he'd been to see Brocco on the *Vermillion* to get some new clothes. Corey and Ruby had gone as well, and Brocco had been so disappointed when he couldn't get Ruby to wear a dress. And just as soon as he thought it, the memory slipped from him, faded, and Matt was simply left with a feeling of familiarity with the situation, but without reference as to why. It was just a moment of déjà vu, he thought.

Tong brought Matt a set of blue silk robes. As much as

he would rather wear his regular clothes, Matt didn't think he could decline this offering as he had the hairstyle, so he thanked Tong and put them on. Tong helped him tie the sash properly and noted with pleasure that he looked almost Chinese.

When Matt came out of his room he found Gaga, Haha, Uncle Chuck, Albert, and Belamie also clean and changed into silk robes in the Chinese fashion. His mother looked quite beautiful in purple silk with wide, draping sleeves and her hair swept up in a bun, held by two crossing sticks. Her face was powdered and her lips painted red. The rest of the group looked a little odd and quite uncomfortable. Uncle Chuck's hair had been slicked back into a ponytail, and his gray beard had been trimmed and braided. He kept jutting out his chin to see the braid. Gaga's short silver hair had been wrapped around an ornate headpiece. Her face was powdered white and her lips painted red. She wore a blue dress that matched Haha's robes. Haha kept tugging at it self-consciously. Albert's robes were a little too long at the hem and sleeves, so he had to keep holding it up as he walked, which his servant kept telling him not to do. Of course, Albert didn't understand so he kept doing it, and round and round they went.

But when Jia came out, the whole room went still and quiet. Matt felt he could have been knocked over by a feather. He almost didn't recognize her, and for a split second he thought it was someone else. She was wearing white silk robes embroidered with silver and blue flowers. Her hair was swept up and adorned with white lotus blossoms. Dainty pearls dangled from her ears. She glided out of the room, holding herself tall and proud. She looked every bit the part of a princess, and Matt suddenly felt he should have known all along who she really was, that she was no orphan or ordinary girl.

Jia stopped in front of him and smiled. "*Nǐ hǎo*, Mateo."

"*Nǐ hǎo, Gōngzhǔ*."

Jia blushed and looked down at her dress. "It's not really me, is it?"

Matt cocked his head, studying her. "It is if you want it to be," Matt said. "I think it suits you very well."

Jia smiled. "Thank you. You look very handsome. So smart. My father will like you."

They stood there just staring at each other for a moment, until Gaga cleared her throat and they both jumped, remembering that there were other people in the room. Matt looked around and saw everyone staring at them. Gaga was smirking a little, and his mom was looking quizzically between him and Jia.

"Are there rules we should know before we attend dinner with the emperor?" Gaga asked. "I shouldn't like to get my head chopped off for not eating the proper way."

"Yes," Jia said. "It is fairly straightforward, and your servants will assist you, but the basic rule is that you do nothing before the emperor. You do not sit until the emperor sits, you do not eat until he eats, you do not speak until he speaks and only if he speaks directly to you."

"What do we do if he speaks to us and we don't know a lick of Chinese?" Uncle Chuck said, clearly agitated by the thought of not being able to communicate.

"Matt or I will translate for you," Jia said. "Don't worry. It's going to be fine."

Somewhere from inside the house a gong sounded.

"That's the signal," Jia said. "It's time."

Matt felt a small fluttering in his stomach as Jia took him by the arm and they walked out together.

It was evening now. The sun was setting, casting a pink glow over the city. The air was cool with a slight breeze. They had to walk to another building within the city, and this time they had many more eyes on them. News must have spread of the strange visitors within the walls of the Forbidden City. Women and children and servants lined the streets to watch them pass. Matt listened to their chatter. Some of them laughed at how pale some of them were, or their wide eyes, but many seemed to be most curious about Jia. Who was this beautiful girl they were calling a princess? Who was the boy at her side? Matt scanned some of the faces as they walked, wondering if the younger Jia was among them.

"Jia," Matt whispered. "I didn't rescue you today."

Jia frowned. "I know. Maybe I wasn't remembering right. Don't worry about it. I'm sure it will all make sense."

Matt nodded. "Okay." He kept his eye out for a younger version of Jia. He didn't see her.

They entered another building with rooms simpler in design than the Hall of Supreme Harmony but still elegant. They were led to a room with a large square table in the center. One golden chair was elevated at the head, clearly the seat of the emperor, while chairs were set lower on the other three sides of the table.

A gong sounded, and all were quiet as the emperor entered the room, followed by a young man Matt knew could only be Yinreng, the crown prince. Perhaps it was the way Jia had described him, but Matt definitely thought there was something evil about him. He gave Jia a look of pure venom. Jia ignored him, kept her chin held high, but the look sent a chill down Matt's spine. He hoped they would not have to deal much with him.

The emperor looked at Jia, nodding his approval at her appearance. His eyes then shifted to Matt. He asked Jia if this was the supposed time traveler she had mentioned earlier. Matt couldn't help wincing on the word *supposed*. Clearly, the emperor did not fully believe who they were or why they had come.

"*Shi*," Jia said. "This is Mateo Hudson."

Hudson! That was the name. Hudson. He repeated it in his

head. Hudson, Hudson, Huuuuh . . .

"Do you speak Chinese?" the emperor asked him.

Matt started a little. Whatever he was thinking about quickly left him. "*Shi*," he said. "I am learning."

The emperor nodded, clearly pleased.

"Father," Yinreng interrupted. "I still do not trust these people. If they say they are time travelers then I think they should offer us proof."

The emperor nodded. "It is a fair request my heir makes. May we witness how you travel?"

Again, Matt looked to Jia.

She shrugged. "Just . . . travel forward a few minutes?"

Matt took out his compass. Yinreng stepped closer, trying to get a look, but Matt didn't want him to see it for some reason. He kept it cupped in his hand and tilted toward his chest as he turned the time dial just one click forward. He was sucked away, and then a moment later (but perhaps five minutes for the others) reappeared. He was a little off-balance, but Jia caught him by the arm.

The emperor clapped his hands. "Remarkable!" he said excitedly. "Well done."

Yinreng looked stunned. He clearly didn't believe that Matt could time-travel, but now that he did, Matt wasn't sure he was glad of it. He thought he could see the wheels turning in Yinreng's mind, plotting. He tucked the compass beneath his robe.

"Oh, thank goodness," Gaga said, clutching at her chest. "I thought you'd disappeared for good. Just like Marcus."

"Who's Marcus?" Haha asked.

"Our son!" Gaga said.

Uncle Chuck shook his head. "You mean Mathis?"

"Mathis? No, that's not his name. Don't you think I know my own son's name?"

Matt opened his mouth to correct them, then felt a sudden fog descend upon his mind, and he promptly forgot what he wanted to say. He shook his head. His brain felt so fuzzy.

"Who are your other companions?" the emperor asked. "I assume they also traveled through time with you?"

Matt nodded. He introduced Gaga as his grandmother, Haha as his grandfather, and Uncle Chuck as his uncle. If the emperor was confused at all about their age differences, he didn't show it. Perhaps he had guessed that in cases of time travel, these sorts of things were not unusual.

"And you are?" the emperor asked, now addressing Albert.

"He's a friend," Matt said quickly, before Albert could introduce himself as a hostage or enemy. It would have been more accurate, but he felt that would needlessly complicate things. When the emperor came to Belamie, though, Matt faltered. He looked to Jia for help, but she didn't seem to know what to say any more than he did. How was he supposed to introduce his mother who didn't remember him or believe she was his mother? Belamie, sensing their hesitation, seized the moment to make her own introduction. She stepped forward and bowed before the emperor.

"I am Captain Belamie Bonnaire, of the ship *Vermillion*," she said in somewhat stilted Chinese. "I have traveled very far in order to speak with Your Majesty and hopefully gain some of your knowledge and wisdom."

"I am honored," the emperor said. "I should be very glad to share any wisdom that I can. After I eat. No one is wise when hungry." With that he turned and stepped up to his elevated seat, assisted by two servants, leaving Belamie looking a bit confused.

After the emperor was seated, Matt and the others were led to their seats as well. Yinreng was seated to the right of the emperor, Jia to his left. Matt sat next to Jia, and his grandmother sat next to him and Haha next to her. Belamie, Uncle Chuck, and Albert were seated on the other side, with Belamie seated farthest away from the emperor, which clearly annoyed her. She glared at Matt with something like jealousy. It pricked his heart and made him just a little afraid.

As soon as they were all seated, a whole parade of servants poured into the room with steaming dishes. They set them carefully on the table, bowing to the emperor before they left.

Matt was amazed at the feast before them, not just the array of dishes, but the artistry of it all. There was jasmine rice garnished with blossoms, dried fruit, lotus root, dragon-headed prawns, chicken and broth, steamed fish, dumplings and pastries, and all kinds of rich delicacies that Matt had never even seen before, some molded and carved into shapes like dragons and flowers.

A servant began to play a harplike instrument in the corner of the room, a slow, soothing melody. Another servant put a little of each dish on a plate and tasted it himself. Matt realized he was testing the food for poison.

After the servant had tasted everything and deemed it safe, he served the food to the emperor, who took a bite, signaling that others could eat as well. Albert fumbled with the chopsticks and spilled a dumpling and sauce all down his front. Yinreng cast him a derisive glance.

Matt was starving. He ate as quickly as he could without seeming impolite. Much of the food was unfamiliar to him. He pointed to a dish that looked like gray crumbly cheese and asked Jia what it was.

"Sheep brains," Jia said. "It's a delicacy."

Matt felt himself go a little green, but nevertheless nodded and dished himself some. He wasn't about to look like a squeamish child in front of the emperor. He took a bite and chewed for a moment. It tasted like very soft tofu.

"My daughter tells me you have come in need of help," the emperor said, speaking to Matt.

Matt had to swallow the brains before answering. "*Shi*," he said, glancing at his mom. "We've come because . . . there have been certain unintended consequences to our travels, some that have caused a fair amount of trouble."

The emperor nodded. "That seems logical. Time is a delicate tapestry, easily torn and unraveled. I would imagine traveling through it would cause a great deal of trouble."

Matt thought it interesting that he used the word *tapestry* to describe time. He thought of the scraps of Corey's and Ruby's time tapestries. He had them tucked in the pocket of his robe. He had an itch to touch them in that moment, but he resisted. There were too many eyes, and he felt that those small scraps were somehow sacred and perhaps the only link he had to his brother and sister.

"We are searching for something to fix that tapestry," Belamie said, clearly unable to stay quiet any longer. "Something called the Aeternum."

The emperor stopped eating. His eyes darkened and narrowed on Belamie. "*Yhongzeng*," he said, speaking the Chinese word for "eternity."

"Yes!" Belamie said. "You know of it?"

The emperor nodded. "My ancestors called it by another name. *Jìnzhǐ Suǒ*."

"*Jìnzhǐ Suǒ*," Belamie repeated. "That means . . ."

Matt was sifting through his own vocabulary. He thought *suǒ* meant "lock," but he wasn't sure about *jìnzhǐ*.

"Forbidden lock," Jia supplied.

"It is an ancient legend," the emperor continued, "one

that has been mostly forgotten over time. *Suŏ* is the force that binds the three pillars of our universe—time, space, and matter. It is the power that creates order and rhythm to our world. The earth turns in its orbit because of *Suŏ*, the sun rises and sets, the seasons come and go, and we are born and age and die, all because of *Suŏ*. In order to change events of the past or future, you would have to break this lock, disrupt the order of time, space, and matter. But of course, this thing is forbidden."

"Forbidden," Belamie said, "but not impossible?"

The emperor studied Belamie. "Tell me, why would anyone wish to break this lock, the very thing that binds our universe together?"

"To make a better world, of course," Belamie said. "The world is cruel and unfair. If there is a way to make things better, to change them, why shouldn't we do so?"

The emperor was thoughtful for a moment. "How would you make this a better world? By making things exactly as you wish?"

Belamie hesitated, as though she sensed a trap. "Why shouldn't I make things as I wish? I would take away chaos of the universe. I wouldn't allow people to needlessly die or suffer."

The emperor nodded. "And what of other people's wishes? Would you make things as they wish?"

"I could. If I deemed their wishes worthy."

"Worthy according to you," the emperor added. "And by granting some wishes and rejecting others, you will create division, and therefore discontent, and so no matter what you do you cannot hope for a better world, only a different kind of chaos. The universe is cruel, yes, and often unfair, but it is foolish to suppose you can manage better than anyone else. To rule is a terrible burden. To do it well is more pain than pleasure. And often the more pleasure you take for yourself the more pain you lay upon others, and so let us be truthful. You seek not for a better world but for your own content. A better world is something that is achievable without the help of any mystical powers or magic."

"By what powers, then?" Belamie asked. "It seems to me power and magic is the *only* thing that has made things better."

"But you just admitted that it has made things worse. Otherwise you would not be here. Confucius said, 'Wisdom, compassion, and courage are the three universally recognized qualities of men.' Sadly, as far as I have witnessed, these qualities are scarce in mankind. They are only concerned with their own comforts and wishes. This is the cause of the world's chaos and pain. We are our own worst enemies. To believe that somehow breaking the universe can solve that is delusion."

Belamie frowned at the emperor, but gave no response. Matt felt a small prick in his soul at the emperor's words. Was he only concerned with his own wishes and comforts? Did he care anything for the rest of the world so long as he got his family back? Was he any better than Vincent? He wanted to believe he was. He *did* wish to right the world. It was Vincent who had made the real mess of things, who had clearly broken the "forbidden lock." But who was he to say he could fix it? What if he only made it worse? And worse. And worse.

The emperor wiped his mouth with a silk cloth and stood. A servant was there right away to assist him. He stepped down from his raised chair and looked as though he would leave them all, but at the doorway he stopped and turned back around. "Quejing, you and your friend will accompany me."

Jia stood immediately. "Yes, Father." She looked down at Matt. He suddenly realized that he was the friend. He stood, knocking the table a little.

Gaga, Haha, and Uncle Chuck stood as well.

"The emperor has asked to speak to just Jia and me," Matt said.

"Over my dead—" Gaga started.

"Please, Gaga," Matt said in a weary voice. "It will be fine."

Gaga folded her arms. "What are you going to do? And what are we supposed to do while you're off doing . . . whatever it is you're going to do?"

As if in answer to this, the servants that had assisted them in their quarters came and started chattering away about all the things they would do for them back in their quarters.

"I promise no harm will come to Matt," Jia said. "My father's servants will be glad to entertain you with music and games, and they can give you a skin treatment that will make you look twenty years younger."

"Oh," Gaga said, fluffing her silver hair. "Well, that should be fine. But if you're not back in one hour . . ."

"Gaga . . . ," Matt said impatiently.

"Two hours! If you're not back in two hours, we will personally raid this entire city until we find you. You have been warned." She glared around at all the servants.

Both Haha and Uncle Chuck looked a little uncertain about this plan, especially as they eyed the armed guards by the emperor.

"Don't worry," Jia said. "We will see you very soon."

"It will be fine," Matt assured his family as he followed Jia out the door. He glanced back at his mom one last time. She was still staring down at her plate.

But it was Albert who disquieted him most. He gazed at Matt with that cold, calculating look that told him to be on his guard.

20

The Summer Triangle

The emperor led Matt and Jia outside of the building and again through the city. The glow of candlelight could be seen through some of the buildings, but mostly it was dark and quiet. A few guards and servants accompanied them as they walked through small alleys and narrow roads, then to the outer edge of the city along the wall. They came to a small door and Matt realized they were going to go outside the city. He looked at Jia, wondering if he should be concerned at all, but she seemed calm and followed her father without question or hesitation.

"Is the forbidden lock truly what you seek?" the emperor asked as they walked.

"No," Jia said. "We've come because it has already been found."

"And broken," Matt added.

The emperor nodded. This information did not seem to

surprise or rattle him. Somehow he must have known.

The door opened to a tunnel lit by torches. Matt had to hunch down a bit as they entered.

"The woman at dinner, then," the emperor said, "she is not truly one of your companions."

"Yes and no," Matt said. "She's my mother, but before she's really my mother. Our timelines got disrupted, and now she doesn't remember me." He felt something hitch in his throat.

"It's a long story," Jia added.

"Then you had better start telling it," the emperor said. "It appears time is not on our side. Tell me all that has happened to you and all that you have done."

And so they did. Together, Matt and Jia told the emperor all they could remember. It was not a smooth story. Seeing as they were dealing with time travel, and their paths diverged and twisted around each other. There was no rational order of events, and they sometimes had to circle back and clarify certain things. Matt thought perhaps he was forgetting some details, and sometimes he and Jia disagreed on what happened and when, but the emperor listened patiently. He didn't interject or ask questions. He just listened.

When Matt and Jia had finished telling everything, or as much as they could remember, the emperor remained quiet. He seemed to be absorbing all the information. They'd been walking through the tunnel for at least a mile, when at last they came to a set of stairs. They climbed up several flights.

The emperor stopped at a door, also guarded, and told them to wait outside. Matt only caught a glimpse of what looked like a library. The emperor was back in less than a minute carrying a large cylindrical tube. He motioned for them to follow him again, and they continued up the stairs a few more flights, until they were once again outside.

They were on a rooftop. There were several large sculptures spaced around the floor, and Matt wondered if this was something of the emperor's private art collection, but as he looked more closely, he realized they were not there for mere visual appeal. It was an observatory, the emperor's private astronomy tower. There was a celestial globe, an armillary sphere with the sun represented at the center and the rings forming a sphere around it. There was a sextant as tall as Matt, more spheres and telescopes and instruments that he did not have names for but understood by their design that they were for measuring longitudes and latitudes and celestial navigation.

There were others up on the tower, white men with long beards dressed in black robes and tall hats. The emperor went to one of them and spoke to him.

"Who are they?" Matt asked.

"Jesuit priests," Jia said. "They have been something like tutors to my father. They have taught him much about astronomy. They also built this observatory."

"It's amazing," Matt said. He knew very little about

astronomy, but as someone who loved math and science, he could appreciate all the angles and lines and spheres, the way they fit together. His mind started to immediately calculate and piece together what each instrument was for and what it could do. It felt familiar somehow. He wasn't sure why. He knew he'd never been here before. Maybe he was foremembering.

The emperor finished speaking with the priest and returned to Matt and Jia. "Come this way," he said. They went to a corner of the roof where there was a table with a few hanging lanterns to give them light.

"May I see your compass?" the emperor asked. Matt looked to Jia first. She nodded, and Matt reached inside his robe and pulled out the compass, holding it out for the emperor to see. The emperor reached in his own robe and put on a pair of spectacles. They made him look very scholarly. He leaned down so his nose was inches from the compass, but he did not touch it. It seemed to Matt that he was not eager to possess such a thing but rather studied it with the keen curiosity of a scholar, nodding and humming at the dials, the numerals and symbols.

"It appears to be identical," the emperor said, "or at least an identical design."

"What do you mean?" Jia said. "Have you seen the compass before?"

The emperor smiled. "You are not the first time travelers to pay me a visit, nor is your mother the first to ask after *Jìnzhǐ Suǒ*."

Jia looked at Matt, alarmed. "Who did you see?" Jia asked, though Matt was fairly certain he knew exactly who.

"Captain Vincent. The very man you have traveled with all these years. He paid me a visit just yesterday, in fact. I didn't think it could be coincidence that you should come so closely together."

"Yesterday!" Jia gasped. "Is he still here?"

"Not in the Forbidden City," the emperor said, "but perhaps still in China, somewhere, seeking for what I could not give him."

Matt glanced at Jia. He must still be here in order to pick up Jia, unless Matt brought her to him outside of China. But Vincent told Matt he picked up Jia in China. He just left out that minor detail that Matt was the one to bring her to him. Maybe Matt had told him not to mention it, just like he told Jia.

"What did Captain Vincent say to you when he visited?" Matt asked.

"Our conversation was very similar to the one I just had with your mother," the emperor said. "He also wanted the Aeternum so he could change the world as he pleased. He also was not pleased with my response. But, it seems he found what he was looking for anyway, despite my warnings. Please, may I see the inner workings of the compass? Just to satisfy an old man's curiosity."

Matt took off the compass from around his neck and set it on the table. He removed the top piece, revealing the innards of the compass, the many cogs and dials and pathways. "Ingenious," the emperor said. "And this is all your design?"

"Yes, though truthfully, I saw it before I made it, so I'm not sure I can say it's totally original."

"But of course it's original!" the emperor said. "You are a time traveler, and so it was inside of you all along, even this observatory was clearly inside of you, though you had not yet been here when you built the compass."

"The observatory? What do you mean?"

"You have never been to China, correct?" the emperor said. Matt shook his head.

"Never been to China, never seen this observatory, and yet see how you have captured its design, the various astronomical instruments, all inside of your compass!" The emperor pointed to the inside of the compass. Matt leaned in and studied it, trying to see it with new eyes. He looked up at the various instruments on the roof, then down at the compass. He looked back and forth and each time was more and more astonished. The compass held every astronomy instrument in miniature form.

"See the sextant and equatorial armilla," the emperor

pointed excitedly, "and the armillary, ecliptic armilla, altazimuth, quadrant altazimuth, and azimuth theodolite."

Matt was speechless. How could this be? He'd had no idea
at the time what he was doing. He had been designing it all
with some kind of intuition. Yes, there had been drawings
and formulas and equations, but he hadn't considered any
outside sources or designs. It all just came from inside of him
somewhere, and yet here he was, staring at his design in giant
form, in seventeenth-century Imperial China.

"Incredible," Jia whispered.

"The only thing that I don't see is the celestial globe," the
emperor said. "A significant piece, but ah! I am thinking that
the compass itself is the celestial globe! If I am not mistaken,
the rings of this device can separate? This spot here," the
emperor said, pointing to the divot in the center. "This is the
center, where the sun would go."

"That's where the Aeternum should go," Matt said. "Where
it did go. Captain Vincent put it there, and then it unlocked
the rings and made a sphere."

"And broke *Jìnzhǐ Suǒ*," the emperor added.

Matt remembered that moment, how everything had
stopped and they'd all been flung back in time and then
everything fell apart. Unraveled.

"Is there any way we can fix it? Is there any way I can bring
back my family? My brother and sister? My mom and dad?"

The emperor shook his head. "I don't know. I don't

understand all this myself. Some of your story has con-founded me. There are clearly missing pieces. You had *Jìnzhǐ Suǒ* all along but did not know it?"

"Yes," Matt said.

"And you do not know who gave it to you or how it was formed?"

"No. I didn't know what it was then, and it was inactive, but then I met my future self, and when our hands touched it somehow activated it, and then Captain Vincent took it."

"And you did not stop him?"

"I couldn't," Matt said. "I don't know how to explain it. It's not that I wanted him to have it. I just *couldn't* stop him. And now my mother doesn't know me anymore. She's forgotten my father, her two other children—my brother and sister—who all disappeared right before my eyes. I didn't want that!" He nearly shouted at the emperor. The anger was rising in him, though he wasn't sure why. He felt he'd had this conver-sation before with someone, but he couldn't remember who it was or when it had been. He only remembered the feeling of being accused of something in which he had no defense except his own feelings.

Jia placed a hand on his arm.

The emperor waited for Matt to calm. "Now you say after this Captain Vincent put *Yhongzeng* inside of the compass, he was able to change things, manipulate time, space, and matter? You saw him do this?"

Matt nodded.

"But *how* did he do this? By what means? This is important."

"I don't know . . ."

"The time tapestries," Jia said. "Show him the time tapestries from Corey and Ruby."

Matt had almost forgotten. He reached in his robe and pulled out the two scraps of fabric that he knew belonged to Corey and Ruby. The emperor leaned in closely to inspect the scraps. Though they had noticeably faded, the pieces of fabric gave off a subtle glow in the dark.

"What is this material?" the emperor asked.

"The captain called it a time tapestry," Matt said. "It's supposedly all the events of our lives woven together—everything we've done, everywhere we've gone, everyone we've met. Or will meet."

"Extraordinary. It's like silk woven from water and light."

"You should see it when it's whole and unmarred," Jia said. "It's the most beautiful thing I've ever seen."

"These are pieces of a greater whole, then?" the emperor said.

Matt nodded. "I think this is how Captain Vincent is changing things. I always imagined he would have to travel around the world all over time and change things, but it seems it's simpler than that. He just pulls out a person's time tapestry and changes whatever he wants."

"But not without help," Jia said. "We think someone is assisting him in the destruction of the time tapestries. Remember the man we saw on the *Vermillion* with the captain?"

Matt nodded. He'd almost forgotten that too. He was forgetting too much, too quickly. "He had some kind of explosive. We think that's what the captain is using to change certain things. We don't know who he is, though."

"Albert knows," Jia said.

"But he won't tell us," Matt said bitterly.

"I think he'll come around if we treat him with respect. Albert's not all bad, you know."

Matt scoffed. "He doesn't deserve respect. Maybe we should beat it out of him. I'll bet he'd talk faster then."

"Violence is always a weak solution, if it is any kind of solution at all," the emperor said. "You'd do better to follow the advice of my daughter."

Jia beamed with obvious pleasure at her father's praise, and for some reason it made Matt feel even more irritable. Maybe he was feeling jealous. Jia had her father. He was the orphan now.

"Even if Albert does come around at some point," Matt said, "there's no guarantee that man will help us or even know how. And by then it might be too late. I'm starting to forget them. My family. I can't see their faces in my mind. I can't remember what they sound like, and there are things about them that I don't know, but I feel like I should, like their birthdays. Shouldn't I know my own brother and sister's birthday? How long before I forget their names? That they're my brother and sister? That I care? That they exist at all?" Jia took Matt's hand. It was only then that he realized he was shaking.

"Your brother and sister are twins you said?" the emperor asked.

Matt nodded, wiping at his tears. "Is that important?"

"I don't know," the emperor said. "Maybe. Maybe not. In China, twins are a symbol of luck, boy and girl twins are especially powerful, they are yin and yang, symbolizing balance in the universe. But your brother and sister are not alone. They have you. You are also significant, I think. You are the inventor of the compass! You are an orphan but somehow came to this particular family. Why? It is not coincidence, I do not think."

The emperor took the cylinder he had been carrying. He opened the top and retrieved a large scroll. He unraveled it and placed it on the table, using some stones to hold down the corners.

Matt almost forgot his anger and grief at the sight of it. He was instantly mesmerized. It was a star chart, very complex. Three layers of circles, one inside of the other, very much like his compass (he couldn't help but notice the similarity), and inside of each were hundreds of constellations. Lines had been drawn, the constellations were labeled. Matt didn't recognize most of them as they'd been labeled in Chinese characters, but he recognized a few—Hercules, Virgo, Cassiopeia.

"Now," the emperor said. "I have been studying astronomy for many years and keeping a careful record. The stars and planets can tell us a great deal about our universe, and lately my priest friends and I have noted certain disruptions. Many constellations have dimmed or disappeared completely, and new ones have begun to appear, but one has remained constant through it all." He pointed to a place on the chart where three points formed a triangle. "The Summer Triangle. Astrologers have interpreted it in many ways over the centuries. There are stories and legends, and of course, the number three is significant in many cultures and religions. It is a holy number, a number of luck. But in more scholarly circles, the Summer Triangle symbolizes the three pillars of the universe—matter, space, and time. Together they bind or lock our universe, create order and symmetry. *Suǒ.* Now you say this Captain Vincent has found a way to break the lock by means of a compass you built and a stone that you gave to him."

"Yes, but—"

"Even if it was your future self, it *was* you, and you did it for a reason."

Matt had no response. What reason could there be other than to destroy his own family?

"Come," the emperor said. "I want you to see this in the real stars."

They left the star chart and walked to the other end of the observatory that overlooked the Forbidden City. There were more buildings than even Matt realized. There had to be thousands of them. There were a few glowing lanterns, but mostly the city was dark, and his gaze was naturally drawn upward. The sky was scattered with so many stars.

"They never stop making me feel both small and large all at once," the emperor said. "That I am both nothing and everything, both the center of the universe and an insignificant insect."

Matt had nothing to say to this, only it felt true. There were times when he felt like everything revolved around him, that he was important and powerful, and others when the universe seemed completely indifferent toward his existence. At this moment he felt like nothing more than a speck.

The emperor approached one of the instruments. One of the priests was making adjustments. He stepped aside as they approached and told the emperor that it was ready and in position. The emperor looked through the telescope and then motioned for Matt and Jia to come.

"Look!" he said.

Matt looked through the telescope.

"The Summer Triangle," the emperor said. At first Matt

just saw a jumbled mass of stars, but slowly they started to organize themselves and he drew lines between the stars in his mind. He saw the three points, equilateral, though two were dimmer than the third.

"In all my years observing the skies," the emperor said, "the three stars of the Summer Triangle have always been equally bright, until recently we noticed two of them beginning to dim."

"You think it's because of what Captain Vincent did? Because he broke the lock on the universe?"

The emperor nodded. "I cannot help but think there is something in your relationship with your brother and sister that is significant in all that has happened. The three of you together, in some way, represent the three pillars of the universe. The balance needed. You must bring them back. Only the three of you together can mend the lock, I believe, restore order to the universe."

"But how? And how am I supposed to bring them back? I told you, they're gone! I don't even know what's happened to them. They just unraveled right before my eyes! All I have are these scraps of fabric and they're unraveling too!" He held out the pieces of fabric. One of them fell, and when it hit the ground the threads started to unravel and disintegrate. Matt felt an invisible thread inside of himself simultaneously doing the same. He bent down and quickly snatched it up. He pressed it to his chest.

"You are an intelligent boy," the emperor said. "You built this compass not even knowing exactly what you were doing. You have power and intelligence inside of you that even you are not aware of, but more importantly you have a good heart."

Matt nearly rolled his eyes. A good heart. What did that matter in this situation?

"You think the heart does not matter," the emperor said, seeming to read his mind. "But it matters more than anything, more than the forbidden lock, more than your compass. Your heart is your true compass. Let it guide you, and you'll never be truly lost."

Matt and Jia were escorted back to their quarters by two palace guards. They walked in silence most of the way. Matt's mind was turning in circles. His dad, Corey, and Ruby had disappeared because the order of the universe had been disrupted, its lock broken, and in order to fix it, he needed to get Corey and Ruby back. But he had no idea how to get them back! It made no sense.

Jia also seemed lost in thought, but he didn't think she was thinking about the same things. She seemed peaceful, happy. After the emperor had told Matt to "follow his heart," he'd turned his attention to Jia. He asked her to tell him about her travels, what she had seen and done, the things she had learned. They talked for nearly an hour, barely acknowledging

Matt unless he happened to be part of the story, which he often wasn't since Jia had been on the *Vermillion* for years before he arrived. Matt watched as Jia spoke to her father, the way she lit up, the way the emperor listened so attentively, clearly admiring his daughter. Matt couldn't blame him, but it was hard not to feel jealous, like he'd suddenly been replaced.

Matt was exhausted. He was hoping he could just walk into the house and disappear into his room. He just wanted to lie down and sleep, but he knew that wasn't going to happen the moment he entered the house. As soon as the guards left them, they heard a crash in the next room.

"Hold him! Hold him!" Matt heard his mom shout. He looked to Jia. They both ran into the main room and stopped short at the scene before them.

At first Matt thought his mom and Albert were fighting with his grandparents and uncle. Belamie had Gaga by the upper arm and Haha by the hair, while Albert had wrapped himself around Uncle Chuck's leg. Uncle Chuck was stumbling around the room, bumping into furniture and walls, knocking things over. When he turned around, Jia gasped. His face. It was blurry. They were all blurry. They were fading, unraveling. Vincent had struck again. He was erasing the rest of his family.

"No!" Matt shouted. He ran to Gaga.

"Oh!" Gaga said. "I feel so strange!" Her arm blurred so

Belamie lost her grip. Gaga faded and disappeared.

"I guess this is really it this time," Haha said as he disappeared too. Belamie pitched forward.

"Uncle Chuck!" Matt called. "Don't go!"

Uncle Chuck was still stumbling around with Albert attached to his leg. "It's okay, Matty," he said calmly. "I'm just going to the next adventure. You gotta stay and finish this one." And he disappeared. Albert fell in a heap on the floor.

Matt gasped and clutched at his head. He started to shake.

Gone. All of his family was gone now.

"What happened?" Jia asked.

"I don't know," Belamie said. "One moment they were all sitting there, normal as can be, and the next they were . . . fading. We tried to help them, but there was nothing we could do. I've never seen anything like it."

Matt had. "It's Vincent," he growled. "He erased their existence."

"Erased their existence?" Belamie said. "That's impossible. Not without . . ." She trailed off, glanced at Albert.

"I told you," Albert said. "I told you all along. They're lying to you. They brought you here under false pretenses."

"Albert . . . ," Jia said, her voice full of disappointment.

Albert said nothing, only stuck his nose in the air.

Belamie looked at Matt. "It's true then. Vincent really does have the Aeternum, doesn't he?"

Matt looked at his mom. He could see there was no hiding

it now. The cat was out of the bag. "You have to understand," he said, "that's *not* what you wanted. Before all this happened, you were fighting *against* Vincent. *He's* the enemy!"

Belamie shook her head. "Vincent would never hurt me. He loves me. And I love him."

Matt felt like he was going to vomit. "No, you don't!" he shouted. "You chose someone else! Vincent went back in time and destroyed your family and made it so you can't even remember them. You can't even remember that I'm your son! *That's* the truth."

Belamie's gaze drew inward, like she was searching for the truth. Matt thought he might have convinced her, but then Albert had to open his big mouth.

"If you didn't want any of this to happen," Albert said, "then how come you gave Captain Vincent the Aeternum?"

"What?" Belamie snapped.

"Albert," Jia said in a warning voice. "Stop."

"He did!" Albert said. "I saw it with my own eyes. So did Jia."

Matt shook his head. "It wasn't supposed to be that way. None of this was supposed to happen."

"It seems that it *was* supposed to happen," Belamie said. "It looks as though this is exactly how you wanted things to be."

Matt shook his head. "No. I didn't. And it isn't how *you* wanted things to be. Can't you understand? You *left* Vincent. But he changed everything. He erased your husband, and the twins . . . my brother and sister"—he tried to remember their names—"Corbin and Rita? Casey and Judy? No. those weren't right. It was all shrouded in fog. "He erased them! He's changed your entire life when you didn't want him to!"

Belamie pressed her fingers to her temple. "But it *isn't* my life. Maybe it's your life, but it isn't mine, whatever you say. I didn't choose this."

"But you *did* choose it!" Matt shouted. "Maybe not now, but in the future you choose it. You *chose* my dad. You chose *me*. And my brother and sister." Why couldn't he remember their names?! "You loved your family more than anything in the world, and you would have done anything to protect them. You did. You gave up everything—the *Vermillion*, the Obsidian Compass, your quest for the Aeternum, saving your parents. All of it. For us. Because you love us. But I guess you don't anymore. You don't care about me or my dad or . . . or . . ." He slammed his own fist into his head. What were their names?! "All you care about is power and immortality."

"And what's so wrong with that?" Albert said. "What is a 'family' but just a group of people guaranteed to let you down? It's better this way, you know. You should be grateful."

"Albert, how can you say such a thing?" Jia said, frowning. "You saw the Hudson family before this. You know how close they were, how much they loved each other. You can't possibly think what Captain Vincent has done is right."

Albert seemed to hesitate just a little, but he held his head high. "It doesn't matter what I think. I am not a traitor."

"No," Matt growled. "You're just a pathetic *loser.*" He lunged at Albert, tackled him to the ground. Matt was not a fighter, but he felt something crack open inside of him and the rage poured out like the fiery breath of a dragon.

"Stop!" Jia shouted. "Matt, stop it!"

Matt didn't hear her. He punched and slapped and clawed with everything he had. Albert mostly tried to protect himself. Only once did he retaliate, weakly swatting at Matt's neck and head and then curling up into a ball as Matt pummeled him.

"I got it! I got it!" Albert shouted.

"No, you don't," Matt said. "Not yet." He continued to hit Albert until his mom pulled him off. Matt twisted free but lost his balance. He stumbled sideways into a table holding a porcelain vase. The vase fell and shattered.

"I got it!" Albert shouted. "Let's go!"

Matt pushed himself off the ground. Porcelain shards bit into his hands, but he hardly felt it when he saw the scene before him. He felt at his chest. The compass. Albert had gotten the compass! He must have pulled it off him while they were fighting.

"Hurry! Let's get out of here!" Albert handed the compass to Belamie who immediately started turning the dials.

"Mom! Don't!" Matt shouted.

Belamie looked at Matt, and a shadow of regret flickered over her face. "I'm sorry, but I'm *not* your mother!"

She made the final turn of the dial. She reached out for Albert, took him by the hand. Albert looked at Matt and smiled triumphantly.

"Mom! Mom!" Matt ran to her, tried to grab on to her, but too late. She and Albert disappeared.

Matt fell on the spot where they had just been. "Come back! Please come back!" he shouted into the air as though she might be able to hear him.

Matt began to tremble violently. Someone knelt down in front of Matt, but he couldn't see them clearly. He felt his body convulse, spasming out of control. Spots appeared in the corners of his eyes. He heard a rushing in his ears, like the sound of waves crashing, getting louder and louder, and then he blacked out.

21

Asleep

Jia sat by Matt's bedside, watching his chest move up and down. He had been asleep for an entire day. She had tried everything to rouse him, even slapped and pinched his face to near bruising. The servants had administered tonics and powders, but nothing worked. Every now and then Matt twitched, and Jia thought maybe he was waking, but he was just seizing again. She had witnessed one of Matt's seizures only once before, and never had she witnessed anyone else seize, but she still thought it was strange. It was almost like he was flickering in and out like a lightbulb.

Jia stayed with Matt every minute. She barely took her eyes off him. She had this increasingly dark feeling that she and Matt wouldn't be able to stay together for much longer, that he would disappear right before her eyes, or she would. Things were changing. She could feel it, and see it too. While Matt slept, China began to experience time rifts. At first, they were slight. The servants brought in stories of people mysteriously showing up in the midst of the Forbidden City, foreigners who couldn't speak Chinese and wore very odd clothes. The guards thought they were spies that had infiltrated the city somehow, but then things happened that were less easily explained. Buildings in the Forbidden City started to disappear, and new ones started to take their place. That evening Jia looked out the window and could see the tall spire of a building she knew belonged in Paris. The Eiffel Tower.

Jia wrote a note to her father. He had asked her to keep him informed of any new developments or unusual happenings. Belamie's abandonment, the disappearance of Gloria, Henry, and Chuck, and Matt falling into a coma were certainly new and unusual developments, not to mention the time rifts that were clearly happening, which surely the emperor knew about. Jia didn't really expect the emperor to respond. Perhaps he would send one of his advisers. But within the hour of her message being sent, the emperor himself came.

Jia was surprised at how comforted she felt by his presence. She hadn't felt that kind of comfort since her mother died. She'd always been afraid of her father before. He had always been a stranger to her. But when they had talked the other night in the observatory, the way he had listened to her, asked her questions, she felt a bond form that she knew would not be easily broken, and she began to wonder what her future would be.

Her father brought with him his royal physician, an old man with a bald head and thin mustache who smelled strongly of eucalyptus and ginger. He inspected Matt thoroughly and then declared what Jia already knew. The boy was in a deep sleep. He had suffered a great trauma that his heart and brain could not cope with consciously. So he shut down.

Of course, Jia knew it was the shock of his mother leaving him. That was the last straw. It broke him, and she was starting to fear he would never wake, or if he did he would never truly recover. If Jia ever saw Albert again, she swore she'd strangle him. This was his fault. He'd been scheming with Matt's mom last night. They'd been planning to steal the compass all along, and it had broken her friend's heart, the purest, kindest heart she had ever known.

"When he wakes," her father said, "he will be different."

"Different how?"

"He will be lost. The Summer Triangle continues to fade. The priests and I have been watching it closely, as well as other movements. I don't think it is without meaning. Things are changing. They will continue to change and the world will go into deeper chaos, unless the lock is repaired. Your friend here is the only one who can do it. He will need you to help him find his way, do what he needs to do. If he doesn't, I fear we'll all be lost."

"I don't know how to help him," Jia said. "I don't know what to do."

"What are your strengths? What do you do well?"

Jia's response was immediate. "Fixing things. Machines and structures. I like building and repairing, making things work better."

This seemed to please her father. "That is a useful skill in all situations, especially when so many things are broken."

Jia didn't answer. How could she fix what she could not see, what was not physically in front of her?

"What do you think of Yinreng?" her father asked.

Jia was startled by the questions. She did not know how she should respond. She knew exactly what she thought of Yinreng, but she was not certain if she was walking into a trap or not. It was treasonous to speak of the emperor or his heir with anything less than respect bordering on worship, but Jia had been gone for so long, the rules were not as entrenched in her, and she felt a sense of boldness that she had never felt in all her days in China before. So she told her father the truth.

"I believe Yinreng is unfit to be emperor. One of your servants is more worthy of your throne than he is."

She held her breath, waiting for her father's response, his anger or disappointment, at least, but to Jia's surprise her father laughed. "I suggest you don't share your feelings with your brother," he said. It was a warning, she realized. Yinreng had it out for her. She knew just by the way he had looked at her last night at dinner. It seemed her father suspected as well. She thought of her younger self, wandering around the Forbidden City, hiding and spying. Matt was supposed to send her on the *Vermillion*. She thought that should have happened already, but what if it never happened now? What if too much had changed and so her very life would change? She couldn't remember, exactly, all that had happened before, but she wasn't sure if that was because it was so long ago, or if her memories were being erased. What if she started to forget things, forget everything that had happened, forget Matt?

"I believe this belongs to you," the emperor said. He held something out to her. It was the Qing dynasty amulet. "So you can always return home."

Jia took the amulet, pressed it to her heart. She knew this was a great sign of trust. And respect. She bowed to her father.

"We cannot fix everything, Quejing," the emperor said. "We do what we can. We try to do what is right, but not everything will be perfect. Sometimes we make mistakes, and sometimes sacrifices have to be made. We all have to sacrifice for what is right and for those we love."

Jia felt her heart clench, fearing what those sacrifices might be.

Her father left and she continued her vigil at Matt's side. She had one of the servants bring her the bag in her room. She changed back into her pants and tool vest. As pretty as the dress was that she'd worn to dinner last night, she felt more herself in her regular clothes. There was another change of clothes in the bag, too, clothes that were not her own. She had a vague memory of borrowing them from someone, Matt's sister. What was her name again? Riley? Trudy? She shook her head. She should know her name, should remember what she looked like, but it was stuck in some part of her brain that she couldn't reach.

She found Pike's book, too, among her things. She knew it was really Matt's book, but she associated it with Pike so much, it was now more her book than Matt's. Having nothing else to do, she started reading it from the beginning, reading all about famous scientists and inventors in time. Many she had read or heard about before, such as Galileo, Albert Einstein, Oppenheimer, Thomas Edison. Others were new to her. She'd never heard of Steve Jobs, though of course she had seen all the fancy computers and phones he made in the future. Wiley had stolen one for her once. It didn't work unless they were far into the future, twenty-first century, and then there were all kinds of things you had to have, like something called a network and a data package. In the end she simply enjoyed taking it apart and trying to understand how it all worked. She still didn't completely understand. Some people's brains . . . she would never stop being in awe of what humans could create and invent, and with no one was that truer than Matt. His mind was like a world unto itself.

She turned the page to Alfred Nobel, a Swedish chemist who had invented an explosive called dynamite. Jia had heard of it. Brocco had piles of the stuff on the *Vermillion*, she recalled. He loved to blow stuff up any chance he got. Once, when they were on a mission somewhere in Africa, he'd blown up a section of a mountain that Wiley said was a known diamond mine in the future. They'd cleared out a sizable amount of rough diamond. After, they'd had a wonderful celebration in Nowhere in No Time. Shortly after that, they discovered Pike on board the *Vermillion*. Pike, Pike . . . why did she leave? Was it just the familiarity of Captain Vincent and the crew? Or was it something else?

Jia turned the page and looked at the pictures of Alfred Nobel, his laboratory. They were all black-and-white photographs, but even so, she thought he looked vaguely familiar to her. She couldn't think where she had seen him before. It felt recent, but also long ago.

Jia looked up. Matt was awake.

22
Forgetting

Matt was between worlds. No, that wasn't quite the right way to describe it. That made it sound like he was dying, and he wasn't dying, he was pretty sure. It was more that he was split in two. He felt part of him was together, solid, lying still in bed, while the rest of him was separated, floating all around like a bunch of dust particles in space, another realm. Definitely not earth. He was in endless space. There was no horizon, no sky, no earth or water. But there was the essence of something more, a kind of presence that he couldn't see but felt sure was there.

He heard a voice, distant and fading.

Hold on, Matt! Don't let go!

He wanted to reach out, grab on to whoever was calling out to him, but he had no strength. He wasn't really here. That other part of him that was still solid and together was pulling him down. These two parts of him struggled against one another. The solid part of him wanted the particles to come back together, and the particles wanted the solid to fly apart. The solid part of him must have won out eventually, because when he woke he was fully together in his bed.

No, not his bed, he didn't think. He was somewhere else. He'd forgotten where. He looked around at the blankets, the tapestries, the furniture. A tapestry of a dragon hung on the wall. On another wall was a series of paintings of Chinese emperors. He was in China, in the Forbidden City. He'd just met the Kangxi emperor yesterday, who just happened to be Jia's father.

And then he remembered what had happened, what had sent him into a seizure. His mother . . . she had left him.

I'm not your mother.

A sharp pain lashed through his head. He gasped and clutched at his head.

"You're awake!" Jia jumped up, dropping some book she'd been reading. He hadn't noticed that she'd been sitting right by his bed. She was back in her regular clothes—pants and a T-shirt with her vest, the many pockets bulging with tools and supplies. Matt decided, even though she had looked beautiful in her dress last night, he liked her better this way. Last night she had been Princess Quejing. This was Jia, his best friend.

Jia rushed to his side. "Does your head hurt?" she said.

"A bit," he said in a raspy voice. But it was much more than a bit. It felt like someone had dropped a twenty-pound bowling ball on his head. "How long was I out?"

"All night and then some. It's noon now."

The events of the previous night came back to him slowly, but remembering them didn't make him feel any better. It wasn't just his mother who had left him. Albert had stolen the compass for her, effectively working around her solemn oath to him that she wouldn't steal it, and they just . . . left. And Gaga and Haha and Uncle Chuck. Vincent had taken them too. How long before he forgot them? There were others that had left him, he thought, but he wasn't sure who. His memory felt clouded. His head ached. He pressed his fingers to his temples.

"I'll get you some tea," Jia said. "You're probably dehydrated."

Jia forced about ten cups of ginger tea down him, claiming it could cure any headache, but the pain persisted, as did the fog in his brain. Maybe those particles were still a bit separated, buzzing around inside his skull like a bunch of gnats.

"Matt, I'm so sorry," Jia said.

"It's okay," Matt said, his voice hollow. "It doesn't matter, really." And there was part of him that felt that was absolutely true and another part of him telling him that it was a complete lie. It was like there were two beings inside of him, fighting for control.

"Oh, Matt," Jia said. "Of course it matters! It's all right to feel sad, you know. And you must know your mother truly loves you. She's just . . . not herself right now."

Matt nodded, even though he wasn't sure what that meant. What did it mean to be yourself or not yourself? Was he himself now? Would he become someone else eventually? Marius Quine . . . and who was he?

Jia picked up the book she'd been reading. It was a book about scientists. It looked vaguely familiar to Matt. He remembered Pike had been reading it somewhere, sometime. But where? Maybe on the *Vermillion*. The book must be from Wiley's library.

"Doing some research?"

"A little. I found something I thought you should see." She opened the book and pointed to a picture. "Doesn't he look familiar to you?"

Matt squinted at the black-and-white photograph of a man, then looked at the caption. "Alfred Nobel? I've certainly heard of him. He invented dynamite, and there are very prestigious prizes named after him." Ever since he'd learned what they were, Matt had secretly wished to win a Nobel Prize in physics or chemistry or mathematics someday.

"But I think we've seen him before," Jia said. "He was the man on the *Vermillion*, wasn't he? The one who was with Vincent when he was chasing us."

Matt studied the picture again and realized she was right. Nobel was the man he'd seen on the *Vermillion*, the one holding the case of the strange dynamite.

"I think he's the reason Pike left us," Jia said. "I think she knows him somehow."

Matt nodded. "Pike could definitely be Swedish."

"Anyway, I think he has something to do with what's been happening, your family disappearing, the forbidden lock breaking. I think if we could visit him, he might be able to help."

"Or not," Matt said. "Clearly he was helping Captain Vincent."

"We don't know what he was doing," Jia said. "Or why."

"Well, it doesn't matter, does it? We can't visit him. Nobel's not alive yet, and I don't have the compass anymore." Matt felt at his chest where the compass should have been. It didn't just feel like something was missing from the outside, but from the inside too.

"I've been thinking about that too," Jia said.

Tong interrupted them with a tray of food. Matt was doubly grateful, both because he really did not want to discuss losing the compass and because he was starving. Plus, he desperately needed to pee. Triply grateful.

Matt got out of bed and hobbled to the bathroom. His legs felt like they would crumple beneath him, like dry pillars of sand. But he managed to hold himself together. After he was finished in the bathroom, he glanced out the window and did a double take.

"Is that the Eiffel Tower?" he said.

"Yes," Jia said. "It showed up while you were asleep, among other things. China is experiencing time rifts. The emperor says it will only get worse."

Matt frowned at the tall metal spire reaching above all the buildings of the Forbidden City. This was not a good sign.

"Listen, Matt," Jia said. "I've been thinking. Maybe you don't need the compass to time-travel."

"What do you mean? Of course I do. No one can travel without the compass."

"Marius Quine can," Jia said.

Matt frowned. That was true. Marius Quine could apparently travel without the compass. He could make himself disappear and reappear wherever and whenever he wanted. Matt remembered the time he'd accidentally traveled to him in the future. Quine said he would teach him how to do it at some point, but it wasn't until this moment that Matt realized what he might have meant is that he would teach himself.

"You're right," Matt said, "Marius Quine can disappear and reappear, but it's not helpful to me at the moment, because I'm still Mateo. I don't know how to do it. I wouldn't even know where to start."

"I think you do."

Matt scoffed. "You think you know what I know better than I do?"

"I know you are constantly underestimating yourself. Just

think about it, Matt. You built a time-traveling compass in your grandmother's basement at the age of twelve. Don't tell me you can't do incredible, even impossible things, because we already have proof that you can."

"Okay, fine," Matt said. "Yes, I built the compass, and yes, it was incredible, but I had something to go off of. I'd already seen it. I knew it could work, so it was like a self-fulfilling prophecy."

Jia threw up her hands. "So is this! You've already seen yourself disappear and reappear, so you know you can do it!"

"But I was much older when I saw myself do it. Maybe it takes years and years to learn. Maybe I won't be able to do it until I'm, like, fifty."

"I think you could do it right now if you wanted," Jia said. "In fact, I think you've already done it before, and you didn't even know it."

"What are you talking about?"

"I'm talking about your seizures. You once told me that doctors never could find any reason for them, right?"

Memories suddenly flooded Matt's mind—the antiseptic smell of hospitals, the prick of needles, drawing blood, brain scans, endless waits, and nurses giving him stickers. In his memory he was all alone, but that couldn't be right. Someone had to have taken him to the hospital—his mother or father—but he couldn't remember. He wasn't even sure he had a mother or father. "Yeah, so?"

"So, maybe they couldn't find anything wrong with you because there's nothing actually wrong with you," Jia said. "Maybe your seizures aren't really seizures, but something else entirely."

"I'm not following."

"You haven't seen yourself having a seizure, but *I've* seen it. Twice. I'm telling you, you don't just shake and twitch. You flicker in and out like a shorted lightbulb. It's like your body is trying to do something it *knows* it can do, but your brain doesn't yet, at least not on a conscious level, so it fights it. Remember when you blacked out when we were in Nowhere in No Time, and when you came back you were convinced you had traveled, but none of us had seen you travel? What if you *did* travel, but it happened so quickly we just couldn't see it for what it was. You were just . . . flickering."

Matt considered this. He had never understood how he had traveled in that moment when he'd gone to see Quine in the future. At the time he thought maybe Quine was the one who had manipulated it all, but Jia's hypothesis was pretty interesting. He felt she was probably on to something here. He *did* feel like he was having some kind of out-of-body experience when he had his seizures. The problem was, he hadn't done any of it on purpose. It had just happened. He had no control over when his seizures happened or how long they lasted. He explained all this to Jia.

"Have you noticed any pattern to your seizures?" Jia asked.

"Like when they come on?"

"They usually occur during moments of high stress or excitement," he said. "Like when I get an adrenaline rush." It was one reason why his mom had been a bit of a helicopter parent toward him in particular, always making sure he was calm and safe. He was more likely to have a seizure and black out if he was anxious or scared.

"Maybe your seizures are some kind of fight-or-flight response," Jia said, "but much stronger, so your body loses control? But what if you could learn to control it?"

"It's an idea," Matt said. "But how are we supposed to test it—put me under a lot of stress or something?"

Jia looked like she was thinking just that. He could almost hear her brain coming up with all the ways she could torture him and make him have a seizure.

"Look, let's not worry about it," he said. "I'll figure it out eventually, won't I? You said it yourself. It's a self-fulfilling prophecy. So it will happen when it happens."

Jia nodded, but still she was frowning. He didn't like the look on her face at all.

Later, when he was alone, Matt tried to make himself dissolve, just as he had seen Quine do before. He tried to focus on his body, produce that feeling when he was having a seizure. He always thought of it as a fuzzy feeling, but also jarring, like he was being tossed around a room, hitting walls. Maybe that was his brain fighting it. If he could relax himself into it, maybe he could make himself disassemble the way Quine did.

Come on, he told himself. *Break apart!*

He felt nothing, except maybe a bit silly for trying to make himself disappear with nothing but the power of his mind. He was smart. He'd even concede he was a genius, but he wasn't a freaking superhero in a comic book.

Comic books . . . someone he knew once really liked comic books. . . . Matt felt a tug somewhere in his chest, and a small voice in the back of his head saying, *Don't let go!*

But it was getting harder to hold on. (Hold on to what?) Throughout that day and into the next, the fog in Matt's brain only thickened. His memories continued to unravel. Some memories remained sharp and clear, like his favorite ice cream flavor (mint chip), the periodic table, and the first time he met Jia on the *Vermillion*. But other things were in a shadowy haze. More and more of the threads of his memory seemed to be disintegrating, along with the bits of time tapestries he kept with him at all times. He couldn't remember exactly where they'd come from, but when he held them in his hand he felt the fog lift ever so slightly, and he remembered that he had a brother and sister. (Or was it two brothers or two sisters? And what were their names? Connie and Ruben? Rudy and Casey?)

The morning after his mother had left (Was she really

his mother? Why did she leave him?), Jia brought up Alfred Nobel again.

"Why don't you just read about him," Jia said, handing him Pike's book. "Maybe something will spark your memory. Or your forememory."

So Matt read, more to appease Jia than anything else. Nobel was a brilliant student, quiet and serious. He spoke five languages. In his younger years he'd wanted to be a writer, a poet, but his father had demanded that he be practical and focus on academics. After many years of hard study and work, he had success in creating an explosive with nitroglycerin, a substance ten times the power of gunpowder. Unfortunately, in the fall of 1864 an accident with the nitroglycerin in his lab resulted in five deaths, including his younger brother, Emil Nobel. Devastated by his brother's death, Alfred Nobel became a recluse. Few people saw or heard from him for several years, but in 1867, Alfred succeeded in the invention of a very powerful and more stable explosive, dynamite, which would make him very rich, but also heavily criticized. A French newspaper, mistakenly reporting Nobel's death, printed *"Le marchand de la mort est mort." The merchant of death is dead.* Nobel was reportedly horrified that this was how he would be memorialized. Most believe this is the reason why he left most of his large fortune to create the Nobel Prizes that would honor those who made significant advancements and contributions in physics, chemistry, medicine, literature, and peace.

Matt had to admit, after reading about Nobel, he felt a certain kinship to him and saw many similarities between them. They both spoke five languages, they were both scientists and inventors, and they both had invented something incredibly powerful that had changed the world—sometimes in tragic ways. Nobel had lost his brother. Matt couldn't fully remember but he had the dim sense that he'd also lost a brother at some time or another. Had he been responsible for his death too? Did he really die?

That evening, after Jia and Matt had eaten dinner, Jia challenged Matt to a game of chess. Jia said it might help if they tried to take their minds off of things. Matt was thinking that was the exact opposite of what he needed, seeing as he couldn't seem to keep his mind *on* anything, but he didn't want to say no. He felt he'd done nothing but disappoint Jia ever since they'd come to China, and he hated the look she gave him every time he said something wrong, like that time he said something about Captain Vincent being his father. She reacted as though he'd just declared the devil himself was his father. It seemed a bit of an overreaction in Matt's mind. Vincent wasn't so terrible, was he? He'd always been nice to him, hadn't he? And one day he would inherit the *Vermillion* and the compass from him. He was his heir. But he certainly wasn't going to say any of that to Jia.

So here they were, playing chess. It was the Chinese version, which was much like American chess but with different pieces and slightly different rules. Jia explained it all and said he'd get the hang of it after a few games. Matt beat her on the first round in six moves.

"Okay," frowning a little. "Good job. Beginner's luck. Go again?"

The next game Matt went a little easier on her and won in eight moves, but she still seemed annoyed. He had a feeling she was used to winning this game. On the next round he let her win, but then Jia guessed he'd let her win, and she was even more annoyed. She said it was an insult to let her win. She insisted they play again and commanded Matt in her most princessy voice to do his very best. So he did, and he beat her in four moves.

Jia just laughed in disbelief. "How are you doing that? Are you cheating now? Did you cheat?"

Matt put up his hands. "No! I promise. The only time I cheated was when I lost on purpose."

"Okay, what am I missing?" Jia said. "Teach me, genius. What am I doing wrong?"

"Nothing wrong. You're just thinking a little too straightforward. You're only considering the present play, but chess requires you to think in terms of the whole—not just the present move, but forward and backward and sideways and even sometimes in a circular fashion."

"Okay, that makes sense, I guess," Jia said. "Like time travel."

"What?"

"Time travel. You know, when you can time-travel you don't just go forward, you can go backward, too, and sometimes sideways. Always when planning a mission, we had to think about that."

"Yes, that's right." Matt leaned over, looking a little closer at the game board and the various pieces. Something about the way Jia compared this to time travel sparked something in him.

"Anything else I'm missing?" Jia asked.

"You need to make sacrifices," he said, still focused on the board. "You're too concerned with protecting all your pieces. You have to be willing to make sacrifices in order to win."

A sacrifice must be made to win this game . . .

"Matt?" Jia asked. "Are you okay?"

Matt felt something shift inside of him and click into place.

"I've been thinking about everything all wrong," he muttered. He'd only been thinking about going forward, how to move in a chronological way. But he was not in a forward-thinking, chronological game. This was an every-direction, all-time game! Forward, backward, sideways, up and down, all around and everything in between. This was time travel. This was *eternity*.

"Matt?" Jia repeated. "Are you feeling all right? You look a bit . . . fuzzy."

He looked down at his hands. Indeed, they looked blurry, out of focus.

The front door opened. A servant hurried into the room, bowed to Jia, and handed her a message.

Jia opened it and frowned as she read.

"What's wrong?" Matt asked.

"The emperor has asked to see both of us," Jia said. "Immediately."

23

The Emperor's Will

Jia's heart raced as they moved swiftly to the Hall of Supreme Harmony. There was something about her father's message that felt off. She wasn't sure what it was. Maybe it was their mixed-up surroundings. On their way, they passed a small village of Tudor-style homes, and then a flock of colorful birds she knew were not native to China, and of course there was the Eiffel Tower. It stood like some alien creature in the courtyard in front of the Hall of Supreme Harmony.

"Are we in Paris?" Matt asked, looking up at the tall spire.

"No," Jia said. She could tell Matt's memories were unraveling even faster than hers.

They mounted the steps to the Hall of Supreme Harmony, and the closer they came to the doors, the harder Jia's heart pounded. When they arrived at the top, Jia reached in her vest pocket and took out her amulet, the one thing that had kept her connected to her home, her family.

"Matt," she said, "I need you to take this." She pressed the amulet in his hand. "You need to make sure to rescue my younger self, take me to the *Vermillion*, and give that to me. You can't forget."

Matt stared down at the amulet, then frowned at her. "Why? What's going to happen to you?"

"I don't know," she said. But something was wrong. She could feel it. "You can't forget," she said again. "Promise?"

Matt nodded. "I promise."

The guards opened the doors and ushered them through.

Jia approached slowly, trying to compose herself. She was in her tool vest and pants still. She should have changed before she came, but it was too late now.

Her father was sitting on his throne, but as she drew closer, she saw that it wasn't the Kangxi emperor on the throne at all. It was Yinreng.

"Sister," Yinreng said, a sly smile on his lips.

"Yinreng," she said. "What are you doing? Where is Father?"

"He's gone," he said.

"Gone where?" Matt asked.

"Nobody knows. He has disappeared, along with many others."

Jia glanced at Matt. What could that mean? Had he been displaced in time? Had Captain Vincent erased his existence? No, that couldn't be, because if her father didn't exist then she wouldn't exist, or Yinreng.

"So you've gone ahead and made yourself emperor?" Jia said. "It is treason to act in the name of the emperor without his blessing, without knowing for sure what has happened to him."

Yinreng only smiled at her. "Did you know," he said, "that the emperor has a box, locked and hidden away, containing the name of his heir? It is only to be opened upon the emperor's death, to name his successor."

Jia had heard of this. It was meant to ensure that his will was carried out after his death, that his successor was named without any confusion or contention.

"Well?" Jia said. "Is it not your own name inside the box? Everyone knows you are the crown prince, heir to the throne."

"I should be," Yinreng said, his lips curling with derision. "But the emperor has been strange since you showed up. He speaks of you a great deal. 'Is not Quejing intelligent?' he says. 'Doesn't she seem like a strong, fair-minded woman?'"

Jia could not understand why these compliments would anger her brother so much. What was it to him if their father thought her intelligent? Yinreng was his heir, unless . . .

"You think the emperor changed his mind," Matt said. "That he's going to name Quejing as heir, not you?"

Jia's heart began to pound. Surely the emperor wouldn't name *her* as his heir!

"It's preposterous," Yinreng said. "A woman cannot rule

China. But yesterday, before the emperor went missing, I heard him ask one of his advisers to bring him the box."

"And?" Matt said. "Did you open it?"

"I can't," Yinreng said. "It is in the possession of Father's advisers. Only they can open it, but I've asked them to wait."

"Wait for what?" Jia said.

"I want to make certain assurances first. You've made the emperor believe you're truly his daughter, somehow traveled back to him from the future."

"I *am* his daughter," Jia said. "You know I am."

"Maybe," Yinreng said, "but I couldn't help but wonder, what would happen if the young Quejing were to tragically die? What would happen to you?"

Jia's blood ran cold. She felt Matt grip her arm.

"You can't do that," Matt said.

"Can't I?" Yinreng said. "No one would miss her. No one cares about her."

Jia began to quake. This was true. With the death of her mother she had largely been forgotten, and there was no one in the Forbidden City who truly cared for her. No one who loved her. She needed to run. She needed to find her younger self, tell her to flee. But the instant she took a step, Yinreng made a signal and the guards standing on either side of them suddenly seized both Matt and her, yanking them apart.

"Bring me Princess Quejing, the *younger* one," Yinreng told one of the guards. "She's usually skulking around in the carpenter's quarters or the blacksmith."

The guard bowed to Yinreng and left.

"Jia!" Matt called. "Stop! Let me go!" He fought with the guards, his face wild with rage. One of the guards hit him across the face. Still, he fought. He twisted and kicked and pulled.

Jia could see him starting to shake, to flicker.

"Matt!" she called as she was dragged away. "You have to get to me, to my younger self! You're supposed to take me to the *Vermillion*! You have to travel, Matt! Don't fight it! Let yourself go! Fall apart!"

"Jia!" Matt shouted, but she was dragged away until she couldn't see or hear him anymore.

She was locked inside a dark room with nothing but cold stone walls. She didn't cry or scream. She knew those things would not help her. But what could? What could she do? Nothing, she realized. All she could do was wait and see. Either Matt would succeed—he would find her and save her life—or Yinreng would kill her.

Jia slid against the stone wall and sat on the floor. What had happened to her father? Where had he gone?

She was not sure how long she waited, if it was minutes or hours. She lost sense of time.

Her legs began to tingle. At first she thought it was just the sensation of her limbs falling asleep from being in her cramped position, but no matter how she moved, the tingling continued and intensified. It moved all the way up her body, to her arms and fingertips, even to her head. She felt like she was being pricked all over by a million needles. Was she dying? Disappearing? Had Yinreng killed her younger self? Was this the end of it all?

She started to have trouble breathing, and then she was hyperventilating. She felt like all the air was being sucked out of the room. She must be dying now. She rocked back and forth on the floor.

This was it. Matt had failed, and Yinreng had killed her younger self. Her existence was about to end. *It's all right, it's okay*, she told herself. Maybe this was the way it had to be in order to get Matt to do what needed to be done, to fix the lock, to save his family and the world. Like her father said, sacrifices needed to be made.

24

Falling Apart

"Jia!" Matt screamed. "Stop! Let me go!" He wrestled against the guards holding him. One of them struck him across the face, but the pain barely registered. He kept fighting. All he cared about was Jia. He couldn't lose her. She was all he had now, but she was being dragged away, and he couldn't get to her.

"Matt!" she called. She was trying to tell him something, but he couldn't hear above all the noise of the guards and his own spitting rage. "You have to get to me . . . don't fight it . . . fall apart!"

"Jia!" Matt screamed, but she was dragged out of sight, and he couldn't hear her anymore. He jerked his body, tried to kick one of the guards. They both yanked his arms so hard he was certain they dislocated both of his shoulders.

Matt began to tremble, his limbs twitching and jerking. Spots formed in the corners of his eyes. He was having a seizure. His head was suddenly filled with a strange buzzing.

He was about to black out, but then he remembered what Jia had said.

What if your seizures aren't really seizures? What if you could learn to control it?

He remembered the epiphany he had, when he and Jia had been playing chess. This wasn't a forward-thinking game. It was forward and backward and sideways. He needed to go in all directions. He couldn't fight the seizure. He had to give into it. He had to let himself fall apart.

Matt released himself. His thoughts moved faster than light speed, a million miles a minute, and it wasn't just his brain that was thinking. It was *all* of him. Every cell, every atom, was coming alive, realizing its own individual energy and power, yet still connected to the whole.

"What's happening?" one of the guards said. "What is he doing?"

His hands felt tingly, like they were falling asleep. He held them up to his face. They were blurry. He focused on them and his fingers dissolved, disappeared, and then slowly came back together. Matt felt the connection in his brain. He could feel those individual cells separate, yet still communicate with each other. It didn't hurt. It sort of tickled, and it took a great deal of concentration just to make his hands disappear, but once he did that the rest seemed to naturally come together, or apart, rather.

"Hold him!" Yinreng commanded.

"I can't!" the guard said. "He's . . . he's *melting!*"

Matt dissolved right through the hands of the guards, slipping from their grip like fine sand.

"Where did he go?" said a voice. It sounded like it was coming through a tunnel. He could see the person, too, though it was like looking through a giant kaleidoscope, thousands of the same image in changing patterns, so it took him a moment to recognize who he was seeing. It was Yinreng. He was turning all around, looking like a boy lost in outer space.

"He just disappeared!" one of the guards said. "He turned to dust!"

Matt was dust. He was nothing, and yet he still existed. He was still alive and himself. He felt all his cells spread out around the room. It was a strange feeling, like swimming with a giant school of fish. Separate, but together. Wild and free, and yet instinctually ordered.

Time, too, was different. It felt different, and in this state he could see his own time tapestry spread out before him like an intricate web. There were holes in it, missing threads, but he found he could travel along as though being pulled in a current.

He saw flashes of things, bits of memories of his life, though much of it was blurred. He couldn't see the people clearly. They were more shadow, intangible. There were two in particular that seemed to follow Matt wherever he went, and he knew these were the shadows of those whose time tapestries he had. They were with him throughout his child-hood, when he first boarded the *Vermillion*, when he went to Paris and stole the *Mona Lisa*. They were with him in India at the Padmanabhaswamy Temple, and in England when he met Queen Elizabeth. There were moments where he breezed through and others where he lingered, like when he was stranded on a barren island in the middle of the ocean. Matt couldn't remember why he had come to this island, but those two blurred shadows were with him, like phantoms, and they huddled on the beach together, shivering all night. He felt the panic rising in himself, the hopelessness, almost as if he were experiencing it again in this very moment. He was afraid. He didn't know what to do, even though he could see very clearly what he needed to do. He had the Aeternum right with him, the stone tied into his bracelet. Didn't he know how it worked? Maybe in his panic he'd forgotten. Maybe he just needed to be reminded. He had a vague memory of being helped, of someone or something pointing him in the right direction, but no one came and nothing happened. He saw himself spi-raling, losing hope. And then he remembered that it was his future self who had helped him at this time, and now it was time to make that come to pass, to finish the loop.

He lowered himself to the island, pulled together the cells of his arm, and wrote a message for himself in the sand.

You know how to call the compass, Mateo.

He wondered if he was breaking the rules. Maybe a

little, but what was the benefit of being a time traveler if you couldn't help yourself out a little every now and then? Not too much though. A little was the key. There needed to be a balance. It was all about balance, because somewhere along the line the balance had been disrupted. The pillars of the universe had been broken. He could see it quite clearly now, like he was viewing the whole universe through a giant telescope. He could see how disordered it was, jerked out of alignment.

But he couldn't fix that now. He still didn't know how for one, and there was something else he needed to do. Someone besides himself that he needed to help.

Jia.

He pulled himself back into his time tapestry and went back to where he had been in the Hall of Supreme Harmony.

"Don't worry about him," Yinreng said. "Find Quejing. She's the real enemy. We cannot let her get away."

But Matt knew they wouldn't find her, because she was already gone by this point in time. Jia had told him he'd come and taken her away very shortly after they'd arrived. He hadn't understood this when she told him, but now he saw it all laid out in his mind's eye like a choreographed dance. He saw many things now that he hadn't before. In this state, he sensed everything in a totally different way. Before he had been a mouse on the ground with no sight or sense of direction. Now he was an eagle in the sky with an aerial view of the world. Past, present, and future were spread out before him, not in a single line, but an intricate web, a sphere. He traveled along the threads to different events and points in time quite easily. His compass had merely been a mechanism to do what his brain could do much faster and easier.

He traveled back in time, to the day he'd first arrived in China. Still in his disassembled state, he followed Jia inside the Hall of Supreme Harmony where with quaking knees she met with her father and Yinreng. He was tempted to take Jia away then, save her here and now from Yinreng's evil plot. But he knew that was not what was supposed to happen. The Jia he needed to save was hidden behind one of the tapestries. He could just see a small piece of her face poking out. He floated toward her and waited until the hall was cleared. He pulled himself back together. It was easier than he would have thought, like his cells all knew their proper place and order and came together simply by thinking about it. Within a minute he was standing in full physical form before the young Jia. She was so small, no more than six or seven, about Pike's age, he thought. Her hair was shorter, and her eyes did not hold the brightness that always greeted him. The tunic she wore, though made of fine silk befitting a child of the emperor, was dirty and ragged. She looked thin. He wondered how long she had been hiding from Yinreng in these tunnels. He could well believe she was actually an orphan.

Jia was alarmed by Matt's presence, at first. She held tight to her little hammer, and for a moment Matt thought she might hit him with it, but her fear seemed to dissipate when he spoke her name, not her given name, but the pet name her mother had called her.

"*Nǐ hǎo*, Jia."

She lowered her hammer. "Who are you?" she asked.

"A friend."

It was not hard to convince her to come with him. Jia had told him that she felt she knew Matt from the beginning, that she foremembered him, and that she believed he would take her to her mother. All he had to do was tell her he would take her away from the Forbidden City and she practically jumped in his arms.

He was uncertain how he would travel with her, but he found it was not a problem, that when he disassembled himself he could take her with him, in a similar way that Blossom or the *Vermillion* could take all passengers wherever and whenever they went. He was the vehicle now. He traveled back a day, as the emperor had said that was when Captain Vincent had come to visit him. He floated around the Forbidden City, invisible, holding on to Jia, until he spotted the *Vermillion* sitting in the moat surrounding the gates of the city. It, like Blossom, had turned into a junk, but the sail bore the flag with the compass and *V* at the center.

Matt landed on the deck of the *Vermillion*. He pulled himself together, and at the same time Jia formed as well. She teetered a little as her feet touched ground. She looked at her hands and wiggled her fingers, then looked around.

"Where are we?" Jia asked.

Matt knelt down next to her. "You will be going on a long journey."

"With you?"

Matt shook his head. "Not now. I will come later. But I won't remember you then. And you will have to pretend you don't know me either. Do you know how to pretend?"

Jia smiled and nodded. "It's my favorite game."

"Then this will be the best game of pretend ever. You will be an orphan. You have lived in an orphanage your entire life. No one was kind to you, but you like to build and fix things."

"I *do* like to build and fix things! See?" She held out her little hammer.

Matt smiled. "Good. Some things you will not have to pretend." He held out the amulet the older Jia had given to him mere minutes ago. Her eyes grew wide at the sight of it. "Do you know what this is?"

Jia nodded. "That's the emperor's. He only gives them to important people."

"You are very important, Jia." Matt pressed the amulet into her tiny hand. "Keep it safe. You'll need it when you return home."

Jia nodded solemnly, clutching the amulet in her fist.

Footsteps sounded from behind. Matt stood and turned to be faced with Captain Vincent, Brocco, and Wiley. "What are you doing on my ship?" Captain Vincent had his sword drawn. Brocco put his hands on his guns, and Wiley clutched the books he was carrying in front of his chest as though they might protect him from attack. They all looked a little younger than Matt remembered. Matt had to recalibrate his brain a bit, thinking of what had happened to this point and what hadn't, what Vincent knew and what he didn't. This was years before Mateo first boarded the *Vermillion*, even before he was born, but after his mother had left, of course, because Vincent had the Obsidian Compass now. It was hanging at his chest on the gold chain. Something twitched inside the captain's jacket. A white rat poked its head out, sniffed, then scurried onto the captain's shoulder. Upon seeing Matt he hissed, bearing long yellow teeth.

"A pleasure to see you, too, Santiago."

Captain Vincent seemed startled by Matt's familiarity with his pet rat. He studied him a little more closely and a look of recognition settled. "You . . . ," he said. "I've seen you before. You snuck onto the *Vermillion*."

That was right. The captain had seen him only once before, when Matt accidentally came on board the *Vermillion*, just after he'd first built the Obsidian Compass.

"That's interesting," Matt said. "I've seen you many times before."

"Who are you?" the captain asked.

"A friend from the future," he said.

Captain Vincent looked skeptical. He glanced at Jia. "And the girl? Who is she?"

Matt bid Jia to come forward. She did so hesitantly, looking between the three men. "This is Jia. I want you to take her on board as one of your crew. She will help you."

"Help me how?"

"In your quest for the Aeternum."

Captain Vincent lowered his sword and raised an eyebrow. "How do I know you're not trying to trick me, that you're not just planting a spy on my ship?"

"You don't. It's entirely possible she is a spy. You can discard her if you want, but you won't get the Aeternum without her. I promise you that."

The captain stroked his short beard, calculating. In one swift movement, he stepped forward and pointed his sword directly at Matt's neck. "Who are you, truly? What is your name? Don't play games with me, boy."

Matt could feel the point of the sword right at his throat, but he wasn't afraid. In fact, he was rather amused. He smiled at the captain. "Sometimes I am called Mateo Hudson. Other times I'm called Marius Quine."

Captain Vincent looked stunned. "Mateo," he breathed. "Marius Quine . . ."

"It will be up to you which name I claim forever." And even as he said this, he knew it was true. His identity was at a crossroads. It could go either way. He had felt that in his time tapestry. His life was not as concrete as some, but whatever was done with the Aeternum would seal his fate forever.

Matt dissolved himself.

Captain Vincent dropped his sword.

"Crikey!" Brocco shouted. All three men staggered back, searching all around them. Matt hovered just above their heads, invisible.

"What just happened?" Wiley said. "Where did he go?"

"Is he a ghost?" Brocco said. "Are we being haunted?"

"Perhaps," Captain Vincent said. "A ghost from the future." He picked up his sword, put it in his scabbard. He then looked down at Jia as though he'd nearly forgotten all about her. "And what am I to do with you?"

Jia just stared back up at him.

"Perhaps we should leave her, Captain," Brocco said. "I don't think we should trust a ghost. What if she is a spy?"

"Mighty small spy, don't you think?" Wiley said. "How much trouble can one little girl be?"

The captain stroked his jaw, still gazing down at Jia. "We'll take her with us," he said. "For now. We can always discard her if she doesn't prove useful, if she does indeed turn out to be a spy. Come along." He held out his hand to Jia. "You'll have to learn English."

"I'll teach her!" Wiley said. "I'll teach her to speak and read, just like you taught me."

"Very good," Captain Vincent said. "Prepare for travel."

Matt waited, invisible, until the captain had turned the dials, and the *Vermillion* disappeared with Jia on board.

She was safe. For now, anyway. He still needed to save the older Jia. That would perhaps not be as easy as saving the younger Jia had been. He had no blueprint for that. He didn't know how it was supposed to happen, or if it would.

He felt his way back along his time tapestry to when he and Jia had faced Yinreng. He took himself to just the point after he'd disassembled and left to go save the young Jia. Now he followed the older. The guards pulled her down a corridor and locked her in a cell, then stood guard outside the room. Matt slipped right through the door. The cell was pitch black. He couldn't see Jia, but he could hear her breathing. She sounded like she was having a panic attack. He swirled around the room until he felt her form huddled on the ground.

Footsteps sounded from outside the door, and voices grew louder. One of the voices sounded angry.

"Open the door at once," said the angry, commanding voice.

There was the sound of clanking keys.

There was no time to explain to Jia now. He did not want her to face Yinreng again. He was certain he would kill her, and Matt knew if that happened, he would not be able to bring her back.

The door clicked. Just as it opened, Matt dissolved himself and Jia with him.

25

Alfred Nobel

1874
Stockholm, Sweden

Matt and Jia landed in the middle of a cobblestoned road. He pulled himself together right in front of a horse. The horse whinnied and reared up on its hide legs, and Matt knew he was about to be trampled by its hooves when Jia smartly yanked him out of the way and they rolled to the side of the road. The driver shouted something at them and cracked his whip and moved on.

"*Nǐ hǎo*, Jia," he said.

"Matt? Oh, Matt!" She attacked him with a hug so tight, Matt could hardly breathe, but he didn't mind. In fact, he kind of wished she would never let him go.

"I was so frightened!" Jia cried. "How did you do that? How did you get me out of there?" And then she gasped, releasing him. "You figured it out. You learned how to make yourself fall apart?"

Matt nodded. "Yes." He held up his hand and made it dissolve and reappear.

Jia gasped again, covering her mouth. "And did you save me? The younger me, I mean."

Matt nodded. "You're safe on the *Vermillion*," Matt said. "And we're far from China now. Yinreng can't hurt you."

Jia smiled at him. He smiled back. He almost thought she was going to kiss him. Or was he supposed to kiss her? This seemed like one of those moments, but he didn't know what to do.

A car sped past, spraying mud all over them.

"Ack!" Matt wiped the mud off his face. He glared at the yellow sports car racing down the road, swerving around the horse and carriage that had nearly trampled him.

A car . . .

Matt looked around. There were cars in the streets, both old and modern, even models that looked like they'd come from his future. There were carriages and bikes, too, but the cars weren't the only thing that seemed out of place. There were clashing fashions and buildings and languages. Across the street, a man was selling hot dogs from a cart. Matt could smell it from here and it reminded him of New York City and Mets games and . . . and something else, a memory he couldn't quite reach though it tickled at the corners of his brain.

In the distance Matt could see a building he knew very well. The Empire State Building stood like a glass and metal behemoth amongst the smaller structures.

"Where are we?" Jia asked.

"Sweden," Matt said. "Or I thought so anyway. I came here so we could visit Alfred Nobel." Now he wondered if he would even be here.

"I guess this place has suffered time rifts too," Jia said.

"I guess."

A boy was selling newspapers. Matt hailed him and glanced at a paper. He couldn't read any of it, but he noted the date. It was July 20, 1874.

"Is that date significant for some reason?"

"Not specifically. I wanted to come some years after Nobel had invented dynamite, so we could ask him what he did for Captain Vincent."

"That makes sense. Maybe the boy will know where he is."

Matt asked the newsboy, as well as he could, about Mr. Alfred Nobel. The boy just stared back at Matt, then held out his hand.

"I think he wants some money for his information," Jia said.

"I don't have any. Do you?"

Jia rifled through her pockets and found a small bronze coin that looked ancient. The boy studied it with suspicion but must have decided it was worth something. He placed the coin in his pocket and pointed in the direction of the Empire State Building. He said something Matt couldn't understand, but he thanked him and he and Jia struck off in the direction the boy had indicated. They had to ask a few more people along the way where he could find Mr. Nobel. Everyone pointed in the same general direction until Matt finally realized they were all pointing to a mansion on the hill, just behind the Empire State Building. It was a grand and imposing brick house with many windows and three chimneys.

The hill was much higher and steeper than it looked from the base. By the time they reached the top, they were both breathing hard. They took a few minutes to catch their breath and then they both stepped up to the door.

"I guess we just knock?" Jia said.

"I guess."

He knocked three times, and a minute later the door swung open and a man peered out.

It was Alfred Nobel. Matt recognized him from his picture. He was pale with light blue eyes that were somewhat bloodshot and a scraggly beard that needed trimming. He looked careworn and disheveled. "Ja?" he said, along with another question in Swedish that Matt was guessing was something along the lines of "Can I help you?" or "What do you want?" Matt did not speak or understand Swedish. He would, at some point, he was pretty sure, but he knew that

Alfred Nobel spoke perfect English.

"Mr. Nobel," Matt said. "I'm sorry to disturb you, but we've come to you for help. You once worked for a man named Captain Vincent. He—"

But Matt did not get to finish his sentence. At the mention of Captain Vincent, Alfred Nobel slammed the door.

Matt and Jia looked at each other. "Now what?"

"We can't just leave," Jia said. This time she knocked on the door. "Mr. Nobel? Please! We need your help!"

"Go away. I want nothing to do with whatever it is you are trying to accomplish."

"Please, Mr. Nobel!"

Nobel did not answer. The door remained closed.

"Maybe we should disassemble ourselves and break in?" Matt said.

Jia shook her head. "I don't think that will build trust with him, and we need him to trust us."

"Maybe we need to go back further," Matt suggested. "Maybe before Captain Vincent came to Nobel?"

"What good will that do?" Jia said. "You'd only be able to warn Nobel of Captain Vincent's arrival, and I'm not sure how helpful that will be."

Jia was right. He needed to understand what Nobel had done for Captain Vincent in order to figure out how to fix it.

Matt sat down on the doorstep and Jia sat next to him. The sun was lowering in the sky, and the Empire State Building looked like it was on fire. They'd been sitting there for ten minutes or so when a young girl came up the path, her arms loaded with packages. Matt squinted at her. She was pale with white-blond hair. Her head was down so Matt couldn't fully see her face, but as she neared them on the path she looked up at Matt and Jia with ghostly blue eyes, very familiar. She smiled at them and waved.

"Pike!" Jia shouted. She jumped up, but at that very moment the door flew open and Nobel stepped out with a rolled-up newspaper.

"Get away!" he shouted, swatting them both with the newspaper. "Don't you talk to my niece!"

"Ouch! Your niece?" Matt said, trying to shield himself from the newspaper baton. "Pike is your niece?"

Pike rushed toward them. She jabbered something in Swedish and all three of them froze. Matt couldn't have been more surprised if he had seen a fish speak French. Pike was speaking to Nobel. She sounded excited and passionate and she was pointing at Matt and Jia. Nobel spoke back to Pike, looking warily at Matt and Jia. From his tone, Matt guessed that he was telling Pike that he and Jia were dangerous and not to be trusted, but Pike was adamant. She stomped her foot then blew past both Matt, Jia, and Nobel and went inside.

Nobel sighed, then cast a dark look at Matt and Jia. "Come on, then," he said in a bit of a growl. "My niece insists."

* * *

Alfred Nobel's house was modest but comfortable. There was a sitting room to the right and to the left a dining room. Before them looked to be the kitchen area. Matt saw no signs of a laboratory, or anything remotely related to chemistry. In fact, most of the house had been turned into a giant library. Everywhere there were books, books lining the walls, piled on the floor and stacked on tables. It reminded him of Wiley's library on the *Vermillion*, all the books stacked into towers and buildings from around the world. He remembered how he'd gone to visit him to find some information, and how kind and helpful Wiley had been to him. There had been others with him then, he thought, but he couldn't remember who.

Pike was unraveling the packages she had been carrying. Matt was not at all surprised to see that it was all yarn. Looking around the house now, he saw evidence of a lot of knitting. Baskets of yarn and knitting needles, blankets and sweaters and socks and hats.

Matt was still marveling at Pike's presence here, the fact that she was Alfred Nobel's niece. Now he understood why Pike had been so fascinated with that book. She'd seen Alfred Nobel's picture and recognized him as her uncle. That was why she had leaped over to the *Vermillion*. It wasn't because of Captain Vincent or any sense of loyalty to him. It was because of her uncle. What he didn't understand is how she got on the *Vermillion* in the first place and what, exactly, was her purpose in being there.

"Marta says you are friends to her," Nobel said, still looking at them with distrust.

"Her name is Marta?" Jia asked.

"You don't know her name?"

Matt and Jia both shook their heads. "We always called her Pike," Jia said. "It's a nickname one of the crew on the *Vermillion* gave her. I've never heard her talk before."

Nobel grunted. "Well, she understands English perfectly, and a good deal of German and French as well, but Marta is a stubborn girl and will not speak anything but Swedish."

Pike—or Marta—spoke something in a tone that Matt felt was somewhat cheeky. "What did she say?"

"She said Swedish is the tongue of her mama and papa and she will never speak another."

That explained it, then. As far as Matt could remember, they'd never traveled to Sweden while on the *Vermillion* and none of them spoke Swedish.

"Come and sit," Mr. Nobel said, motioning to a chair in the sitting room.

Matt sat in the chair. A photograph of a young man sat on the table next to him. He looked much like Alfred Nobel, though younger and clean-shaven. Matt was guessing this was his brother, Emil, the one who had died in the explosion in his laboratory.

"You have a lot of books," Jia said.

"Literature was my first love," Nobel said. "I wanted to be a writer, a poet, but my father thought it was impractical. And he was right, in many ways. It is impractical, but the desire is irresistible, to link words into rhythmical phrases that carry powerful meanings and ideas . . ." He brushed his hand over a book sitting beside him.

"Science and chemistry have poetry, too, I suppose. The combination of the earth's elements in various ways has its virtues and beauties, to make possible what was once thought impossible."

Matt understood that feeling. Everything that had happened to him he had once thought impossible. Some of it had been good. He never would have met Jia if he hadn't built the Obsidian Compass, but he also knew terrible things had happened. Great losses, even though he couldn't remember exactly what those losses were. He pulled out the bits of fabric from his pockets. They were more like a jumble of threads now, and they were faded, but even so, they still had an otherworldly quality to them, a faint glow.

Nobel leaned in and Matt heard his breath catch. "Time tapestries," he said.

"You've seen this before?"

"Yes, though I have never been able to touch or access it myself. Captain Vincent was the only one who seemed to be able to touch it, manipulate it."

"And you were hired to help him destroy it," Matt said.

A shadow fell over Nobel's face. "I didn't want to," he said. "But he gave me no choice. His power. The things he could do . . ." He glanced at the photo sitting next to Matt and unmistakable pain slashed through his stoic features.

"Is that your brother?" Jia asked.

Nobel nodded. "Emil, Marta's father."

"He died in an explosion," Jia said. "We read about it."

Nobel stiffened slightly. His already pale face became white as a sheet. "You did, did you? Well, that was only his first death. I'm guessing the book didn't tell you about his second."

"His *second* death?" Matt and Jia spoke at once.

Nobel glanced at Marta, who was now busily knitting with her new yarn, her little hands flying with the needles in a smooth, speedy rhythm. "I had better start from the beginning, if there is a beginning," Nobel said. He removed some books from the chair across from Matt and Jia and sat down.

"Many years ago," Nobel began, "when I was a young and hopeful chemist, I had a dream to create the most powerful explosive the world had ever seen, fifty times more powerful than gunpowder. I had been experimenting with nitroglycerin for years. Most people thought it was too dangerous, that it couldn't be compounded and stabilized for safe production and use. I could see it had potential, and so despite warnings and criticisms I forged ahead. Emil was always by my side assisting with the work. We succeeded beyond anyone's expectations. I invented dynamite, and the railway and mining companies were in awe when we showed them the tests. And then one day, the lab exploded." He paused. His eyes went glassy. "I blamed myself. I wasn't there. If I had been there, I believed it never would have happened. I would have taken the proper precautions. Emil was intelligent and a hard worker, but he and my lab assistant were sometimes careless. The nitroglycerin had to be kept under a certain temperature. I was always careful to keep it well below, but something must have happened. Our burners must have overheated, gotten too close to our nitroglycerin stores. I don't know. There was an investigation and the explosion was officially reported as an accident, but still I came under great censure. Everyone blamed the accident on me. I had tampered with things that should not have been touched. One French paper even called me 'the merchant of death.' I was horrified. I fell into a deep depression. I moved to Paris to try to get away from it all. I vowed I would never touch explosives again, but the heaviness of Emil's death stayed with me. I had no peace. No rest. And then *he* showed up."

"Captain Vincent, you mean?" Matt asked.

Nobel nodded. "I'll admit, I felt wary of him from the beginning. Perhaps it was the shoes. Ridiculous shoes, something a clown in a circus would wear. But he told me he could bring back Emil, that he could make it so the explosion never happened at all. I thought he was a lunatic, but he showed me the most incredible things, impossible things. He took me on board his ship. He took me to the future. He showed me how he could manipulate time and space. I thought to myself that this man was either an angel from heaven or the devil himself, but I didn't much care who or what he was so long as he could save Emil. I begged him to do it, and he said he would but only if I would help him. I said I would do anything. That's when he showed me the time tapestries. I'd never seen anything like it. He pulled them out of people and sometimes animals. I could not understand its chemical makeup. It wasn't solid, exactly, but neither was it liquid nor gas. It was something out of this world. The captain had the power to manipulate the fabric, to cut and rearrange and change certain things, but he wanted to find a way to destroy the fabric entirely. He wanted me to find a chemical that would effectively erase the time tapestries forever. He told me my dynamite had come closer than anything else, but it was still not quite right. Some semblance of the tapestry still remained. He wanted me to find a way to get rid of all of it."

"And you agreed to do this," Matt said.

"How could I refuse?" Nobel said. "He said he could save Emil. He said he could bring him back and make everything right, but only if I helped him, only if I succeeded with destroying the time tapestries. He's my brother. How could I refuse? How could I?"

Matt didn't blame him. There were some people you would

do anything to save. Anything to bring back. Matt thought of his grandparents and Uncle Chuck. His mom. There were others, he was pretty sure, but he couldn't remember them. He couldn't see their faces.

"But how did you do it?" Jia asked. "How did you destroy the time tapestries?"

Nobel shook his head. "I don't know."

"But the explosive worked," Matt said. "We saw you on the *Vermillion* with it, and then Captain Vincent changed things, erased people."

"He took away Matt's family," Jia said.

"I know," Nobel said. "I know I must have done it somehow, but I don't remember *how* I did it. I don't know if Captain Vincent changed my own memories so I wouldn't remember. Maybe he knew you two would come looking for me. Maybe he didn't want me to be able to tell everything that happened, but then why would he allow me to remember anything at all? I do not know. I was not in the best shape after Emil's death. Captain Vincent insisted I come on board the *Vermillion* with him, that I conduct my experiments there, so he could track my progress and offer any resources I might need. It seemed like one day Captain Vincent just showed up and the explosive finally worked as he wanted. But I honestly don't remember what I did differently. I've looked over all my notes. I checked all my chemicals and ingredients, but I can't see that I changed anything from the time Emil and I worked together, and then before I knew what was happening, Emil was back, just as the captain promised. The accident never happened at all. It was like it had all just been a nightmare. Little did I know that the real nightmare was just beginning."

"What do you mean? What happened?" Matt asked.

Nobel scoffed. "What do you think? Things started to change all over the place. Buildings and people from other times and places. As you can see, Sweden is no longer Sweden, and I have heard reports that other places have suffered similarly. And Emil . . ." Nobel's face darkened. Matt saw him put his hands into fists. "Well, let's just say bringing Emil back was not a gift. It was almost worse than having him dead. He was different. I'm sorry to say he returned a little more like me, unhappy and stubborn. He was not the brother I knew. It was as though he knew he wasn't supposed to be there. When he understood what I had done, what was happening with the world and the role I had in it, he was angry with me. He said I'd tampered with things that should not have been tampered with. I tried to make him understand, but he refused to hear me, refused to have anything to do with me or my business. He left, fled to Paris. I never saw or spoke to him again. I sent him letters, but he never responded, and then a year later I learned that he had died of cholera. His wife as well. This time I did not ask Captain Vincent for his help."

Nobel grew silent and seemed to retreat into a dark space in his mind.

After a few awkward moments of silence, Marta spoke, still focused on her knitting. Nobel gave a ghost of a smile.

"What did she say?" Jia asked.

"She says I am forgetting the happy ending when she was brought to me."

"Wait," Matt said. "Pike—or Marta—was born *after* Emil was brought back?"

Nobel nodded. "Yes. I did not know of her existence until after he died. The second time."

Matt and Jia shared a look. He was sure she was thinking the same thing as him. If Captain Vincent had never brought back Emil, changed the past, Marta would never have been born, and if Matt, by some miracle, was able to fix the lock and bring back the people Captain Vincent had erased, what would happen to her? Would she cease to exist? Would she continue living?

Marta looked at Matt with her ghostly eyes, like she knew just what he was thinking. She didn't stop her knitting.

"She is a strange little thing," Nobel said. "I've always thought she had an otherworldliness to her, like a sprite or an elf. She's always disappearing and reappearing, as though she's slipping between realms. I sometimes think she, too, does not belong here, and that she knows it."

Matt remembered he'd had that same feeling about Pike

when he'd first met her. He'd always thought she was a bit spooky, partly because of how pale she was and partly because she never talked, but now, thinking about her origins, Matt wondered if there was something else about her that made her different. Her existence was brought about by a change in the space-time continuum. That had to make you different.

And then there was her seeming obsession with tying knots, knitting and weaving. He used to think that was just some kind of compulsion, a tic she couldn't help, but now he wondered if there was more to it than that.

"Marta," Jia asked. "How did you come on board the *Vermillion*? Who brought you there?"

Marta spoke, and Nobel translated. "She says you brought her there," Nobel said, nodding to Matt, "that you transported her there from the jungle city."

"Me?" Matt said and at the same time Jia said, "What jungle city?"

"She says a place with three circles, the place where you were born, where everything begins and ends."

Matt felt chills run down him. She had to be speaking of Ciudad Perdida, the Lost City of Colombia. That was the place he'd been found and adopted, though he couldn't remember *who* had adopted him. Captain Vincent? And Captain Bonnaire? It seemed right but also wrong.

"You were there?" Matt asked. "What happened?"

Marta shrugged and spoke.

"She says she doesn't remember," Nobel translated. "It's all a blur to her now. Maybe Captain Vincent altered her memories too."

"Did Captain Vincent understand why you were on board the *Vermillion*?" Jia asked.

"She says no. He suspected her presence at first. He threatened to discard her, but after she unlocked your safe and brought him the box with the letter, he trusted her fully."

"Why did you do that?" Matt asked.

"Because you told her to."

Matt's mind was racing to put together all the pieces, what his future self was thinking, what his goal was. *Who* was he? He looked down at the frayed and fading bits of time tapestry.

"Do you know who they belong to?" Nobel asked.

Matt shook his head. "I can't remember. I only know that they were important to me, but even that feeling is starting to fade." He couldn't remember who they were, couldn't remember their names or picture what they looked like, but he felt the pain of the loss as though he'd lost both his arms. He felt the phantom twitches of their presence. But he knew time was running out. If he didn't find them soon, he feared they'd be gone forever. He would forget.

Forget. Was there a sadder word in any language? If there was, he couldn't remember it.

"You truly don't know what you did to make the dynamite work the way it did?" Matt asked.

Nobel shook his head. "Nothing that I can think of. I suppose it's possible Captain Vincent erased my own memories for this very purpose, so I would not have the ability to tell you."

"Possibly," Matt said. His mind began to whirl.

"What are you thinking?" Jia said.

Matt shifted in his chair. "Nothing, really. Except I wonder if someone else could have done something to the dynamite? Changed it somehow, to make it work the way the captain wanted? Or at least *appear* to work."

"You mean he hired someone else besides Nobel?" Jia asked.

"No," Matt said. "I'm thinking maybe someone could have changed it without Nobel or Captain Vincent knowing. Someone from the outside."

"They would have had to be extremely sneaky," Nobel said. "The dynamite was never out of my sight."

Yes, Matt thought to himself. They would have to be pretty much invisible.

He glanced at Jia. She was frowning at him like she knew he was cooking up some harebrained idea. And he was. He was cooking up what was possibly his most harebrained idea yet.

"Your brother, Emil," Matt said. "When did he die, exactly?"

"September 3, 1864," Nobel said.

"And you boarded the Vermillion how long after?"

"I can't say precisely. A few months, perhaps."

Matt nodded. He could work with estimates. It was dark now. Through the window, Matt could see the twinkling lights of the jumbled city. Matt thanked Mr. Nobel and said that he and Jia should be on their way, but Marta wouldn't hear of it. She insisted that they stay the night and would not accept no for an answer.

Matt looked to Jia. She was bleary-eyed. Her entire body sagged. She looked like she could fall asleep standing up.

With all that had happened, Matt knew he should be exhausted, too, but he wasn't. Every cell in his body seemed to be alert and energized, ready for action. He knew he wouldn't be able to rest. There was too much to do.

Nobel fixed them a meal of potatoes and sausages and greens. Matt didn't realize how hungry he was until he started eating, and then it was like he couldn't stop. Disassembling himself took a lot of energy, apparently.

They didn't talk very much as they ate, though Marta looked at Matt with such a piercing gaze, he had a feeling she knew exactly what he was about to do. It was possible, he realized, that she knew everything that was about to happen even more than he did.

After dinner, Nobel showed Matt and Jia to a room where they could sleep. Jia yawned and flopped down on the bed, her eyes drooping. She fell asleep within seconds.

Matt immediately prepared to leave. He hated to leave Jia behind. He knew she would be furious with him, but this was a mission only he could perform, and he had to do it now, before it was too late.

He turned, ready to dissolve himself, but came face-to-face with Marta. She was standing in the doorway, staring at him with her ghostly eyes. Matt put a finger to his lips. She mimicked him, and then he disappeared.

26

Self-Destruct

He traveled back to September 3, 1864, the day Emil Nobel died in the explosion. As Matt suspected, it had been no accident. Brocco had set their stores of nitroglycerin on fire, causing it to heat above the temperature required for stability.

Nobel, brooding over his brother's death, moved to Paris, and a few months later, Captain Vincent appeared with his promises to save Emil. Nobel boarded the *Vermillion* and commenced his work for Captain Vincent. Matt, traveling through the time tapestry, watched him try different chemical combinations, different materials.

Every day, Captain Vincent ran his experiments. He experimented on people who they picked up at different times, and sometimes animals, whatever Brocco and Wiley were willing to bring on board—mice and rats, dogs, cats, and chickens. They, too, had time tapestries. It seemed all living things did. Matt could tell that Santiago, Captain Vincent's pet rat, did not like this one bit, especially when they experimented on the rats. Captain Vincent didn't seem to care about the feelings of the rat. Only the time tapestries. He wanted to destroy them completely, but at the end of each experiment, no matter how he burned, sliced, or shredded the time tapestries, some semblance of it still remained. The creature might disappear from sight, but they could also reappear at random, which was not at all what the captain wanted. He wanted complete erasure. Total nonexistence. This, Matt realized, was what Captain Vincent had done to the two people whose time tapestry remains he held. Somehow, he'd managed to erase them. Or so it seemed. But what if it wasn't what it seemed? What if there were other forces at play?

At night, while Nobel and the rest of the ship slept, Matt, still invisible in his disassembled state, slipped into the cabin where Nobel slept with all the stores of dynamite. He moved around the dynamite, spilling his cells over and around it. What he was about to do would either be the most brilliant thing he'd ever done, or the most idiotic.

Here goes nothing, he thought to himself.

Matt poured himself into the piles of dynamite, infusing his separated cells into all the nitroglycerin. It felt cold and hot at the same time. It was disorienting at first. His cells went a bit berserk, like eggs thrown on a hot frying pan. They seemed to sizzle and pop, and he did feel like maybe he was burning, but he didn't die. At least he didn't think he did. He remained aware and himself. And here he waited.

The next morning, Captain Vincent requested more experiments. Nobel wearily brought his crate of dynamite to the deck of the ship. Matt moved with it. His senses were a bit dulled. He couldn't see much in this state, his cells all separated amongst the several sticks of dynamite, but he could tell that Brocco brought the captain a black top hat and inside was some furry white creature. "Thought we could make the rabbit disappear inside the hat! You know, like a magician?"

A rabbit. They were going to experiment on the rabbit.

"No need for theatrics, Brocco," Captain Vincent said. "This isn't a magic show."

"Seems like a magic show to me," Wiley said, puffing on his pipe. Matt couldn't see the pipe, but the sweet scent of the smoke seeped into his cells inside the dynamite.

Captain Vincent pulled the time tapestry from the rabbit. He wrapped a stick of dynamite inside the time tapestry.

"Light her up," Captain Vincent said.

Nobel struck a match and lit the wick. When it caught and started to burn, Matt's cells immediately contracted, like he was recoiling from imminent pain.

"Back up!" Nobel called. They all quickly backed away from the rabbit, its time tapestry, and the dynamite.

When the dynamite went off, Matt exploded with it.

27

Don't Let Go

Being blown up from inside of dynamite felt like shooting off in a rocket, or more like a trillion rockets all shooting off in different directions. It was hot, disorienting, and completely wild. Yet, Matt was still connected, still part of the whole. He could still feel the rest of his cells pulsing in the other sticks of dynamite.

He was connected to the rabbit, too, or its time tapestry. When the dynamite had blown up the tapestry, Matt's cells attached to its unraveling threads, clinging to them like drops of water on a spider's web. When he moved his cells through the air, the threads moved with him. He could feel the essence of the rabbit, its existence, its feelings and desires, almost as if he *were* the rabbit. He pulled all the threads into himself, taking the white rabbit's existence right along with him.

From above, still invisible, Matt looked down at the rest of the *Vermillion*. They were all fragmented in his mind's eye, but he could see that the rabbit had disappeared. The black top hat was empty.

"Crikey!" Brocco said, staring into the hat. "It all disappeared this time, Captain! Just like magic!" He popped the hat onto his head and grinned, his diamond tooth sparkling in the morning light.

The captain was very pleased. "Well done, Mr. Nobel," he said.

Nobel was scratching his head, clearly confused.

"If it works on the Hudsons," Captain Vincent said, "you will have your brother back, as promised."

The Hudsons . . . the name sparked something in Matt, a small thread of memory. He couldn't quite reach it.

The *Vermillion* traveled, and Matt went with it. Most of him traveled inside the dynamite, though part of him followed along outside, carrying the unraveled threads of the rabbit's time tapestry. The travel was chaotic. They seemed to be bouncing throughout time, chasing something or someone. Matt didn't have much sense for time or place. Captain Vincent used more of the dynamite, and whenever he did, Matt's cells exploded with it and attached themselves to the unraveling time tapestries.

He was swimming in a sea of glowing threads now, the remnants of those Captain Vincent had unraveled. He did not know who they were, and he was not sure he could take them all with him. He could feel his cells were tiring out. But as he swept through the threads he felt a pull, like some of the threads had a magnetic energy attracted to his own. They wrapped around him, wove themselves into him. He recognized their energy. It was the same as those scraps of time tapestry he'd been carrying. Perhaps they recognized the remnants of themselves.

Matt pulled on those threads. He gathered every last strand, wrapped them in and around himself like a cocoon. It all felt so warm and safe, familiar. By the time he'd gathered it all, he was exhausted. He knew there were more threads, but he couldn't get it all now. What energy he had left he needed to pull himself back together. Otherwise he feared he might be stuck in his disassembled state forever. So he would have to leave some of the other threads behind, and that meant he needed to leave part of himself behind. He would have to come back to it later.

He traveled back to Sweden, to Jia, and Mr. Nobel, and Marta. Marta must have known what he was going to do, because she seemed to be waiting for him when he returned. She was standing in the middle of the room, looking up toward where he was hovering in his invisible state.

Matt slowly pulled himself together. It was difficult, so much harder than it had been before. It felt like all his cells were moving through a thick gel. He wasn't sure he'd be able to come back together without letting go of all the threads he'd carried with him.

Don't let go!

He didn't let go. He could feel inside these threads the existence of people he needed, people he loved. He clung to them and pulled. It felt like wading neck-deep through a thick swamp, then climbing a sheer cliff. Every cell was trembling with the effort. He was grasping a narrow ledge of the cliff by his fingertips. He felt himself slipping, the threads falling away.

Don't let go!

He found his grip again. He mustered every last quark of energy in every last cell he possessed. He pulled, and pulled, and pulled. Slowly, slowly his cells went back into their proper order, and as they did, those threads he'd clung to so fiercely began to pull through and separate from him, coiling in glossy strands on the floor. Marta instantly grabbed them and began to weave with impossible speed. It was as though she'd been practicing for this very moment. Her tiny hands flew, tying knots and loops with the iridescent threads. As she worked, Matt felt things changing, like threads were being woven together inside of himself, holes he didn't even know existed being filled.

As Marta wove, Matt continued to pull himself together, but still he held tight. To what, he wasn't sure. Something important, or someone. He just knew he wasn't supposed to let go.

When he was all back together again, he fell to the floor in a heap, gasping for breath. He felt like he'd nearly drowned. He was disoriented. He was trembling all over. He wasn't even sure where he was.

"Matt?" He looked up to see Jia, sleepy-eyed, peering down at him from her bed. "What happened? Are you—" And then she gasped and covered her mouth.

Matt looked down at himself. He was still a bit blurry, like he hadn't been able to pull all of himself together. Except his hands. His hands were solid and in sharp focus, and they were firmly grasping on to something. Or someone. Two someones.

Matt looked to his right and to his left. He closed his eyes and opened them again to make sure what he was seeing wasn't a hallucination or a dream. Lying on either side of him, grasping tight to each of Matt's hands, was a boy and a girl.

It all came back to him in an instant, like a tsunami of memories crashing over his brain. Memories of scavenger hunts and picnics in Central Park, birthday parties, baseball games, and trips to museums. Running down Fifth Avenue after school, the smell of hot dogs and gyros and garbage and exhaust. Memories of arguments and shouting and games and laughter. And love. There was overwhelming love threaded through every single memory. All this spread through him like wildfire, burning up any fears or doubts. He was not lost. He was not alone. He had a brother and sister, and they were here.

"Corey? Ruby?"

Corey flopped over and groaned. He sat up and shook his head, so dust flew off his shaggy hair. "What just happened? It felt like I was melting or something."

"We're still here," Ruby said, holding up her free hand in front of her face. Matt hadn't let go of her other hand. "We're still here. I'm not dead. Or am I? Are we dead?" She wiggled her fingers, then felt her face.

"You're not dead," Matt breathed, still staring at his brother and sister, not quite believing any of his senses. But they were back. Real, solid, alive Corey and Ruby. "You're not dead!" he shouted. His heart swelled nearly to bursting. He felt lighter than air. He was trembling so much, he thought he might fall apart again, but he needed to hold himself together so he could attack Corey and Ruby with a hug. And he did. He wrapped his arms around both of them and knocked them back down to the floor. He hugged them as tight as he could. They were so real. He was never going to let go. If he could, he would weld all three of them together and they'd stay like that forever.

"Oof! Matt, get off of me!" Ruby said.

"Dude, what is your deal?" Corey said. "And why do you smell like fireworks?"

"It's dynamite," Matt said. "I blew myself up!"

"Huh— What now?"

"Matt, I can't breathe!" Ruby cried.

Matt still didn't want to let go, but he had to reason that suffocating his brother and sister would be counterproductive to his goals. He released them, and Corey shoved him away. He fell back against the bed where Jia was still gaping at the impossible scene before her. She rubbed at her sleepy eyes and blinked a few times.

"Corey? Ruby? Is that really you?" Jia stumbled out of bed.

"It's us," Ruby said. "But I'm not sure what just happened."

"Matt's gone crazy, that's what just happened." Corey rubbed at his shoulder where Brocco had shot him. Matt must have aggravated the wound with his hug attack. He only felt a little bit bad about it.

"Where are we anyway?" Ruby asked, looking around. "This isn't our apartment. And this isn't New York, is it?" She was looking out the window. "Oh, but maybe it is. Is that the Empire State Building? Where's Mom and Dad and everyone else?"

"They're not here right now," Matt said.

"What did you do?" Corey said in a growling voice. Matt winced, his joy dissipating ever so slightly at the anger on his brother's face, the bewilderment on Ruby's. Matt recalled the moments before Corey and Ruby had disappeared. They'd been fighting. They'd just found out Marius Quine and Matt were the same person and believed he was on Vincent's side. There had been such confusion and anger. Corey had attacked Matt, and then everything had happened so quickly.

It appeared no time had passed for Corey and Ruby since that moment, and Matt had to rewind his brain to meet them where they were at.

"I know everything is confusing right now," Matt said. "And I know I owe you some explanations."

"More than some," Corey said.

"Where did Pike come from?" Ruby said. "Last time we saw her she had gone with Captain Vincent on the *Vermillion*."

"And what is she doing?" Corey asked. "What's that stuff she's playing with?"

Marta was standing in the corner of the room. She was still weaving together more of the time tapestry threads that Matt had carried with him from the dynamite explosions. A shadow began to form, faint and blurred at first, and then slowly it grew sharper and more defined, something small. A minute later a white rabbit appeared. It looked to be the same one that Captain Vincent had first experimented on with the dynamite.

Marta squealed with delight. She swooped the rabbit up in her arms. "*Kanin!*" she said, which Matt assumed was Swedish for rabbit.

Corey and Ruby both stared in amazement.

"Wait, Pike *talks*?" Corey asked.

"Only Swedish," Jia said. "Her real name is Marta Nobel."

"*Nobel?*" Ruby said. "As in . . ."

Ruby stopped talking as creaking footsteps sounded from outside their door. A moment later the door flew open. It was Mr. Nobel. He was wearing an old-fashioned nightgown and a cap. Definitely not twenty-first-century pajamas.

"What is all this noise you are making? I am trying to sleep!" Nobel stopped short, seeing that there were two new strangers in his home.

"Dude," Corey said. "It's Ebenezer Scrooge!"

"*Kanin!*" Marta said again, holding up the rabbit and beaming at her uncle.

Mr. Nobel went red in the face. "Would someone care to explain what the devil is going on?"

"I'd like to know the same thing," Jia said, folding her arms and giving Matt a steely look that made him flinch.

"Me too," Ruby said. She rested a hand on the hilt of her sword as though she thought she might need to fight.

"Me three," Corey said. "Time to spill your guts, *Marius Quine.*"

28

Hinges

Everyone started asking questions, and they pelted Matt like a hailstorm.

"What are we doing here?"

"Where's Mom and Dad? And Gaga and Haha and Uncle Chuck?"

"Where did you go? How did you get Corey and Ruby back?"

"*Kanin!*"

"Why does my niece have a rabbit?"

"Matt, why are you so *blurry*?"

Matt could hardly process what anyone was saying. He was too excited. He was still trembling, bouncing on the balls of his feet. Corey and Ruby were back. *Corey and Ruby were back!* The fog that had hovered over his mind for however long had cleared.

"Matt, are you listening to us?" Corey asked. "*What is going on?*"

Matt put up his hands. "I'll tell you everything, I promise. Just please be patient."

Corey grumbled and muttered something under his breath. Matt was sure it was something about how he hated being patient. Ruby lightly slapped his arm. "We can be patient."

"Yeah," Corey said. "But make it quick."

Matt grinned. Just that small interaction gave him a fresh wave of affection for his brother and sister. He wanted to hug them to the floor all over again. But he resisted. Corey, Ruby, Jia, and Mr. Nobel all looked at him expectantly. Marta, too, had settled herself on the bed with the rabbit, like she was ready for story time.

Matt told everyone what had happened. It wasn't quick, but no one interrupted or complained. Even Corey listened quietly as Matt described how their dad and Corey and Ruby had disappeared during the time rift in New York, and how their mom reverted back to her younger self with no memories of her husband or children. Jia helped fill in parts of the story too. Corey and Ruby were both shocked to learn that she was really the daughter of an emperor. Jia told most of what had happened to them in China, including what they had learned there about the forbidden lock, the Summer

Triangle, and how the emperor believed that Matt, Corey, and Ruby were supposed to fix it somehow.

Matt told them how Gaga, Haha, and Uncle Chuck had mysteriously disappeared in China, and then how Albert had stolen the compass and he and Belamie had abandoned them. This resulted in an outburst of rather crude insults from Corey until he saw the look on Alfred Nobel's face, and he cowered a bit.

He told them about Yinreng's threats, how Matt had figured out how to disassemble himself, and how he had rescued the younger Jia, placing her with Captain Vincent in order to save her life and also help them.

"Wait," Corey said. "So you can do the disappearing trick?"

"Is that why you're sort of blurry?" Ruby said.

"Prove it!" Corey said. "Do it right now!"

Matt was so exhausted, he didn't think he had the strength to fully disassemble and pull himself back together, but he held up his hand and made it disappear.

Corey laughed like a little kid seeing a magic trick. "Whaaaat! You're like a comic superhero!" Then his face suddenly fell. He knit his brow and frowned at Matt. "Or villain. Still not sure."

"He's not a villain, Corey," Ruby said. "He's our brother, and he saved us from nonexistence, remember?"

"Maybe," Corey said. "But remember how he's also Marius Quine, possibly related to Captain Vincent Quine? And from all we've seen they seem to be on the same side. And he still hasn't told us *how* he rescued us. Maybe it was a fluke and he's just playing it off like he saved us. Mom and Dad still aren't here, you know, and Gaga and Haha and Uncle Chuck. Where are they now?"

Everyone looked back to Matt. "I think Mom is with Vincent right now," he said. "She doesn't understand what's going on. She doesn't remember us or Dad. And Dad's still hanging in some kind of limbo. I think I can bring him back, but he might not remember us either. As for Gaga and Haha and Uncle Chuck, I'm not entirely sure. I saw them disappearing, but it wasn't the same as when you two disappeared. It seemed different for some reason. More like . . . how I disassemble myself." He was trying to think why that might be . . .

"How did you bring us back?" Ruby asked.

"Yes, I would like to know this," Mr. Nobel said. "What happened to the dynamite? Did you see why it worked differently?"

"I did," Matt said. "I put myself inside the dynamite."

"You *what*?" Jia screeched.

"What do you mean you put yourself inside the dynamite?" Ruby asked.

"Yeah," Corey said, "not sure how that fits."

Matt explained as best he could what he had done and what had happened. How he'd put himself in the dynamite, and then when Captain Vincent blew up the tapestries, his own cells attached to them.

"I could feel you two the strongest," Matt said, "I think because I had those pieces of your time tapestry. It was like you clung to me, and I couldn't let go. There's still more. Other people, I mean, but I didn't have enough energy to gather them too. That's why I'm fuzzy, I think. Part of me is still with them, or still inside the dynamite." Even as he said these words, he could feel that small portion of him far away, like his very being was split between realms.

"Wow," Ruby said.

"Yeah," Corey said. "Wow."

Jia seemed to be lost for words. He could tell she was battling between being impressed with him for what he'd done, but also upset with him for leaving without telling her.

"Incredible," Mr. Nobel said. "And Marta, she helped?"

They all turned to Marta. Both she and the rabbit were now asleep on the bed.

"I couldn't have done it without her," Matt said. "Somehow she knew exactly what to do, how to weave the time tapestries back together so Corey and Ruby could come back."

"I always thought she was maybe a ghost," Corey said.

Matt nodded. "Maybe she sort of is. Not a ghost, exactly, but not really part of this world."

Nobel frowned at his sleeping niece. "I'm afraid she won't be in this world much longer," he said, his voice a bit raspy.

"What do you mean?" Jia asked.

Nobel didn't seem to be able to speak.

"She was born to Emil after he was brought back to life by Captain Vincent," Matt said gently. "If he hadn't done that, she never would have been born, and if we are somehow able to fix the lock . . . I don't know what that will mean for Marta."

Jia's eyes widened as she understood what he meant. She shook her head, eyes gleaming.

Mr. Nobel went to the sleeping Marta and gently picked her up in his arms, the rabbit too. He carried her out of the room, leaving Matt, Ruby, Corey, and Jia in tired silence.

"We can't just let her . . . die, can we?" Ruby said in a small voice.

"It's not exactly death, is it?" Corey said. "I mean, technically she wasn't even supposed to be born."

"Is anyone *technically* supposed to be born?" Jia said. "Does Marta have less right to live just because she was born in a different reality than ours?"

"No, that's not what I'm saying," Corey said, "I just . . . sheesh, this is complicated. It's like math. I hate math."

Yes, it was complicated, but Jia was right. Marta had just as much right to live as any of them, and yet Matt didn't know how to solve for that. It was just one more riddle to add to the steadily growing pile.

"I think she maybe has a role to play in fixing the lock," Matt said. "All her weaving and knot tying, the way she helped bring you two back, I think she'll be able to help us fix the rest, somehow."

"How are we supposed to fix the forbidden lock, anyway?" Ruby asked. "We don't even know where it is or what it looks like, do we?"

"We don't know much," Matt agreed. "But I think it's very likely that it's in Colombia, or that the place has something to do with it, anyway."

"Why Colombia?" Corey said.

"Obviously because that's where Matt was born, duh," Ruby said.

"And it would make sense that his birth would have something to do with the forbidden lock," Jia said. "Everything seems to be connected to Matt. Your family, time travel, the compass, all that has happened, begins and ends with Matt's birth."

"Not my birth," Matt said. "My adoption."

"What do you mean?" Ruby asked.

"In our reality Mom and Dad were the ones to adopt me, but that could change, theoretically, couldn't it? With the Aeternum, Captain Vincent could make it so *he's* the one to adopt me, make me his child instead. And then I really will become Marius Quine and you two won't exist at all."

Corey let out a long sigh. "To think this world could exist without *me*. It would just be so dark and . . . boring."

"This isn't a joke, Corey," Ruby said.

"I'm not joking! I'm, like, essential to the earth's well-being."

Ruby rolled her eyes.

"You're essential to me," Matt said. "You both are. I don't want to be Marius Quine. I don't want you two to go away. I don't want any other family. I want *our* family. I want Mom and Dad and Gaga and Haha and Uncle Chuck."

"Maybe you don't have a choice," Corey said. "Maybe it's not up to you. Our fates are out of our hands."

Matt felt an ache begin in his chest. The thought of being torn from his family, of truly not knowing or remembering them . . . it really would be a world of darkness.

"What if it is your choice?" Jia said.

"What do you mean?" Matt asked.

Jia had a pensive look on her face. "I'm not sure. I'm just thinking about the things my father said about you three being the key to repairing the forbidden lock. What if it's up to you three what happens? Maybe it's simpler than you think."

Corey snorted. "None of this is simple."

"The problems are not simple, but that doesn't mean the solutions can't be. Think of it in terms of mechanics. This door, for example." Jia stood and went to the bedroom door. She swung it open and closed and open again. "Look. A large, heavy slab of wood. If it were just that it would be very difficult to open it, but it's the small hinges that make it work so easily. Small mechanisms can have huge effects. Matt, you of all people should know this."

He did. So many things that seemed big and overwhelming originated from the smallest thing. Even his ability to atomically disassemble himself came from such a small space in his brain. You just had to know where it was and how to activate it, make it light up.

"Maybe you need to think of yourselves as the hinges in all the larger stuff that's happening," Jia said. "Don't over-think it."

Easier said than done, Matt thought. He could barely think at all right now. Blowing himself up and bringing Corey and Ruby back into existence was just a tad tiring. Corey and Ruby looked exhausted as well. But Matt didn't think there was any way they could sleep now. He feared that if he closed his eyes he would wake and Corey and Ruby would be gone again, and he'd forget them completely. And their parents . . . his dad was still hovering in a state of nonexistence, and their mom was in the clutches of Captain Vincent, totally unaware of what he'd done to her and her family. And there was Gaga and Haha and Uncle Chuck. And beyond that, beyond his own family, there were all the time rifts throughout the world, the destruction of cities and entire civilizations, families separated, and people displaced in space and time. Matt knew the fate of the world was at stake, and if they didn't fix the lock soon, get those pillars of the universe back into place, everything would fall apart. There was not time to rest. They had to push on.

"So what now?" Ruby asked. "Do we go to Colombia, try to head off Captain Vincent?"

"Soon," Matt said. "First we need to gather our troops."

He didn't think he'd be able to get his parents back quite yet, but there was still Gaga and Haha and Uncle Chuck. Matt had a feeling he knew where they had gone and how to get them back.

Nobel helped them prepare to leave, gathering whatever food he could for their journey. In less than an hour, they were all outside, ready for departure. Or nearly. Corey and Ruby were standing on the edge of the yard, noting the odd mixture of buildings and vehicles in what was supposed to be nineteenth-century Stockholm. It was nearly dawn now. There was a purplish glow on the horizon. It looked to Matt as though more buildings had disappeared in the night, and others had appeared.

Jia and Marta were crouched in the garden, feeding handfuls of clover to the rabbit. Matt stood in silence with Nobel, watching the two girls who had become something like sisters. He was trying to work up the courage to ask Mr. Nobel for something he was certain he would not want to give.

"Do you know what you will do once you reach Colombia?" Nobel asked Matt.

Matt shook his head. "Not really. Search for the forbidden lock. And myself, I guess."

Nobel gave a wry smile. "Ah, the eternal quest. I've been searching for myself my entire life, and yet the more I search, the more lost I become."

Matt nodded in agreement. "It's like a riddle, isn't it? I feel like a riddle that I don't know how to solve."

Nobel seemed startled by this for some reason. He opened his mouth, but before he could say anything, Marta dashed right past them, chasing after the rabbit.

Matt took a breath. "Mr. Nobel, I need to ask you for something."

"You need my niece to go with you," Nobel said, still watching Marta wistfully.

Now it was Matt who was startled. "How did you know?"

"Marta told me she would be going with you," Nobel said, "and I have never been able to stop her from doing her own will. She seems to know she has a mission to perform."

"You could come with us, too," Matt said. "So you can stay with her . . . as long as possible."

"No," Nobel said resolutely. "I've always known Marta would walk paths I could not follow. This is her fate. And I must live with my own as the merchant of death." He spoke these words with a bitter sadness that made Matt feel very sorry for him.

"I'm probably not supposed to tell you a whole lot about

your future," Matt said, "and who knows if your life will even fully turn out the way I've read about it in the history books, but for what it's worth, I don't think you're the merchant of death. You're a great scientist, and there are still great things you can do. Things that will help people and the world. Even after you're gone, you can leave a great legacy that people will celebrate for centuries."

Nobel brightened just a little at these words, or at least some of the bitterness seemed to soften. "Thank you. I will think on that."

"Hey," Corey called from across the yard. "Are we leaving or what? I think I just saw an entire house disappear. We might want to get on that whole saving-the-world mission sooner or later. Sooner's probably better."

"Coming," Matt said.

"I have something to show you before you go," Nobel said. He went inside his house and returned in less than a minute carrying a small leather notebook. He flipped through the pages until he found what he was looking for.

"I started writing this ages ago," Nobel said, "when I still had dreams of being a poet like Lord Byron. I never finished it. I'd almost forgotten about it, but something you just said sparked my memory. I wrote it in English. I wasn't sure why at the time. That's just how the words came to me. Well, you read it." He shoved the notebook at Matt.

Matt took it, not quite understanding, until he saw the

title of the poem written at the top of the page in a sprawling cursive.

A Riddle
You say I am a riddle—it may be
For all of us are riddles unexplained.
Begun in pain, in deeper torture ended,
This breathing clay what business has it here?
Some petty wants to chain us to the Earth,
Some lofty thoughts to lift us to the spheres,
And cheat us with that semblance of a soul
To dream of Immortality, till Time
O'er empty visions draw the closing veil,
And a new life begins . . .

"This poem seemed to flow through me," Nobel said, "almost as if it was coming from another sphere, another time. And maybe it did. Maybe we were always meant to meet and solve the unsolvable riddles, both within ourselves and the world."

A riddle . . . the closing veil . . . a new life. Matt didn't understand everything in the poem, but it sparked something in him. It rang true. He remembered how Quine had told him that, above all, poetry must speak truth.

"Thank you for showing this to me." Matt handed the notebook back to Nobel.

"Safe travels, Mateo." They shook hands.

Alfred Nobel went to Marta. She had caught the rabbit and now held it captive in her lap. Nobel knelt down in the grass and spoke softly to his niece in Swedish. Marta handed her uncle the white rabbit like a parting gift, then hugged him tightly around the neck.

Matt, Corey, Ruby, Jia, and Marta all gathered together.

"Ready?" Matt said.

"Let's do this," Corey said. Ruby and Jia both nodded, while Marta simply looked expectantly up at Matt.

"Everybody hold on to me."

They all crowded in and grasped Matt's hands and arms and shoulders, intertwining themselves. He started to dissolve himself, then slowly moved that same energy through everyone else. It was a chain reaction, a domino effect. Once he had the process started, he could keep it moving to anyone physically connected to him.

"Whoa," Corey said. "This feels super weird."

Ruby squirmed a little. "It tickles! I feel like I'm turning to sand!"

"It's okay," Matt said. "Just hold on. I won't let go."

Matt dissolved himself and everyone with him.

Alfred Nobel stood in his yard for a long time, gently stroking the rabbit while staring at the place where his niece had disappeared. Finally, he released the rabbit in the yard and went inside.

29

Gathering the Troops

It wasn't easy, carrying four extra people in a disassembled state. It was like swimming with heavy clothes on plus a backpack full of books. But Matt knew things were only going to get heavier. His load was only going to increase. So he held tight and pushed on.

He traveled to China on the day that he had first arrived in the Forbidden City. He found Blossom sitting in the moat around the walls of the city. Matt pulled himself together, releasing the others as he did. Corey, Ruby, Jia, and Marta all took shape as they spilled from Matt's grasp, like water taking the shape of its container.

"Whoa," Corey said as soon as he was fully formed. "That was so weird."

Ruby shook her hands and stomped her feet. "Gah! I feel like my whole body is asleep!"

Jia stretched her fingers and shook her head. Only Marta

seemed unfazed by the journey.

"I'm going to go get Gaga, Haha, and Uncle Chuck," Matt said. "You three wait here."

"Shouldn't we come with you?" Jia asked.

"No. It will be easier if I'm by myself. I promise it will be fine. I'll be back in no time at all."

Matt dissolved himself again. He traveled to the moment just before he and Jia returned to the house from their time with the emperor at his observatory. He entered the house and saw Belamie and Albert sitting together, whispering. Matt knew they were conspiring to get the compass from him, but he couldn't worry about that right now. His mission was only to get Gaga and Haha and Uncle Chuck. He knew now that it hadn't been Captain Vincent who made them disappear. Matt had done it. It hadn't made sense to him at the time, but it did now. He could see the bigger picture. He had fit together more pieces of the puzzle.

Gaga was sitting in a chair, drinking tea. Haha and Uncle Chuck were playing chess. He gave a silent apology for the scare he was about to give them.

Matt spread his cells between his grandparents and uncle and began the process of atomically disassembling them all. He could feel he was low on energy. It would take him longer this time, and then he worried, even when he got them all disassembled, would he be able to pull them all back together?

Gaga noticed first. "My face is tingling," she said, patting at her cheeks. "I think that treatment they gave me is irritating my skin."

"Funny," Haha said. "My face is tingling too." He rubbed at his jaw.

"My foot's asleep," Uncle Chuck said as he tapped his foot.

Haha turned and looked at Gaga. "Gloria!" He stood and knocked over the chess table.

"Oh, Henry!" Gaga cried. "Your face is melting!"

Belamie and Albert rushed over. "What's happening?" Belamie asked.

"Help!" Haha cried, holding up his fading hand. "I'm disappearing!"

"Albert, hold on to them!" Belamie grabbed Gaga and Haha while Albert grasped on to Uncle Chuck's fading leg. He crashed into a table, knocked over a porcelain pitcher, and the rush of movement further drained Matt's energy. He didn't know how he was going to be able to finish this.

And then Matt came in. The past Matt. Present-Matt could feel his presence. It gave him an odd boost of energy, like his past cells were recharging his present cells.

"No!" past-Matt shouted while the invisible Matt started to work more quickly.

"Oh!" Gaga said. "I feel so strange!" Matt disassembled all of Gaga and went on to Haha.

"I guess this is really it this time," Haha said.

"Uncle Chuck!" past-Matt called. "Don't go!"

"It's okay, Matty," Uncle Chuck said calmly. "I'm just going to the next adventure. You gotta stay and finish this one." He dissolved and disappeared.

Matt watched his past self clutch at his head and start to shake. He saw the flickering, like a lightbulb, just like Jia said. He felt a bit sorry for himself but also knew this was necessary. He had to hit rock bottom before he could fully fall apart.

Matt carried his grandparents and uncle with him back to Blossom. He touched down and released them from his hold. Their cells spilled onto the floor and reformed. All three of them gasped and fell to their hands and knees.

"Whoa," Corey said as Matt appeared next to him. "That really was no time at all. You were gone for, like, less than a minute."

"What just happened?" Haha said, getting to his feet.

"Did we die?" Gaga asked.

"Matty, is that you?" Uncle Chuck said.

"Oh, Mateo!" Gaga said. "How did you get here? I thought you and Jia were having some secret meeting with the emperor?"

"We did," Jia said.

"Fast meeting," Haha said. "Did you learn any secrets?"

"A few," Matt said.

"I feel like I'm missing something," Uncle Chuck said. "What am I missing?"

"Who are all these children?" Gaga said, looking at Corey and Ruby and Marta. And then her eyes widened. Matt could see the fog lifting from her memory as she took in Corey and Ruby.

Gaga gasped and covered her mouth. "Oh . . . oh!" She swept Corey and Ruby into a hug. "Corey! Ruby! You're okay! You're here!" She grabbed each of them by the face, kissed their cheeks, and crushed them with more hugs.

"Urgh!" Corey grunted. "Not so tight, Gaga!"

"I'm sorry," Gaga said, releasing the twins. "But how . . ."

"Matt brought us back," Ruby said.

"By blowing himself up," Corey said.

"What?" the three grown-ups said at once.

Matt did not have the energy to explain one more thing to anyone. Luckily, Corey was eager to tell the tale. He made a few embellishments that made the whole thing sound like a comic book adventure, but Matt didn't mind. It wasn't far off the mark.

"Is that why you're so blurry?" Uncle Chuck asked. "Parts of you are still in outer space or something?"

Matt shrugged. "More or less."

"Well, that's a relief. I thought my eyesight might be going."

"So what are we doing now?" Haha asked. "Have you figured out how to beat that maniac yet?"

"Almost," Matt said.

"We need to go to Colombia," Ruby said. "We need to find

Matt as a baby and keep Vincent from adopting him, because if he does, he'll make him his own son."

"And then we'll really be in deep doo-doo," Corey said.

"We won't *be* at all, actually," Ruby said.

"So . . . we're going to fight?" Haha said, looking a little uneasy. Uncle Chuck and Gaga did too.

"You don't have to come with us," Matt said. "I can take you someplace safe, and you can wait until it's all over."

"And let you children go off on your own to fight Captain Vincent?" Gaga said. "Are you kidding? That maniac messed with my family. I'm not going to hide when I've got the chance to mess with him. Right, Henry?"

Haha smiled at his wife with glowing admiration. He took her hand. "Right, Gloria. I'll fight with you and for you, all the way to the end."

Gaga blushed a little, but she patted Haha's hand in appreciation.

"Me too," Uncle Chuck said resolutely. "Nobody messes with the Hudsons and gets away with it. It's time to take this maniac down."

Matt felt an overwhelming love for all his family right now, but at the same time, a pang of sadness that they weren't all here. His parents . . . he needed them. He didn't care what state they were in, if they remembered them or not. They needed to be together.

"We need to get Dad back," Matt said. "I think Mom needs

to see him, to remember, or foremember, at least. I think that's important."

Ruby nodded. "We can help her remember too. If all of us are together, she'll have to feel it somehow."

"Yeah," Corey said. "It's, like, destiny."

But Matt still wasn't sure. Captain Vincent had the Aeternum. The lock was broken, and Matt still did not know how to fix it, where it was, or even what it looked like. But they had to move forward. He had to believe that answers would reveal themselves along the way.

"All right, bro," Corey said, "Let's get out of here. Work your magic."

"It's not magic," Matt said. "It's science, cellular manipulation."

"Tomato-potato," Corey said. "Just do it."

Matt dissolved himself.

"So freaking cool," Corey said.

Matt spread his cells throughout Blossom, breaking it all down, pulling it all into himself and into the web of space and time. Somehow it was easier to carry an entire vehicle full of people than it was to carry a bunch of individual people, just like with the compass. It was like mass-time-travel transit. He was the driver, the captain, and they were on their way to war. He just needed to pick up one last passenger before they reached their final destination.

As they traveled through the web, he felt for those other

cells still hovering in that state between existence and non-existence, clinging to those other threads. He connected the rest of his cells to them, pulling them along for the ride. It didn't feel as hard this time. Maybe because he was getting better at it, or maybe having the rest of the family with him somehow helped, like the collective energy of all their cells was somehow helping him gather and hold on. This time Matt didn't have to wait to weave the threads together. Marta was ready. Even though he couldn't see her, he could feel her weaving those threads, pulling them back into existence as they traveled.

30

The Undoing of Santiago

1880
Neuschwanstein Castle, Bavaria, Germany

Santiago was hiding in a chest, gnawing on a bag of peanut butter–filled pretzels. He was getting dangerously close to the end. Soon he would have to venture out to find something else to eat. He dreaded it. He did not want to cross paths with *her*. That woman, the one Captain Vincent had obsessed over for the past twenty years.

The Hudsons were no more. The captain had unraveled the father and thereby the two children, leaving only the mother and the boy Mateo (who wasn't really Mateo). Captain Vincent said they would soon forget the life they'd had. They'd forget that they'd ever been Hudsons or had any other life. Everything would be as it always should have been. For the captain, anyway. Santiago wasn't so sure about himself.

The Hudson woman hadn't appeared to them right away.

Captain Vincent started to worry. Santiago could feel it. Perhaps they'd made a mistake. Perhaps they'd done things wrong and erased the woman too. But then she appeared, quite out of nowhere, with Albert in tow. Albert, of all people! He had been the one to bring her back to them. Apparently she had gotten stuck somewhere in China. It was all very confusing, but the captain didn't seem to care so much about all that. His Bonbon was back! There was such happiness and celebration! The captain embraced his Bonbon and she embraced him, and Santiago was feeling all the happy feelings between them until the Hudson woman laid eyes on him sitting on the captain's shoulder. She screamed so high and loud it pierced his ears and vibrated through all his fur.

"There's a rat on you!" she screamed. Before Santiago knew what was happening, she shoved him off the captain's shoulder. He fell to the floor, feet up. The woman looked down at him with pure disgust.

"Oh, poor Santiago," the captain said, though he made no move to help him.

"Don't tell me you have a *name* for that creature."

"Don't be cross, Bonbon. He really is an intelligent fellow. Very helpful. He cleans, you know."

"I don't care if he's a ballerina. I'll have no rats on *my* ship!"

"Of course not, Bonbon, whatever you wish." And unbelievably the captain kicked Santiago out of the room. Actually *kicked* him with the toe of his ugly red shoes!

Santiago rolled and landed on his feet. He turned around and hissed.

The woman pulled out a dagger and threw it at Santiago. It didn't hit him, but it shaved one side of his whiskers.

Captain's Bonbon evil! Ugly! Poop! Stink! Santiago screeched all the ugly human words he could think of.

The captain only laughed. "Off with you, Santiago. Go and find something to eat."

Santiago obeyed. Angry feelings aside, he was still the captain's most loyal companion. And so here he was, hiding in a dark chest, gorging himself on peanut butter pretzels. Only a few left.

Santiago had been banished. Replaced. The captain might as well have discarded him.

He reached the end of the peanut butter pretzels. He swished his tail back and forth, tried to stay hidden, but that bottomless pit of hunger overwhelmed him. He needed more food.

He crawled out of the chest, climbed up the wall and scurried between the rafters. He heard the voices of the captain and Bonbon.

"I don't like this crew," Bonbon said. "Only Albert will follow my orders, and even then, he defers to you. Am I no longer captain of this ship? Where is Demetria? Where's Neeti and Tui?"

Santiago could feel the captain's thoughts spinning. He'd been so focused on finding the Aeternum, destroying the Hudsons, getting back his Bonbon, he had not prepared for the questions she might have upon returning. "They were traitors," the captain lied smoothly.

Bonbon gasped. "Traitors? Impossible!"

"It's true. They mutinied against you, stole your compass, and had you discarded. But I fought for you. I discarded *them*. I found my own loyal crew, and then I found the Aeternum in order to bring you back to me."

Santiago could feel the captain was expecting gratitude from his Bonbon, for a sweeping romantic gesture and for his gallantry, but none came. "Traitors," she said again. "I don't believe it."

"We will forget them," the captain said. "We don't need anyone but us. Now come, I have a surprise for you."

"You know I don't like surprises."

"You'll like this one. I promise."

Santiago scurried away. He didn't like surprises either. But just as he got to the pantry, he heard the bell for travel. Santiago felt the walls of the *Vermillion* start to shift. He clung to one of the rafters as the Vermillion turned into a boat, sailing along a winding river between green mountains. Ahead, a castle stood high on a mountaintop, its many towers and turrets sparkling silver in the sunlight.

"Neuschwanstein Castle," Captain Vincent said, placing his arm about his Bonbon's waist.

"It looks just like a fairy tale," she said.

"And we shall live there happily ever after. As king and queen."

Bonbon smiled, but it faltered. "Doesn't this kingdom already have a king and queen?"

"No," the captain said. "We're king and queen now. All this is our kingdom."

And his word made it true. The captain claimed the castle and the kingdom within hours of their arrival. They only needed to pull a few time tapestries, shift a few things around, and the deed was done. The captain was King Vincent now, and his queen, Queen Belamie. No one questioned it, not the servants and advisers or lords or ladies or peasants.

Santiago questioned it, however. He hated the castle. The instant he entered he was attacked by a flock of swans! They came honking and flapping right at him. One even bit at his tail! He overheard Wiley say something about how the former king had loved the birds and kept them in the castle. Santiago tried to complain to the captain-now-king, tell him to banish the evil birds, or better yet, make them not exist at all, but the captain was preoccupied with his Bonbon. He didn't even seem to hear Santiago anymore.

He found the castle food stores. He gnawed through the

bags of flour and the sugar and ate and ate and ate, trying to fill that bottomless pit he knew could not be filled, all while the captain was occupied with his Bonbon who really shouldn't have been his Bonbon at all, and the kingdom that really wasn't his.

Only a week after their arrival at the palace the king and queen held a ball. Guests arrived in great swarms, dressed in their silks and furs and jewels, but it was the new queen everyone admired, dressed in a glittering gown and crown. Santiago overheard Brocco boasting to Wiley that her dress was his finest achievement. "*Finally*, we got a dress-wearing female on board the *Vermillion*. She's fabulous, isn't she?"

Wiley shrugged. "She doesn't seem too happy to be here," he said, looking at the queen as another guest bowed to her.

"Probably just the shock of everything that's happened," Brocco said. "She'll adjust."

"Maybe," Wiley said, but Santiago thought perhaps Wiley was right. The new queen didn't seem happy. She didn't smile at any of her new subjects. She pressed a hand to her head as though it ached.

There was a feast, and then there was music and dancing. Santiago stayed well-hidden, but in a place where he could see most everything and be in close proximity to the food. He feasted on a meat pie while he watched. The king smiled and laughed all night long, but the queen didn't so much. She kept

405

looking around like she was looking for someone, or maybe lost something, like a glove or a hairpin. She wandered out of the ballroom, and then Santiago noticed the king was looking for her. Santiago saw this as an opportunity to show his loyalty and usefulness, so he went to the king and pointed him in the right direction.

"Thank you, Santiago," the king said and went after the queen.

They found her wandering the castle corridors like she was lost. She had her fingers pressed to her head, her brow knit in pain. She was humming to herself, and every now and then she muttered the words of a song, something about stars.

"Bonbon, what are you doing?" the king asked. "I've been looking for you everywhere. Come back to the party."

"I was only away for a day or so, wasn't I?" she said, frowning. "But in some ways it feels longer than that. It feels like so much has happened that I can't remember."

"I told you. Much has happened," the king said. "You were lost to me. I had to go to the ends of the earth to bring you back."

"With the Aeternum," she said, glancing at the place where the glowing stone now resided in the king's chest. "You changed things?"

"Of course I did," the king said. "Wouldn't you do the same for me?"

She nodded. "Of course. Of course I would," but she

continued to frown. "My parents . . . can we save them? Bring them back?"

Santiago felt possessiveness flare up inside the king. She had been asking this every day since she'd come back, but the king was not keen on the idea. He had his own plans, and he was not eager to share his Bonbon with her parents.

But he smiled. "Of course, Bonbon," he lied. "We will save them very soon, just as we'd always planned. But first, we must attend to other things. We can't think only about those we want to save from the past. We must also think of those we must save in our future."

"The boy, the one I saw on the ship?"

"Yes, our son."

"Annie said he was my son. *He* said he was my son, but he said you weren't his father. He said he had another father."

The king stiffened. Santiago felt his self-assurance diminish ever so slightly. He raised one eyebrow. "Do you want him to have another father?"

"No, no, of course not," the queen said. "I'm just so confused . . . I feel like I have a fog in my brain." She rubbed at her head again.

"Of course, you're confused. Think of all you've been through. Listen, Bonbon, there are forces at work, evil people who are trying to break us apart. We must fight it! We must fight to stay together! Do you agree?"

The Hudson woman nodded. "How do we fight it?"

"We must go and get our son. To complete all our happiness, to lock our eternal destiny in place, we must claim him before someone else does."

"Where will we find him?"

"In Colombia. In Ciudad Perdida. Our son told me himself that we had to go and find him there. If we didn't, then all would be lost. Now come back to the party. Your subjects are waiting for their queen."

They began walking together back to the ballroom, but Santiago hissed at the king so he held back.

"What is it, Santiago?" the king said impatiently.

Bad plan. No Mateo.

"For the last time, Santiago, Mateo—*Marius Quine*—is on our side!"

Bad plan, Santiago repeated. *Mateo evil.*

"This is the only way. Making him our son is the only way to complete my eternal destiny! Without him everything falls apart!"

Mateo bad. Hudson woman bad. Discard.

He shouldn't have said that. Santiago wasn't sure if it was referring to her as "Hudson woman" or the fact that he called her bad, but it triggered something in the king. He lunged at Santiago and snatched him up by the tail. He wriggled and screeched.

Down! Santiago down! Mean king!

"Yes, perhaps I am a mean king." The king pressed a finger

to Santiago's stomach, and then he pulled that shimmering cloth from inside of him. Santiago was instantly paralyzed.

"I'm sorry it has to come to this," said the king. "You've been a faithful companion, but I won't have a *rat* getting in the way of my eternal happiness, so I'm afraid it's time for you go."

He pulled out one of those burning sticks. Santiago felt himself unraveling. His senses began to fade, and his lovely sentient thoughts. And his hunger, that bottomless pit, miraculously closed itself up. What a relief! All of him seemed to be unraveling into sweet oblivion. The only thing that remained was his hatred. He clung to it with every fiber of his being. Whatever fibers remained. He hated that Hudson. He hated Brocco and Wiley and the evil swans. He hated the whole world and everyone and everything in it.

But mostly he hated King Vincent.

31

The Final Glitch

Matt landed Blossom on a grassy terrace surrounded by lush green mountains and jungle. As he pulled himself back together, Blossom appeared in her bus form. She revved her engine and honked her horn, announcing their arrival. Everyone pulled back together.

"Oof," Ruby said as she slammed into a seat.

"So weird," Corey said, shivering a little as his body re-formed.

Everyone shook their limbs and checked to make sure they were all there. Matt looked around, counting the passengers—Corey, Ruby, Jia, Gaga, Haha, Uncle Chuck . . .

"Where's Marta?" Jia said, looking around the bus.

Matt checked the back, but she wasn't there. He knew she'd been with them through their travels. He'd felt her, and he'd felt someone else too. Another time tapestry, or maybe two even, that had been blown up by the dynamite at some point. Matt thought he'd pulled them through, but now he wondered if maybe they'd gotten lost somewhere along the journey. Had he dropped them? Were they lost in that web of time and space?

Something fell from the roof of Blossom and hit the ground. They heard an *oof* and a loud groan.

"What was that?" Gaga asked.

Corey pressed his face against the window. "Uh . . . it looked like a person just fell off the car."

And then a small pair of pale legs dangled over the windshield.

"What the beetle juice?" Uncle Chuck said.

"Marta!" Jia cried. "How did she get up there?"

Marta hopped down from Blossom and ran around the car. They could just see her little towhead bobbing up and down along the windows. She stopped on the side of the car where the other person had fallen.

Haha opened the door. There was Marta, standing before a man who was just pulling himself up off the ground, brushing himself off.

Ruby gasped. "It's Dad," she said.

"Sort of," Corey said.

Matt breathed a sigh of relief. It was their dad, though he was younger by a good twenty years, just like their mom.

That must have been when Captain Vincent blew up his time tapestry.

"Marta, what is that you have?"

Marta had her hands full of iridescent threads. "*Råtta*," she said.

"Time tapestry threads," Matt said. "She must have pulled someone else through with her." She was still weaving it together, her hands methodically tying the knots in the fabric.

"Who is it?" Ruby asked.

"I have no idea." Matt could not remember anyone else the captain might have erased, but whoever they were, they were angry. Matt could actually feel the rage buzzing around his cells that were still attached to the threads.

"Where am I?" Mr. Hudson said. "How did I get here?" He looked at his surroundings, then looked at all the people crowded in the orange bus. He squinted, then his eyes lit up with recognition and surprise.

"Mom? Is that you? And Chuck?"

Matt realized he wouldn't know Chuck as being his brother right now. Chuck seemed to realize this, too, so he just waved and said, "Hey, Matty."

But then Mr. Hudson looked at Haha, and here he had the biggest surprise of all. "Dad?"

Haha smiled. "Hey, son."

"How did you . . . where did you . . . ? I . . . I don't

understand. What just happened? What's going on? I was just in New York. I was looking for someone, and then this crazy guy attacked me. It was like he was ripping out my throat or something." He rubbed at his neck, and then another realization seemed to don on him. "Am I dead? Is this the afterlife or something?"

"You're not dead, sweetie," Gaga said gently. "But things are a little mixed up right now. It's hard to explain."

Mr. Hudson nodded. "I think I did something foolish. I think I got mixed up in something I wasn't supposed to, and I messed things up."

"Hey, it's not your fault," Haha said.

"The maniac who attacked you has hurt all of us," Uncle Chuck said.

"But we're going to make it right," Ruby said. "That's why we're here now."

Mr. Hudson looked at Ruby when she spoke, and then he glanced at Corey, then Matt, then back at Corey, who strongly resembled his father. Matt could almost see the wheels turning in his brain. Clearly, he saw something familiar about the children before him, even if he did not fully understand their connection. He turned around, surveying the view before them. "Where are we?"

"The Lost City of Colombia," Matt said.

"It's beautiful," Gaga said.

The ancient ruin was a series of green grassy terraces,

layered one on top of the other and held up on the sides by rough stone walls. They were standing on the highest terrace on one end overlooking the rest, with lush green mountains and jungle in the backdrop, all blanketed by a thick mist.

Matt had done some research on Ciudad Perdida, after his mom had told him he'd been found very near here. The Lost City of Colombia had once been a thriving civilization that existed more than a thousand years ago, even older than Machu Picchu. The people had been called the Tairona, and they'd lived peacefully until Spanish conquistadors invaded, spreading disease and killing off most of the population. Survivors abandoned the city. What was left had been overgrown by the jungle and hidden until explorers discovered it in the 1970s. Matt knew he had been found near the Lost City by some tourists around this time, but he had no other idea where or when he'd come from, or why he'd been abandoned in the jungle. Now, standing here, he had this feeling of connection, to another time and life. To a people long gone. Just a gentle echo in his heart.

"It's so still," Jia said.

It was, Matt realized, and quiet too. The trees did not move. He neither saw nor heard any signs of animal life. There were no calls of birds, no rustling of shrubs or vines. He couldn't even smell the earth. It was as if the place itself had been paused in time.

"Hey, look at this," Ruby said. She had climbed down to

the next terrace. She was standing by a flat-faced boulder propped up against one of the walls. It was about as tall as Matt and had a series of lines carved into it, with larger dots chiseled in at several intersections.

"Is this, like, an ancient game of connect the dots?" Corey said.

"Almost," Jia said. "It's a star chart."

She was right. Matt traced his fingers over the lines, the patterns. Toward the center he found three dots connected by equilateral lines. The Summer Triangle. An image suddenly flashed through his mind, unbidden—a man and woman, dressed in rough woven cloth, standing on the highest terrace of this city at night. The man was observing the stars through some kind of ancient astronomy instrument. The woman was carving lines into a huge boulder, likely the very boulder he was touching.

"Matt," Jia asked, putting a hand on his shoulder. "Are you okay?"

"Yeah," he said. "I'm okay."

He dropped his hand from the star chart, feeling a curious energy running through him. It was like he was remembering things of which he had no previous knowledge. He wasn't sure how he knew, but he did. The ancient Tairona had been astronomers. They must have noted the fading of the Summer Triangle as well, and, just like Emperor Kangxi, knew something terrible was going to happen, something that could destroy their entire civilization and the world. He could almost feel their fears inside himself, like they were channeling it down their timelines to him.

"So . . . what now?" Corey said. "Aren't we supposed to find baby Matt?"

"Doesn't look like a place to find a baby, does it?" Ruby said.

It did not. The place was empty, still and silent. Were they supposed to search for him in the jungle? What if he wasn't here yet? Or what if Captain Vincent had already taken him? No, he couldn't have. He wouldn't be standing here if he had. He wouldn't think of himself as Mateo Hudson, but Marius Quine.

A deep rumbling sounded in the distance. Matt felt a slight vibration in his feet.

"What's that?" Ruby said, looking around.

"Feels like a mild earthquake," Mr. Hudson said.

The vibrations grew stronger. Matt started to teeter. Jia grabbed on to him as she lost her balance and nearly fell.

"Or more like a big earthquake," Uncle Chuck said as he struggled to stay upright. Gaga and Haha held on to each other.

And then the earth cracked open, splitting down the center of the city. A large pole shot out of the ground, spraying dirt and rock in all directions, and then another and another. White sails unfurled on three masts. The very top of the tallest mast bore a black flag with a white compass and red *V* at the center.

"What in the world . . . ?" Mr. Hudson said.

It was the *Vermillion*. The whole ship rose out of the ground, sailing on waves of dirt, and settled on the opposite high terrace of the city. It looked like a beached whale.

"You don't see that every day, do you?" Mr. Hudson said.

"Some people do," Corey said.

A rope was thrown over the side of the ship, and one by one, the crew came down. Brocco first, then Wiley, Albert, and Captain Vincent. Last to come was Belamie Bonnaire. She was dressed in a loose white blouse, black leather pants and boots, her sword at her waist. Her long dark hair was tied back from her face. She looked fierce, ready for battle. The crew of time pirates jumped down from the terraces and walked toward the group of time castaways. As they did, dark clouds gathered above and the sky let out a low rumble.

Corey and Ruby came to either side of Matt. Ruby drew her sword. "What are we supposed to do?" she asked, her voice a bit panicked.

"I . . . I don't know," Matt said. He wasn't ready for this. He thought they'd have more time. Time to find the forbidden lock, to figure out how to fix it. "Just . . . stick together."

"Seriously?" Corey said. "That's all you got right now? *Stick together*?"

It was. He racked his brain, trying to think of any

possibilities, any escape, but every path was a dead end. They couldn't run or hide anymore. They had to face Vincent and all Matt could think was to hold on to his family, to Corey and Ruby.

"It might be enough," Jia said. "Remember, small hinges."

"We're all with you," Haha said. They pressed closer together.

Captain Vincent, Belamie, and the crew stopped about ten feet from them. Matt glanced at the compass hanging around Belamie's neck. She'd chosen it over him. She'd chosen Vincent. The memory of it sliced through him like a blade.

Matt flinched as fat raindrops splashed on his face. He looked up. The sky, which had been clear and bright just moments before, was now dark and foreboding. Matt knew they must be causing a glitch with all these out-of-sync meetings.

Captain Vincent glanced briefly over their group. He stopped at Mr. Hudson. His eyes flashed, and his jaw pulsed. He reached for his sword, but then Belamie spoke.

"You," she said, looking at Matthew Hudson with a puzzled expression. "I've seen you before."

Matthew ran a hand through his windblown hair. "Yeah. I was . . . sort of looking for you, but things got a little crazy." His eyes flickered toward Captain Vincent.

"This is the one I was telling you about, Bonbon," Vincent said. "He's the one who's trying to tear us apart, take away everything we've worked for."

"No, I didn't . . . ," Mr. Hudson started.

Belamie glanced at the others, then did a small double take when she saw Ruby, who looked like a miniature version of herself, especially with her sword in hand.

"Are you . . . ?" she started, and then trailed off.

Ruby nodded and smiled. "I'm your future daughter."

"But I'm your future *favorite* child," Corey said, "just FYI."

Ruby rolled her eyes. "He's the worst, but you *do* love him."

Belamie's mouth twitched with a smile.

Belamie looked at Matt, and her cheeks colored as though she was embarrassed or ashamed or maybe both. She reached for her compass and her gaze drew inward for a moment. She muttered some words under her breath. It was very soft. Matt had to strain to hear, but he recognized it immediately. She was singing the lullaby.

When you feel lost and all alone
Look to the sky and you'll find home

She looked back at Matt, then again at Matthew Hudson, and it was like the final piece of the puzzle clicked into place.

Matthew Hudson's mouth tugged into a half smile.

Belamie Bonnaire's eyes brightened.

Captain Vincent bared his teeth. "I suppose I'll have to fix things the old-fashioned way after all." He drew a dagger from his waist and threw it. The blade soared through the air straight toward Matthew Hudson's heart.

"No!" Belamie cried, lunging toward him, but someone else jumped in front of Matthew at the last second.

Gaga screamed. "Henry!"

Haha fell to the ground, clutching at his side. Gaga whimpered as she knelt down next to him. Matt couldn't comprehend what he was seeing. Blood soaked Haha's shirt surrounding the hilt of the blade between his ribs. He'd thrown himself in front of his son. He'd taken the dagger for him.

The sky rumbled. Lightning crackled across the sky in the distance. The rain fell more steadily now.

"Vincent," Belamie said, staring in horror at the bloody scene before her, "what have you done?"

"What had to be done," Captain Vincent said coldly. "This is what I was trying to tell you before, Bonbon. All these people are trying to tear us apart. I'm only protecting you."

Belamie stepped away, shaking her head. "You aren't protecting me. You're protecting *you*. I did leave you, didn't I? And you couldn't handle that. You could never handle anyone leaving you behind. You could never come in second. So you got the Aeternum and you . . . you changed everything."

"Bonbon—"

"Stop calling me that," she snapped. "I've always hated that name."

Captain Vincent set his jaw. His eyes darkened. "You mustn't believe their lies, Belamie. Don't let them win."

"You're the liar!" Corey shouted.

Belamie shook her head. "No, Vince. This isn't right. I'm done. I don't want this." She turned away from Vincent, toward Matthew Hudson and her future children.

Vincent's face twisted into a venomous rage. He drew his sword.

"Mom, watch out!" Corey shouted.

In a flash, Belamie drew her sword and whipped around, slashing Vincent across his neck. The skin parted, exposing flesh and bone, but no blood appeared, and then the skin knit itself back together and smoothed over. Not even a mark remained. Belamie backed away, staring in horror at Vincent's throat.

Captain Vincent grinned. "Don't you wish you'd found the Aeternum first, Bonbon? If you hadn't left for that imbecile, you might have." He whisked away as though on a wind and then suddenly he was right in front of Belamie, less than a foot apart. He leaned in, as though he was going to kiss her, and then he grabbed Belamie by the neck. He wrenched out her time tapestry with such violence, her entire body arched back. She dropped her sword and froze.

"No!" Mr. Hudson shouted. He ran toward Captain Vincent. Brocco cocked his guns and aimed. At the same time Ruby lifted her sword and slashed down on Brocco's hand, slicing through his fingers. The guns fired but missed their target.

Brocco dropped his guns and hopped around, pressing his hand into his jacket. "Oh! My beautiful fingers!"

Mr. Hudson rushed at Captain Vincent, who whisked himself away again, holding on to Belamie's tapestry. He reappeared right in front of Mr. Hudson, punched a fist inside his stomach, and yanked out his time tapestry. Both Belamie and Matthew were paralyzed.

Then everything happened at once. Ruby raced at Captain Vincent with her sword. "Let them go!" she shouted. She stabbed her sword at him, aiming for the heart.

At the same time Corey picked up one of Brocco's guns. "Get away from my parents!" he shouted, and pulled the trigger. The bullet hit the captain square in the chest at the same time Ruby's sword pierced his heart, or where his heart should have been. Neither the gun nor sword had any effect. The captain whirled like a tornado, taking Matthew and Belamie with him, spinning into both Ruby and Corey. He yanked both of their time tapestries out of their heads so they hung like dolls from his hands.

Captain Vincent didn't stop. He was on a rolling rage. He tore through the rest, ripping out time tapestries right and left. He yanked Uncle Chuck's from his beard. He took Jia's from her back, and Gaga's and Haha's. He even took Albert's and Brocco's and Wiley's. He took them all, yanked and pulled and twisted them all together.

Matt watched all this in a trance. He couldn't seem to move. He stared at his parents, his brother and sister, Jia, Uncle Chuck, Gaga, and Haha, who was frozen with the dagger still in his ribs, the blood now soaking most of his shirt. All their time tapestries flowed out of them, ghostly shadows and images floating inside the shimmering fabric. It looked so fragile, so tenuous, and all Matt could think was how could anyone expect to hold on to anything in this world when it was so easily broken, when everything you loved could just be ripped away from you in an instant?

Captain Vincent turned to Matt, his hands full of the time tapestries. Before Matt could so much as blink, the captain whirled right to him.

"Don't worry, Marius," the captain said. "It will all work out in the end." He plunged his hand between Matt's ribs and tore out his time tapestry.

It felt like he was ripping Matt's lungs right out of his chest. All the air was knocked out of him. His life literally flashed before his eyes, every moment, every joy and pain, all the way to the very end. Because this was the end. He could feel it.

The captain wrenched all the time tapestries. He twisted them together and wrapped them around a pile of dynamite.

"Goodbye, Hudsons," Captain Vincent said as he struck a match and lowered the flame to the wick of the dynamite. It sputtered and caught.

Just then Marta came running with a wriggling mass of white fur in her hands. "*Råtta!*" she said excitedly.

It was Santiago. That was the other time tapestry Matt had pulled through with him. The captain must have gotten rid of him for some reason. Or he tried to. Santiago squirmed in Marta's grasp until he noticed Captain Vincent, and then he stilled. He focused his glowing red eyes on the captain and hissed. He leaped from Marta's grasp and flew at the captain, startling him just enough so his hold on Matt's time tapestry slipped. It spun back into him. He took a huge gasping breath, filling his lungs, just as the flame reached the end of the wick.

Matt only had a split second to dissolve himself.

Boom!

Searing heat rushed at Matt. His cells scattered and whirled in currents of energy. He felt everything unraveling, disintegrating, including himself. It was all falling apart. His family, himself, the world.

He tried to pull himself together, but he couldn't. He was too weak. All his strength, the energy of every cell, was sapped.

He was fading. He was starting to lose consciousness, and he knew once he did, it would be over.

Don't let go!

But what did he have to hold on to? He felt those around him, the other threads he'd unraveled with. His family. Corey and Ruby, especially. They were always there. He felt their beings, all their threads and cells weave in and out of his own, creating links and loops within him and between them. He felt it go on and on, this eternal chain, outside of time, beyond space, more substantial than matter. They pushed and pulled him together. At every point they were there. He could not hold himself together on his own, but they could.

And he suddenly knew what he had to do.

Don't let go!

It wasn't just about holding on to each other in the moment. They had to hold on for always. Forever. They had to stick together in the past, present, *and* future. A triangle in time. Matt, Corey, and Ruby, the three of them together.

Matt traveled through his own time tapestry. He sped through his future, touching down from time to time to gather his army. It didn't take much. It was a domino effect. Once he got it started it just kept going. If he told one, then he told them all, and he knew they would all come because if they didn't, they might cease to exist.

Matt traveled back to the Lost City. With the very dregs of his remaining strength, he pulled himself back together. His feet hit solid ground. He felt his lungs expand, his heart pumping blood.

He made it. He was back. Alive. But he was alone. Everyone was gone. There was no Corey or Ruby or any of his family. There was no Jia or Marta. No Brocco or Wiley or Albert, not even Santiago. There was only Captain Vincent. He stood in the center of the torn, ruined city.

"So," Captain Vincent said. "It's just us now."

Matt's hope vanished. He must have missed something, done something wrong. It hadn't worked.

Crack!

"Ah! Stupid bushy plants!" Someone stumbled out of the brush in the nearby jungle, cursing the plants. They turned and jogged toward them. "Hi! Sorry if I'm late." It was Corey. But different. He was slightly older, Matt thought, maybe by a few years. He was taller, a little more gangly, and he had braces. He looked around and frowned at the empty space. "Oh, dang. Am I the first one here? That's lame. Now I have to wait for everyone."

"Heaven forbid," said another voice, "you should have to wait every now and then, as if the rest of us haven't had to wait for you basically your entire life." It was Ruby. She appeared out of thin air right next to Corey. She also looked older, even older than the older Corey, like early twenties. She had her hair pulled up in a messy bun. She was wearing stretch pants and a tank top, like she'd just come from yoga class.

Another Ruby appeared behind the first, looking more or less the same as the Ruby Matt knew, only different clothing, her hair in a braid. And then another Ruby came, and another and another, each of them at varying ages and fashions. There was Ruby with blue streaks in her hair and heavy eyeliner, Ruby in jogging clothes, Ruby with a sword at her side, Ruby wearing a suit and glasses, Ruby dressed up fancy like she was going to the prom. All of them were different, and yet they were all Ruby.

More Coreys appeared, too, though most of them after Ruby. His sense of fashion didn't change much. He almost always wore a T-shirt and jeans and kept his hair long and shaggy. One version of him was even sporting a ponytail.

And then Matt saw himself. He appeared again and again, but instead of any random order, each version of himself seemed to appear in an orderly ascension, each Matt a little older than the last. He watched the evolution of his own life like watching a plant grow in fast motion. He got a little taller (though not as tall as he hoped), a little broader, then older and gray and shorter again.

"Hello," said one of the older Matts. "Good to see you all again. Always a pleasure. Ah, and Captain Vincent! Look at you! You never change. Exactly the same after all these years. Please, won't you share your secret? If I could bottle that up, I'd make a fortune!"

Captain Vincent just stared at the bizarre sight, completely stunned.

It had worked. They were all here, a version of themselves each year in the future. It was like a bizarre future family reunion.

"Dude," said a wiry ponytailed teenage Corey to a middle-aged version who was a little more rotund. "What did you do to me?"

"Don't judge, dude. You will be this before you know it."

An older Corey with thinning hair and glasses shook his head. "Don't worry. It's only a phase. You'll get yourself together eventually."

"Oh, joy, look at all I have to look forward to," said the youngest Corey, the one Matt knew best.

The earth started to rumble. Matt could feel the ground start to shake.

"Can we get this over with?" said the Ruby in the suit and glasses. She looked sharp and professional. "I have a meeting I can't miss."

The teenage Ruby wearing heavy makeup and blue streaks in her hair rolled her eyes. "Seriously, did you forget we're, like, trying to save ourselves here?"

"We'll have you back in time," said an older Matt wearing a hoodie and glasses, his hair a mess. Clearly, hygiene was not his top priority at this point in his life. Matt felt that familiar buzz in his chest as he spoke.

More and more of them came. Twenty, thirty, forty Matts, Coreys, and Rubys. The wind picked up. The rain lashed down. Lightning cracked across the sky like a whip. And still they kept coming, growing older and older, until they were stooped and gray and looked like they were a minute from death. But still more kept coming. Not Matt, Corey, and Ruby, but there were more children, more teenagers, more adults in all stages, and he realized this must be the future generations of the Hudsons. These were their children, grandchildren, great-grandchildren, nieces and nephews. They went on and on, seemingly forever. Matt thought it was the most beautiful sight he had ever seen or would ever see for his entire life.

The earth shuddered and groaned. Lightning flashed, illuminating the Lost City and the surrounding jungle. It was all shifting, breaking apart. The terraces rose and fell and then rose again, and the hills and mountains in the distance rolled like tsunami waves in a hurricane, crashing down, swallowing the jungle.

All the Coreys and Rubys and Matts circled one another, weaving in and out of each other. They spread around the city, shifting with the time storm as they surrounded Captain Vincent. The rain lashed against their faces. The earth shifted and groaned, and the wind blew in powerful gusts, enough to pick up Blossom and the *Vermillion* and send them careening into the raging jungle. But Matt and the rest remained steady. They moved with the storm. They were the storm.

Captain Vincent turned all around. He didn't seem to comprehend what was happening. The ground split beneath him, and he stumbled and fell to his knees.

"You wanted immortality," Matt said. "You wanted the powers of eternity, to rule the world, but you misunderstood the true key to unlock those powers. Eternity is not a power that can be held by just one person. Eternity is holding on to someone. Eternity is family. Eternity is friends. It's connection. It's sacrifice. It's love. *We* will go on forever, because we have each other. You are the weak one. Because you're alone, and no matter what you do, you can't rip us apart. We refuse to let go."

Matt clasped hands with Corey and Ruby on either side of him, and they clasped hands with those next to them, and on and on. All the Matts, Coreys, and Rubys held on to each other, forming one giant triangle around Captain Vincent.

Matt felt a buzz run through him like an electric current. It rushed through every part of his body, every vein and cell, and it continued to Corey and Ruby on either side of him, and on and on.

The three of them weren't just supposed to fix the lock. They *were* the lock. And in order to fix the lock, they needed to break time. They had to make one giant glitch.

The earth began to spin. Matt trembled as the current grew stronger. They were all shaking. Matt wasn't sure how much longer he could hold on. He felt as though bolts of lightning were flashing through his body. But he knew they must not let go. Not yet. He doubled down. He squeezed Corey's and Ruby's hands.

"Don't let go!" he shouted. "Hold on!"

Corey and Ruby squeezed him back. They held on as

though they were melded together. The current running between them grew stronger, hotter. It burned inside his very bones, but Matt held on. His grip was ironclad. The world would fall apart before he let go.

And it did. The whole universe seemed to crack and implode on itself.

The sky ripped open, and stars fell from the heavens. They shot toward the Lost City in hot-blue streaks. But they weren't stars, Matt realized. They were time tapestries. They came tumbling through the air, falling in gauzy, iridescent streams, and when they hit the earth they flashed and formed into people.

First came their parents, the young Belamie Bonnaire and Matthew Hudson.

"Oh!" Belamie said. "What's happening?"

More time tapestries fell from the sky. There was Uncle Chuck, and Gaga, and Haha, still wounded and bleeding, but still alive.

Jia appeared, and Marta carrying a wriggling Santiago. Brocco, Wiley, and Albert came too. A time tapestry touched down on the high terrace of the city, and the Eiffel Tower bloomed into being. On the opposite terrace appeared the giant Ferris wheel from the Chicago World's Fair. Someone hopped out of one of the rotating carriages. It was Annie Oakley, rifle in arms. She ran toward them.

"I'm coming, Captain!" she shouted.

Another time tapestry fell and Queen Elizabeth I of England appeared, wearing a golden gown, her red hair blazing in fiery waves all around her. She looked younger than when Matt had seen her.

"Elizabeth!" Belamie shouted.

"I warned you that man was no good," she said, pointing her scepter at Vincent.

"I know!" Belamie said. "You were right all along! I should have listened to you!"

Another time tapestry touched down and another woman appeared. She was bundled in furs, a spear in hand. It was Tui, come back from the Ice Age.

"*Rubbana!*" Tui shouted. "I'm sorry, *Rubbana*! I shouldn't have betrayed you! I was wrong. So wrong."

More and more time tapestries fell, almost, it seemed, as many as there were stars. The Brooklyn Bridge appeared in the jungle beyond, an army marching across with shields and swords and spears. Next to the bridge appeared the golden Padmanabhaswamy Temple from India, and next to it a castle that looked straight out of a fairy tale. There was the Metropolitan Museum of Art. Napoleon Bonaparte stood on its steps with his legion of soldiers.

"*Le château est à moi!*" he shouted.

And the Kangxi emperor appeared in his golden robes. He was holding on to a telescope.

"Father!" Jia called as she ran to him. He held his hand out to her.

The Louvre appeared next to the Met, and then a painting flowed out of one of the time tapestries. The *Mona Lisa*. A small man appeared. He wore a white coat and had a thin dark mustache. The Italian thief Vincenzo Peruggia! He grabbed the *Mona Lisa* and shouted, *"Per l'Italia!"*

A herd of woolly mammoths came charging through the city, followed by a roaring T. rex.

Last to come was a kitchen sink. It fell from the sky right before Captain Vincent in the midst of the human triangle with a resounding *crack*. The faucet was miraculously running. The sink filled up and overflowed, and then it was like a dam broke and the water gushed faster and faster. It pooled around Matt's feet and ankles, soaking his sneakers and pants. A whirlpool formed around Captain Vincent. It grew bigger and bigger, deeper and deeper, and it began to pull at Captain Vincent, sucking him down with it.

"I'll save you, Captain!" Brocco shouted. He ran to the captain, but before he could reach him, Annie aimed her rifle and shot him in the foot.

"Ooh!" he said, hopping around. "You little demon woman! I'll blow your head off!" He reached for his own guns, then remembered that he'd dropped them. He backed away from the captain, away from Annie Oakley and her rifle.

The whirlpool spun faster. It was up to the captain's waist now. He fought against it, grasping for anything that could save him. "You think you can trap me, defeat *me*?" Captain Vincent snarled at all the Matts, Rubys, and Coreys before him. "I have the Aeternum! I can go anywhere, anytime. I can destroy all of you. I can change *anything*."

"You can't change yourself," Matt said. "With the Aeternum, you will be the same forever and ever."

"You'll never change," Ruby said, "and so you belong in a place that also never changes."

"A place that goes on forever," Corey added. "I like to call it Nowhere in No Time."

Real fear came across the captain's face now as the force of Nowhere in No Time continued to pull him in. He couldn't resist it.

Matt felt a jolt like nothing he'd ever felt before, like a bolt of lightning shooting through every cell in his body, and he knew it was time.

"Let go now!" Matt shouted. He pulled his hands away from Corey and Ruby, and the universe seemed to snap back into place.

Captain Vincent roared like a wild beast as the vortex pulled him down and closed over his head.

The storm still raged, and others began to disappear. One by one, all the future Matts, Coreys, and Rubys left, sucked away into their own time tapestries, back to whatever time and place they'd come from. All the people and everything that had appeared now began to disappear. Queen Elizabeth, Tui, and Vincenzo Peruggia, holding the *Mona Lisa*. They folded back into their time tapestries and shot back into the sky.

"Father!" Jia cried, reaching for the emperor as his time tapestry wrapped around him and carried him off.

The Eiffel Tower went, and the Ferris wheel, taking Annie Oakley with it. The Louvre and the Met and the Padmanabhaswamy Temple. Brocco went, too, though clearly not willingly. He tried to pull off his own time tapestry as it wrapped around him. Albert shouted with terror as he was picked up off the ground, his time tapestry wrapping around his legs. Wiley caught him and held on to him.

"I got you," he said. "Just hold on to me. We'll be okay." Their time tapestries intertwined and disappeared together.

Blossom suddenly came charging through the air, revving its engine. The *Vermillion* charged forward as well. Both vehicles spun around each other like boxers in the fighting ring. They shifted again and again, into ships, cars, buses, trains, and airplanes, each circling the other faster and faster, until Matt lost track of which was the *Vermillion* and which was Blossom. A small blur ran toward the two battling vehicles.

"Marta!" Jia called. Marta paused for just a moment. She smiled and waved at Jia, and then she jumped right into the fray of the two vehicles as they melded together. Matt had a feeling she would next show up in a pantry on the *Vermillion*, eating a sack of sugar.

The jungle waves softened and stilled, returning to their natural hills and mountains. The Lost City was re-formed. The terraces rose and the ground smoothed. The rain and wind stopped, and the sky cleared. The earth gave a deep shudder and all was quiet.

Ruby let out a breath. "Did we do it?" she asked.

"I think we did," Corey said.

Matt walked over to the spot where Captain Vincent had been, right in the center of the city. All that remained was a small puddle of water. Something caught the sunlight and sparkled beneath the water's surface. Matt reached down and picked up a small, shiny black stone. He held it in his hand. It was smooth. There were no markings on it, but he knew exactly what it was.

Jia gasped. "The Aeternum?" she whispered in a reverent tone.

He nodded. Even now he felt its stabilizing effects, like it was grounding him, holding him together. It must have been formed by all their collective cells coming together, that searing jolt. He slipped it inside his pocket.

Matt heard a groan. He looked to his right and saw two forms on the ground. Matt raced to them, Corey and Ruby too. "Mom? Dad?" They were still their younger selves, but right before their eyes they began to change. Both Belamie and Matthew clutched at their heads as their bodies shifted ever so slightly. Mrs. Hudson held out her hands before her, watching them age. Her eyes shifted, too, as her brain seemed to expand and reclaim the memories she'd lost. Matthew Hudson touched his face as a few wrinkles settled in his eyes and the lines around his mouth deepened. His hair grew a bit longer, his shoulders rounded as all his years of reading and research caught back up to him. He glanced at the woman beside him.

"Belamie, are you all right?"

She nodded. "I . . . I think so. You?"

Mr. Hudson nodded, and then they both looked at the children before them. Belamie glanced at each of them in turn. Her chin quivered, her eyes brimmed with tears, and then with one swift motion, she gathered all three of them in her arms, crushing them against her chest. Mr. Hudson wrapped his arms around them from the other side, so all three children were sandwiched between their parents. Matt felt all the love and happiness in the world existed right there in that moment.

They broke apart, though, when they heard someone crying. Matt soon saw the source, and his heart turned to ice. Gaga and Uncle Chuck were on the ground, each of them holding Haha, who was propped up against the side of the lower terrace. He still had Captain Vincent's dagger in his ribs. Jia was there, too, kneeling on the ground in front of

Haha. She had some strips of cloth that she was gently pressing over the wound, trying to stanch the bleeding that was starting to soak into the ground beneath him. She had torn the sleeves off her shirt, Matt realized.

"Dad," Mr. Hudson said, kneeling down. Haha was pale and gasping for breath. Gaga was also gasping for breath as she cried. She looked up at the rest of them in desperation.

"Please do something," she cried. "Please save him!"

"He needs a hospital," Mrs. Hudson said. "I can transport him right away. I can get him there in moments." She still had the compass around her neck.

"I think moments are all he has," Mr. Hudson said.

"It's okay, Gloria," Haha said with effort. He reached for Gaga's hand. "This is how it's supposed to be."

"No, Henry," Gaga said. "We're going to get you help. You're going to be okay." But she cried all the harder as she spoke.

"Yes," Haha said, his voice little more than a whisper. "I'm going to be okay. I'm okay. When I was stranded, and I . . . didn't think I'd make it," Haha said, gasping for breath between his words, "all I wanted was to see you one more time. All I wanted was . . . my family."

Family. All Matt had wanted to do was save his family, for them all to be together. Shouldn't he be able to save all of them? Shouldn't Haha get to live too? "We can still save him, maybe," Matt said. "I can pull his time tapestry. We can go back and . . . and . . ." Matt wasn't sure what he was saying. He knew he was grasping at straws, but he had to do something. He had to try. He felt for the threads of Haha's time tapestry, pulled at them from his hands. The tapestry was barely there. It was nothing more than a faint, shimmering mist. He couldn't see any images inside of it, and he realized there wasn't anything he could do. Haha's time tapestry hadn't been blown up, destroyed, or damaged. Matt's cells were not attached to it in a way that he could pull it back together. It was simply fading, because Haha was fading.

Haha took a breath, and his next words seemed to take every last ounce of energy he had. "I love you," Haha said, his voice fading. "I love you all . . . so much."

Gaga grabbed his hand. She pulled it to her chest. "I love you, Henry," she said. "We all love you." Henry smiled, squeezed his wife's hand. He closed his eyes, took one final rattling breath, and was still. His time tapestry began to fade. Gaga reached for it, brushed it with her fingers, until it was gone. She fell over him and cried.

32

Baby Beginnings

They buried Henry Hudson on the edge of the Lost City. Gaga said he would like it, being buried in a jungle, no gravestone to mark his whereabouts. Uncle Chuck and Mr. Hudson dug the grave, while Gaga and Mrs. Hudson wrapped Henry Hudson in some of Uncle Chuck's colorful crocheted blankets.

"Henry loved to be in nature," Gaga said as they all gathered around the burial site to pay their respects and say goodbye. "He liked the feeling of being lost. Sometimes I told him to get lost, and he didn't seem to mind following my orders." She laughed a little through her tears. "But I'm glad we found him in the end, even if just for a moment."

Mr. Hudson and Uncle Chuck shared stories, things they remembered about their dad from when they were little, how he loved to play board games, and give the boys "horse rides" on his back, and take them hiking and fishing in the Catskills and give them candy and soda and told them not to tell their mother, which all sounded very familiar to Matt. Gaga laughed at this, and then cried. They all cried. But it was a good cry.

When all was said and done, there was quiet for a time. Matt felt strangely peaceful, like all was right with the world even though he was sad at the loss of his grandfather. They stayed for a long time. No one seemed to want to move.

Finally, someone said something about going home. Matt wondered if they still had a home. Would it be the same? Would everything be back as it was before? Or would there still be battles on the Brooklyn Bridge and in Central Park? Would dinosaurs still be roaming the subway and flying around the Statue of Liberty?

They all made their way up the stone steps that led to the Lost City. Gaga moved slowly. Burying her husband seemed to age her twenty years, and the other adults stayed with her.

"Go on ahead," Mrs. Hudson said. "We'll be there in a minute."

Matt, Corey, Ruby, and Jia made their way back to the grassy terraces of the Lost City. It was as empty as it had been when they arrived. Only Blossom stood in the center. Well, it was *mostly* Blossom. Oddly, she had a mast sticking out of her with the flag of the *Vermillion*. The two vehicles seemed to have melded together in the battle, and Matt thought his theory that they were one and the same was probably correct. Just as he and Marius Quine were one and the same, and every now and then they overlapped.

Corey climbed onto the roof of the bus. "Hey!" he said. "Our names aren't here!"

"You'd better carve them in then," Jia said. "Or else how will you know when you're supposed to stay?"

"I don't have anything to carve it with," Matt said.

"I lost my sword in all the chaos," Ruby said.

Jia reached inside one of the pockets of her vest and found a small chisel. She handed it to Matt, along with her little hammer. He took them. "Do you want to come?"

She shook her head. "No, it should just be you three." She smiled, but it was a sad smile. Matt had this feeling he knew what her sadness was about, but he wasn't ready to hear it. Not yet. Maybe not ever.

Matt climbed on the top of Blossom, and the three of them carved their names into the mast. Matt was sure to use his signature *M* with the lines crossing each other, forming an *X* at the center. When they finished, he was filled with that familiar feeling of déjà vu. Everything was coming full circle now. This was the end, but also the beginning.

"It feels like lifetimes ago, doesn't it?" Ruby said. "When we first boarded the *Vermillion*."

"Yeah," Corey said. "Do you really think it's all over? Is Captain Vincent really gone?"

"He won't bother us again," Matt said. He felt certain of that, though he wasn't certain of anything else. What would the future bring them? What parts of their past would come back to haunt or delight them?

The adults finally made it to the top of the city, and they were all gathering, getting ready to head home, when Matt heard a very strange sound coming from somewhere behind him.

"What's that sound?" Ruby asked.

They all stopped and listened.

"It sounds like crying," Corey said. "Like a baby."

Matt, Corey, and Ruby all looked at each other, clearly wondering the same thing. They searched for the source of the crying. It buzzed in Matt's ears and seemed to echo like it was inside a cave.

They came to the huge boulder with the star chart carved into it. It had been cracked in half during the battle, and between it was a wriggling, squalling bundle.

Mrs. Hudson gasped and covered her mouth.

Matt felt himself go a little fuzzy.

"It's Matt, isn't it?" Corey said.

Corey was right. This baby was him. But how did he get there? He looked around. There was no one else here.

Mrs. Hudson knelt down and scooped up the crying infant in her arms. She cuddled and cooed to the baby, and then she started to sing the lullaby. The baby instantly stopped crying, and even Matt felt soothed.

"Aw, he knows his mama," Uncle Chuck said.

"But . . . how?" Matt asked. How did he get here?

"You must have pulled yourself out of your own time tapestry, somehow," Ruby said. "During the time storm."

"So . . . basically he orphaned himself?" Corey asked.

"I . . . I didn't mean to," Matt said.

"Or maybe you did," Corey said. "Maybe even as a baby you knew where you belonged. Right here with us."

He had orphaned himself? But why? Was he supposed to put himself back? Was that even possible? Matt felt his mind whirling, trying to think of all the answers, all the possibilities. Maybe this was the only way to fix things. Maybe this was the sacrifice that needed to be made. Himself. His own timeline.

Mr. Hudson knelt down next to his wife, smiling at baby Mateo, who was now sleeping.

"Aw," Jia said quietly. "You were a cute baby, Matt."

"I wish we could keep him with us," Ruby said.

"As much as I'd love that," Mrs. Hudson said, "I think it might cause a few problems."

"Plus, he poops his pants now," Corey said. "Love you, bro, but I don't want to change your diapers."

"I don't want you to either," Matt said.

"We'd better get him to his parents, shouldn't we?" Mr. Hudson said.

Mrs. Hudson pulled the baby tighter to her chest. She looked at her husband like he'd just suggested they abandon the baby to a pack of wolves.

"I meant us!" he said. "We should get him to the adoption agency, so they can, you know, give us a call?"

"Oh," Belamie said, relaxing a little. "Right." But she still looked reluctant, as though she wished she really could keep him with her now.

"Make sure they tell you the baby's name is Mateo!" Ruby said.

"Yeah," Corey added. "We wouldn't want you naming him something else, like Marius or whatever."

"Well, I think that's up to your brother, isn't it?" Mr. Hudson said. "What's it going to be, kiddo?" he said, looking at Matt.

He didn't hesitate for a second. "I'm Mateo," he said. And that felt truer than it ever had. He was Mateo. Mateo Hudson. And this was his family. He didn't need to have all the answers. He didn't need to know where or when he had come from. No one really knows that anyway. They just know when they've found home. They know who their family is. And Matt had found his. This was how it was always meant to be.

They all gathered inside of Blossom. Mrs. Hudson cradled baby Mateo gently in her arms. She couldn't take her eyes off of him. Just as Matt was about to get inside of Blossom, he realized Jia wasn't there. He turned around. She was still by the cracked boulder, staring at the star chart.

Matt went to her. "Jia? What's wrong?"

"Nothing . . . I . . . I just . . ."

Ruby stepped up beside Jia. "You need to go home," she said. "To China?"

Jia cast her eyes down at her feet. Matt felt his heart fall into his stomach. He'd known this was coming, probably for longer than he wanted to admit, but that didn't make it any less painful. "Why?" he asked.

Jia looked up at him. "Because it's home, and . . . and I think my father needs me."

No. Matt wanted to tell her to forget China. Forget her father. She could live with them. They needed her more. He needed her. But then he realized he wasn't thinking about what Jia needed. He was being selfish. He wanted to keep her to himself, not realizing that she had her own family and home, and it was time for her to go back.

Mrs. Hudson appeared then. She handed Mr. Hudson the baby, then took the Obsidian Compass off from around her neck and handed it to Matt.

Matt understood. He handed the compass to Jia. "Here," he said. "You take it. So you can come and visit whenever you want."

"Oh," Jia said, her eyes widening. "I couldn't possibly. It's yours, Matt. It belongs to you."

"But I don't need it," he said. "I can get everyone home myself, and I want you to have it."

"But what about your mom?" Jia said, glancing at Mrs.

Hudson. "Aren't you supposed to give it to her at some point? What if something happens and you never get it back?"

"You'll bring it back," Matt said. "Someday." He placed the gold chain around Jia's neck. She gently touched the compass, then looked up at Matt with tears in her eyes. "I'll never forget you," she said. "Any of you."

"Of course you won't forget us," Corey said. "We're totally unforgettable."

Jia laughed and wiped at her tears. She hugged each of them and told them goodbye. She hugged Matt last and longest but still not long enough.

"Goodbye," she said. "I'll see you all again. I promise." And before Matt could beg her one more time to stay, she turned the dials, and she was gone.

The space where she had just stood suddenly felt so empty. More empty than empty. Like a black hole. Matt felt the emptiness in his heart too. He knew it would never be filled.

"I'll miss her," Ruby said.

"Me too," Corey said. "But Matt will miss her most." At first Matt thought he was teasing him, but then Corey put a hand on his shoulder and squeezed, and he knew he was trying to comfort him.

"It always hurts to say goodbye to those we love," Gaga said, her voice a little hoarse. "But it's a good kind of pain, because it means we are living well."

They took baby Mateo into Santa Marta, and his parents

found the adoption agency where they'd adopted Matt twelve years earlier. The rest would take care of itself, he knew. Still, his mom looked extra worried after they'd left him, and she gave Matt an extra-long hug before they left for home, like she was worried he might disappear on her any moment. And he could, he realized. Anytime he wanted, he could just disappear and go anywhere, anytime. But he didn't want to. He just wanted to be here right now, with his family.

Epilogue
Peanut Butter and Bubble Gum

April 26, 2039
New York, New York

It was a perfect day in Central Park. The air was warm with a gentle breeze and the sun shone through the trees. Mateo Hudson was sitting on a park bench. Ruby sat next to him, a cup of coffee in hand. They were both gazing at a skyscraper in the distance. It was still under construction, but it was already a marvel. It was straight and sleek until it peeked above the surrounding buildings, and then it split and curved into loops.

Ruby looked down at her watch, then turned around, searching.

"He's on his way," Matt said.

"He's always late, and I have an appointment in thirty."

"Give him a break. He's got a lot on his plate right now."

"So do I! What makes his time more valuable than mine?"

Matt gave her a look.

"Okay, okay."

"There he is." Matt nodded toward Corey walking down a path pushing a double stroller with two toddlers, not more than two years old, a boy and a girl. "Hey, Henry! Hi, Gloria!" Matt waved at his little niece and nephew, both of them dark-haired and rosy-cheeked.

Corey ambled toward them slowly, like he was pushing a heavy load. His Superman T-shirt was covered in various stains, some that looked like ink and paint, and others Matt didn't really want to know. His hair was long and shaggy. His face had a few days' worth of stubble and his eyes had dark circles under them. "Sorry I'm late," he said, unfastening the seat belts while the children squirmed to get out. "Henry peed his pants, and then Glory was hungry, and she's a total pig. Took forever."

"Don't call my niece a pig," Ruby said. She reached in her bag and pulled out two lollipops. The two children squealed and reached chubby hands toward the candy.

"Who's your favorite auntie?"

"Woo-bee! Woo-bee!" they chanted.

"And don't you ever forget it." She handed them the lollipops.

"Oh, brother," Corey said. "That's all they need. More sugar. Are you trying to torture me?"

"Well, you know what they say. What goes around comes

around," Ruby said as she pulled both children onto her lap.

"Hey, share," Matt said. "I'm their favorite uncle." He took Henry on his lap, ruffed up his curls, and kissed him on the head.

Henry responded by popping his lollipop out of his mouth and shoving it in Matt's face. "Yum!" he said.

"Yeah, thanks. Yum."

Gloria wiggled herself off Ruby's lap and toddled over to the playground. Henry followed.

"How's Lana?" Ruby asked.

"Tired," said Corey. "We're always tired."

"Gives you a little empathy for what our parents went through, doesn't it?"

"There's no way I was this much trouble."

Ruby snorted.

"Henry, don't eat the dirt! Yuck!"

"Yum!" Henry said, sticking his lollipop in the dirt and then in his mouth.

Corey went and yanked the lollipop from Henry who immediately started screaming. Ruby ran over and washed it off with her water bottle, then gave it back to Henry. He smiled through crocodile tears.

"Kids these days," Corey said. "No common sense."

Matt never would have thought that Corey would be the first to get married and have kids, but five years ago he'd been at Comic Con, speaking and signing copies of his latest book, when a young woman dressed up like Wonder Woman smiled at him as she walked by, and he was a goner. They were married a year later, and then the twins came. It had been somewhat comical to watch Corey get smacked with parenthood, but Matt also envied him. He had his own family now. Still, he knew nothing would ever come between them. They may be leading their busy separate lives, but they had promised they would always stick together, no matter what. Every Friday afternoon they met in Central Park. It was Matt's favorite day of the week. Sometimes, once a year or so, they'd all get sucked back to the Lost City with all the rest of their selves, past and future. They never knew exactly when it was going to happen, but it always happened when they were together and alone. (Never when the twins were around. Their past selves seemed to have rules about that.) Matt always looked forward to it. It was like a bizarre family reunion.

"Either of you talk to Mom and Dad, lately?" Corey asked as he pushed Gloria on the swing.

"Yesterday," said Ruby. "They're having a grand time in Paris." Their mom had been asked to come work at the Louvre for a year to oversee some restorations and preservation of several pieces of art, including the *Mona Lisa*. Mr. Hudson said he'd tag along for the ride, but he'd kept himself busy with his own projects. He was writing a book. It was a great secret. He wouldn't talk about it, but Matt had a feeling it had something to do with maps and time travel and perhaps two people in different centuries who, against all odds, found each other and stayed together.

"Those two crazy lovebirds," said Corey. "They still act like they're our age."

"They're lucky," said Matt a bit wistfully.

"And aren't we lucky we got them for parents?" Ruby said.

Matt nodded. He counted himself lucky every day, and yet still there were times he felt like something was missing.

"The building is looking good, Ruby." Corey nodded toward the twisting building in the distance. It was, in fact, Ruby's design. She was one of the world's youngest, most promising architects, wowing the world with her unique and daring designs. She was on the cover of magazines and everything.

"Everything on schedule?" Matt asked.

"I think so," Ruby said. "I have an emergency meeting with one of the contractors. We're having a problem with one of our steel suppliers in China, and it's holding everything up."

Matt felt a little flash of pain in his chest. Even all these years later, any mention of China still made him suddenly look around, like he might see Jia just show up. He'd heard nothing from her. She'd never come to visit. He wondered why. He worried something might have happened to her, that maybe Yinreng had done something. Several times he'd resolved to just travel there himself and find her, but he always chickened out. Somehow it felt like it would be an intrusion, like he needed an invitation. He'd searched history books and records for any mention of her name, but there was nothing, except for the records of her name as one of the daughters of the Kangxi emperor.

"I'm sure you'll get them back on track," Corey said. "You always do."

"Thanks," Ruby said. "How's the new book coming?"

"Slow. Turns out having kids really does something to your work time. My publisher is being very patient though."

"That's because they know genius when they see it," Ruby said. Corey was a successful comic book artist. He'd already illustrated several comic books and graphic novels, and every day it seemed like more opportunities came knocking.

"Speaking of genius, how's your research coming, Matty?" Corey asked.

Matt blew out his lips like a horse. "Slow, but I don't have kids as an excuse." Matt was a physicist and a biochemical engineer, of course. He was currently studying the physical and mental effects of time travel on rats. He'd already published a few articles that were garnering quite a bit of praise and attention (and some strong criticism) in the scientific community. Time travel was in its infancy for most of the world. Some people still did not think it would ever be possible for humans to achieve, and those who did debated much over the possibilities, the ethics, how time travel should be regulated, and to whom it would be made available. It was important for everyone to know the costs as well as the benefits. Matt had seen both. He knew it was a big responsibility he could not take too seriously. No one actually knew he was the one publishing his material, because he published under a pen name—Marius Quine.

"We'll throw you a big party when you win the Nobel Prize," Corey said.

"Thanks. I request many balloons. With helium. Enough to make me float."

"You got it."

They played with the twins. Matt pushed Gloria on the swings while Ruby took Henry down the twisty slide.

Ruby looked at her watch. "I gotta go. Don't want to be late for that meeting."

"See you later, then," Corey said.

"Oh, Matt, I found something I thought might interest you," Ruby said.

She pulled out a *National Geographic* magazine and handed it to Matt. On the cover was a painting of a Chinese woman dressed in yellow robes, sitting on an elaborate throne. "Did a Woman Once Rule China in the Early Eighteenth Century?" the title read.

Matt's heart skipped a few beats. He flipped to the article.

* * *

On December 20, 1722, Kangxi, emperor of China for sixty-one years, was on his deathbed. Records claim he gathered seven of his sons to his bedside, presumably to pass on his throne to one of them. There had been many disputes over the years as to who would inherit the throne. Historians had long believed he named Yong-zheng his heir, and though we know Yongzheng did in fact rule China for a period, recent documents discovered have given historians reason to believe that the emperor passed his throne not to one of his sons but to a daughter.

Matt paused for a few moments. His hands began to tremble a little. He read on.

"It's an almost unthinkable break from tradition for a woman to officially rule China," says Ann Huang, a professor of Imperial Chinese History at Columbia University and the leading researcher of the discovered documents. "Surely no one would have supported the decision, but neither would they have dared to go against it. The emperor was like a god. You couldn't go against the heavens."

The throne was initially meant to go to Yinreng, his second son. But Yinreng was an extremely volatile and power-hungry young man, and the emperor soon realized he was not fit to rule. Kangxi removed him as crown prince and declared that he would place the name of his successor inside a box kept in the Palace of Heavenly Purity to be opened only after his death. Several of his sons began to vie for the throne, each plotting against the next.

Historians always believed that his first son, Yongzheng, was then made his successor. There had been some rumors and conspiracy theories of him passing the throne to a daughter, but they were always rejected as they had no sound foundation. These recently discovered documents, however, could confirm the rumors as truth. It appears Emperor Kangxi passed his throne to one of his daughters, Quejing, a princess of the second rank.

Matt paused on the name for several seconds. Quejing. Jia. An empress.

It is unclear why Emperor Kangxi chose Quejing to inherit over any of his other sons or even other daughters of higher rank. She was not the daughter of an empress but a concubine of low rank. However, from the few records that have been discovered, she seems to have been an extremely powerful, intelligent, and just ruler, beloved by her people. During the time of her rule, she brought peace and prosperity to a nation that had long been in turmoil, and especially brought more rights for women, outlawing the brutal practice of foot binding as well as the practice of rulers keeping many wives and concubines. There was also evidence of her possessing some savvy with mechanics and technology. Among the documents found were some designs for a rather sophisticated plumbing system. "Her designs were well beyond the technology of the time," Professor Huang said. "It was almost as if she had visions of the future."

Empress Quejing ruled closely with her brother Yongzheng. He often took charge in Quejing's stead when she traveled, which she did often and extensively, another key part of her success as a ruler. The empress never married and bore no heirs, though there is some evidence of correspondence between her and some man who has remained unknown. Empress Quejing held many secrets, and not even those closest to her seemed to be privy to them.

Yongzheng succeeded Quejing as emperor when her rule ended around 1740. An exact date of her death is unknown. There is no burial site or tomb for her. There are conspiracy theories she was murdered by one of her brothers or their supporters for the throne. There is no evidence to support either theory. It remains a mystery that historians may never uncover.

"What is clear," says Professor Huang, "is that Empress Quejing was highly influential and still is, even if people don't really know who she is. It is a common theme in women's studies. We don't know the women who are changing and shaping the world. Their efforts are either undocumented or attributed to men. In this case, it was almost as if Empress Quejing wanted to remain anonymous, for whatever reason."

Matt closed the article and studied the picture again. He noted the gold chain hanging around her neck, and the large, shiny black stone sitting at her chest, accented with bits of gold. In her hands she holds a piece of paper. A map, Matt realized. They never did find out who made their father's map. Maybe it had been Jia. Or perhaps it had still yet to be created. There was still time for that. There was still time for a lot of things.

"Makes you wonder, doesn't it?" Ruby said.

Matt just nodded, still unable to take his eyes off the picture.

"Anyway, you keep that. I have to get to my meeting."

"I should go too," Corey said. "Lana wants us to have family dinner, though I'm not sure why. They just throw food everywhere."

"How about I come watch the twins sometime this week so you and Lana can go on a date?" Ruby asked.

"How about so we can just have a nap?"

"Whatever you want. Either way, please change your shirt."

Corey looked down at his stained Superman T-shirt. "Yeah, this one could use a wash, I guess."

"All right, see you guys later." She held out a fist. Matt and Corey both put theirs in and they gave their three-way fist bump, as natural as anything.

After Ruby and Corey had gone, Matt walked alone through Central Park, the baseball diamonds, along the roads where horse-driven carriages pulled tourists cuddling beneath blankets. He came to the Metropolitan Museum of Art and watched people go in and out, step into self-driving taxis and flying cars. He watched children splashing in the fountains, laughing and shrieking, tossing coins in the water for luck and wishes. He reached in his pocket, found a coin, and tossed it in.

Matt heard some sniffling behind him. He turned to see a kid, maybe nine or ten, sitting next to his bike, crying. It was one of the latest models with hovering capabilities and glow-in-the-dark wheels.

"Hey there," Matt said. "Can I help you with that?"

"I can't get it to start," he said. "I just got it, and my mom'll ground me forever if I break it!"

"Let's take a look. I'm pretty good at fixing things." Matt knelt down and took off the cover to the operating system. "Looks like one of the circuits shorted. Hmmm . . . this would be easier with tools."

Out of nowhere a wrench dropped down onto the sidewalk. "What the . . . ?" Matt picked up the wrench and looked around.

"Maybe you should try putting some peanut butter on that bike," said a voice.

Matt whirled around, dropping the bike and nearly knocking over the kid. He could hardly believe his eyes. It was Jia. She looked exactly the same, except older. She was wearing her old tool vest, and the Obsidian Compass around her neck.

"Peanut butter?" said the kid. "On a bike?"

"Yes," she said, still looking at Matt. "And bubble gum. It's a magical combination, you know." She knelt down and picked up the bike. "Oh, I can give this a good tune-up." She brought out her wrench, tightened the brakes and the seat, then brought out a small jar of peanut butter–bubble gum mixture and greased up the chain and the gears. "There you go. Good as new!" She lifted the bike and spun the front wheel.

The boy clicked the button and the bike sputtered to life. It rose off the ground a little. "It works!" he said. "Thank you!" He hopped on his bike and sped away, jumping over trees and swerving around pedestrians.

Jia turned around to face Matt. He still could not speak. He was afraid if he did, he would wake up and find this was all a dream. Jia, after all these years, was there standing before him.

"*Nǐ hǎo*, Mateo," she said.

"*Nǐ hǎo*, Jia."

Jia smiled a smile that was pure light and joy. Matt felt that hole in his heart close up.

All was right with the world, in the past, present, and future.

Acknowledgments

The end already? It came too fast, and at the same time it's been a long journey. I do feel that I've traveled through time and space with a crew of amazing people who supported me and helped me tell this story with all its quirky characters and adventures. I know it's my name on the cover, but there are so many people who contributed to the Time Castaways trilogy. To Melissa Miller, thank you for believing in me, for sharing your brilliant ideas and allowing me to take them and run. It's been a joy and an honor. Thank you to my editor, Mabel Hsu, for jumping in with enthusiasm and for your incredible patience. Thank you to Amy Ryan for the amazing design work, to Robby Imfeld and Lena Reilly for getting these books into the hands of readers. Thank you to Lindsay Wagner, Kimberly Stella, Tanu Srivastava, and all the team members at Katherine Tegen Books and Harper-Collins for your efforts on this book and series overall.

Thank you to my agent, Claire Anderson-Wheeler, for having my back through this whole process, reading and commenting at the drop of a hat when I needed it, coaching me through the rough spots and talking me off the ledge.

You've been a true champion of my work, and I'm so grateful.

Thank you to all the wonderful teachers and librarians who have championed my books. I know I wouldn't be where I am today without you. And to the readers, thank you for sticking with the Hudsons' adventures to the end. Or the beginning? It's hard to tell . . .

So many friends have helped me through this series. Shout-outs to Katie Nydegger and Lisa Allen on this one. You saw me at my worst and haven't discarded me, so I know it's true friendship.

To my children, Whitney, Ty, Topher, and Freddy, thank you for being my biggest fans and the most wonderful children a mother could hope for. You inspire me every day and have brought so much joy and love into my life. Scott, where would I be without you? Lost. Sad. Totally bonkers. (I know I'm a little bit bonkers.) Thank you for keeping me laughing through my tears, for holding my hand and putting up with the many late nights and weekend work. Let's all stick together forever.